The Fall
of
Blood and Snow

RENEE M. PALSTRING

ACORN FOREST PUBLISHING

ISBNs

978-1-959414-05-6 (Hardcover)

978-1-959414-04-9 (Paperback)

978-1-959414-03-2 (eBook)

Published by Acorn Forest Publishing

For David—
without you, this book would still be in the drafts

CONTENT WARNING

The Fall of Blood and Snow is intended for a mature audience, as some content may upset readers. This content includes; graphic sexual scenes, graphic violence/death, some swearing, and attempted sexual assault.

PRONUNCIATION GUIDE

<u>Names</u>

Ina - E-nah

Alaric – Al-a-rick

Neo – Knee-o

Rainer – Rain-ear

Batair – Bah-tar

Damon – Duh-mon

Acacia – Ah-kay-suh

Sil – Sil

Ala – Aa-la

Catrine – Cat-trine

Aspen – As-pin

Sam – Sam

Eli – E-lie

Alis – A-lis

Azima – Ah-zee-ma

Aeson – A-son

Ellary – El-lah-re

<u>Places</u>

Artico – Art-tee-co
Rivelia – Ree-vel-e-ah
Woodland – Wood-land
Aplela – App-lee-la

CHAPTER 1

A cold breeze swept through the mating room, causing the numerous flames decorating the altar to flicker. Shadows danced on the cavern walls, as if in mockery of the unlit candle in my hands. The same one I had ceremoniously held for hours next to this year's brood of females.

We had stood in a line as male after male entered, covering our hands with theirs, seeing if the spark would ignite, to see if the *Gods* had destined us together. I stood there and watched as the fires came to life and the crowded room lessened. I stood until I was the only one left, and there were no more males to enter this *sacred* room—an anomaly within itself. Typically, one or two other females remained—the ones who were on their first or even their third ritual. At least that's how it had been for the seven years I had participated in the ceremony.

Still, it was another year, and my mate had not been found. It was another year wasted of being paraded around to convince more males to join the yearly ritual, all so I could finally be wed off and make the future alpha.

I gripped the jar tighter, raising it over my head, wondering how much force it would take to break it into a million pieces so even the most skilled glassmaker wouldn't be able to mend it, forcing my father to commission a new candle to be made in Rivelia—a feat that would take a year. It would spare me from at least one mating ritual, depending on how long it took for the caretakers to notice mine was missing. At least it would, if my father had not decided that this was my last year, that this year—if the Gods did not *bless* me with a mate—a tournament would be held, and the victor would be awarded a forced mating bond with me and the title of beta, then alpha with my father's passing.

A soft knock came from the wooden door that covered the mouth of the cavern, followed by a soft, familiar voice. "Ina, are you still in there?"

I sighed heavily, knowing there was only one reason for Ellary's presence in the cavern.

Humans knew that these grounds were sacred and should only be walked upon by wolves and a select few servants, but even then, it was rare for them to enter.

She had come because the start of the tournament was nearing.

"Come in, Ellary," I replied, placing the candle back on the altar, allowing it to live another day.

Light beams slowly filled the cave, Ellary's mumbled prayers accompanying them, thanking the gods for the miracle of the Protectors—the Artico Pack—that guarded her village just below the mountain.

I shifted my attention back to my candle, making sure my name was facing toward the door, allowing Ellary's intimate prayers to only be heard by the gods. The same gods that had listened, in past years, to my wish of not finding a mate but were now silent to my plea to stop this tournament.

If I had known they would grant only one wish, I would've been more careful with my wording and asked to never be bonded. The thought of having a male claim me as theirs made me retch.

"I am sorry that the gods did not bless you," Ellary whispered, scared that her voice would taint the holiness of the cavern.

"Thank you, Ellary," I replied, faking sincerity.

I had never told anyone of my prayers. To wish what I wanted, as the alpha's daughter, was taboo. It was believed the gods created mates to show us how to create the strongest pack, whether that be in a powerful couple or amazing offspring. Of course, for others, it was still allowed to reject your mate or refuse to participate in the mating ritual all together, and in some rare cases, it was encouraged.

"Do you still need time?" Ellary asked, her voice closer now. "I can request that the tournament be pushed back for a few more hours. Everyone will understand."

I bit my lip, stopping an involuntary laugh, making the short sound appear more like a sob.

Time would not make this easier. I needed to get this over with.

I met Ellary's face, which was filled with pity.

"That won't be needed. It would only delay the inevitable and postpone the festivities that will follow. I'm sure those that were mated today are ready for the celebration," I declared, keeping my voice even.

Ellary nodded then stepped to the side, allowing me to lead the way.

CHAPTER 2

The comforting smell of old leather and burning wood filled the arena as Ellary and I walked through the stands to the Alpha's Box. It was the safest area in the arena, as it was strategically placed in the center, middle of the stands, so the alpha and his family were surrounded by the pack. However, it was more for show than anything. The pack never faced threats in this age. Of course, we had the occasional thief, but none were foolish enough to try to take on a wolf, let alone the most powerful one in the pack and the second most—me.

I had taken on every single warrior in the pack and won. I had outrun them, outwitted them, and no matter what form of combat, I knocked them down. I was revered in the pack. It made me forget my fate, made me think it could change. However, I didn't feel like that now.

The straps of my ceremonial red, silk dress fell with every swift movement. The black cloak, meant to warm the flesh that the thin dress left exposed to falling snow, dragged across the ground, occasionally getting stuck on splintered wood. I had to stop every couple of steps and ask Ellary to free me. It was embarrassing.

I yearned for my leather pants and wool tunic, but tradition was tradition. The females who participated in the mating ritual had to wear the red dress until the moon was full or until it was taken off to add to the lust of the night.

"It's good to see you in a dress again," a strong, kind voice chimed a few steps above.

I raised my head to meet a pair of glistening blue-grey eyes that matched mine, grey hair swooping across a wrinkled face, and despite the scars that decorated it, a smile so big that it could reach across the continent.

I raised my fist to my heart, slightly bowing my head, giving the respect one should when greeting the alpha. "Father," I whispered before raising my chin. "I'm glad someone finds this dress pleasing, because I certainly don't," I remarked as I passed him, heading for the chair that seemed like a toy next to the towering monstrosity that was placed next to it—the seat of the alpha—intricately carved with the wolves of the past, the gods' faces, and symbols so old that the meaning of them had been lost to the years.

"Do not look so glum. Today is a day of celebration." The throne creaked as my father sat beside me, and Ellary took her place on a cushioned stool behind us. "We celebrate the new year to come, the full moon, the new mating bonds that will be created tonight, and we celebrate—"

"And we celebrate the chosen male whom I will be *forced* to bond with." I raised my brow as I looked in my father's direction. His chest was already filled with the air he needed to calm himself, to prepare for a fight we had numerous times already.

"Ina," he growled through gritted teeth, trying to keep his voice low. "You know why we cannot wait for the gods to give you your mate. I am growing old."

I rolled my eyes. "Not that old if you can still participate in morning spars." His brows furrowed. "I could smell Artico's Fang mixed with steel from the cavern this morning."

"You've always had a good nose," he replied with a smile, touching the necklace around his neck that had been passed down every generation to the strongest of the pack. Well, the strongest of the males. Otherwise, it would have been mine, along with the title it carried.

I continued to eye the necklace, taking in the ancient smell, a force drawing me in, as if its spirit were calling to me. Noticing, my father tucked it into his tunic, removing it from my view.

I leaned back in my chair, grinding my teeth. "I've always had a good *everything,* including better skills than any of the males competing today."

"I know," Father softly muttered.

"Then, you should agree that the necklace and the title it comes with should be mine," I hissed, keeping my eyes on the males warming up, predicting their movements, picturing how I would counter them.

"It doesn't matter what I think. Tradition dictates Artico's alpha must be a male. Have you forgotten what will happen if I pass and you are not mated?" he whispered.

I sneered, sinking my canines into my cheek, knowing all too well what he spoke off.

Though the Artico Pack had my heart in every way, there was one thing I hated about us—the exchange of power from one alpha to another. There were two ways it could happen. The first was when the current alpha passed naturally, or he knew he was growing weak and willingly passed the title to whoever he named his beta. Typically, it would be his son or his daughter's mate. The second option was for a challenger to step forward and win against the alpha, taking his title. However, with the latter, there would be opposition.

Many wolves believed that only someone of the original bloodline could be alpha. Therefore, when someone outside of the ancient lineage proved they were the strongest in the pack and had every right to lead, they were expected to somehow bring the original bloodline into their family no matter the cost. Which in my case, as I was the only child of my father, if a male challenged my father and won, he was expected to sire a child with me immediately. If he didn't, whether my womb refused to participate or from lack of trying, the very religious of my pack would take it as a sign from the gods that the male was not blessed to lead, thus causing more opposition in the pack and more claims to me.

It was a barbaric practice. It was why when my mother died, before she could grace our family with a male heir, my father made me participate in the mating ritual as soon as I was at the eligible age of eighteen. It allowed for a greater chance at finding my mate, and if I found him—the one that was picked by the gods—the change of power would be like the first option. It would be controlled, safe, and with minimal resistance. It was what many alphas of the past wanted to do for their daughters, even if they had to get her a mate through a forced mating bond.

However, the forced mating bond was rarely used, since there were so many conditions that needed to be met. First, the ritual for the forced mating bond had to happen on the night of a lunar eclipse. The second was that the gods needed to approve of the mates, to agree to cut and retie the strings of destiny. This was requested by the couple mixing their blood together in a bowl and having a priestess—possessed by a god—taste the blood. If the taste satisfied her, then the couple would be mated. However, if it didn't, the bond would not be made, and the couple would have to wait three years for the next lunar eclipse to either try again and hope that the gods changed their opinion of them, or they had to find a different partner to obtain a false bond with. Due to the lengthy wait time, it was always vital to have a strong connection to your partner, so the gods would be more sympathetic to your case or go through the ritual with someone who was your equal. It was why my father was now hosting a tournament, because from all those options and all my *failed* attempts to find my mate year after year, he decided it was best to have me go through a forced mating bond, so he could name his heir now.

And I hated it.

I knew the rule about females becoming alpha was unchangeable. I had looked through document after document, scoured through all the history books, and there was no mention of a way to change the rules. But I always hoped that I would find something, do something so incredible that the idea of my ruling would not be questioned. However, according to my father, my time was up.

"How could I? You remind me every day, but we still have time before you must give up your title. You don't have to name your beta now." I crossed my arms as the mountain breeze started to chill my skin. If it got any colder, I would have to shift. "And do not use the excuse you are getting old. We've already established you were at this morning's spar."

Father exhaled deeply then slowly looked around, making sure no one's eyes were on us. "Just because I was sparring doesn't mean I'm not getting slow." He lifted his cloak, revealing cream-colored bandages wrapped around his forearm.

I stopped breathing.

Never had I seen my father wounded by the warriors of the pack in a fair fight. I couldn't even touch him.

"Who delivered the blow?" I frantically whispered, my heart speeding.

"Rainer," he replied, pulling his cloak tight against his arm, "and luckily, he was the only one paying attention."

My jaw clenched. No male infuriated me more than Rainer. He was the only male who made me break a sweat when we sparred, the only male I had to fully concentrate on my movements with. He was the one who all bets were on tonight, and Rainer knew it. It was probably why talk of my father's arm hadn't started yet. If Rainer won the tournament, won the right to my hand in the forced bonding ceremony that would occur three months from now, the title of alpha in the future would pass to him much quicker and cleaner than if he were to challenge my father now.

"Are you certain?" I asked, eyes darting for any threats.

Father nodded, calmly. "If anyone else had, I would have you running by now." He leaned back in his seat, taking a sip from one of the two goblets between us.

Rainer was going to be my mate, and there was no way out of it.

CHAPTER 3

A gong sounded, summoning the warriors to stop their warm up and to stand side by side in the arena, facing the alpha. They sheathed their weapons, one by one racing to the edge of the stands, trying to take a place in the center of the line.

I scoffed as I watched the males try to discreetly push one another, heard their low snarls and their empty threats. Any sign of the honorable warriors they were was gone. They had turned feral, all because this was their chance to be alpha. If they had any sense left in them, they would know that a true alpha didn't need to fight for respect, that it was—

The warriors went still, craning their necks ever so slightly to see a giant of a male approaching the line, effortlessly tying up his shoulder-length, wheat-colored hair, disregarding the silence his presence brought upon the crowd, as if this event was no more than a mere day of training.

He strode straight to the center of the line, pausing, waiting for the two toned males to move. They gaped at one another, stalling for enough time that the male looked up from the sleeve he was rolling up. One brow cocked up, a challenging half smile on his face as he looked between the two. They shuttered, lowering their heads slightly before shuffling away. The male took his place between them, his feet shoulder length apart and his hands clasped behind his back. He craned his thick neck up, so his storm-grey eyes met mine, intensely holding my attention, daring me to look away. I didn't, refusing to give in to him. He smiled darkly before his eyes began to lower, following every curve of my all too exposed body. My breathing sped, and my cheeks flushed as our eyes once again connected and he mouthed the word, "mine".

I gripped tighter to the armrest, keeping myself from running down and pommeling the male.

The male named Rainer.

The tournament went quickly and as expected. Rainer had won each of his matches with little to no effort, embarrassing many of his opponents. The crowd had stopped placing bets on who would win in the third round and started to bet on how short the bouts would be. Even now, minutes before the final round, all bets were placed on Rainer, and if I were to join, mine would be too.

As much as I hated him, as much as I hated the way his eyes were constantly on me before and after every fight, as if to check I was still in mint condition, I could not deny how good of a fighter he was. I could not deny that out of all the *male* wolves he should to be the next alpha.

I grabbed the wooden chalice off the table, chugging the deep red wine, a bit of it trickling down my face, refusing to be sober when he officially announced his claim on me. I heard a shift behind me and saw Ellary moving for the jug that sat next to the servants. I held up my chalice, allowing her to easily refill it before calloused hands enclosed the rim, pushing it back down.

"Only my glass, please, Ellary," my father said with a smile as I silently bared my canines at him.

"Yes, Alpha Batair," Ellary quickly replied, giving me an apologetic glance as she retreated to her stool before another quarrel with my father began.

"Everyone will be filled with drink when night falls," I sneered, slamming my cup down. "Why does it matter if I start early?"

He took a sip of his refilled chalice before answering, "Because I need you to stand and consent to this promise when Rainer wins."

"I think I can manage a simple nod no matter how many drinks I've consumed." I reached for my chalice. If my father wouldn't permit Ellary to fill it, I would do so. It wasn't beneath me. However, he was quicker. He snatched it off the table and placed it on the floor beside him.

"You'll have to swear the oath." My whole body whipped to my father. "I promised him, after this morning's spar, that you would swear to bond with him under the next lunar eclipse."

"I will not say such embarrassing things in front of the pack. I will not promise myself to Rainer until it is truly time to do so. No male will come near me in fear that Rainer will rip their heads off."

"As is any males' right if he feels another is encroaching on their mate. As is your right and any other female to do the same." Father leaned in so he may talk at a whisper. "Ina, he's only asking for the rights any other normal pairing would result in until they can be bound. He's not the villain. Not yet. Please, for once in your life, just do as I say."

"I would rather—" The gong sounded in the arena again, our priestess standing in the center with it. "An alpha is a leader of the people. He must be strong, intelligent, and able to lead. He must also be able to *compel* those in his pack who go against him. It is why this last test will not require the contestants to be in human form but in their wolf form." My breathing hitched, realizing what the last challenge was. "The contestants will try to compel one another. They will attempt to make the other bow."

I shook my head at the impossibility of the task.

Compelling was a skill only a true alpha could have and was typically passed down through a bloodline. With it, a wolf could order his pack members to do whatever they wished. It was a rare skill to obtain. Even

I hadn't been born with it. It was even rarer for someone outside of the family to have it.

This would end in a stalemate, unless Father knew one of them had this power, that Rainer had this power.

CHAPTER 4

I watched Rainer along with Kovu enter the arena from opposite sides. Still in human form, they made their way to each other. I half expected Rainer to break their eye contact, to look up at me as he did with the past rounds with a grin filled with arrogance. He never did. It was as if he was nervous about this challenge.

Kovu and Rainer both stopped five paces from Shaman Azima. She gave them a brief nod then looked to my father for permission to continue. The stands fell utterly silent, waiting for his response, waiting to see if he allowed one of these warriors to show their true power, waiting to see if he'd allow Kovu or Rainer to show the pack that they had just as much right to the title of alpha as he. It was like watching a man walk to the guillotine as he grievously nodded.

Was this also one of Rainer's requests to ensure that our bonding would happen?

I was going to kill him for forcing my father through this embarrassment.

Shaman Azima stepped back, allowing enough room for them to shift. "You may call upon your wolves," she announced, her voice booming though the stands.

Rainer and Kovu bowed their heads, saying a silent prayer to the gods. In a blink of an eye, two wolves—thrice the size of normal ones—stood where the two males had. Their hackles and tails raised whilst they bared their fangs. The challenge had begun.

There was not a sound or movement in the stands as we all looked upon them, wondering if one of them had the ability. A couple minutes passed when Kovu snapped at the air, snarling as if in pain. Rainer's stare narrowed, and his claws dug deeper into the earth—the same stance my father did when he needed to compel stubborn pack members.

This wasn't possible.

Kovu shook his head, whimpering, his tail lowering until it was between his hind legs. He snapped once again at the air, as if he could attack whatever invisible force was infiltrating his mind. Then his ears lowered, his nose touched the ground, and he bowed to Rainer.

He had been compelled.

My throat closed as the wheat colored wolf turned toward the stands, his eyes passing over me, landing on my father. There was deafening silence as exchanges passed between them. Eventually, Rainer shifted back to his human form, his hand resting on the hilt of the sword strapped to his waist. My father stood, reaching his hand out to me, willing me to take it.

I wanted to fight it, to shake my head in protest, but after that display of power, I knew all my challenges would be futile. There was nothing I could do but go along with this.

I did as my father bid, squeezing his hand far too tightly for support. I felt all eyes on me, heard the incoherent whispers.

I hated this attention. I hated this.

I bit my lip hard before raising my head and meeting those storm-grey eyes. The pain distracted me just enough to get the first words out.

"To the gods, I swear. I swear that the male before me will be my mate, that one day we will be bonded, and—"

My breathing hitched, the rest of the oath refusing to leave my lips. I placed my hand on my chest, trying to calm myself. I needed to finish it. I needed to let the pack hear the rest, or there would be chaos. But I couldn't bring myself to speak. I couldn't stop the world from spinning.

"Finish it," someone snarled.

I looked for the person who was so loud that they seemed to be in my head but found no one close enough who matched the voice. I looked to my father to see if he was just as perplexed, but he still waited, just like everyone else in the stands.

He hadn't heard the voice. No one had. Only I could hear it.

"Look at me," the voice growled again.

Without thinking, without my permission, my head slowly turned, and my eyes drifted down to the center of the arena where Rainer stood.

He was compelling me.

"Finish it," he commanded again, my silence too long for his liking.

My throat bobbed at the ferocity in the words that sounded inside my head, at the knowledge that he could now control me as the rest of the sacred oath danced over my lips. "I will pledge my mind and body to him on that day."

Rainer's hold on me released as the last word rang out, and he mimicked the words, allowing my body to slack and for me to fully feel my shattered pride.

CHAPTER 5

The stands were quiet except for the pitter patter of feet that were slowly making their way to the party and the distant cheers. But it was all noise that faded away, as my attention continued to linger on the empty ring where Rainer had stood, where he had compelled me. He was finally stronger than me. He was the strongest wolf in the pack, and I was second best.

He was overall better than me, and he knew it. He would flaunt it in my face, just as he always did in the sparring ring anytime he came close to beating me, asking if I was getting slower or if he was getting better.

I couldn't live with that for the rest of my life.

I needed to go practice.

Sweeping up the ends of my cloak and draping the excessive fabric over my arm, I began the trek down to the arena where weapons had been carelessly discarded, since they were not allowed at any festival ever since the last incident a couple years ago. It had involved two males who were too drunk to transform and far too consumed by their male arrogance. They had decided to spar to decide who would get the *honor* of kissing a playful, willing female. The fight had ended with both males and a couple of their friends in the healer's hut for a month, forcing the patrolling guard to take double shifts. Father had been furious. The entire patrolling guard had been too. But there was little punishment father could deal out, since all parties involved were consenting adults, and the lust that caused the lack of sound judgement was expected because of the mating ritual and the revelry. It was in the wolves' blood to act this way, to act as if we were all in a mild heat. It was the gods' way too to ensure there would be more of us, and we would never be punished for the natural animalistic tendencies that came with our blessing of the wolf. We could only prevent harm from happening because of it. Thus father decreed that weapons were banned at festivities. It was a much-needed benefit of tonight, as I would have my pick of any item in the armory, and since everyone had been so swept up in the excitement of learning who would be their future alpha, no one had bothered to wait to guarantee I would attend the party tonight as well.

"Ina," a cheerful voice called, accompanied by three pairs of feet.

Well, not everyone.

Pivoting, I found Ala, Catrine, and Sil hurrying toward me, their identical cloaks to mine fluttering in the wind. Ala, out of breath, was the first to reach me.

"Those two are the slowest," she huffed, tucking her golden-blonde hair behind her ear, looking up at me with the purest smile.

"We don't want to look disheveled just yet," Catrine calmly voiced as she and Sil caught up.

"Exactly. The disheveling is reserved for our mates tonight," mused Sil, causing a blush to form on Ala's cheeks. "Oh, come now, Ala. You knew this was going to happen when you found your mate." Sil patted Ala on the shoulder. "You're finally going to dirty those white sheets of yours." Ala's cheeks grew to an impossible shade of red, provoking a laugh from Sil and a small scold from Catrine as she tucked Ala under her arm.

I chuckled with a soft smile at the three females I had grown up with, the females I barely saw nowadays. We had all chosen different paths when we reached the apprentice age of sixteen. Ala spent all her time in the gardens, learning the names and uses of the herbs in our region. Catrine devoted her time to learning the scripts and being Priestess Azima's apprentice. Sil, well, she loved to be under the moon and the stars making people smile, so she worked in the tavern down in the human village as a singer. And I sparred every day, readying for the day when Artico's fighters were needed. However, that didn't dull the feelings amongst us. No matter how long we spent apart, it felt as if no time had passed, that we could pick up where we left, and that we were still sisters of the soul. It was why lying to them was going to be hard.

"Speaking of mates, all of *yours* are probably waiting for you," I cajoled, trying to rush their departure and allow me to unsuspiciously lag.

"They've waited for years. They can wait a little longer," Catrine chimed. "We wanted to walk over with you. It's been our tradition after all."

I painfully eyed the scattered weapons. I needed to practice, but Sil was right. Ever since we all started participating in the mating ritual, we walked over to the festival together, hand in hand as Ala, Catrine, and Sil pretended that they were unaffected by another failed mating ritual, whereas I feigned sadness. I had always felt guilty when they pushed away their own sorrow and tried to raise my spirits. They always thought my grief was greater than theirs, as they began to partake in the ceremony five years after my first one. In reality, I was celebrating and only felt grief for my friends who sought their destined match.

"It will be our last walk together before we are all bonded," Ala proclaimed, taking my hand in hers.

I winced at the melancholy in her voice.

How was I supposed to say no to that?

"You're stalling." Catrine stepped forward blocking my view of the javelin I was eyeing.

I forced a smile. Catrine had always been preceptive, but after her time with Priestess Azima, it was much harder to hide things from her. It was a wonder how she never caught on to my feigned sadness throughout the years.

"You don't have other places to be, do you?"

I tilted my head, my smile growing larger, trying to think of any excuse to get away. "Well, you see, I—"

The wood panels behind me groaned.

Turning my head, I saw Ellary shifting from one foot to another, twiddling with her hands whilst my father talked to an elder behind her.

My stomach twisted as air rushed past my lips at the realization that I had forgotten to dismiss Ellary. Though she had served my family for years, this was her first time working the day of a mating ritual—a day that banned all humans from our village after nightfall, as our better judgment was hazed—and dusk was nearing. With her human legs, she'd be caught in the mountain after dark, whereas a wolf could make it down in half the time.

My forced smile turned real.

I had found my excuse and a way to clear the guilt due to my negligence.

"I need to take Ellary to her village," I uttered, watching the three pairs of lips lower, their mouths tightly shutting.

I knew they wanted to tell me to find someone else, that Ellary would be alright on the trek alone, but it went against our first law—a wolf must protect humans.

My excuse was flawless, at least I thought so, until a deep voice came from behind.

"I'll take her."

"Alpha Batair," all three of my sisters spoke simultaneously, bowing their heads.

I balled my hands into fists.

The gods really did have a vendetta against me tonight.

"You four are young and should enjoy the festivities. I'll take Ellary down, Ina. Go enjoy time with your friends." Ala, Catrine, and Sil smiled brightly, thanking him as my father pushed me forward. "And Ina"—I looked back to find narrowing eyes—"don't worry about the abandoned weapons. I've already ordered the wolves who are on patrol tonight to lock them in the armory."

I ground my teeth as my father flashed me one more smile before turning to Ellary and linking his arm with hers.

Pack members danced around the bonfire, hips swaying to the alluring beat of a drum accompanied by drunk laughter and muffled moans. The scent of ale, mead, and wine filled the air, overwhelming my senses, making it easier to forget my disappointment and be present for my sisters.

"It's already gotten quite *heated*," Sil yelled as the music tried to drown out her voice.

"It was the tournament. You know how a good fight gets the blood pumping," Catrine pointed out as she untied her velvet black cloak, revealing her bare arms and the tops of her breasts to the falling snow.

"I know your wolf will warm you, but it can only do so much unless you're fully transformed, Catrine," I yelled at her as Ala nodded.

"You know, once we start dancing, all of you will be taking off your cloaks as well. It happens every year." Catrine tossed the fabric over a stack of hay, wiggling her arms as if she was already affected by the chill and didn't want to admit it.

"Or are you just trying to get to the night's end already?" Sil wrapped her arm around Catrine's shoulder. Catrine rolled her eyes playfully as another blush formed on Ala's cheeks.

Words weren't needed to explain what the *night's end* entailed, especially now that we were mated. Well, for the three of them at least. It was the reason why the festivities were so loud. It was to block out the sounds of those who were bonding tonight, those that were too impatient to wait for their female mate to go into heat or to plan a bonding ceremony—the human equivalent to a wedding.

"You're not going to make me blush, Sil." Catrine filled glasses from the ale barrel we had walked over to until we all had a cup. "I've always planned to enact the bond on the night I matched, since my heat comes just a week before the next annual mating ritual. I am not waiting that long."

"Have you talked to Eli about it yet?" Ala asked, her soft voice barely audible.

I cocked my chin to our usual standing area through the years. It was far from the band but still close enough to enjoy the music, without it blaring in our ears, and for others to know we wanted to partake in the various *activities* of the night.

Catrine shook her head. "I didn't get to talk to him much before the tournament began," she worriedly replied as we headed for our spot.

"Well, I think you have nothing to worry about, especially with these out," Sil squealed, grabbing Catrine's ample bosom.

We laughed in unison as Catrine covered her chest, running ahead of us to avoid Sil's icy hands.

"And what of you, Sil? What are your plans?" I asked as I noticed her eyeing Ala who shyly looked away, not ready to say what we all expected of her.

"Me? I'm not sure yet."

Mine and Ala's mouths both dropped open.

"Don't look at me like that," Sil defensively groaned.

"But you were teasing just a moment ago how you were going to be disheveled tonight," I quipped, further calling her bluff.

"You know I'm all talk and not any bite." I stopped in my tracks and faced my friend, earning a sigh and further explanation. "I enjoy a good night of warmth, but this is different. This is the bond we're talking about, and if I give him that connection, I want to make sure...well...you know."

Sil bounced on her toes. "I haven't ever spent time with Aspen," she nervously whispered.

Ala rubbed Sil's arm tenderly. "I'm waiting. I've already told Sam, and he gets it. I'm sure Aspen will too."

Sil's shoulders loosened as a soft smile formed on her face.

My heart warmed hearing all their plans, knowing how long they dreamed about this day, how long they had waited. They deserved this, and the males they were paired with deserved them.

I had trained with all three of their mates and knew they were good males. They were kind and gentle, and I knew each of their unique qualities would complement my friends' personalities perfectly. It made me almost believe that the gods knew what they were doing when they paired wolves at birth. Yet I still wouldn't change my prayers of the past. I didn't want a mate. I didn't want anyone that was *chosen* for me, particularly someone that I had seen as a competitor since childhood.

"Ina, did you hear us?" I looked up to see three worried pairs of eyes. Frantically, I tried to figure out what was asked.

"Well, that answers that," Sil sighed out.

I tilted my head in utter confusion.

"How are you feeling about being mated to Rainer?" Ala asked, her hand on top of mine.

"I feel," I stammered, trying to find the least offensive words in case curious ears were around. "I feel—"

"Awful? Terrible? Mad that he can compel?" Sil sputtered out before Ala covered her mouth.

"I mean, isn't this better than getting your mate?" Catrine whispered.

My pupils dilated at the words that came out of Catrine's mouth. She was the friend who believed most in the teachings. She huffed a laugh.

"Out of all the years we've known you, you really didn't think we couldn't hear your sigh of relief when they announced there were no more males to test each ceremony?" I looked at each of them as they offered me a shrug.

I opened my mouth, trying to find words to defend myself, but none came. It wasn't as if I was scared to tell them my secrets. I trusted these three with everything. It just felt wrong, disrespectful almost, to tell these three—who strongly believed in mates—that I didn't want one, that I believed it wasn't right for our emotions to be swayed by the gods' will.

"Ina, it's okay," Catrine continued as if hearing my concerns. "We all have our own beliefs. It's alright if you don't like the idea of mates, and it's alright if you don't want to share your beliefs with us. It's why we've been quiet about it." Ala and Sil nodded in agreement, the only reassurance I needed to know that they were telling the truth. Instantly, my body felt lighter. "But you are now promised to be bonded to Rainer, which is almost the same as finding your mate at a ritual. We want to make sure you're okay, that you know you don't have to go through this alone."

I stiffened seeing all three of them look at me with worry. They earnestly wanted to know, to comfort me, and now that my secret was out, I wanted them to. I wanted to tell them I was angry, that I didn't want to be here, that I needed to be in the ring. I wanted to tell them that I needed to train because it was the only thing I could control, but I knew that would only make them worry more, that they would comfort me and let me go to the ring. They may even follow like the good friends they were, and I couldn't let them do that. I wouldn't take away the magic of this night for them. One more night of repressed feelings wouldn't hurt.

I dropped my shoulders, breathing out. "It could be worse." I gripped my cup, trying to keep my hands from shaking, putting on my best show.

"Oh, Ina," Ala extended her hand, seeing right through my act, when robust laughter a few feet away caught our attention.

A horde of males stood in a circle, ale sloshing out of their cups, their faces blood red, and their mouths open so wide that their canines could be seen from a mile away. All of them pushed to be closer to the male who stood in the middle, Rainer, regally holding his mug like he hadn't had a single drop, like he was already alpha and everyone was his to control.

My blood began to boil once again, my breathing turning heavy.

As if he could feel my rage, his smile faded. He craned his neck left then right, scanning like he was on patrol, looking for the nearest threat. It wasn't long until his eyes fell on me, and his alert exterior changed. One side of his lips raised, and his eyes filled with excitement for the challenge of me.

Sneering at myself and him, I looked away. The former because I shouldn't have let him see my anger, that he affected me. It was the first lesson of combat—don't show your emotions. It's how enemies took advantage of you. And it was a thing I struggled with, as I led with my heart.

"There you all are," a husky voice came from behind.

Turning, I found three males—Sam, Eli, and Aspen—heading toward us, toward their mates. I glanced at my sisters and found them all to be bright red while they clutched their cups closer to their chests. Their worry for me was temporarily gone, replaced with nerves and excitement they had no control over, exactly as it should be on a night so special to them.

I muffled a laugh as the three males reached us. If only my friends knew that these males were the softest of warriors. Not in strength, of course. I would never let my sisters go to someone who couldn't protect them. They were the softest because they—unlike the majority of the pack's warriors—constantly talked about finding their mates and the day they'd be able to hold their cubs.

The three males stood in front of their mates, waiting for them to say anything, but all three females stood awestruck. They were an intimidating sight, particularly since the other males in their field were mere ants next to Sam, Eli, and Aspen, but it didn't lessen the urge to giggle.

I sucked in my lips as both sets looked at me, waiting for me to assist in this awkward encounter. I only shrugged as my smile grew.

This was far too entertaining to end just yet.

A burst of pain ran up my shin, causing me to stumble and my teeth to dig deep into my lip. I yelped, looking down to see Sil's foot retracting.

"Really?" I mumbled so only she could hear.

Her eyes darted to the males then back to me, begging. I shook my head, smiling foolishly. I suppose they had been tortured enough for the night, but Sil would pay for that kick.

"For warriors, you were awfully slow to greet your mates. Maybe I should ask Alpha Batair to give you some extra training." I crossed my arms, cocked my head to the side, and spread my feet so they were shoulder-length apart, taking the persona I took when father left me in charge of training, otherwise known as hell days.

The three males shuddered, making Ala, Catrine, and Sil's eyes widened.

"Please, no," pleaded Sam.

"It's all the scents in the air. We couldn't smell where you were," Aspen added as Eli nodded rapidly.

Ala, Catrine, and Sil's lips parted slightly, amusement twinkling in their eyes, seeing that even these males could be frazzled just like any other.

I took a sip from my cup, hiding my gloating as I realized my plan was working. All that was left was to ensure Sam, Eli, and Aspen were comfortable.

"I don't quite believe you." I glanced at the bonfire where couples danced, their breathing ragged from the demanding songs that were often played tonight. "Perhaps if you survive three or four songs, I'll consider your cardio sound."

"That'd be easy," Eli stated, a smile forming on his face, on all of the males' faces. They loved challenges too much.

"It would be, but you'll need a partner." Sil tensed up. Though she performed at the human tavern, her acts were mainly stationary, as she was never graceful on her feet. "These three seem to be available," I chimed, waving toward my sisters.

Sam, Eli, and Aspen grinned, holding out their hands to their respected mate. Catrine was the first to accept, next was Ala, leaving Sil.

"I hate you for this," Sil grumbled into my ear.

I smirked at her. "Don't kick me next time, and I'll be nicer with my help."

She glared at me but then examined Rainer. "Will you be alright alone? He doesn't look like he intends to come over soon."

I discreetly followed her gaze. Rainer, now sitting smugly on a hut's railing, was still surrounded by the drunk males, smiling at the praise that was flowing through his ears. Sil was right. He wouldn't be leaving *that* anytime soon, but that was more than fine with me. The last thing I needed tonight was for him to seek me out.

"I'll be fine. I've always been great at entertaining myself." I gave Sil a playful push. "Now, go. Have fun."

Sil gave me one last smile as Aspen nodded in thanks. Then they headed over to the bonfire. I watched quietly, letting the music fill my ears, remembering all the nights Sil, Ala, Catrine, and I danced to the song. It had been our song for many years, but it was theirs now. It was one more thing that was going to change tonight, and hopefully, the final change.

CHAPTER 6

Four songs had played since I sent my sisters and fellow warriors to the bonfire. It was all that was needed for them to smile in each other's arms, for them to push aside their nerves and give their heart to their mate.

Each of my sisters' eyes sparkled, and a rosy blush painted their cheeks. They wouldn't look for me the rest of the night. They were wholly enchanted by their mates, and I was truly happy for them, but it was a reminder of why I didn't want that bond. Naturally or forced. They had barely talked to them before tonight, and now they were utterly infatuated with each other. It didn't make sense.

I set my cup down on a barrel nearby and made my way back to the arena. The weapons wouldn't be out, but I still had one trick up my sleeve or rather my dress—a dagger that I always kept with me no matter what.

I trudged through the snow that covered the ground like a blanket, admiring how pristine it was. It barely had a mark, except for the handful of footprints that led to different huts, left by the couples who had waited as long as they could in the cold and were now being warmed by either their mate or a temporary lover.

Pausing to look up at the clear night sky, I inhaled deeply, allowing my nose to be refreshed from the smell of drink, my lungs to wake with the cold, brisk air. For the first time tonight, I felt at ease as the scent of pine trees circled around me.

At least I'd always have this. The bond would never change my feelings on these small things.

Fingers wrapped tightly around my forearm, pulling me into the darkness that lay between two huts, the movement far too fast for my ale filled body to react before I was pinned between a wall and a bulging chest. I reached for my dagger, trying to level the field, but another hand caught my wrist and held it above my head with my other hand.

"You're not supposed to have that," a taunting voice, I knew all too well, chided as the cold hands readjusted, so only one hand encompassed both of my wrists, allowing the other to trail up my thigh, pulling the knife from its sheath before throwing it deeper into the darkness where no passerby would find it.

I glared into storm-grey eyes, a string of curses dancing out of my mouth as I realized the hold Rainer had put me in. It was the only one I could never get out of when faced with a bigger opponent. There was no point in fighting. I had to wait until his guard was down or to find a weakness caused by tonight's revelry.

"Well, when one is greeted in such a brutish manner, it comes in handy." I kicked, testing to see if the drink had turned his legs soft. It only made his leg push farther between mine, making it rest against my entrance.

"It doesn't look to be that *handy* when it's all the way over there." He cocked his head down the alley, an arrogant smirk on his face.

I chewed on my cheek. If this had been a fair fight, he'd be on the ground already bruising.

"What do you want, Rainer?" I growled, wiggling my wrist to see if there was enough sweat between our skin to slip out from his grip.

"I just wanted to talk." He tightened his hold with a raised brow as if to ask me *really*.

"You couldn't have talked to me like a normal person?"

Rainer rolled his eyes. "We both know you would've walked away."

"I don't think you would've given me the choice," I spat, "seeing as how happy you were when you compelled me last." I thrust my body forward, only to be squashed against the wall again, bringing Rainer's mouth so close to mine that I could feel his hot breath.

"I wouldn't have to do it if you behaved."

I sneered. I didn't want to be compelled, but I most certainly did not want Rainer to think that I would bend to his will. "Go ahead, and do it. I will never act how you want me to."

Rainer's grip tightened, and his lips formed into an even tighter line. I braced myself for him to enter my mind, but he only snapped his head away in agitation like he had been defeated.

I perked up in confusion but did not dwell too long on his actions, realizing that his attention was on other thoughts, just enough for me to try something.

I kicked hard into Rainer's shin and thrust my forehead forward, hitting the bridge of his nose. Instinctively, his hands cradled it, freeing my wrists. I pushed on his chest, successfully creating a gap large enough between us that I could throw a decent punch. I aimed for his gut, but where I should've hit his stomach, I felt his coarse palm.

Damn the effects of ale.

Rainer's hand engulfed my fist, spinning my arm around my back as he pushed my chest into the wall. "Gods, Ina. Calm down. If someone sees us like this, there will be so much talk tomorrow that it won't matter if we took an oath. Can you be clear headed for one second? Think of your father."

I exhaled slowly, calming my boiling blood.

I hated that he was right. The pack would expect some anger from me, but if they saw an all-out-brawl, they would think I was planning on running, and the change in power would be hastened.

"Fine. Just stop pushing my face into this wall," I somehow managed to say with only a bit of aggression.

"I will, but only if you stop hitting me and *trying* to run."

Begrudgingly, I nodded, ignoring his emphasis on the word trying.

Rainer's hold loosened. However, as I spun around, he planted his hands on the walls by my hips, trapping me in. I bared my fangs in warning but did nothing more, knowing I could easily escape when I wanted.

"Alright, talk. I want to get on with my night," I barked, crossing my arms over my chest, backing into the wall so I stood as far away from him as I could.

Rainer straightened. "I just wanted to make sure you weren't going to run."

"That's it? That's what you wanted to ask when you pinned me to a wall?" I scoffed, "Unbelievable." Still, Rainer looked on, waiting for an answer. "No, I won't. I understand, probably more than you, what that would mean." I pushed against his arm, singling to him I wanted to leave, but he didn't budge. "Move. The less I see your face the better," I snarled.

"Is it really that bad to be promised to me?" Rainer took a step forward. "I thought, after these past years, after you chose me to help with your heat again and again, you might be joyed a little that I won."

I flexed my fingers as my body recalled how Rainer had made me feel during my yearly heat, another thing the gods *blessed* us with. For two weeks out of the year, females were fertile and with that came impossibly strong pheromones and a weakened wolf form. It unlocked the unbonded males animalistic need to mate, making them feral. Of course, most males that were part of a pack had control over their urges due to the training they had to take once they reached adulthood, along with the accountability other wolves held them to. It was what was expected. Rape was never tolerated in our society. However, the males did burrow their eyes into the females and breathe a little too deeply whenever they were near. The heat made males lose focus, compete for the female's attention, and sometimes made them physically be in pain depending on the natural attraction they had for the female in heat. It made life a bit irritating but still doable, unless you were me.

Since most of our attack force consisted of males, my heat affected the entire unit during training, meetings, and patrols. Our plans and teams had to be reorganized anytime it happened. I had to either work strictly with the bonded males—they typically stayed close to the pack for their mates and cubs, meaning my choices in missions was limited—or work in isolation. I hated it. I especially hated it when I had been tracking a band of thieves and had to be taken off the mission, since it was easier to replace me than the six unbonded wolves who I was partnered with at the time. While it made sense, it didn't make me feel any less terrible. It gave me another reminder of my fate, that because I was female, I was treated differently, just like when it came to the change of alphas. After that day, I swore I would never let my heat affect my life like that again, and there was only one way to do that. I had to sleep with an unmated male. In doing so, my body would be appeased and halt any production of pheromones. The wolves inside of the males would stop being affected by me, and I would carry on with my life. It was like this for every female, and it was our choice to do so as long as we were happy about it. It was why casual sex was never frowned upon in Artico. However, this solution did come with a risk.

The false mating bond. The worst type of bond for a wolf shifter.

They were unpredictable. Some lasted for a couple days, while others would last for months. Some felt as real as a mating bond, while others felt like a silly infatuation. Either way, when it broke, you were left with a melancholy feeling and felt like something was missing. For some, the feeling was so strong that they tried to make the relationship work after the false bond ended, but more times than not, it ended in a disaster. The wolves who were bonded either realized the strong feelings between them were all created by their false bond, or one of them would find their mate.

It was quite the gamble, which was why I chose Rainer two years after I tired of all the *accommodations* made for me.

He had seemed the least affected by my pheromones, and with the fact that we were competitors, I highly doubted the false bond would be more than a tiny infatuation. I wasn't sure why he agreed to it or even bothered to keep it a secret, though. Rainer always got better missions when I wasn't there. But if I had to guess, I suppose it was because he got some sick pleasure knowing that he was helping me and that he was a part of a secret that I didn't want anyone to know about, a secret he could use against me. Even though it was common for females to take lovers during their heat, sleeping with a male who I swore was my rival seemed like a good thing for people to tease me about. Either way, after the first time, I found my prediction to be right and that began our yearly tradition of Rainer visiting me at the start of my heat.

"You know why I chose you," I spat, placing my hand on his chest, trying to keep the space between us from growing smaller.

"I know the reason you told me each time and all the times you *needed* me during the false bond, but you forget that I was with others before you. You forget that I can tell when a female is enjoying me or her wolf is. And you, Ina, always fell into that first category."

My breathing grew shallow as my body betrayed me. My arm trembled and began to bend, allowing Rainer to close the space between us.

I cursed. Rainer was great in bed, acted like he had something to prove, but I still didn't want him more than just physically, and I had told him that each time he teased that I might. I had been abundantly clear about it, and each time he said he was fine with it. Because of that, I had always joined with him when I had the urge to, but now was not the time to give into those urges. Not when he was allowed to claim so much of me, was claiming so much of me already, taking a title that should have been mine.

"You're wrong," I mumbled as he leaned in, his nose grazing my neck.

"Then, tell me why you smell the way you do," he said in a guttural tone as his hand slipped under my silk dress.

My entire body tightened at his touch.

I needed to stop him, but my hand only gripped tighter to his tunic, and my head pivoted so his hair tickled my nose, so his alluring scent flooded my senses.

Taking that as an invitation, Rainer nipped the lobe of my ear. A small whimper escaped my lips, but it was permission enough for Rainer to close the space between us. His hand cupped my sex with only my thin undergarments between them as his mouth found mine.

I tried to remain still, tried to act like I didn't like it, but my body had other plans. My fingers ran through his hair, my tongue slipped into his mouth, and my hips ground on that deliciously strong hand.

Whimper after whimper came as my body craved more, pleaded for more. It had been so long since I had been touched like this.

I shouldn't have ever wanted him like this. I shouldn't want him like this now. Not after the tournament. I needed to stop this. I would—

My head jerked back, and my breath became lost to me as Rainer's fingers curled inside me, his thumb circling the bundle of nerves just above my entrance.

This was what I needed.

I moved my hips in sync with his fingers, urging him to go faster, but his other hand pressed against my hips, pinning them to the wall as he pumped his fingers tantalizingly slow.

I growled.

Why? Why was he teasing so much?

I looked up to find him peering down at me, his breathing completely ragged, his eyes ravenous.

He wanted me. So, why was he going so slow?

Kicking off the wall, I attempted to free my hips but was pushed back. I glared only to find him smiling.

"Ask for it, Ina."

My throat bobbed. Never, in all the times that we had lain with each other, had I done *that*. I just needed to summon him and undress, then we would go on with our business without a word. It made our transaction so much less humiliating for me.

He placed his lips on the base of my neck, slowly moving them up with the occasional tender nip. "Ina, tell me you want it."

My stomach twisted but not at the command. It twisted at the hint of begging behind his words, as if he wanted to hear me ask, not to humiliate me, but because he wanted to turn this into something more.

I bit my lip, suppressing the words the lust in me wanted to say.

It would never work out between us. We both wanted too many of the same things and did not want to share. It would only lead to strife unless something had changed, but there was something so satisfying about Rainer begging.

I shook my head, fighting myself, but couldn't anymore as Rainer looked at me with earnest eyes.

Maybe we could learn? Maybe this could be something more?

"Please," I whimpered.

His body slacked for a moment as if he was relieved, then he smiled devilishly before kneeling in the cold snow at my feet. Both his hands climbed up my legs, reaching my undergarments, and with all his force, he tugged them down.

I leaned back and spread my legs, giving him permission to do whatever he wanted.

Rainer looked up at me, victorious possession in his eyes. My gut twisted instantly, but not in the pleasurable sense.

"You're going to be mine, Ina. I'll be the pack's alpha, and more importantly, I'll be yours."

I shook my head. I was wrong. He had to be the strongest. He wanted to be more powerful than me and be able to control me.

"I'll be the strongest in the pack all so I can—"

I raised my knee in one swoop, ramming it hard into his nose.

"I don't belong to anyone, and I don't belong to *you*." I pulled my cloak closer to me, returning my undergarments to where they originally sat and headed for my blade "And you may be able to compel, but in a fair fight, I would win. I will always be stronger than you. Don't you dare try to belittle me." I sheathed the dagger away. "And just so you know, it was the drink that made me ask for you. I won't ever do it again," I declared, watching a few drops of blood drip from his nose.

Rainer reached for me as I walked to the exit of the alley, only to have me kick his hand away.

"Ina, that's not what I was—"

His words faded away as the stench of iron filled the air.

Blood. Lots of it, and it wasn't Rainer's.

"Ina, are you listening to me?"

I held up my hand to silence him. "Do you smell that?" I asked in a tone I reserved for missions.

Rainer wiped the blood from his nose and turned his head up before sniffing the air. His nose wrinkled, and his eyes grew.

"We should—"

Screams cut him off.

Screams of the pack.

We didn't even look at each other as we instinctively shifted.

CHAPTER 7

We raced toward the bonfire as screams turned to shrieks. I prayed that this wasn't an attack, that it was some weird misunderstanding, but even as we ran, all traces of merriment were gone. All signs pointed to an attack, but none of them prepared us for the sight we beheld when we stopped running.

Huts were burning, blood drenched the snow, pack members—too filled with drink, unable to call upon their wolf—cowered as pale figures resembling humans stalked toward them. I sniffed the air, trying to figure out what they were, but the smell of blood was too great.

An all too familiar scream sounded.

Sil's scream.

My sisters were in danger.

Frantically, I scanned the area, but all too late.

Sil and Ala trembled behind Aspen—still in human form—who was covered in blood. His own or others, I couldn't tell. Sam and Eli, their bodies lay still a couple feet away from my terrified friends, their lifeless eyes still open, making it appear that they were staring at something. I followed them, scared that they would lead to the last missing person. Sure enough, they did.

Catrine was captured by one of the pale humans. One of his hands was shoved through her stomach, the other wrapped around her neck. Hot tears streamed from her eyes, and her entire body shook. I raced forward, claws out, ready to kill, but I didn't reach her in time before the monster sunk his fangs into Catrine's neck and fed.

I froze. There was only one type of monster that drank blood like that.

Blood demons—creatures that appeared human but were anything but.

Unlike wolves, who lived for thousands of years, they lived for eternity, thriving in the world with their unnatural strength and agility. Their skin never sagged or blemished once they lived for a quarter of a century. They just stopped aging. They were left to live beautifully forever, but at a horrendous price. They needed blood to live.

They were our ultimate enemy. The world's ultimate enemy, and they were supposed to be extinct. We hadn't seen or heard of one on the continent since the Blood War ended nineteen years ago.

Eradicating the demons had been the purpose of the hundred-year war but at a great cost. The Blood War had decimated our numbers and the numbers of wolves on the continent, leaving only a few packs scattered around it. Packs that, even after nineteen years, still refused to communicate, work together, or answer to the King of the Wolves. It had destroyed our way of life. It was a life I had barely known as I was only five when the war ended, but nonetheless, it was a crime within itself. A crime we hadn't recovered from.

The demons couldn't be back. It couldn't be.

Rage and fear fueling me, I jumped on the demon, claws digging into his back, ensuring that if he moved, I went with him. He dropped Catrine to the ground, shrieking, his arms flailing as he tried to separate me from his back, but it was useless. I bit down on his neck, his blood gushing into my mouth. I fought the urge to vomit as I spat it out, along with the demon's mutilated head whilst I watched his squirming body, waiting for it to collapse. I needed to make sure that the lessons were true, that if you separated the head from the body the immortal monsters would die.

Thank the gods, it was.

"Ina," Catrine beckoned, reaching out to me as snow fell on her exposed innards. "It hurts," Catrine mewled, the words struggling to come out.

I pushed my snout against her hand, my heart breaking as I took note of her labored breathing, her pale face, the intestines that lay half inside her and half on the ground.

I looked at Aspen, hoping he didn't agree with me, but he shook his head with hope abandoned eyes. Catrine would die, and it would be long and painful. There was nothing we could do, at least, nothing to heal her.

I nodded at Ala and Sil who stood still as stone, making sure Aspen saw. He nodded back, knowing what I was about to do.

I waited as he mumbled something to both my sisters. Sil shook her head viciously. She tried to run toward me while Ala looked on in shock, but Aspen held her back, pushed her face into his chest as she slammed her fists into him over and over. Aspen, still fighting Sil, urged Ala to turn. She did, but all the light from her eyes was gone.

I looked down to Catrine, wondering how to explain what I was about to do, only to find her painfully smiling at me. "Take away the hurt, Ina."

I choked back tears. She knew. Of course she knew. Catrine was the smartest out of all of us.

I bent down to lick Catrine's cheek, my nondominant paw nudging against her hand, and held her gaze. She nodded shallowly, giving me permission again, before I quickly shoved my claws into her heart.

The light faded from her eyes, her chest ceased to move, and I knew the pain was no longer there.

I knew Catrine was no longer here.

CHAPTER 8

"**B**ehind you!" Aspen roared.

I spun around to find red eyes above me, fangs ready to seep into my flesh. I braced myself for the impact but felt a rush of wind hit me as wheat colored fur flooded my vision.

Rainer and the blood demon tumbled to the ground. A symphony of growls and screeches sounded as their bodies twisted and collided with one another. The demon's arms wrapped around Rainer's neck, the grip growing tighter, threatening to snap the delicate bones.

I lunged as I did with the previous demon just as Rainer's eyes started to close, aiming for his back, but he saw me coming and flung me away with a small flick of his wrist. I collided with the ground, felt my wrist turn unnaturally. Still, I stood. As much as I hated him, I wouldn't let Rainer die. There had been too much death already.

The demon barely shifted his focus my way, treating me like a mere nuisance and nothing more. My anger flared, and I lunged again. The demon laughed, thinking he'd deflect me like he did before. He threw up his arm waiting, and as he swung, I pivoted, opened my mouth, and clamped down.

"Let go, beast! Let go!" the demon cried as he pushed on my snout, trying to gain any distance from me.

My eyes widened. They could talk. These demons, from my memories, I only remembered them screeching. Still, I held on until Rainer came to and started sprinting, canines bared. He tore the head cleanly off, dropping it just as fast as I dropped the demon's arm, spitting out the vile blood.

Once composed, Rainer nodded to me in thanks, knowing there was no time for rivalry, for us to pretend we didn't need help. This was a real battle, and though we had trained for combat since we were sixteen, nothing could have trained us for this, to finally face the blood demons who we thought were extinct. Yet here they were, stronger than we had ever been told.

"We can't leave her. We can't!" Sil screamed, clutching Catrine's body as Aspen tried to hush her, tried not to attract the attention of the other blood demons that were busy feasting on pack members we failed to save. But their blood wouldn't last much longer with the way the demons were guzzling it down. Sil and Ala needed to leave now. It was the only way that they would survive.

I moved closer, ready to tell Aspen to retreat with one of the silent signals we memorized to communicate with in wolf form, but Sil screamed, "Stay away, Ina. You killed her. She was still alive after he let go, and you killed her," stopping me in my tracks.

I felt an arrow pierce through my heart, felt immense pain at the hatred in Sil's eyes, the growl in her voice I had never heard. She had never been this angry at me before, and she was the temperamental one of the group.

Ala knelt next to Sil, giving me pitiful looks, attempting to calm Sil as Aspen held her back. "She was gone already, Sil. No number of herbs and stitches would have fixed her," Ala whispered between Sil's sobs.

Ignoring the emotional turmoil inside me, I took advantage of Sil's focus shifting to Ala and tucked my tail between my legs as I flattened my ears and jerked my head to the woods—the signal for retreat.

Aspen shook his head. "I can fight too." He closed his eyes, trying to summon his wolf, but no matter how hard he tried, not a single hair emerged.

I gestured again, making sure to point to Sil and Ala, telling him they wouldn't survive on their own in the woods.

Aspen breathed deep, looking around at the carnage, at the dead bodies, at the huts that were collapsing, at the wolves who were pinned down, and at the lost village. His fists tightened, and his knuckles turned white. He was a warrior, and it was his job to fight, but it was also his job to recognize when a battle was a lost cause, when it was time to run and live another day. I hoped he remembered that.

Thankfully, he did.

Aspen solemnly nodded before standing and trying to drag Sil away from Catrine's body.

"Come on, Sil," he growled, taking on a warrior's voice. Sil clung harder, Catrine's blood staining her golden hair.

She wasn't going to leave.

My heart sped. Aspen would have to force her off the body, wrestle Sil perhaps, but that would attract the attention they needed to avoid. I needed to think of something fast. But before I could, a low growl came from behind.

Rainer stood not a foot away, his eyes narrowing, claws digging into the dirt. Sil stood, baring her canines but turned, grabbing Ala's hand, and willingly headed into the woods.

Aspen's throat bobbed, and his neck bent as if he wanted to bow in thanks for Rainer's power, instead he hastily swore, "I'll protect them until we meet again. You two better survive," before following Sil and Ala to the woods, staying in the shadows.

Never did I think I'd be grateful that Rainer could compel.

Rainer and I searched for anyone breathing, anyone we could rescue. We took on the demons that were by themselves, not risking taking on more than one at a time between us, and snuck by the ones in groups, listening to our cornered pack members' pleas as they saw us run past them. We listened to their screams as we nudged the ones we could save toward the forest, urging them to flee. It was all happening too fast. It was all too chaotic, and my head was spinning. Still, I urged myself to keep going, to ignore the breaking of my heart as I saw familiar faces lie still in the snow.

Find, assess, decide if to kill or to run; those were the actions we took until there was nothing left but dead bodies, a handful of wolves that managed to turn, us, and the remainder of the blood demons who tripled our numbers.

The blood demons stalked toward us with red-stained fangs.

It was time to retreat or the few of us who had stayed behind wouldn't survive.

We backed away slowly, making our way to the woods. We were four steps away from the edge when several shrieks sounded just outside the dining hall, when several wolflings raced out the crumbling building.

The demons' eyes widened, confused at what caused the shrilling sound, but when they saw, they smiled broadly, smiled at the easy prey. They turned their backs to us.

No.

I had watched too many die tonight. I would not let the blood demons take the lives of those who had barely lived.

I lunged, digging my claws into the back of the closest fiend. He shrieked, trying to alert his comrades, but they were too consumed by bloodlust. They continued their hunt, getting closer and closer to the cubs.

No, no, no.

I bit down on the demon's neck, cursing him to die quicker, when the rest of the wolves jutted forward. Half of them raced to the cubs, forming a protective circle around them, as the other half jumped over the demons and blocked their path, allowing the wolflings to escape with the first group.

I joined the second group, content to battle, to die here if that ensured the wolflings would survive. No matter—

"We can't leave Alpha Batair," an unshifted wolfling cried as she was picked up by the scruff of her tunic. "He's in the hall still. He hid us there until a demon came in. He's still in there fighting it."

My fur stood on end, guilt-ridden that I had not thought of my father until now. I was so used to him being strong and being able to stand on his own that I had not given a thought as to where he was. I had assumed he was in the village down below, evacuating the humans, as he had taken Ellary down not a couple hours ago. It never occurred to me that he might have returned, that he had been fighting by himself when his strength was waning.

I analyzed the crumbling building. I had mere minutes before it came tumbling down.

I needed to get to him, but I couldn't abandon this fight. Father would never forgive me if I abandoned the people he was supposed to protect to save him. That wasn't what an alpha was supposed to do.

I surveyed my surroundings.

The children were nearly engulfed by the forest, the demons were distracted by the grown wolves in front of them, and Rainer was giving orders to retreat once the children were gone in hopes of preserving most of the warriors here. I would make my move then. With all of us running in separate directions, it would send the demons into a frenzy, allowing me to rush into the fiery hall.

I stood on the tips of my toes, keeping my paws light as I watched the children disappear into the darkness. Then, finally, I watched as Rainer's ears went flat and his tail lowered between his legs. I didn't wait to hear the scrap of claws against the ground or for all the adult wolves to turn before I headed for the falling building, my fur already singeing.

"Ina, turn back," Rainer growled in my head, using the tone I heard at the tournament.

My paws slowed.

I cursed.

I would not turn away from my father. I would not be compelled.

"Now, Ina," Rainer ordered. "It's too late for him. Run to the woods and run far from here."

I felt myself pivoting.

I bit down on my cheek, the pain pulsing through my body. My mind focused on how to stop it and less on Rainer's commands.

Pain.

I could use pain as a distraction.

Before Rainer had time to issue another command, I threw my sprained paw into the fire, howling as it burned my flesh, keeping it there until the pain was enough that my mind could focus on nothing else.

I flashed a look to Rainer who stood on the forest's edge in the stance that meant he was trying to compel. His thoughts didn't reach me. In fact, I felt nothing.

I signaled for Rainer to retreat, and his fur bristled before I raced toward my father.

CHAPTER 9

My body screamed at me to stop as the heat rose and the soot turned my white fur black. My paw throbbed with pain, but I kept running, kept sniffing, trying to track my father, but I only inhaled smoke.

I wouldn't let him die here. I wouldn't. It wasn't his time yet.

"Where is she?" a deep unfamiliar voice roared. "Give her to me."

"You won't find what you seek here." My father's voice was strained. "This attack will only cause pain."

I sprinted to the voices.

My father lay on the ground, a demon's long legs straddling his body as its fingers twisted in my father's hair, forcing their eyes to meet. I froze with fear as I looked upon the demon and sensed his prowess. He wasn't like the demons I had fought outside. He didn't have ravenous eyes, and his garments were clean, void of any shade of red as if he hadn't feasted on a single living thing tonight, as if bloodlust hadn't taken over. He held himself in such a regard he looked human, and I would have thought it too if it weren't for his crimson eyes.

"This is your last chance," the blood demon threatened, drawing a dagger from his belt. "Tell me." My father glared in response to the roaring voice. "Have it your way, then. Your death will be long and painful." The demon raised his dagger, the action helping me out of my stupor.

I rushed through the flames that had been hiding me, biting the demon's forearm. Black blood spewed out. I shook his arm hard, my teeth tearing through his muscles. I had nearly reached his bone when his knee hit my chest, flinging me breathless on the floor beside my father.

"Who's this?" the demon calmly asked, as if he wasn't in any pain.

My father crawled over my body, shielding me from the eyes of the approaching demon.

"Leave her, Marcellus. This is between us," Father growled, removing Artico's Fang from his neck then sliding it over my head, tucking it into my tunic.

Marcellus's eyes gleamed. "She resembles your coat from ten years ago." I made a move to stand but was pushed back down by my father. "If I had to guess, she's just who I've been looking for," Marcellus honeyed out. "It's time for your line to end, but only after I make her scream a bit." Marcellus licked his lips.

I shivered, actually shivered, but I refused to be a coward. I wasn't raised like that. I was the alpha's daughter. I tried to stand once again, but Father shielded me further, blocking my view. I fought against him, wondering if the fire had clouded his mind. He would never want me to cower from a fight, not one I could win, and I was sure I could with this one. It was only one demon after all.

"I'm going to attack him, and when I do, you *will* run." My father's voice echoed in my mind, compelling me. I shook my head, looking at him with bewilderment, willing him to see reason. To run while he distracted Marcellus was to sentence him to death. "You do not know who you deal with. You cannot win," he assured me, as if he had heard my previous thought. "If you go now, one of us will live. Leave me." I extended my paw, reaching for a pile of burning wood, refusing to accept his command. I would not lose my father today. However, before the fire could even singe my fur, my father's grip tightened, stopping me from moving. "Run until you reach the Castle of Rivelia," he ordered, his voice so much harsher, all of his compelling power thrown into it. "Go nowhere else. If you do, you will not make it. Once you get there, tell King Damon what happened today. He will protect you."

Rivelia.

My nose scrunched at the name.

It was the home of our allies long ago. It was once the gathering place of the wolf packs across Aplela, ruled by *King* Damon—the leader of the wolves. At least that's how it was until the war, until the packs were decimated, until King Damon closed their gates and lived a solitary life, leaving the remainder of the packs to fully govern themselves.

Why would they help?

"Where should I make her bleed first?" Marcellus stalked toward us, a sickening grin on his face as he twirled the dagger in his hand without a worry that it would cut him.

Father straightened his back, his eyes forming a watery coating.

"Run," he commanded as he let out a frightening growl and shifted into his wolf form, his claws aiming for Marcellus's head. "Run," he commanded again, and I did, unable to fight him.

CHAPTER 10

My feet had a mind of their own. No matter how badly I wanted to turn, to run back, I couldn't. I ran out of the fire past the dead bodies, past the blood-soaked snow, past the wolves that were being dragged away by demons to only the gods knew where. Then I ran into the woods, deep into the woods, hating myself the entire way.

I was halfway down the mountain when I heard the dining hall come crashing down, when I heard maniacal laughter and psychotic cheers. I was halfway down when my feet stopped, and I realized my will was my own again.

Father. He had...

I would rip Marcellus apart.

I changed my heading, too fueled by rage to see the demon sprinting toward me. I fell to the ground. Warm blood dripped onto my fur as fangs came toward my neck. Adrenaline kicking in, I pushed the demon off, ignoring the pain of my sprained, blistering paw.

His red-brown eyes—more on the brown side—examined me as he unsheathed a dagger. "Finally, a wolf not yet eaten from. Your fur will make a nice coat for my daughter," the demon cajoled. "I'll be careful not to stain it while I'm cutting you up."

I huffed impatiently. I needed to get to Marcellus. I needed to find him and exact revenge for my father, for everyone, but I still had enough common sense that I knew I had to face this demon first. It wouldn't be the best strategy to have someone following from behind when I charged in. I just needed to finish this fast.

With a growl, I rushed forward. The demon held his ground, his dagger solidly held in front of him. I had him. I'd finish him the same way I did the others who had underestimated my speed, but just as my mouth opened, the demon rolled with immeasurable speed, his blade the only part protruding from the ball his body had formed. I cocked my head, surprised at the speed that I had not seen from any of the demons yet. From the demon's attacking stance, I didn't think he had that much power nor had I scented a spectacular prowess on him as I did Marcellus. I only smelt the blood of wolves on him, in him. Yet, I had barely dodged the demon's counterattack, had barely lifted my leg in time so his dagger only nicked my upper arm.

Was I that tired? Or did the demon have something on him to make him more powerful that I couldn't detect?

The demon began to snicker, pleased with the tiny cut he had made.

"Soon, I shall have my prize," he sang to himself.

These demons were so deranged. A cut like that was nothing to be—

Pain.

Pain like nothing I'd ever felt danced on the cut. It was like fire, and it was spreading.

What in the gods' name was happening?

As if hearing my question, the demon licked my blood from his knife, revealing the material it was made of.

Silver.

It was the wolves' greatest weakness.

We couldn't hold the material without yelping, without dropping it immediately. Being cut by it, having the microscopic silver shavings—that separated from the blade when it tore open flesh—in our blood would result in silver sickness.

The body would feel incalculable pain where the silver struck. It'd grow weak—unable to shift or hold wolf form—then the wound would fester, and the pain would turn into a deadly fever. According to books, a small wound like this would take a few days to fester, however, given my already weakened body, I wouldn't be surprised if it came much faster. Much, much faster.

Damn it all. I could already feel my wolf growing tired.

I needed to run. I needed to survive. But Marcellus...

No. I had to push aside my feelings and urges, just as I had told Aspen to do, because now I knew with absolute certainty that I could win no more battles today.

I would find Marcellus another day and rip his head off, but first, I needed to kill the demon before me, or he'd catch up to me in no time.

"She's going to love her new coat. Or will it be a cloak?" the demon pondered, waiting for me to go unconscious, his guard clearly down, too confident in the silver. But he didn't account for my will to live, my anger.

I gathered the remaining of my strength and leapt. My mouth engulfed his head before he had time to shriek, then I ran again.

I ran for hours. I ran until the smell of blood and smoke dissipated. I ran through the pain until my tail disappeared, my fur shed away, and my paws turned to feet and hands. With labored breathing, I pulled my cloak close to me, sinking to the ground, tucking myself under the branches of a willow tree as the world faded to black.

CHAPTER II

Every part of my body ached as I shifted away from the light protruding through the willow tree's leaves. A soft wind wafted the smell of soot and blood that lingered on my body up to my nose, reminding me of the terrors of last night.

Sitting up, ignoring the consuming urge to keep resting, pain shot through my upper arm. Groaning, I shifted my cloak, revealing the cut from the silver dagger.

The wound was severely inflamed and gleamed red. Yellow-green liquid bubbled out of the cut and dripped down my arm. The smell was rancid, like rotting meat. I covered my mouth, swallowing, pushing back down what little food I had eaten before the attack.

I needed a poultice and fast.

But with what herbs?

I had studied little about the plants that could heal, confident that I would always have access to a healer or Ala.

I wished I had paid attention now.

I ripped the bottom of my silk dress, careful not to irritate the sprained wrist or my blistering hand, and made a couple bandages. I wrapped one around the festering wound and tied the others around my uninjured wrist for later use. It wouldn't heal the wound, and it certainly wasn't the cleanest dressing, but the cloth would prevent any further debris from getting inside the flesh, giving me just a little more time to find help or the Castle of Rivelia.

With shaking quads, I stood, stepping cautiously out of the willow tree's protection. I didn't recognize this place. Even the majority of trees and vegetation were foreign to me. The snow was completely gone, and the air was warmer and wetter than what I was used to. I had run so far last night—the distance of a two-day journey for a human—and this was proof of it. I should be close to the Castle of Rivelia, but it was hard to say as I had paid little attention to ensure I was heading directly toward it.

Turning my nose up, I inhaled deeply, searching for any sign of civilization or even a landmark to get my bearings.

Hearty potatoes and saffron filled my nose. I sniffed again.

Stew.

I was smelling stew.

I was close to someone or a tavern perhaps, based on the faint scent of ale. I shook my head. Specifics didn't matter right now. All that did was I now knew where to find help.

CHAPTER 12

After hours of walking, I reached for the handle of the tavern only for the door to swing toward my face. Thankfully, I sidestepped just in time to avoid getting knocked over. The patron leaving, reeking of ale and farm work, looked me over. His lips pursed in disgust as he grunted and shimmied past me, treating me like a rabid dog.

I stood in the doorway, realizing that the rest of the patrons inside were looking at me in the same way, except for one who sat at the end of the bar. He stared with curiosity and a glimmer of pity. I knew I had to be covered in dirt, perhaps some dried blood, but the people in the tavern were covered in dust, their scents reeking of manure. They had little room to judge. Pushing past the condemnatory looks, I took a step forward, making my way to the bar where I could explain my situation. However, as I passed a mirror on the way, I froze.

Twigs and leaves were snared in my hair. My face was covered in dirt that had almost turned to mud from the cold sweat that dripped down my brow, and my exposed knees were stained green from my many falls on the walk over here.

I didn't care too much about my appearance, as I mostly looked rugged from all my patrols, but this, my appearance as it was, I understood why the customers had looked at me the way they had.

I pulled my cloak closer to me, covering my head with my hood, as if it could erase the patrons' memories of what they had just seen before continuing my walk.

"What do you want, *witch*?" a stout man hissed.

Too tired to correct him, I replied, "I am in need of a healer."

"There's no healer here. Best be on your way." He crossed his arms, gesturing toward the door with his chin.

My eyes narrowed, irritation growing in me. If he knew I was a wolf, a protector of his kind, he'd regret his hostility. But I wouldn't point that out, not just yet. That wasn't our way. We protected the humans, and they treated us with respect by *choice*. Still, this treatment was boiling my blood. No one in my condition should be turned away like this, but I didn't have the strength to argue. I would just get information then be on my way.

"How far am I from the Castle of Rivelia?"

Silence swept over the tavern.

"You mean that pile of stone where those *filthy* mutts live," someone interjected.

I stilled, looking the man up and down with shock, words unable to leave my mouth. Never had I heard a human use such foul language when talking about *their* protectors.

The barkeep sneered at my apparent disgust in his word choice. "I suggest you leave." There were several creaks behind me, the sharp sound of weapons partially unsheathing. "We don't associate with the likes of them or their *sympathizers*."

I straightened, eyes jumping around the room, taking in the ten men ready to fight me. If I wasn't injured and sick, I could take them, but that would also go against wolf code.

"Just tell me which direction to head, and I'll be—"

"Get out," the barkeep roared, raising an old sword that was hidden under the counter to my throat. "Get out, now."

My eyelids fluttered.

"What," I stammered, wanting to ask what was going on, but before any more words could come out, I felt the men from behind closing the distance between us.

Their message was clear. One more word and they'd attack.

I raised my hands in defeat, taking a step back so the blade no longer touched me. "Alright," I whispered, "I'll be on my way."

The barkeep nodded, and the men stepped to the side, giving me a clear path to the exit.

I slumped on the steps, head in my palms, confident no one would follow so soon after my dramatic departure.

The humans in the Artico region welcomed any sort of wolf and immediate servant to us with open arms without question. These people despised wolves.

What was going on? Better yet, what was I to do now?

With the silver sickness weakening me with every passing moment, I couldn't rely on my keen sense of smell to locate the castle. I couldn't get directions from the only form of life that I knew was nearby, and I certainly wouldn't be given a map. I could wander, follow the paths until I found the castle or another tavern or village where the humans would be friendlier, but that would require time I didn't have.

I could already feel my body giving out. I could feel my eyelids growing heavier too. If I didn't get help soon, I would...

I didn't want to think about it.

The tavern door screeched open. I jumped to my feet.

"I'm going," I mumbled, wiping away the silent tears that had just started to fall.

"The castle is down that path," a tender voice spoke.

I turned to find a slender, toned man in his early twenties, maybe five years younger than me, pointing to a path that curved left. The same man who had stared at me with pity before.

"It's about an hour-long walk," he informed as he made his way down the stairs.

I looked at the dirt path, sighing heavily. It wasn't that hard of a trek, but with my shaking legs, my growling stomach, and my spinning head, I wasn't sure if I'd make it a third of the way before collapsing.

The man surveyed me as I stared hopelessly down the path. Wondering if it was out of curiosity or disgust, I glanced around my hood, finding his eyes fixated on Artico's Fang, which I had mindlessly pulled out and was twiddling with. I flattened my hand over Artico's treasure, no longer trusting of the humans in this area, even if this one gave the answers I had begged for. I couldn't lose the necklace my father had entrusted me with. I couldn't suffer one more defeat.

The man's hazel eyes grew. He stared up at me, at my white hair, then to the north—the direction of the Artico lands—and for a second, I thought his nose wrinkled as if he was inhaling deeply, trying to pick up a faraway scent.

Quietly, he made his way to a line of tied up steads. "Take this horse," the stranger ordered, untying one. "Her owner is still recovering upstairs from his fun last night. He won't notice until midday that she's gone."

The stranger held out the reigns to me. I backed away, shaking my head. "I can't steal someone's horse."

The man sighed, nervously glancing toward the tavern windows.

"She won't be missed. He was trying to sell her."

"The money will be," I hissed, exerting too much energy. I stumbled back and had to grab the nearby rail for support.

Grumbling, the stranger thrust the reins into my hand.

"Then, leave some," he commanded, though it was filled with fear and worry. "I'll sneak it into his purse." The stranger looked at the tavern door, quiet for a moment so we could hear the voices inside bidding farewell to one another.

The patrons were stirring. I needed to get out of here.

I pushed the reins back into the stranger's hands that waited for the money he thought I had, cursing my moral compass. A horse would make the journey so much easier, even if I wasn't a skilled rider, but I couldn't steal from the humans, even if they were the opposite of the ones I had protected through the years. However, the stranger tucked his hand behind his back before I could.

"I don't have any money," I whined, ashamed.

The male sucked on his lips, as if in deep contemplation, before unclipping a coin purse from his belt and lifting it so I could see how full it was.

"I'll pay," he declared.

My breath caught in my throat, pride getting the best of me despite my impending doom. "I can't," I began.

"It's fine." The stranger positioned himself between me and the window, blocking me from the patrons who were now standing. "You can pay me back someday." He gently pushed me toward the saddle. I resisted, peering over my shoulder at him.

I didn't like owing debts, and I certainly did not like leaving them unpaid without a timeline on when I would return the favor. The stranger, sensing my resistance, mumbled something under his breath before pleading, "Please, go. They are almost done with goodbyes, and they won't be kinder to you out here, and they certainly won't be kind to me if they find me out here talking to you."

I glanced through the window, watching more humans devour their bowls of soup. He was right. They'd finish soon, and then they'd start making their way home. Some may even take the same path as me and would, no doubt, catch up if they were trying to or not.

Scared of what they may do, scared that I wouldn't have enough strength to defend myself and the stranger without harming the humans, I climbed up the horse. "How do I get the money to you?" I asked.

A victorious smile swept across his face. "I'm certain our paths will shortly cross again. It's a small continent."

My brows furrowed, knowing Aplela was anything but. "Tell me your name so I may seek you out when I have the means to."

"You'll learn soon enough," he chuckled, slapping the mare's backside to get her running. I gripped tightly to the reins, focusing on my balance, fully out of practice for this mode of transportation. "Just follow the path, and you'll see it soon," the mystery man yelled. "Oh, and when you get there, don't tell the guards I helped you, and be sure to—"

He screamed something else, but his words were swept away by the fierce wind traveling through the lands.

My body was swaying by the time I had gotten to a stone bridge that led to a wall. It was so high that I was surprised I could see the towers that soared behind them. It was like nothing I had ever seen. It made the grandest hut, even the dining hall back in Artico, look like a shack. It was obvious that this was the meeting place for the wolves before the Blood War, that this was the Castle of Rivelia. I could have marveled at it all day, however, that was near impossible as my condition worsened the closer I got.

My head felt disconnected from my body by the time the mare's hooves touched the stone. Unable to sit up straight, I leaned forward, hugging her thick neck as I kept my eyes on the large steel gate, clutching Artico's Fang, asking it to give me strength.

"State your business," a voice ordered from above.

I groaned, pivoting my neck up, only to be blinded by light that bounced off glistening gold armor. "I am Ina of the Artico Pack. I seek shelter," I mumbled, my voice growing weaker with each word.

"Do you have a letter granting you permission to enter?"

I weakly moved my head left to right, confused as to why I needed a letter. I was clearly in pain, a refugee. I knew Rivelia lived in solitude, but surely, they would help.

I opened my mouth to speak, to fight to come in, but as I did, my heart palpitated. Breathing became harder, my body felt like stone, and I couldn't make out the features of the guard.

The silver sickness was taking hold.

If treatment was delayed any longer, the strongest herbs wouldn't be able to heal me.

"Please, I need a healer," I begged, my hand dropping from the necklace to the horn of the saddle, trying to keep myself up.

"There are healers in the village nearby. We don't take in strangers here," the guard replied.

I opened my mouth to further object, but words would not come. My mouth was too dry, my muscles were too weak, and my throat burned from just breathing. I was out of time.

"Leave," the guard sounded again, but I just slumped further onto the mare's neck, shaking my head. I couldn't be turned away again. I couldn't. "Last warning." The sound of a string on a bow stretching echoed through my ears.

Was this how I was going to die?

"Stop," a robust voice growled. "Lay down your bow."

"But—"

"I know what orders I gave, but now, I am giving you new ones," the voice roared. "Look at the necklace. It's the—"

The rest of the words faded away as I felt my boots slip from the stirrups and my bottom leave the saddle.

CHAPTER 13

Sunshine pierced through my eyelids, beckoning me to wake. However, the soreness of my body told me to remain asleep, allow for more time to heal. I pulled my knees toward my chest with full intent to listen to my body's advice, but the pain was too immense. It wasn't the normal soreness I felt after a day of sparing.

With my eyes still closed, I racked my brain for what I could've done, but as I lay there and thought, memories of screams, blood, and fire flashed in my head. Images of slain wolves and fangs made me shiver. Images of blood demons.

I shot up, fully remembering everything that had happened. The attack, my father's last command, the running, and...and the archer.

I had made it to Rivelia. They had tried to turn me away, tried to shoot me, but now, I was...

I calmed my heart long enough to survey my surroundings.

Looking around, I found that I was in a room no more than ten feet across and wide with nothing but the simple bed I was on, a barred window, and a wooden door.

I had escaped a massacre, only to find myself in a prison.

But why?

Father had told me Rivelia would help. Instead, I was in *here*.

Could it be that this wasn't Rivelia as I had thought? Or had the king been overthrown?

I sniffed the air. Cedar with hints of musk filled my nostrils. Wolves were nearby and lots of them.

Fear coursed through me.

Despite my weakened state, I was certain I hadn't gone off the trail enough that I had found another pack this large. The latter of the two theories had to be correct.

Whoever waited on the other side of this door would be the greatest foe I ever faced. I needed to figure out what was going on, look for something to use as a weapon.

Trying to ignore the pain that was igniting like wildfire with every movement, I stood, but as I did, I noticed that I was dressed in loose, raggedy clothes that were not mine and that my body was void of any dirt or blood. I looked down at my arm. The burns on my hand were gone, and the wrist I had hurt was bandaged. There was little to none swelling. I lowered the collar of my shift to examine where the demon had stabbed me. There was nothing, save a thin red line covered in some type of salve.

I grazed my hands over the scar, completely in awe at how it healed. Only a skilled healer could have pieced me back together this well. Whoever my captor was, they didn't want me dead. They wanted answers for something.

The door slammed open and two guards in golden armor stalked inside. One of them held cuffs. The other gripped the hilt of his broadsword tightly.

"Who are you?" I snarled, backing away, trying to hide my surprise and dodge the cuffs aimed for my wrists.

The first guard gave the second an annoyed look, bobbing his head in signal for something. Quickly, the second guard slammed the hilt of his sword in my gut. I fell to the floor, saliva dripping from my mouth as I gasped for air, unable to stop the first guard from shackling me.

I tried to call on my wolf as the guard hauled me up, pulled me to the door, but it wouldn't come. My body was still healing. I cursed. I should have inspected my body faster. Whatever fate awaited me, I would meet it defenseless.

The walk, to wherever only the gods knew where, was long and tedious, especially for my aching body. However, it didn't stop me from taking in my surroundings, from memorizing where every door and window was. Though the task was much harder than I had anticipated and not because of the pain.

Everywhere I looked, my attention was ensnared by glistening marble floors, and sparkling golden embellishments placed throughout the halls we walked. Everything unnecessarily shimmered. It was unlike the stronghold of the Artico Pack. I wanted to scoff, to laugh at the blatant waste of money, however, as we turned a corner and were met with a full-length window, my heart stopped.

A river cascaded down a cliff. The powerful water pummeled into the rocks below, some of it jumping up and turning to mist only to reveal a rainbow overhead. Around the water was lush green grass, vibrant violet flowers, shining yellow dandelions, colors that were rarely spotted in Artico. Everything was so beautiful, so mesmerizing that I hadn't realized that two grand doors were opening in front of me.

The guards shoved me forward. Unable to regain my balance, I fell to my knees with a great thud. I bared my fangs, pushing off the floor, ready to tear into the males, but before I could lunge, sharp steel rang and the coldness of it soon caressed my neck.

"I would think twice before you consider harming *my* people," a voice warned from behind, sending shivers throughout my body.

I followed the blade of the sword to the hilt with my eyes, finding strong, tanned hands linking to a steady arm. I trailed it too, examining each defined vein and sculpted muscle, wondering who had caused these rare shivers, until I met unwavering hazel eyes. They were beautiful, reminded me of the rich dirt that created the earth—strong and reliable—despite the promise of death in them.

A low growl escaped my lips at the threat, my desire to hide my skills until I had a chance to escape or to learn what was going on wavering. The male cocked his head, pushing the blade closer to my throat. A dribble of liquid warmed my skin, trying to extinguish whatever fight I had in me, but I only smiled. Though he had the body of a warrior and towered over me, he was still smaller than the largest male—Rainer—I had fought. With a squat and a throw of my fist, I could easily reverse our places.

"Enough. I've waited long enough for her to heal. I will not have her hurt now, not until I have the answers I desire," a stocky male who shared features with the armed male—with the exception that his ebony hair had silver streaks—ordered. His voice boomed in my ear, even though he sat on a throne across the room planted on a dais that also held two other smaller chairs.

One of them was empty, while the other hosted a smaller male, adorning a loose olive-green tunic that he didn't quite fill out. There wasn't a hint of threat in him. However, as I raised my gaze to see his face, my breathing hitched. Before me was the male from the tavern, the one who had insisted I take a horse, sitting calmly on the dais. I balked, wondering why he, someone who seemed so kind, had sent me here.

Had he known what hostility waited for me?

Clearly seeing my confusion, he mouthed *later* before holding a singular finger to his lips.

A gust of wind whipped against my shoulder as the muscular wolf aggressively sheathed his sword, clearly unhappy with his orders, before making his way to the chair beside the stocky wolf.

The older wolf grunted his approval, but the younger wolf did not acknowledge it. Instead, he burrowed down, glaring at me, promising to unleash whatever skill he thought he had if I moved. I didn't look away, not when I wanted to make my own promise to humble him, that was until the older wolf held out a necklace with a white pendant—Artico's Fang.

My hands flew to my neck, patting my chest, refusing to believe that the artefact was in an unknown male's hands. My blood went cold as I felt nothing, as I squinted at the necklace and acknowledged that it was truly real.

"Good," the older wolf growled. "Your panic means you know the worth of this necklace, that it didn't just fall into your hands. Tell me why you had this, so I know I didn't waste precious resources on keeping you alive."

I sat in silence, fighting every instinct that demanded I attack and pry the necklace from the stranger's hands. It was the last symbol of my people, the last task my father gave me. I needed to keep it safe, but I reminded myself that in shackles, I would not be able to make it up the dais before the guards caught me. I took a breath, calming myself. I couldn't let my emotions get the better of me.

"Because it is mine," I said flatly, not wanting to give too much information.

The male laughed, dangling the pendant in front of him, watching it spin in the air. "Don't lie to me, *wench.*"

I ground my teeth, my anger taking a turn for the worst. "My answer remains the same," I said through gritted teeth. "The necklace is mine."

The male stared at me unnervingly. I stared back, wishing we were in Artico, wishing I could handle this with a fair fight.

"Well, then, tell me how this necklace became yours," he commanded mockingly.

I chewed on the inside of my cheek, sneering. I wouldn't tell him a thing, not when I had no reason to trust him, not when I thought him some usurper who would take advantage of the alpha blood I carried in my veins.

The male cocked his head. "You refuse to answer?" I raised my chin in response. "Fine, then. I've already wasted enough time healing you. I will not waste anymore waiting for you to talk." The male stood and waved his guards over. "If you want to be silent, do so in the ground. I'll find other means to get the answers I want."

"Father," the male from the tavern exclaimed, panic clear in his voice.

My heart raced. I thought he would send me back to the dungeon, see if my spirit broke before interrogating me, giving me time to plan my escape, but it was clear by the younger male's tone that the usurper's threat wasn't a bluff.

"Surely, we should wait and see if a few days without food will break her," the male from the tavern continued.

The stocky male ignored him and let his guards continue their walk to me.

The male from the tavern began to sweat. He leaned back so he was out of his father's view, his throat bobbing. *Tell him,* he mouthed, *tell him.*

I slid across the floor, dodging the guards, debating.

I couldn't die here. I had to avenge my father. I had to see if any of my people had survived, and if they had, I needed to find them. But I didn't trust these people. I didn't trust the male from the tavern. The smaller male's begging could very well be a ploy to get me to talk.

Hands wrapped around me, forced me to my feet. I tried to shake them off, but I was too weak to fight them. They began to drag me away.

My stomach tightened, and my posture slacked as I convinced myself it was better to be alive and deal with the next problem than to die without trying. "Wait," I screamed.

The older male held up his hand, stopping his guards.

"I'll tell you everything," I whispered.

Silence echoed through the room as I finished my story. I had told them everything, with the exception that Batair was my father and that I had come here to seek King Damon. However, I didn't know if it was enough for the male as he gripped the necklace like it was a lifeline. I was always terrible at lying, even if it was just bending the truth.

"They were feeding on them," the male who had held the sword to my throat breathed in disbelief, breaking the silence. His expression, for once, changing from hostility to pure terror.

The stocky male slammed his fist down. "We need to double the guard on the gate," the male ordered a guard. He then turned to the muscular male and the one from the tavern. "No one is allowed to enter or leave the city. That includes you two," he growled, narrowing his eyes on the one from the tavern, "especially you."

Despite my worry over what would become of me, now that the truth was revealed, disgust filled me at the pure self-preservation that the usurper had planned, the lack of worry for those outside Rivelia.

The male from the tavern replied, "Of course, Father. You know I've given up on that life for a while. I haven't been outside these gates since the last time I was allowed."

The bigger male scoffed, but the stocky male—content with the answer—headed to a balcony door with Artico's Fang without another thought of me.

Was I free to go?

I looked around the room. The guards made no movement to grab me, and the two younger males stood as if ready to leave at any moment.

I inhaled deeply, utterly confused. The situation had been so intense, and now, well, I suppose priorities had been shifted. However, it hadn't for me.

I needed to confirm if I could leave now. I couldn't waste another moment.

"And what of me?" I asked, stopping the usurper in his tracks.

He turned, and with one eyebrow cocked, he looked me up and down in contemplation. "You seem to be of no threat, and you've brought us valuable information. You may stay in Rivelia, refugee. However, if you cause trouble, your punishment will leave you in a state far worse than when you arrived," he proclaimed, turning without waiting to hear my reply, as if that was the option I would ultimately decide.

Shaking my head, I sneered, "And if I choose to leave?"

The stocky man bristled like his hackles were standing on end. "You may do so, but you will not be permitted to enter another time. The gates will not open again, not until the continent is rid of blood demons."

The ember of anger that I had been trying so hard to stifle flared.

Who was this awful male to forsake the teachings of wolves?

Keeping my anger from erupting, I peeked at the swords of the guards to remind myself I could not win against all of them.

"That is fine," I replied flatly, hiding the disgust in my voice. "I'll just need my necklace, and I'll be on my way."

The stocky man let out a singular laugh, snapping at his guards then pointing to me. "You've got bravery for making demands of me, but you'll be on your way without it." He tucked the necklace into his tunic. "This necklace belongs with people who are worthy of it."

The guards grabbed my forearms, dragging me to the door. With every ounce of strength I had left, I planted my feet firmly and pushed against them. But just like last time, with my weakened state and the slick marble floor, I was unable to stop their momentum.

Second by second, we were getting closer to the door, and Artico's Fang was getting further away. My stomach dropped. A smarter wolf would have taken the loss, leave the necklace behind for now, but I couldn't depart without it. I couldn't leave it in the hands of a male like this, he was the complete opposite of what Artico stood for.

I had to do something to get it back.

Anything.

Unable to think clearly about the repercussions of releasing my suppressed emotions any longer, I screeched, "That necklace is my birthright, and I demand that it leave with me."

The men kept pulling, but the usurper froze. Slowly, he turned back around, examining my snow-colored hair and my tan skin. He swayed slightly.

"Stop," he whispered his voice shaky, but the guards did not hear him, not when they were focused on my kicking. The usurper took rushed steps forward, calling forth worried expressions from the males beside him, and this time, he yelled the word. The guards stopped immediately, both of them tensing. "Are you," the shocked wolf mumbled, but the words faded away as he reached out his hand to me but didn't dare touch.

My skin crawled at the sudden worry and care in his voice, but I carried on my strong façade. "I am Ina, Daughter of the Alpha of the Artico Pack—Batair—and that necklace is *mine.*"

The male's pupils doubled as he shook his head. "But you don't smell anything like him. You—" He sniffed me closer. I sunk back as far as I could, my neck straining so far away I thought it would snap. "The mud and blood covered up your scent when you arrived. Now the herbs and salves do the same, but underneath, there is a faint smell." The male's knees trembled, and in a swift movement that I could not dodge, his arms wrapped around me in a warm embrace. "You are his child. Thank the gods," he whispered. "I thought they had succeeded in taking everyone dear to me."

I cringed at his close proximity, at the tears that fell to my shoulder. I didn't understand his sudden change of attitude, nor did I care to find out. I just saw a weakness, an opportunity to get the symbol of my people back.

I wedged one of my palms between his chest and mine, clutching the pendant, as my other glided down to the hilt of the sword strapped to him. Without a glimmer of suspicion, I pushed the male away, ripped the necklace off him, and drew the blade, pointing it at his throat. The guards and the two males lurched forward but stopped as I pushed the blade further toward my target.

"Ungrateful bitch," the male who had held a blade to my throat snarled. "I should've slit your throat after the first sign of disrespect you showed."

"Quiet," the older wolf growled.

I smiled. At least one of them knew they now had to behave. "I'll be leaving now. No one will try to stop me. Understood?" I asked, pivoting so I was closer to the door, using the older male as a shield.

"Why don't we talk about this?" the usurper whispered. "There have been some misunderstandings."

"The only misunderstanding was that you thought I would leave without this." I held up the necklace.

"Watch it," the male on the dais barked, interfering again.

The stocky male sent him another scathing look. "I told you to be quiet."

"Father, I—"

"I am your King, Alaric, as I am to all the wolves. You will obey me."

The male on the dais frowned, his body shaking as he bit his lip. I almost laughed at seeing his flame extinguished, but history lessons rushed back to me.

This stocky male had declared himself king of the wolves and called the snarling male Alaric—the name of King Damon's eldest son, born nearly a hundred years ago.

I specifically remembered that name because of the stories about him. He had fought in the Blood War at the mere age of fifteen with little training under his belt. However, he was one of the most skilled fighters, a natural born killer, and with time, he only got better. He would be called upon for the worst battles, the ones everyone knew the wolves would lose. Yet, when he arrived it was like the gods fought with us. The tide of the battle changed, and we would win with a third of the expected casualties. He was death himself.

But this male, this male who was smaller than Rainer, he couldn't be him.

Could he?

No. It couldn't. Alaric was loyal to his father without fault. He would never join a new pack, let alone one that was led by a usurper who now called himself King—his father's title—unless...

I examined Alaric then his father. Both wore the golden rings imbued with magic so they could only fit the true King of Rivelia and his successor. I swore my heart stopped beating.

How could I miss such a crucial detail?

Gods, if my skills failed me like this during recovery, I would never get injured this badly ever again.

"You're King Damon," I stuttered, sword lowering in shock.

"Yes," he muttered.

I shook my head. I knew that Rivelia had closed their gates, but I didn't think it was this bad, that they would be so hostile. I figured that *closing their gates* was a figure of speech. I figured that they didn't host meetings any longer, that they would do a search before new people entered, as opposed to the times when people could freely come in and out. I didn't think that they'd turn people away with a mere thought at the gates.

"My father sent me here to ask *you* for help?" I asked aloud, too in shock to keep my thoughts silent.

King Damon smiled, taking my concerned question as a relieved statement. "I'm glad he did," he beamed. "I loved your parents so much. I am honored your father trusted me with you."

King Damon tapped my shoulders, embracing me again. I didn't dare step back this time, now knowing who he was, but a sense of unease formed in the pit of my stomach.

Nothing was making sense.

Damon pulled back, noticing my stiffened posture, blushing as he held me at arm's length. "I'm sorry. You must be so confused. You woke our prisoner, and now I'm hugging you like a daughter."

I gulped, trying to collect my thoughts, baffled by King Damon's sudden change in attitude. It was like I was talking to another person. Every sense in my body told me to run, to get as far away from here as possible. But father had told me to come here, that I would find help. His advice was rarely ever wrong. I needed to fight those urges. I needed to trust him and see how this played out. Perhaps King Damon had a reason for his ways. They were a central city for wolves after all.

"So, you'll help?" I asked, ignoring the pit in my stomach.

Damon's smile grew. "Of course. I'll have the servants prepare your mother's old room in the west wing."

I shrunk back. I hadn't known Mother had resided in the castle before she came to Artico. All I knew was that she came from a well-known family in Rivelia. Though, for granted, I didn't know much about Mother at all since she passed when I was five.

"Father, I don't think this will be a good idea. Rivelia and Artico are opposites now. She won't be happy here," interrupted Alaric, his voice steady, opposite of his worried eyes.

"Are you questioning me again?" Damon raged, reverting to the character he was before learning of my identity.

My skin crawled. If he were to return to hostility, we wouldn't be able to plan anything.

"I don't intend to stay long," I interjected before things could escalate. Damon's wild eyes turned to me. "I just need somewhere to plan for a bit, borrow some of your troops—with your permission, of course—to find any surviving pack members and to reclaim our home, then we can rid the blood demons from this continent again."

"You intend to face them?" the male from the tavern—Neo, the second son of Damon—asked, casually interrupting as if he hadn't stayed quiet this entire time.

"I do," I said, trying not to trip over the words, curious at the glimmer in his eyes. "With Artico and Rivelia combined, we could—"

"Rivelia does not join in battles outside of its own domain, outside of these walls," King Damon exclaimed, motioning to the stone structure that encompassed the castle and the town below.

My lip curled in disgust. "But it is our duty as wolves to aid those who cannot defend themselves."

"For you, yes." King Damon responded. "For Rivelia, it is preservation that matters."

"Why?" I somehow managed to ask, despite the bile that climbed up my throat.

"Our species were decimated during the Blood War. We cannot let our numbers get that low again," he replied in a somber quietness.

My throat bobbed.

Fear.

Rivelia lived in fear.

It was why they had not bothered to contact the other packs all these years. It was why they were so hostile when a *stranger* arrived. It was why I would not receive the entirety of the help I wanted, no matter what I said. Perhaps father only sent me here to heal.

"I see," I replied flatly. "I will rest here for a couple days—if that is still permitted—then I'll be on my way."

"You're going out there alone?" the younger wolf asked in awe. "That's a suicide mission."

"Quiet, Neo," Alaric snarled, calculating eyes flickering to King Damon.

"I have no choice," I responded, ignoring the strange interaction.

There was a long period of silence to which all males seemed to have a different response. Neo's eyes sparkled with what seemed like admiration; Alaric looked at Damon with weary, worried eyes; King Damon peered down at the ground. The varying energies around them added to my already spinning head.

I needed to rest and be away from all of this. However, before I pushed for an answer to my question, Damon mumbled, "You're right. You don't."

I turned to the king, feeling fear and anger flood the room.

"Your father trusted me to keep you safe. He told you to come to me. I cannot allow his faith to amount to nothing. From now on, you are my ward."

Alaric stepped forward. "Father, she wants to go. Let her go. This won't be good for—"

"Question me again, and I'll have you locked up," King Damon threatened, silencing Alaric. "I've grown tired of your advice lately."

Alaric shrunk back with tight fists.

This couldn't be good.

"And what does being your ward entail?" I asked, crossing my arms.

King Damon eyed his two guards, his gaze dragging over to me. I whipped toward both of them, backing away, knowing we were about to resume the dance we started when I first met them.

"That you are under my protection," he said with a nod to the guards. They jumped on me, their hands grabbing my upper arm in a way that didn't hurt but ensured I couldn't move.

"What are you doing?"

King Damon sat on his throne, head held high, his two sons still standing. "I know you have plans, but I can't let you go through with them. I can't let the blood demons take one more life that I care about.

You will stay here until the continent is safe once again. I owe that to your parents."

"Keeping me prisoner is not what my father had planned when he said to seek help from you," I yelled, trying to fight the guards, despite knowing my efforts were futile.

"No, but your father didn't always know what was best." King Damon sat back. "Take my ward to her room in the west wing," he ordered, ending the conversation.

CHAPTER 14

I bit into the bread a maid had brought me, surveying the once immaculate room. The tapestries that had covered the walls were now scattered around the floor, the bedsheets were missing—confiscated by the guards when they realized I was trying to make a rope from them to escape—and the numerous dresses that the maids had tried to coax me into were thrown around the room. It was like a storm had passed through here, leaving nothing in peace. And it was only going to get worse if I had to spend another passing minute in this glistening prison.

They had locked me in here for the past two days. Two days that I had not spent looking for my pack. Two days that the blood demons lived in our continent unchecked. All because of King Damon's incessant, unnecessary need to protect me.

I was raised as a warrior. My people were known as warriors. Locking me away was not what my father meant when he said to seek help from King Damon. I was certain of it despite the King reassuring me that it was, which was why I challenged him every chance I got.

I refused to accept the title of his ward, refused to help in the preparations for the ball King Damon wanted to have so he could formally introduce me to his pack. However, that only made him push harder, made him assign more guards to ensure that I stayed put until my head *cleared*. But it was already clear. I knew what I wanted and that he was the delusional one. I also knew he was never going to let me go.

Never.

I had to find a way to escape, but it was becoming more and more impossible by the day. Even with all my years of training, I couldn't take on the ten guards that watched my every step alone. I was too used to fighting with a pack, leading that pack. I couldn't take on the whole castle nor sneak out undetected, as King Damon had made the guards memorize my face.

I was thoroughly at a loss.

A knock sounded from the door.

I placed my bread down, wiping the crumbs off my hands, preparing for the next fight about wearing a frilly ballgown, but as the door opened and Neo slid in, I bolted up with enough force my chair nearly fell over.

I had not spoken to him or Alaric since the incident, and as the latter had been so ready to slice open my throat, and the former had not warned me of the hostility I would receive at the castle, I considered them both a threat.

"Good morning," he honeyed out.

I didn't move. I simply glared, trying to guess why he had come to *visit* me.

Neo sucked in his bottom lip. "Understandable greeting," he grimaced, closing the door behind him. "It doesn't make me feel good as the receiver of it, though," he chimed with a half-smile.

My head sunk back. I couldn't be more baffled by the sheer familiarity in his voice. It was like we were friends finally talking after a little tiff.

"Do you mind if I sit?" Neo asked, pointing to the chair that was across from the one I stood in front of. "I just finished a run, and my legs are in a mountain of pain." Neo shook out his legs, each one trembling as they took turns supporting his weight.

My lips parted, and my nose scrunched. Any warrior knew not to show weakness in front of a stranger, let alone a captive.

What was he playing at?

Whatever it was, I would keep my guard up.

I spread my feet, strengthening my stance.

"I'll take that as a no," Neo said with a sigh. "They really do hurt, though." He shook out his legs once again, his sad pup eyes drifting up to me in a silent plea.

I did not move.

Neo's shoulders dropped in defeat. "Alright. I'll talk fast, then." Neo looked over his shoulder at the closed door, nodding in approval before stepping forward and whispering, "I want to help you escape."

I slowly blinked, disbelief filling me at this declaration.

Damon was Neo's father. If he were to help me, it would go against orders, betray the natural urge of a wolf to be loyal to their alpha. There was no possible way his words were real. I looked for the knot in my stomach to tell me that something was amiss, ready to listen to it, unlike when it had happened with the king, but I felt nothing.

"Why?" the desperate side of me blurted out, breaking my silence.

Neo smiled, happy to hear my voice. Assuming we were finally on friendly terms, he hurried forward. In return, I flashed my canines, keeping him from pulling out the chair he reached for. He grimaced but continued talking. "I think it's rather admirable, going against the blood demons to protect the humans." Neo gripped the back of the chair in front of him. "No, not admirable. It's what's right."

I crossed my arms, head cocking, thinking of how Damon had ordered the gates to be shut, how Alaric proclaimed that Rivelia did not partake in affairs outside of these walls.

How could the second son—sired by Damon, influenced by Alaric—have different ideals?

I sniffed in Neo's direction for any trace of excess sweat, checking if he was nervous. There was some, but not the kind that came with lying. I stared into his unfaltering eyes. They were so honest and pure, but I couldn't believe that his opinion differed so much from his kin. I couldn't allow myself to trust wolves that were not from my own pack again.

"Believe me, please," he begged as if he could hear my wary thoughts.

"No," I said shortly, sitting back down, signifying I was done with the conversation.

Neo didn't agree, though. He stepped past the chair he was holding. "What do you mean no?"

Seeing the persistence in his eyes, I answered, "Just that. I don't need your help. I can find my own way out of here."

Neo inched closer so he was parallel with the table, his scent reeking of desperation. "It will be months before you find a way out if you can even find one. This is the quickest option. People may die—*will* die."

I looked down at my nails, refusing to look at his disheartened expression any longer, refusing to acknowledge every instinct in me screaming.

Neo stared at me for a moment more, his jaw clenched tightly. "This is about trust, isn't it?" My subconscious, clearly still begging to find a way to trust the male in front of me, forced me to lift my head to him as if to answer yes. Neo sighed heavily. "Then let me bare this to you. Alaric clearly stated that Rivelia does not concern itself with what happens beyond the walls, that includes the simple act of speaking with humans or the rare roaming wolf for more than just business. When we met, I was in a tavern, a human tavern."

I froze, recalling the encounter I had not bothered to think of, as I had been too consumed with the events of the past few days.

Neo had been amongst humans who had turned me away despite my life-threatening wounds, humans who hated wolves. For Neo to have been accepted by them, or to even go to the tavern and be allowed to stay, he needed to have a good relationship with them, had to like humans. They had to like him.

"I care for them. I've always cared for them ever since I met my first one. I feel my best when I'm around them. I go there—without my father's permission—and just..." Neo pushed the inside of his cheek outward with his tongue in deep thought over the word to use. I perked up as he thought. I knew the feeling that he was trying to give a word to. All wolves did.

It was a feeling that some believed the gods created, ensuring that wolves would always stay close to humans. It gave us sense of ease, and at the same time, it was invigorating, and that feeling only grew as you spent more time with happy humans. It was something that couldn't be obtained with any other species. The only feeling that was greater—so I've been told—was a true mating bond.

"It feels right," I interrupted.

Neo nodded, his shoulders turning inward as he softly whispered, "Yeah."

The longing in his voice broke my heart, made me want to hug him. However, as the memory of him in the tavern became vivid, I recalled the important details lost to the madness of the day I met Damon. Neo had not mentioned that he had met me in the tavern nor vouched for me. And to make matters worse, he hadn't warned me of the hostility I would face when I arrived here. He had sent me alone. Before I could trust him, I needed to settle that issue.

"I know the feeling you speak of and the need for it, however, you sneaking out proves nothing," I bit out, extinguishing the empathy taking root. "I'm sure if he caught you—his son—he'd give you a measly punishment." Neo's temple ticked. "This isn't some game that you can pretend to be interested in then turn away when the repercussions happen, just as you did by pretending not to know me."

"I didn't turn away in fear for myself," Neo hissed, his happy demeanor gone, breaking my stoic façade, "and his punishments for me are not *measly*." Neo's eyes darkened as he stared into the grains of wood on the table, like something horrid was captive in the cracks. His knuckles turned white as his fist became tighter and tighter. Part of me dared to ask him what exactly those punishments were, but the sight before me told me it wasn't my place. "I helped you as best as possible. We can fight all day on the details of it or how I could do better, but I did what I could, and I'm trying to do so now," Neo huffed.

"Is everything alright in there?" a voice beyond the door asked.

Neo rubbed both his hands across his face, inhaling deeply. "Yes," he replied in the cheeriest of voices. "No need to worry."

There was a minute of silence before we heard the shuffling of feet heading away from the door.

"Listen, I didn't mean to raise my voice," Neo whispered, still using a sense of urgency but quieter now. "I just know that I am the only chance you have of escaping here, and I can't let any more innocent people die because of fear. I can't let my family be the ones responsible for it. I don't want the humans to hate us anymore than they do."

My throat bobbed, my instincts bursting forth once again as I took note of Neo's eyes. They were filled with something like regret and sorrow. It was so deep that it was impossible to imitate.

"Alright," I agreed with no small amount of worry, hoping I wouldn't regret this decision.

Neo's eyes lightened, a broad smile emerging on his face causing warmth to sweep through me, just how Ala's smile did.

My chest tightened. I needed her to be alive. I needed them all to be alive. I needed to be out there searching for them.

I kicked out the chair in front of me, the one Neo had begged to sit in before, beckoning him to sit then tensely commanded, "Tell me the plan."

CHAPTER 15

I fiddled with the golden leaves pinned to my olive-green dress as I waited for Neo in the garden. The tulle was unbelievably scratchy, and the plush amount of it was hardly practical when it came to walking around the giant castle with its many winding corridors. The heaviness of it slowed me down, and the billowing sleeves continuously snagged on hinges or anything that was at shoulder level. I wanted to rip it off, wear a tunic and trousers instead. However, Neo insisted that I wear the dresses his father had ordered for me, all so I could show that I was becoming docile and content in Damon's court. Neo swore that the act would allow me to leave my room and would lessen the number of guards who kept watch over me. I hated it, but I did as he bid, as it was phase one of our plan.

I hardly thought it would work, or at least take ages to execute, but sure enough, after a week of *behaving*, I was allowed to walk through the castle with a mere number of five guards. Neo had chimed with a gloating, "told you so," the day it happened and further explained that his father was always quick to act when it seemed he was getting his way. It made my resolve to getting out of here that much stronger. It was irritating to know that the King of the Wolves behaved like a spoiled cub. Regardless of King Damon's disgusting behavior, I was happy that it allowed us to start thinking about phase three, as phase two would be completed once Neo came to the garden today.

"Afternoon," a chipper voice came not too far away. I turned to find Neo nodding to the guards, a beautiful slender female on his arm—Lillian, his mate.

Though Neo was all but twenty—five years from when a wolf's aging slows—he had found his mate already. And while my beliefs regarding mates still stood, I couldn't argue that they were irrevocably in love and completed each other.

Neo loved to talk and had no problem integrating into a new group, whereas Lillian was quiet and shy. It took her ages to warm up to anyone, however, with Neo—so he told me—she was not slow to talk to him. She wanted to converse with him, wanted to go to parties because of him, and he wanted to visit the library because of her. They found themselves loving the things they avoided, simply because the other was there. It was how they discovered they were mates within a month of them meeting.

"Neo. Lillian," I stood, nodding my head in greeting.

Lillian smiled softly in way of greeting, as she was still shy around me. Her soft pink dress billowed in the wind playfully, the exact opposite of Neo's somber expression.

Terrible news was about to come.

I rolled back my shoulders, readying for whatever news he had.

Neo glanced over his shoulder at my attentive guards then back to Lillian who nodded. She began violently coughing. The sound was unbearably atrocious. The guards' attention snapped to her as did mine. Neo slyly held up his hand by his torso, reminding me it was all an act.

"Do you need some water?" Neo asked, supporting Lillian at the waist as her shoulders curled inward.

"I think I need to lie down," she squeaked. "My cold"—the one Lillian had conveniently gotten the day phase one started—"hasn't gone away just yet it seems."

Neo's face contorted into that of the perfect concerned mate.

He really could act. Thank the gods he wasn't when he told me he wanted to help.

"Let me escort you back," Neo offered, guiding her away to entrance of the castle.

Lillian planted her feet, gesturing to me.

"I'm sure Ina can wait a bit longer," Neo stated with soft sternness. I nodded as I always did when we performed this act.

"I'll be fine. It's a short walk," she winced out, coughing once more before pushing away Neo.

He watched her go, waiting until she was barely out of ear's reach before he ordered the guards, "Follow her for me."

The guards looked at me then back at each other, debating whose orders to follow—the king's or the prince's. The former was undoubtedly the right answer, but the king was far away and surely wouldn't notice the few minutes of disobedience. Neo, on the other hand, was right in front of them, and despite his sunny, carefree disposition, he would bite their heads off for refusing to ensure his mate's safety.

Neo growled again, "She is a Princess of Rivelia. You have sworn to guard her. Follow her. I can watch my father's ward until you get back."

The men glanced between each other once again and their surroundings, making sure the king was not around. Once certain, they raced off after Lillian, leaving Neo and I alone.

"How bad is it?" I asked softly but with all the urgency in the world, scared to hear what he had to say.

Neo and I had discussed many elements of our plan in great length, like what I would do if I were to find survivors when I escaped Rivelia. I knew many of my pack members would want to fight, but for those who couldn't, I had to leave them behind. I had to leave them somewhere safe.

Artico was destroyed and would offer zero protection from the elements or any blood demons who would linger. It would take months to rebuild. Leaving the injured, old, and young there was not an option. The only safe place for them would be Rivelia, as that was the only close pack that Neo and I had knowledge of. However, for my pack to enter, I would need to be in Rivelia and vouch for them. Without me, Damon would claim they were strangers that would endanger the safety and order behind his walls. Because of that, Neo and I had decided that we needed to see if there were any survivors before I left Rivelia and get them inside before I left, since even King Damon would not turn out someone he let inside his walls without cause. It would make him look barbaric. Therefore, Neo and I decided to convince King Damon to send scouts to Artico. It had been phase two of our plan.

It had been a difficult request for King Damon to accept. He hadn't wanted to risk his people. However, we had assured Neo's father that it would better my forever life here, allow me to have a few familiarities during the dramatic change in lifestyle. We convinced him that it would make his relationship with me better, and thankfully, he had fallen for it. Though with whatever news his scouts found, I still had to watch my reactions around Damon. If I was too happy that my people were alive, he may feel threatened and think I may take them and go somewhere else. If I was too grievous, he may see it as an insult, as his kingdom was supposed to easily replace my pack. Thus, Neo had obtained the information before my meeting with Damon later today so I could be prepared to act *correctly* when Damon delivered the news.

"The scouts came across a few demons on their way to Artico. They trailed them for a while and found out that they were heading for their old castle, the one they used during the Blood War."

I nodded, grateful I at least knew where to look for them now.

"But," Neo began, looking away, unable to speak the rest of his sentence.

"But what? What of my people, Neo? Did they find anyone?" I asked, gripping the fabric of my dress.

Neo's throat bobbed. "The scouts reported zero survivors."

The world went silent.

No one had survived.

No one.

I had expected some, held out hope that some of my pack had gotten away, but for none...

I was alone in this world.

I was a lone wolf.

My knees wobbled, and my head felt light.

Vengeance was the only thing left for me in this world.

CHAPTER 16

I walked through the quiet hallway, hiking up the excess fabric of the emerald-green dress, hoping that it would allow me to walk faster than a simpering pace. However, the heavy crystals that dotted the skirt tired my toned arms and forced a bead of sweat to drip down my side. I wanted to scream, to let out all my frustration and anger, but the door to the private dining room was open, showcasing King Damon, Lillian, Neo, and Alaric. The sight of them reminded me that I had to be on perfect behavior tonight, needed to be appreciative of my role as the king's ward so phase three could finally begin. It was the step that would finally get me out of here, which I needed more than ever. I didn't know how long I could sit idle with the knowledge that the exterminator of my pack still lived.

"There she is," Neo called a few feet away, pulling everyone's attention from the food and redirecting it to me.

I took a breath, turning away from the thoughts that clouded my vision. Everyone at the table smiled in return except for Alaric. He looked at me with strong resentment.

His hate for me was a mystery, and it bothered me to no end. Anytime I saw him I had the urge to demand an answer as to why. Luckily, my wits were strong enough to tell me that the answer wasn't worth my time. After all, Alaric didn't pose any additional threats to Neo and mine's plan. In fact, he rarely talked to me, sought me out.

If I had any spare time to solve the numerous things I didn't understand in Rivelia, I would find out what had changed the once great Damon. However, I doubted I would ever find out, since the beginning of Neo and mine's final phase was going to begin.

I clumsily curtsied, trying to imitate what Lilian had taught me, fighting the urge to bow as I had all my life, my gut twisting as I did. Damon didn't deserve this respect, nor had it gotten easier pretending that he did in the weeks I had been here, but I managed to sculpt a smile on.

"Sorry to keep you all waiting," I mumbled. "I'm still trying to get used to dressing in"—I examined the fabric prison, trying to come up with a polite word—"the Rivelia way."

"If it meant that we wouldn't starve while waiting on you, I'd rather you dress like you're in Artico," Alaric grumbled, plucking a grape from the various fruits laid around the glazed ham in the center of the table.

My smile tightened as I gave a demure, apologetic nod.

It didn't matter how many legends depicted Alaric as an elite fighter, I would happily take him on and rip his throat out, even if that meant sinking my canines into him, well, that was if the future of my escape didn't rely on playing the wolf the king wanted me to be.

"Leave her be, Alaric," Damon scolded, tired of the hostility between me and his son. "Come sit, Ina." He gestured to the chair between him and Alaric.

I nodded but not before throwing a victorious smirk at Alaric. I knew I shouldn't have, but it was too pleasurable to resist.

"Thank you, King Damon," I sweetly said, turning my body ever so slightly so I couldn't see Alaric from my peripheral.

"Damon," he insisted as he always did. "I don't want you to be just another member of my pack; I want you to be part of my family too. You should address me with familiarity."

The declaration made my body shake in disgust. I had never thought about joining another pack. Never. Even if I had to, being a part of this one, a part of Damon's...

I would rather become a lone wolf, destined to become deranged as I wandered the woods alone, and my animalistic side destroyed my human ideals. It was why phase three was going to be the hardest part for me.

I bit my lip, sucking on my cheeks, trying to lubricate my dry throat with whatever moisture I could find, every bit of my body rejecting what I was about to do.

I fisted my hand under the table before replying, "You're right." Damon froze. "It is odd for your own family to address you with such formalities. I will call you Damon from now on."

Damon silently turned to me, bewilderment and hope in his eyes. "Do you mean," he began but trailed off as a watery lining threatened to fall down his cheek.

I gulped, reminding myself I had to say these words for the plan to succeed. "I gave it some thought, and I have been unwise in my decisions because of my emotions. I want to join your pack. I want to officially become your ward."

Silence misted over the table. The action, though half of the table already knew what I was going to say, expected as joining another pack, even if your former had been eradicated, was rare for wolves. It was an act not taken lightly, as it altered your brain, gave control to the alpha of the pack you were swearing to, and allowed him and him alone to compel you.

Damon's lips reached ear to ear as he reached for my hands.

"Why?" Alaric growled, halting Damon.

My nostrils flared.

If I ever got a moment alone with this male, I'd bite his head off.

I parted my lips, my spine bristling, ready to say something snarky, but Neo's sunny voice sounded.

"This is wonderful." Alaric's hostile attention snapped to him. "I'm so happy. I've always wanted a sister figure around," Neo continued to spew, not allowing anyone the chance to interrupt.

Lillian nodded in agreement, adding to Neo's enthusiasm that was calming any tension created from Alaric's question. Surprisingly, Alaric didn't stop it. He only stared at Neo with calculating eyes.

"I'm glad to hear it," I managed to follow up with, trying to ignore the new forming questions about Alaric.

Neo beamed, allowing a moment for his father to take in our words, the reality that what he wanted was coming true. It took but not a minute for Damon to do so.

"I'm so happy you've come to this decision. You'll be happy here. I promise. I swear it to your mother and father."

I squeezed his hand tenderly, but disgust rippled through me. I didn't know what to say or if I could even muster words. Luckily, it was time for Neo to talk.

"This is something to celebrate!" Neo stood up, appearing to be the over happy pup Rivelia knew him as. "Father, we can finally throw that ball you wanted to celebrate. You and Ina can complete the ritual then."

Damon bounced in his chair, enjoying the idea, however, he looked at me as if to ask me what I wanted—a first since I had been here.

I nodded, using my excitement for our succeeding plan to hide the repulsion that threatened to appear on my face.

Damon tapped my hand. "Then, we shall." He stood and raised his glass. "Let us toast to it."

I followed suit as did everyone at the table except Alaric. He remained seated, finger tapping, debating on saying something.

I held my breath, hoping that whatever comment he snarked wouldn't sour the mood to the point where it may ruin Neo and mine's plan. However, to my surprise, Alaric stood and clinked his glass with ours.

CHAPTER 17

Sitting at the vanity in my room, I braided my hair whilst I thanked the gods that tonight had gone exactly as planned. I was one step closer to escaping this place, one step closer to being able to begin my quest, do what wolves were meant to do—protect those that were weak and rid the continent of the blood demons. I was ready for it, though a sense of unease sat in the pit of my stomach.

Neo and I had thought that Damon would take weeks, maybe months to plan the ball. However, due to his overzealous excitement to have me publicly integrated into his pack, he deemed that the ball would be held in a couple weeks. It should have brought me joy, but with the news that my pack had been slaughtered, I had no idea how I was to do this on my own. It would be certain death if I were to show up to the blood demons' stronghold alone. The coward in me said that it was a pointless quest, that it would result in the eradication of the Artico Pack, that I should stay where it was safe so I could keep our history and way of life alive, but I knew that was fear talking.

No matter what, I would leave here. I would make my way to the blood demons. I would look for allies along the way, but if I still arrived alone, I would accept my fate with honor, knowing I tried. I just needed to make the most of the time I had now.

With a huff, I pushed off the vanity and headed for the giant chest at the foot of my bed. I pulled out a series of items, taking note of what I had and still needed. So far, I had a tunic, trousers, boots, a cloak, and a dagger. It was a seemingly fair number of items for the quest to come. However, I still needed a satchel, food supplies, and a couple of maps. Neo had promised to obtain them before I departed, since I knew little of the intimacies of the castle and was sure to get caught if I tried to get the items myself. However, after a dagger had been noted as missing during one of the weekly armory checks, along with several servants reporting missing personal attire, I wasn't sure if he would be able to hold to his promise.

I rubbed my temple, trying to calm the annoying pulsing. My situation was getting worse and worse. Without those items, the journey there would make an already hard trek that much harder.

A knock sounded through the room, causing me to jump.

I noted the blackness outside, racking my brain for who could be knocking at this hour, knowing that it couldn't possibly be the maids. They had already helped me ready and been dismissed.

I breathed in the direction of the door deeply. The smell of the guards posted outside filled my nostrils, but it was also accompanied by pine and sandalwood—Neo's scent.

He had never visited me this late.

I perked, all my senses alert. However, recalling the events of today, my shoulders relaxed just as quickly.

Neo had to be here to discuss our now expedited plan. I quickly got up, not bothering to put away the items and opened the door fully. But when I did, I found the doorframe filled with hardened flesh and a frame bigger than Neo's. Dread washed over me.

"We need to talk," Alaric coldly demanded.

My throat bobbed.

He was the last person I had expected to visit my chambers.

I attempted to lessen the gap, but Alaric gripped the door, ripping it back open with ease.

"I'm not dressed properly," I said to justify my actions, remembering how prudish the wolves of Rivelia were.

Alaric scoffed, stepping forward so one foot was in my room. I glanced around him, frantically looking for the guards I had scented earlier for help, but they were nowhere to be found.

Alaric's gaze dropped, examining every part of me, like he could see under the plush robe that I wore. It shouldn't have unnerved me; I was used to being ogled by males in far less clothing, but my stomach fluttered, and I felt a rush of heat in my cheeks.

"Why should that matter?" he asked gruffly. "There's nothing to see."

My nose scrunched, and my lips curled back to reveal my canines, the embarrassment that I had felt completely leaving my body.

"If you came to insult me—"

Alaric effortlessly pushed me aside and entered my room.

I stumbled back, holding onto the door for dear life, absolutely baffled.

Alaric was smaller by a fraction than Rainer—someone I could hold my ground against. Yet, Alaric had almost made me fall when I was in a fighting position.

I turned to assess the male, maybe even ask a question, but as I did, my breathing halted. In Alaric's hand was the tunic Neo had gotten for me.

"Well, this shortens the conversation by great lengths," he said in that cold, unfeeling voice, pushing around the rest of the items with the tip of his boots.

Shame pulsed through me. I should've hidden the items, even if I did think it was Neo at the door. A pup would have known to do that, but I had been too excited to see one of my two allies in this place.

"I don't know what you mean," I said, feigning innocence, trying to push past the horror of my mistake.

"These"—he gestured to the remaining—"are the items of someone about to depart on a very long journey."

"Or someone tired of wearing heavy dresses all day," I snarked back, finally able to find my voice again after the shock of Alaric's visit.

Alaric tilted his head, one side of his lips turning up in a vicious gloat. "Is it?" he asked. "My father had thought you started to enjoy them, since you've stopped complaining." Alaric bundled the shirt in his hand and headed for the door. "Perhaps I should go clear that up for him. We are about to be family after all. Secrets should not be kept."

I rushed to the door, blocking Alaric's exit. "Some must," I responded, keeping my head high. "You know your father abhors me wearing trousers. Let me have this. Let me dress how I please in my free time. I'm not hurting any—"

Alaric, quicker than I could sense, wrapped his fingers around my throat and pushed me into the door. I grabbed his forearm, tried to push him off, but he squeezed tighter, coming close to crushing my airways.

"You hurt much more than you know. If you leave and create a mess in your wake, I doubt you know all the problems you would cause."

"I have to," I wheezed, my vision already blurring, pulse quickening. My plan danced on my tongue, ready to race out my lips, realizing it was the only way to keep me from passing out. "I need to, and even if you tell your father"—I panted, trying to find enough oxygen to keep me afloat just a little longer—"I will find a way."

Alaric held my stare, his eyes narrowing, debating as he always did, and as his hand scarcely trembled when his fingers left my throat, I knew it was whether to end my life or not.

Knees wobbling from the lack of air, and my hand firmly planted on the door handle to keep me up, I wearily watched Alaric pace around my bedroom, refusing to flee. If I did, the guards would know something was amiss, and that would lead to questions. I had to see what Alaric had decided, what made him let me breathe.

He paced around for what felt like eternity, hand raking through his hair, then he stopped. He just stopped and turned to me.

My pulse quickened, but I managed to release the door and stand on my own, pretending that I had fully recovered from his choking.

"Fine," he said through gritted teeth. "I won't report you to the king, but you will do as I tell you."

I looked Alaric up and down, debating to agree or to not, despite the fact that I didn't have much choice in the matter. After all, if I said no, I'd be back to where I started. I had to hope his request wasn't too outlandish.

I nodded, and Alaric made his way back over to me, unclipping his belt. *What in the hells?*

A favor like this hadn't even crossed my mind. Was Alaric's scowl so awful that wolves in his own kingdom had denied him to the point where he'd keep a secret from his father for—for—

I raised my fists and lowered into a squat. My volume rising with each word as I raged, "What are you—"

Alaric held out the sword that was connected to his belt, stopping my words. He looked me over once again then rolled his eyes as if to say *not even in a lifetime*, but that was the only acknowledgment he made about my embarrassing confusion before casually demanding, "You need to stop taking things from the palace, therefore this sword is yours."

Taking note of the well forged blade and the leather handle that was starting to wear down, but still had plenty of uses in it before it needed to be changed, I took it, replying, "An inconvenient request but fine." Though the blade wasn't originally on my list of things to get, nor did it completely replace what I needed, I could make do with it. Not to mention, for keeping such a vital secret, this was far from the worst demand Alaric could have made of me.

"And," Alaric added.

I cursed. I should've known better than to think that the measly requirement was his only condition.

"Do whatever you want, but leave my brother out of it. If you don't, I'll make sure you never get out of here alive."

I held my head high, trying to look unaffected by his threat, but I gripped the sword tighter to me and watched his hands intensely in case he tried to choke me again.

"I'm not scared of you," I snarled.

Alaric took another step toward me, sending shivers down my spine.

"You should be." Alaric grabbed my chin, yanking it up so our eyes met. "Do you know how many things I have killed?"

I pulled away, feeling a course of fear rush through me, recalling the stories I had heard about him on the battlefield.

Surprisingly, Alaric didn't reach for me again.

"I don't know, and I don't care," I snarked, trying to hide my shivering, my curling shoulders. "Just get out."

Alaric rolled his neck. "I will, but first, give me what I want."

I bit my lip, refusing to answer him, my stubbornness compromising my safety.

Alaric stalked toward me; I stepped back. He did it again, as did I, until I had nowhere else to go, and I was flush against the wall.

"Swear it," he commanded, his breath hot on my head, daring me to look up. "You will not let my brother help you any longer, and you won't talk to him."

I kept looking down, feeling his body tense around me the longer we sat in silence, fear emitting from us both.

I dared a peek at him, wondering if my nose was fooling me, but just as our eyes met, Alaric roared, "Swear it."

The sound was so harsh, so loud, I snapped fully up and screamed, "I swear."

Alaric held my stare for a moment, held me against that wall, reading my face. Finally, he inhaled and dropped his arms. "Good," he whispered before leaving.

CHAPTER 18

I trudged over to the table filled with pastries and fresh fruit, pivoting away from the wall of windows the sun beamed through. The strong light was almost more annoying than the servant that had woken me earlier than normal, relaying that Damon wanted me at the morning family meal.

I hated the idea, and not just because I had to tolerate Damon more than I did on a standard day, but because I would run into Alaric and Neo. The dread for the latter more so because of the former. I didn't want Alaric to think in the slightest that I was still involving his brother. However, Neo didn't know that our partnership had come to an end, and I was certain that he would talk to me as he did at other gatherings, and with so many present, I wouldn't be able to explain why he couldn't. Well, that was if he didn't arrive first.

Distant footsteps sounded down the hall, and I prayed that they belonged to Neo or Lillian, but then the footsteps stopped and grew distant, seemingly going in a different direction.

I groaned.

Everyone was taking their time this morning, and it was doing nothing for my nerves. I paced the room, only stopping whenever I heard a noise.

"My lady, are you alright?"

I followed the voice and found the servants staring at me. I stiffened, realizing I looked crazy, far from the ward I was expected to be.

I needed to fix that.

I smoothed out my dress, resting my hands on top of one another as Lillian had shown me.

"I like a bit of exercise before each meal," I replied.

The servants nodded but still maintained their concerned expressions.

I sighed, knowing I couldn't pace anymore, but still, my body needed something to do. As slowly as I could muster, I headed back to the table of food, setting my eyes on a plump muffin decorated with nuts and berries.

The warmth of it heated my hands as I moved it from the three-tiered platter to my plate, the smell of it causing my mouth to water. Though everything in Rivelia was wrong, their food was impeccable, far superior to anything we had in Artico. I suppose that was due to the freshness of their ingredients here. Regardless, I would miss it when I was on the road, especially when I knew a well-cooked meal was hard to come by when traveling. But perhaps I could have some of it for the first couple days.

Slyly, I looked over my shoulders.

The guards waited outside the room and the servants, no longer interested in me, stared at the walls of the room, lost in their thoughts.

It was safe to say no one was paying attention.

Swiftly, I grabbed two more muffins and placed them into my pocket.

It wouldn't be enough food to sustain me for more than a day or two, but at least, if this was all I was able to get before the ball, I wouldn't have to stop the first day of my escape to hunt.

"Grabbing some snacks for later," a friendly voice chimed from behind.

I jumped, shocked that someone had been able to sneak up on me, especially in such a quiet room.

I turned to see Neo. The wolf smiled devilishly, proud of his stealth.

I peered around him, checking if anyone else had seen me flinch. All the servants still stared off into the distance, however, Lillian sat at the table and smiled alongside Neo. Pride getting the best of me, I angrily defended, "They're rations."

There was silence, and then Neo moved closer. "I could have gotten those for you."

My pulse picked back up and cleared away my angry pride, allowing me to remember my concerns of earlier.

I really was not suited for a life of secrecy and sneakiness. I was too used to being forward with my actions.

I looked back at the door, standing on my toes to make sure no one else was going to come in for a while.

Now was my chance to explain.

"No, you can't," I began.

"Yes, I can," Neo interrupted, bracing himself on the table so he met my gaze. "Just because everything had been hastened doesn't mean that—"

I looked up at the ceiling, irritated that Neo had cut me off. However, I had little time to be annoyed, as the scent of pine and sandalwood grew, and as seeing how Neo hadn't gotten closer, I knew another royal was about to join us.

I cut Neo off. "That's not it. Your brother"—Neo stiffened, his eyes going dark—"came to my room last night and saw the clothes," I admitted. "He knows. He's promised to keep everything a secret, but I must stay away from you. I appreciate everything you've done, Neo, but I can't have you help me anymore. I can't talk to you either."

There was silence and an unexpected change in Neo's scent. Anger. Pure unfiltered anger was radiating off him.

"Neo," I whispered worriedly.

I had expected some fury, but not this much. After all, Neo knew the wishes of his father and had explicitly told me not to trust Alaric with my escape information. However, the rage emitting from him was more than just the expected frustration of being caught.

"He's still on that side," he mumbled, almost too quietly that I didn't hear, accompanied by a cynical laugh. "They'll never change, will they?"

"Neo?" I whispered again, looking over at Lillian who was starting to get up, sadly sighing for her mate, as if Neo's extreme negative feelings were a normal occurrence.

Neo shook his head, pulling out a tan folded paper. "Take this." I stared at the parchment reluctantly. "It's a map. You'll need it," he urged.

I didn't move.

The paper in front of me had been on my list. It was something I sorely needed, but I couldn't take it. It didn't matter that Alaric wasn't here to make sure I kept true to my promise. I had already sworn that I wouldn't seek help from Neo again, and without anything to my name, all I had was my word, all I had was staying true to the Artico teachings. A promise was a promise.

I took a step back, hoping it would help with the temptation.

"There are only a handful of them in the castle. All of them are either in my father, brother, or the cartographer's room. You won't get a map unless you take this one." Neo closed the space between us. "Accept this one, please," he pleaded.

Neo pushed the map toward me, made it touch my chest. I looked down at it, stared at the markings, at the trails I needed to know. And perhaps it was the desperation that had been haunting me for these past weeks, or maybe Rivelia had started to change me, but I found myself discarding my pervious thought and reached for the map.

"What's that?" a cold voice growled.

I turned to see who it was, but from the shiver that ran down my spine, I already knew.

Alaric stalked toward us, soaked in sweat, his hair ruffled, and fresh scrapes on the side of his cheek, looking as if he had just returned from a fight or perhaps a spar.

My eyebrows rose.

While I was certain Alaric exercised with how he handled his sword the other day and the way he had pushed me out of the way last night, I hadn't expected him to get up before the sun to train or allow scrapes to be made on him.

Neo retracted the parchment, shaking his head before smiling. "Nothing. It's just a list of our traditions. It's to help Ina meet everyone at the ball."

"Really?" Alaric sarcastically asked, reaching for the paper, all the while glaring at me. "That's very nice of you, Neo. Do you mind if I see it? I'd like to add to it."

Neo hid the map behind his back. "I think I've covered everything."

Alaric snickered. "I'm sure you have, little brother, but as her designated *helper* for the next two days, I think I should see the list." I blinked. Noticing the action, one side of Alaric's lips turned up into a sickening smirk. "Oh, I see. The king hasn't told you the good news yet." Alaric ran his tongue over his canines. "Last night, when I was talking to Father, I insinuated that the next two days of appointments and lessons may be a bit overwhelming for his sweet ward. Naturally, I suggested that a friendly face should be there for you, Ina."

"And he thinks that's you're the friendly face I need?" I asked.

Alaric let out a small laugh. "No, not in the slightest." Alaric tucked a hand into his pocket. "But I managed to convince him that this would be good for me and you. We haven't gotten along too well since you've arrived, and the only way to fix that would be to spend time together, which I fully intend to do." I gulped, seeing the glint of cunning in Alaric's eyes. "There will not be a second that I leave you unattended."

"How convenient," I harshly whispered.

"Yes, indeed," Alaric said, head high, nodding to the paper. "So, as you can see, Neo, there's no point in hiding that. In fact, it would better serve Ina if I held on to it."

Neo's smile diminished, and the map crumpled in his hands. "Well, with a teacher like you, I doubt Ina will need my list. You're so knowledgeable, and your notes are *far* superior to mine," Neo sneered, his voice rising to the point where the servants were starting to stare, all ounce of charm within him gone.

Alaric, for a moment, looked hurt, or perhaps it was a trick of the eyes, because his brows, just as quickly as I had seen them simper, scrunched together.

"I won't explain the situation again, Neo. Give me the paper," Alaric stated, sidestepping so he blocked Neo and I from the eyes of the servants. Neo gripped the paper tighter, his young age showing as he huffed. Alaric leaned toward my ear. "I'm allowing grace because I'm assuming you just told him that you don't need his help anymore."

My temple twitched. None of what he was doing was an act of *grace*.

"Encourage him, or I will make my words from last night true," Alaric hastily warned, pulling me from the many curses I wished to scream at him.

My breath left me as I debated, as we all stared at one another, playing a game. It was one that I didn't want to play, couldn't afford to. If I didn't go after the blood demons, no one would. Still, I needed that map.

I thought of ways to barter, to ask for this to be the last thing, but before I could think of anything, King Damon's scent drifted into the room.

Alaric gave Neo and I one last pointed look. Neo did not budge.

Alaric shook his head, his brows lowering. "So be it," he replied somberly, taking a step toward the door, toward Damon.

This wasn't happening. Oh gods, it couldn't. I was so close. Damn the map. I'd figure out something else.

"Alaric," I called, making sure to grab his attention as I snatched the map from Neo and threw it into a fireplace a few steps away. "You're right. Your way is better."

Alaric's chest caved in, as if he had been holding his breath. "Wise choice," he muttered before greeting his father at the door.

I turned back to thank Neo for all that he had done one last time. However, as I turned, I met blazing eyes. They were a fire that burned so strongly, so brightly, that I wondered how long the pyre fueling it had been building, how long it would burn.

I reached out, but Neo shrugged away, rolling back his shoulders. "I can't do this anymore," he mumbled.

I nodded in agreement, but something in my gut told me we weren't talking about the same thing.

CHAPTER 19

I gasped for air as the maid cinched my gown tighter again, cooing, "Just once more."

I gripped tighter to the chair in front of me, cursing with what little breath I had left, reminding myself that tonight was my last night in Rivelia—the night of my grand escape. It was the only thought that kept me from screaming. After all, it was more crucial than ever that I let them treat me like the doll they wanted, especially since I was doing this alone and with a menacing shadow watching over me tonight.

Though Alaric had said he would let me go if I no longer talked to Neo—which I hadn't since the map incident—I wasn't sure what to do. I didn't know if Alaric would intervene if he saw me leaving or if he would turn a blind eye and walk me to the gate. I also didn't trust him to keep his word. Not completely. For all I knew, his threat was a ploy to make sure that my attempt at escape would fail, and his watching me had not helped to alleviate that theory.

In the past few days, Alaric had watched me like a predator watching his prey. He was with me every second, every step. He even waited in the hall when I used the privy. It made me miss the times when it had just been the guards. At least with them, their eyes wandered off, and they whispered amongst themselves when they got bored. Because of Alaric, it had made this morning virtually impossible to prepare for tonight.

My original plan had been to go on a walk around the castle and hide my satchel of supplies near the privy so I could change and sneak out of the castle during the party. However, with Alaric looming over me, it was impossible to smuggle the satchel out of my room or even plant it. So instead, I was now wearing my disguise, sword, and dagger under my chemise and ballgown. It was a feat proving to be much, much hotter than I expected, and the maid *still* tightening the laces did not help at all.

"Is she almost ready?" Alaric yelled beyond the door, causing my eyes to roll.

I couldn't believe he was already back.

He had left me an hour ago to prepare for the ball. It was the longest we had been apart, except when we slept. Yet, it was still not enough time for me to gain any peace of mind from him. He had my heart speeding every second, had my spine tingling whenever the sun rose because I knew he was on his way to my room. It was annoying. I hated the feeling, and I hated him.

"Almost, Prince Alaric," the maid respectfully chimed.

She turned back to me, examining my waist before pulling the ribbons with a strength that had me yelping.

A small laugh came from behind the door. It took all my strength not to growl and hope Alaric could feel my anger.

"Sorry. We don't have any more time to be gentle with it," the maid whispered.

Gentle.

All of the endless pulling and tugging was supposed to be gentle?

My upper lip curled. However, I didn't stew on the question for too long, as I caught a glimpse of myself in the mirror.

The forest green dress gripped tightly to my bosom, dipping down just below to see the tops of my breasts and the space that lay between them where Artico's Fang rested. The luxurious fabric then glided down my arms, turning sheer so it revealed the glitter the maid had dusted onto my body. As for the skirt, it wasn't poofy. It cascaded down my body, down to the floor like water, creating a pool of fabric at my heels. My braided hair was wrapped around my head, each strand perfectly tucked except for two wisps that fell on either side of my part. They framed my face, pulling focus to the bronze wolf head—surrounded by emerald leaves and golden branches—that sat in the middle of my diadem. I hadn't expected to like the headpiece so much. I had even rejected the thought of even wearing one, but seeing it like this, I couldn't stop smiling. I was beauty and power personified.

The click of the doorknob turning caught my attention. I wiped the smile I wore from my face, ready to see Alaric sneer as he did every time he looked at me. However, as the door opened and we were fully bare to one another, he gawked, wide eyes slowly raking over me, taking in every detail as if I was a piece of art. I cocked my head at that, at the impossibility of it. Alaric, in response, rolled back his shoulders and scoffed.

A delayed reaction, then.

"Let's get to it," I prompted, walking to the door with every intention of passing him, but Alaric grabbed my wrist, twisting my arm so it entangled in his.

"Proper females have an escort at balls," Alaric announced without so much as another look at me.

I grimaced.

Of course, that's how it was here.

Alaric tugged my arm, beckoning me to walk with him. I followed, staring forward, focusing on the steps of my plan. However, as we walked, I couldn't help but find something unnerving. I paused, trying to think of what sent my instincts flaring.

Silence.

The hall was silent.

There should have been the clanking of metal suits behind us.

I sporadically spun, searching for my guards, but none were within sight.

Alaric pulled me back in, answering, "Their presence would have caused tension in the ballroom, so I instructed them to take the night off." I looked up at him. "No one but I will watch you tonight, so if you plan to cause mischief before you are sworn into our family, make sure you do it tonight, but remember our deal."

My jaw slacked at Alaric's blatant declaration.

Perhaps I should've had more faith in this male's word than I had.

I froze as the ballroom doors opened for us, and my nose was drowned in rich perfumes along with the smell of pastries, meats, and cheeses. My head grew dizzy at the sight of so many colors, performers dangling from the ceiling, and the people dancing, their movements stiff and perfectly synchronized. It was like some rehearsed act, yet there was almost magic in how many people knew the steps. It wasn't like any celebration in Artico, and I wasn't sure how I felt about it.

"Presenting Prince Alaric and Ina of the Artico Pack, Daughter of the late Alpha Batair," bellowed a man next to us.

The music stopped, and all eyes turned to the staircase. I gulped, and my stomach dropped.

Though I had been used to speaking in public in Artico, I knew that pack. I knew that I had friends there, and they didn't look at me with such judging eyes as the Rivelia Pack did now.

Alaric tugged on my arm once again, breaking the spell I had put myself under. I walked with him, waiting for the wolves to look away but none of their gazes faltered. I became all too aware of my posture, the appearance of my face, and the heaviness of my dress. One small misstep, one piece of fabric under my shoe, and I would collapse in front of everyone. I gripped Alaric's arm tighter, thankful, for once, that he was beside me. To my amazement, he did the same, even going as far to reposition his arm ever so slightly so it offered more support.

I wanted to ask why but stopped myself as we reached the bottom of the stairs, and the silence I didn't think could get any louder did. The people kept staring, their eyes moving up and down. I didn't know what to do or say. I didn't know how I was going to survive this all night.

"Please, pluck your string once more," Neo chirped, emerging from the crowd. "Let us show this Artico wolf our signature dance." Neo grabbed a couple of hands and pulled them to the dance floor where Lillian stood, blushing in the middle.

The quartet started up once more, and Neo led a dance that began in a twirl. His energy beckoned people to join, and soon enough, everyone who had stared intently at me had moved on. I let out a sigh, catching Neo's eyes as he did one more spin. He smiled broadly at me, and I smiled back in thanks. I would miss him and Lillian so much.

"That's enough of an interaction," Alaric growled, stepping in front of me, any kindness that he had showed on the stairs gone.

I rolled my eyes, bothered by his disdain, but I wasn't sure why. It's what I expected from Alaric, all I had ever known from him since I had arrived. It didn't matter if he had been kind for a couple of seconds.

Looking away, I checked the position of the full moon. It still had a third of the way to go until it reached the center of the night sky, until the ceremony would be held in which I was supposed to kneel before Damon and swear my allegiance to him, officially joining his pack. Though in reality, that was how much longer until I made my escape.

That time couldn't come soon enough, not when Alaric was going to act like a brute all night.

"Presenting King Damon," the same voice that had bellowed my name boomed.

A hush fell over the crowd, not the same that had happened when I ascended those steps but one of respect. At least that's what I thought initially.

The more I examined the crowd, the more I noticed shaking hands and lowered eyes.

Respect wasn't here. Well, maybe a bit of it, but it wasn't the main feeling. It was fear and sorrow. Still, Damon's people gracefully moved out of his way and bowed as he strode over to me and Alaric.

Alaric gave a shallow bow as I curtsied, then with a flick of his wrist, Damon summoned the music again—a silent order for everyone to stop staring and join in the dance.

Damon gave Alaric a nod in greeting then turned his attention to me. "You look beautiful," Damon gushed, reaching out to hug me.

It took every ounce of my strength not to flinch.

"Thank you," I lowly said, glancing at the window once again, wishing I could make time go faster.

Damon held my cheek. "You look so wonderful in her dress."

"Her?" I asked nonchalantly, trying to think of a way out of this conversation.

"Your mother," Damon softly stated with a smile, snapping my attention to him, but not before I saw Alaric stiffen and move slightly closer to me.

I knew so little about my mother. I had craved to know her so much that I stared at pictures of her for years, hoping to find something that would give me another clue as to who she was. However, with each passing day that I found nothing and no one to tell me anything about her, that yearning had left. I didn't even know why it had come back today, as Damon had mentioned her when I first arrived, and I had not brought it back up. Perhaps it was all the things that had happened that day, or the warrior in me suppressing my feelings so I could focus on the new battle in front of me. Whatever the reason, the child in me was now overpowering it. It was shouting that we needed to learn everything we could about her, because with my father's passing and my escape tonight, this may be my last chance.

Ever so carefully, I ran my fingers over the skirt, examining it as if I could see her in the fabric. "This is hers?" I asked, the disgust I felt for Damon temporarily clouded by curiosity.

Damon's cheeks turned a rosy color. "Yes, I bought it and the diadem for her when we were still betrothed."

I dropped my skirt. The world went quiet, and my heart hammered away.

Betrothed.

As far as I knew, my mother had always been in love with my father and he, her.

Damon laughed. "I suppose Batair didn't tell you?"

I shook my head, a bit of wariness trickling in. No matter how different Rivelia and Artico were, we were all still wolves at our core—possessive of those we laid claim to.

"That's understandable. Your father and I did get in a couple of brawls when we first found out." I stepped back, wanting distance between us. Damon's mouth dropped. "Oh, no. Ina, everything was fine afterward. You see, I basically grew up with your mother. Her father advised mine, and because of that, she was always visiting the palace. We were purely friends at first, but after many years, I began to form some romantic feelings for her. So, I asked her if she would be mine." Damon blushed. "She said yes, and we were very happy for a time. However, a week before our wedding, when other packs began to gather in Rivelia, she met your father. They had an instant connection and were hardly inseparable, so much so, they asked to be tested as mates."

Damon's blush faded, and only a melancholy smile remained. My heart slightly hurt at the clear pain on his face, at one of the reasons I hated the mating bond.

"I was angry at your father at first. I even challenged him a couple times. He always beat me, though." Damon laughed. "I hated him for a while until I realized she—your mother—was happy with him. That's when I moved on, well, with whom I loved. She will always hold a special place in my heart. Both of your parents do." Damon took a deep breath, closed his eyes, then released it, smiling once again. "It is why I am so protective of you," he overzealously declared, his eyes shining. "You are a memory of them, and I will treasure that. I will make Rivelia safer for you. I will build her walls higher so the past does not repeat itself." Damon touched my cheek once again, looking at me. No, through me. He was seeing something else. Someone else. My mother.

Damon stroked his thumb tenderly against my cheek, inches from my lip. My skin crawled, and my stomach turned sour, clearing away the haze that had allowed me to talk to him. However, the curiosity remained; it was just mixed with anger.

During my time here, I had ignored the way things were done and Damon's reasons for trapping me here. I was sure it was unchangeable without the help of another alpha. But now, Damon's ideals were more than just the wrong way of thinking. They were actions he had decided to take to *honor* my parents. However, it was nothing but. Everything that he was saying, everything that he had done and was doing for them, was an insult to their memory. I couldn't let that stand, not before leaving.

I leaned away. "But why?" I asked, canines starting to show, any thought of restraint falling apart.

Damon's brows raised. "What do you mean why?"

"Why do what you do in their memory?"

Damon's hand dropped from my face. "It should be clear as day, especially with your father's passing. That should have proved the way he chose to handle things was wrong."

I stared Damon down, eyes unwavering. My anger growing by the second. "They wouldn't want this. Nothing you're doing makes sense."

Damon shifted from one foot to another, his hand flexing in the way that meant he was readying to call over his guards.

I raised my head, hand ready to reach under my skirt and grab the dagger attached to my thigh.

If he wanted to fight, I'd make one last show of it before my escape.

"I'm sure nothing makes sense when you've had so much wine," Alaric growled in that ever-condescending tone, gripping the top of my forearm, pulling me behind him. "Father, allow me to escort her to the balcony. She needs to clear her head before the ceremony."

I pulled my arm away, scowling at Alaric. "I'm perfectly fine," I countered.

"No, you're—"

Numerous gasps drowned out Alaric, beckoning us all to abandon the conversation that was about to boil over and look to where the wave of fret had originated.

In the center of the dance floor knelt Neo, fear and worry exudeding from him as his shaking hands held up Lillian's limp body.

In an instant, Alaric made his way to them, the crowd parting. Damon followed. I did too but not before scanning the room, inhaling deeply, and examining each scent, making sure nothing was askew.

"What happened?" Alaric asked, his tone harsh and alert but still caring.

"We were dancing, and she fainted," Neo said between gulps of air.

Alaric gently placed two fingers on Lillian's neck, waiting a minute before nodding to himself.

"All her drinks were tested?" Alaric asked, carefully pulling down on Lillian's chin to open her mouth, getting close to her breath so he could check for any poisons.

"Yes," Neo hysterically blurted out before Alaric could sniff her breath. "I think she's just tired, or her cold from before came back. She told me she was feeling dizzy, but she didn't want to miss tonight, and..." Neo's throat bobbed, his answer causing Alaric to sit up and comfort his brother. "I should've made her stay home," Neo whined out.

A worried mumble came from the crowd. Alaric quickly glanced around, one side of his jaw ticking. "She should be alright. She just needs rest."

Neo assessed his brother, making sure he spoke the truth. Alaric did not break his stare. Finally, Neo nodded.

Quietly, Alaric waved over a guard, whispering so soft that I almost didn't hear, "Help Neo and Lillian to their room, and send for the royal physician right away."

The guard nodded, kneeling with outstretched arms, but Neo shook his head, clutching Lillian tighter. "I got her," he whispered before carrying her out.

The crowd parted, their eyes glued to him. There wasn't a sign that their staring would stop for the long walk Neo had to make up the stairs.

"Come," Alaric growled, gripping my hand. "Father, check in with the priestess." Damon scowled at his son, making it clear he didn't appreciate being ordered around. "She may take this as an omen and stop the celebration. She listens to your pleas the best." Damon stiffened, a hint of fear in his eyes. Alaric, taking that as agreement with his plan, dragged me to the middle of the dance floor and flung me so I stood in front of him. It happened so fast that I didn't have time to protest.

"What are you doing?" I gasped, stepping back as he reached for my waist.

"Shut it, or the party will never continue," Alaric hissed, pulling me flush against him, glaring at the musicians until they felt his piercing eyes ordering them to play.

"Why should it?" I snarled, trying to get out of his grip. "Lillian is sick. We should be concerned," I spat, too worried over one of the only two people in Rivelia who were on my side.

Alaric laced his fingers with mine. "Oh, should we? The last time I checked, you seemed keen on making sure that this ceremony happened. Has that changed? I can't tell anymore after that skiff you had with my father. If that would've continued, he would have had you locked up to contemplate your words."

"He was dishonoring my parents' memories. I had to."

Alaric shook his head. "Your reasoning is void, but it doesn't matter anymore. Thankfully, the situation has already passed without repercussions. I just want you gone. You jeopardize too much." My head shrank away from him, highly doubting I could jeopardize anything of importance for this pompous prince. "Now, take my hand and smile. You need to appear happy to make the pack happy, or the priestess will take it as a bad omen and won't perform the ceremony."

I stilled, listening. Not a single laughter sounded. There were only mumbles and hushed arguing—Damon and the priestess's arguing. Alaric was right.

My hand hovered over Alaric's hand. "I don't know your dances," I whispered, my leg shaking.

"Of course you don't," he scoffed, closing the distance between our hands. "Just follow my steps. It's like working on footwork for swordplay. You can handle that, can't you?"

My nose scrunched at the condescension in his tone. However, it quickly disappeared as a chorus of notes rang out.

Alaric stepped forward, tugging a bit on my dress, telling me to take a step back. I followed, only for him to step right, then back, then left, then forward again. Each of his steps accompanied with those tiny tugs.

I held my breath for each one, trying to guess what the next move was. After a few more steps, I realized that the pattern was repeating.

Forward, right, back, left.

The movement started to come naturally, and the tugging on my dress lessened. I started to smile, to look away from my feet, but that was a mistake.

I was met with the eyes of those who had watched Neo, their quiet mumbles of my steps and appearance reaching my ears. Suddenly, my feet became heavy and reminders that I had never danced like this filled my mind.

I lost count of my steps, of which foot came next, and tripped. I inhaled sharply as my body fell backward, as my eyes met the crystal chandelier above. I pivoted forward but the fabric of my dress and the items hidden beneath it weighed me down. I was destined to fall. But, as gravity took me, Alaric's hand gripped tighter, and his bicep bulged into my side, stoping my fall. With my body still at an incline, he turned us a quarter of a circle before pulling me back up with such a force that I spun as he got me to my feet, my dress flaring. The crowd gasped. Someone even applauded.

"Relax," Alaric whispered in a surprisingly comforting tone, pulling me close to him again. "They'll join in the dance soon enough. Just focus on me."

I nodded, my cheeks warming as I did what he told me to. For once, his features were soft, still observant, but soft nonetheless. It was an expression I hadn't seen from him yet. I marveled at that, at the idea that his eyes weren't always piercing, that his lips weren't always pursed, that he didn't always scowl like I believed him to.

"Thank you," I whispered.

"For what?" Alaric growled, his demeanor going back to how it normally was, as if my gratitude were poison.

"For teaching me to dance and making sure I didn't fall," I replied shortly.

Alaric looked away. "I didn't do it for you. I did it so you wouldn't embarrass my family. I can't have our people seeing my father's ward as some uncivilized wolf from the Artico region who can't perform a simple waltz. Not to mention, I needed to redirect everyone's attention from Neo. Poor Lillian is already going to be mortified from fainting. I knew having you dance with me would be a spectacle and regain the festive spirit. Letting you fall might have done that as well, though. The court does love a good jester. But then you might've been limping for the ceremony, and father—"

I yanked my hand out of Alaric's, pushing him away. He barely budged an inch. He looked down, laughing at the small space between us.

"Tired of dancing already?" he asked in that patronizing tone again, one side of his lips turning up, revealing one of his canines.

I didn't say a word, angry with myself for even thanking such a creature.

"I'll take that as a yes," he smugly said, straightening his lapels, their misplacement the only indication that I had pushed him. "I need a drink," he announced. "Dancing with you made me parched, and with the ceremony quickly approaching, I need to make sure my needs are met for that grueling experience." Alaric headed to the small table of refreshments but stopped momentarily when he came parallel with me and whispered, "I suggest you do the same," before disappearing into the sea of wolves.

I gritted my teeth, sending foul curses on the breeze.

Alaric had to be the most horrendous male to have ever existed. I hoped our paths never crossed again. I would've even prayed for it, but as I looked at the moon and saw that it was almost to the peak of the sky, I knew I couldn't spare a moment for it.

The time had come for me to leave.

CHAPTER 20

I rushed through the hall, going as fast as the heavy skirts would allow, scared to go any slower. Though I had made it out of the ballroom with little to no problems and earlier than planned due to Damon leaving and Lillian's fainting, I was certain that the nosey court members would soon take note of my absence, and the news would quickly reach Damon's ears. I prayed that it wouldn't be too soon, or that if it did, the act of clutching my stomach and covering my mouth as I hurried down the hall would make everyone assume I was sick with nerves, stalling the suspiciousness that were sure to occur. It had to be one of the most embarrassing acts that I had done since I arrived in Rivelia, but the gods knew I needed the extra moments, especially when I was still making my way to the late queen's sitting room. If I were caught, I would never leave here.

I shook my head. I couldn't think like that. After all, the sitting room was only a few turns away.

I breathed deeply, hiking up my skirts further, sweat dripping down my back, and took my next step. However, I did not dare take another as the clatter of armor echoed down the hall.

I held my breath, searching for a shadowed alcove to hide in—knowing well enough that I was too far from the privy that I couldn't use sickly nerves as an excuse—but I found none. The moon had risen too high. Its light illuminated everything, destroying any possible hiding place. I was going to have to fight.

I pressed myself into an alcove, making sure I wouldn't be seen as the guard approached. I inhaled deeply, as I did before every fight, and visualized the movements I'd make to take him out—a punch to the gut to topple him over, then a firm hit to the back of his neck to knock him out.

The footsteps grew louder, and the moonlight was replaced with a flickering red. I raised my fists, prayed that somehow the guard would fail to see me in his peripheral, but when silence, followed by a short inhale, echoed through the hall, I knew they hadn't been answered.

I threw my first punch. However, as my arm began to fully extend, the sleeves of my dress tightened, slowing my speed. I held my breath, willing my fist to keep going.

It hit with great force but not enough.

The guard snarled, anger and surprise written all over his face. He inched closer, debating what to do with me, but as the light from his lantern revealed the diadem on my head, his eyes widened.

"You're the king's ward." He searched our surroundings. "Where are your guards? They or Prince Alaric are supposed to escort you everywhere." I said nothing, my brain too tired to think of an excuse. The guard realizing what was happening, ordered, "Come with me. I'm taking you back to the king."

He attempted to grab my arm. I stepped back, readying a kick, sure that the loose fabric around them wouldn't interfere. I was so wrong.

The excess fabric wrapped around my foot causing me to slip. My knees fell quicker to the marble floor than I could thrust out my arms to catch myself. The male, taking the opportunity, grabbed my wrist. I pulled and pulled against him, but the too tight bodice prevented me from twisting, ensuring that I would never get out of his grip. Panic filled me as he pulled me up. I began to flail, a desperate attempt at freeing myself, but nothing worked.

Tears threatened to spill. I hadn't even gotten out of the castle, and I had already failed my mission. I shut my eyelids tightly, making sure that no one would see them as I felt my feet sliding across the floor, felt my body rising, the guard's grip tightening.

"Hey," a familiar voice snarled, followed by the clatter of armor, the end of the guard's grip on my wrist. "Ina, are you alright?"

Slowly, I opened my eyes.

In front of me stood Neo, shrouded in a black cloak, a sword in his hands, and a pack slung across his back.

"What are you doing here?" I mumbled, the only words that I could utter. "You're supposed to be with Lillian. She's..." My words died off as I put two and two together, and a theory formed in my head.

Neo sheathed his blade. "What do you mean what am I doing here? I'm obviously helping." He knelt, checking the guard's pulse. He smiled softly. "Good, still alive."

"Lillian is fine, isn't she?" I asked.

"Just now remembering our acting skills, aren't you?" Neo answered me, dragging the guard into the alcove.

I crossed my arms, needing more of an answer than that.

"She took a potion to make it appear that she was ill so I could be here. It was actually her idea. She's quite the conniving one. Her sweet personality is such a mask."

My head spun. "Neo, you shouldn't have. Alaric—"

"I'm tired of listening to him and my father. I want to help. I can't stand on the side anymore." Neo stood, an awful gloat on his face. "And even so"—he jerked his head to the male asleep between us—"you can't complain because you needed my help."

I rolled my eyes. Though I was relieved and happy to see Neo one last time, I had given my word not to involve him.

"You're right. Thank you for that, but we need to part ways now."

Neo rested his hands on his hips. "I'm seeing this through to the end."

I rubbed my temple, a headache already forming. Something inside me told me that even if I escaped and Alaric found out Neo helped me after the fact, he would chase me down and deliver the violence he had promised.

"No, Neo. You can't," I began just as a bell rang through the castle.

A warning bell.

Time was up.

Neo tilted his head, asking a silent question.

I groaned. "Alright, fine," I spat out, taking note of the strengthened determination in Neo's eyes. "You can walk me to the escape route."

Neo gripped my wrist as I walked past him. "I'll walk with you to the blood demons' castle."

I stared, loud silence between us as I processed his words.

"Absolutely not," I snarled. I was already worried what Alaric would do if he found out I let Neo walk me to his mother's room. I couldn't imagine what he'd do if he caught Neo with me outside the walls. "You can't come. I made a deal with Alaric." I pulled my hand out of Neo's grip, listening to the bell ring. I would have to sprint to get to the door now. I began ripping off the dress. It was something I should have done long ago, but I had wanted a piece of my mother to stay with me just a while longer.

"You need me," Neo growled back, pulling the strap of the bag on his back forward.

I rubbed my temple, realizing I should've taken note of that earlier as an indication of his intentions, as the bag was far too big to be just for one person.

I unwrapped the cloak I had tied to my waist and draped it over my body, refusing to lose anymore time as I responded, "I can get the rest of the supplies when I travel. I can even tough it out for a few days if need be.

I know how to live off the land. I grew up in the mountains, remember?" I stalked forward, ears open for any clattering armor, not bothering to ask for the bag. "Thank you for everything, Neo."

"The land cannot provide a map," Neo sternly whispered, running after me. I glanced at him, but continued walking, keeping alert. "You forget what we discussed. If my father does send his army after you, you cannot afford any missteps. If you take me, you'll have one. I've studied maps of the continent for years. I know several routes you can use to get to the blood demons' castle by heart. I started memorizing them after we concluded that's where they're probably hiding. I know a way through the forest, one using the main road, whatever you need."

I chewed on my lower lip.

The worry Neo spoke of was only if they came after me, but even if they did, I would do whatever I needed to keep them from finding me. I would even slather dung on myself to hide my scent then run as fast as I could. I wasn't sure if Neo would go to that extent, and even if he did, I knew nothing of his athletic skills. He may very well fall behind. Not to mention, him coming along would heighten the chances of Damon sending his men. The benefit of Neo coming wasn't worth the risk.

"No, Neo," I proclaimed again, walking away.

Neo followed until I stopped in the hall where his mother's sitting room was. I stared at the numerous doors, trying to remember which one led to it. Neo tapped his foot. I ignored him, knowing he wanted me to ask. However, I refused to give him that satisfaction, knowing it would give him another reason to come with me. Despite my stubbornness though, Neo opened one of the doors, revealing a green room with florals painted all around the walls, fabric draped over only what I could assume was furniture.

I walked into the unused room, ignoring Neo's mocking bow, and headed toward the tapestries on the back wall where Neo had claimed the secret escape route—he had found years ago—was. I pulled back the one depicting a horse resting in the field, and sure enough, a wooden door waited behind it. I turned the knob, and a deep musty smell flooded my nose, the strong scent explaining why no one had tracked Neo's smell when he had used it in the past and why I was now confident no one would track mine.

The rest of the way would be easy. I just needed to do one last thing.

I turned to Neo who stood taller and clutched both straps of his bag, still refusing my answer.

"Please don't make me knock you unconscious," I pleaded, already reaching for my dagger, ready to use the hilt.

Neo widened his stance. I sighed heavily and pulled out my weapon.

I didn't have time for this.

"The longer it takes to get to the blood demons, the more people will die," Neo spat out, a bit of panic in his voice.

I froze at his words.

"Take the risk for them, Ina. Take it. We can deal with my father and Alaric later."

My chest tightened at the truth I hadn't dared to think of, knowing that it was nothing I could change as the map was unattainable after my deal with Alaric. I already hated myself for taking so long to escape, for coming to Rivelia instead of trying to find my pack when I awoke after the attack. If I got lost, if I wasted time aimlessly wandering through the land trying to find a map or someone to give me directions, I would never forgive myself.

I needed Neo.

"The journey will be hard. There will be none of this." I motioned to the marble floors and gold embellishments. "You'll need to run hard, and there will be fights." I looked worriedly at his semi-toned body.

Neo chuckled. "My father may have closed the gates, but he still has his sons train as if they go outside."

I rubbed my face. I highly doubted Neo spoke true or knew what skills were needed beyond the wall, but I didn't have time to test him. I just needed to take his word for it. After all, it hadn't steered me wrong yet.

"What about Lillian? You won't see your mate for a while." I paused, hating what I was about to say. "You may not even see her again."

Neo grimaced but continued his argument, unfazed by my words, "Like I said before, she took the potion so I could be here. We've already discussed this at great lengths, and both of us have agreed that I need to go with you."

Neo held my stare, making sure I knew his words were true, that he knew all the risks, all the things he would endure if he came with me.

I had no excuse not to bring him anymore.

I closed my eyes and sent a quick prayer to the gods before nodding and beginning our descent.

CHAPTER 21

Pulling sticks from my hair, I examined the dense woods Neo and I had fallen asleep in. I didn't have a clue as to where we were or even how far we had run. All I knew was that my body ached and that it was tired from a full day and half a night of running. Still, I would've run more if our fur hadn't turned to skin, and our paws to hands and feet in the middle of the night.

It had happened unexpectedly, both Neo and I tumbling as our bodies transformed. We had sat for a moment, allowing our wolves to rest then tried to transform again, scared that we had not run far enough, that the wind hadn't had enough time to blow away our scent to avoid the trackers we were certain Damon would unleash. However, no matter how long we waited, our wolves refused to answer our summons. We were forced to lie down in the forest, covering ourselves in leaves to hide our scent, then, and only then, did we allow ourselves a bit of sleep. Though now that my mind wasn't clouded with fatigue, I realized it had been a dangerous choice.

I should have found a way for us to transform. I should've made us keep going, even if that meant trekking through the darkness in our human form.

Who knew when the wolves would be sent beyond the wall to look for us? How soon they would pick up on our scent?

Turning up my nose, I sniffed the air, detecting only the forest, Neo, and myself. However, the scents—even mine—were muted. They seemed far away, but I knew they were anything but. The forest was all around us. Neo was not too far away either. He slept an arm's distance away from me under a pile of leaves. And I had nothing to alter my personal scent. If anything, it should be stronger. Quickly, I tried to shift. A warm feeling began in my chest, but it didn't grow. It wouldn't stretch to my fingers or to my toes. It didn't begin to melt and change my flesh. I closed my eyes and pushed again. Still, nothing happened. I snarled in frustration, flinging my hand through a mound of leaves. My wolf was still tired, and to make matters worse, the heightened senses I had in human form had dulled.

"I can't shift either," Neo exclaimed, sitting up, only his legs still covered in foliage. ·

I cursed under my breath.

"How long do you think it will be until we can again?" he asked, examining his hands, feeling his teeth for his canines.

In a panic, I did the same. Thankfully, the sharp teeth still remained.

"I don't know," I replied, standing up, brushing the leaves and twigs off my clothes. Neo mimicked my movements. "I've never had this happen before."

Neo gulped, showing the nervousness we both felt. I tried to push the feeling away.

My wolf had slowed in the past after a long day of training, but after some rest, it would be as it was before. Surely, that was the case now. At least I hoped so.

The cracking of a twig not too far away had me spinning, and my heart racing as I tried to peer through the trees, but I found nothing. Still, I felt as though we were being stalked.

I threw Neo's bag over my shoulder. "Are you ok to walk?"

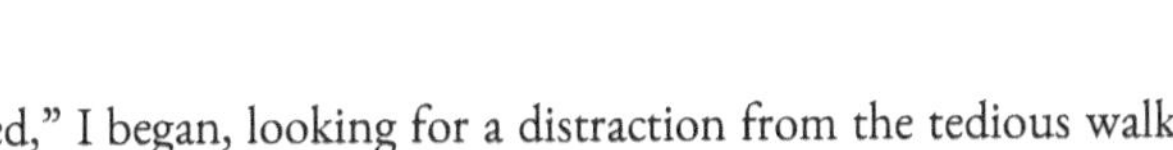

"I never asked," I began, looking for a distraction from the tedious walk through the woods in our human form, "how did you find the escape route?"

Neo looked up from the fallen tree he was awkwardly climbing over. It was strange to see a wolf so uncomfortable in the forest, but I could barely judge, as my feet had started to drag, and unlike Neo, traversing through the woods had been my job.

"It's kind of a sad story," Neo warned.

I looked forward. There was no sight of the river Neo had claimed would be our next landmark, and the woods seemed to grow denser. We still had a long way to go. "That's fine," I mumbled, accepting anything as a distraction.

"My mother died when I was born, so she's always been an air of mystery for me, and I wanted to solve that when I was younger."

My feet came to a halt at the similarities between Neo and mine's efforts in getting to know more about our deceased mothers. Perhaps that was why I had been so fast to trust him.

"I asked around but no one, not even my father or Alaric, would tell me about her. Alaric even warned me not to ask around, but I did anyway." Neo smiled mockingly at himself. "Everyone said they didn't know much or gave me some quick generic answer. They told me she was kind or that she was a good queen. They acted like talking about her was taboo.

"But someone—I can't remember who—told me to check a particular room and that I would find answers there. I looked, and sure enough, I did." Neo came parallel with me. "It was her sitting room, covered in dust, completely forgotten about. I spent hours there, going through her personal belongings that were scattered about the room as if she had just used it. I found letters from her friends, sharing her excitement about her having another child. I found drawings she had made, even a little picture book she had created for me. It was very bittersweet until I found her diary.

"In it, I learned of her favorite places. I learned about the *humans* she called friend." Neo licked his lips. "You see, I had never questioned why I wasn't allowed outside the walls, or why we didn't interact with the humans beyond. I just knew that as the standard. When I read her journal, it was my first time seeing the world the way it was before I was born, before the Blood War, before the separation of wolves and humans. It seemed wonderful."

I clenched my fist as I saw tears form in Neo's eyes.

"I didn't understand why things had changed, so I began asking around. And again, everyone's answers were short, and they ran once they gave me some broad response. They were even more scared to talk about it than they were my mother. Still, I kept trying, expecting someone to tell me or some mystery man to appear again, but no one ever did. Finally, I decided to go and see for myself. I came up with several plans to sneak out beyond the walls, but there was always a flaw in them. I began to think I would never find a way out, but on the off chance that I was examining my mother's tapestries, one fell."

"The one covering the secret door," I surmised.

Neo nodded. "I took it and found that it led to the outside world."

"What happened after?" I asked, fully facing Neo.

"I learned that my mother was right." Neo smiled sadly. "The humans were like us, just weaker." Neo drifted off again, but still, I kept staring, wanting to know more.

If he had seen the humans for what they were, got along with them, then why was he so silent? Why didn't he leave the castle, say he was done with Rivelia's ways only now?

As if hearing my questions, Neo continued his story. "I kept adventuring out and made friends with the humans. However, one day,

I ran into my father too soon after I got back. I hadn't gotten to bathe yet, and he smelt the humans on me. He took me into his office and questioned me." Neo rubbed his thumb across his nails. "He asked me how I got out, why I disobeyed him, and so forth. Being so young, I wanted to tell him. I almost did too, but Alaric was in the room that day. He kept shaking his head, urging me not to say a thing. It confused me, as Alaric never hid things from our father. He obeyed his every word and told me I should as well. It was so out of character for him that I listened."

My head shrank back into my shoulders at the information, at the fact that Alaric had betrayed his father in such a way, especially when it came to humans.

"I staved off his questions again and again until my father finally tired. He dismissed me with a warning—don't sneak out again, or there will be consequences. Alaric did the same but in private. He told me that the punishment father would deal out would haunt me for the rest of my life. I told him I would only listen if he told me why. He wouldn't, said I was too young for the truth." Neo's eyes darkened, and he began to chew on his lower lip. "I was too stubborn back then and didn't listen. As soon as I had the opportunity, I snuck out in a quest to understand. I even told one of the humans I had grown close to what I was and asked him for help. Of course, he agreed. We made it our secret mission. We even traded trinkets as a substitute for a blood oath." Neo played with a simple wood carving of an acorn around his neck. My heart began to hurt, already guessing the end of his story, knowing that objects held scents much longer than living bodies. "I didn't know much about scents back then. I thought I had washed the human scents off, and I attended family dinner as normal. Father didn't even ask me about it. He just shifted and started snarling, destroying everything around him. Alaric couldn't calm him. He couldn't calm me as I screamed about how I didn't understand, how Mother—"

Neo's words stopped as his head dropped, and he held back a sob.

I gingerly placed a hand on his shoulder, offering him any support I could, imagining the terror Neo had experienced.

An alpha's rage knew no bounds. My own father had once shown me a fraction of his wrath when I did something inconceivably stupid, and I had been petrified for weeks as a grown wolf. If I had experienced it any younger, I was sure it would have taken me months, maybe a year, to get over.

Neo tucked the pendant back inside his tunic.

"His punishment was far more severe than I could have imagined."

I studied Neo, debating if I should ask. By the somberness of his voice, I knew it was a memory he didn't want to recall, but I needed to know what kept Neo from fighting his father. I needed to know what Damon was capable of.

"What was it?" I asked, meeting Neo's gaze.

He kept staring, his eyes growing darker by the second. For a moment, I thought he wouldn't tell, but his lips parted.

"If I tell you, promise me—"

Wood snapped, leaves flew up in the air, and a snarl erupted from the forest. I spun just in time to see a massive black wolf emerge from the trees and lunge, barely giving me enough time to raise my arms and prevent its canines from sinking into my head as it took me to the ground.

Alaric had found us.

With what little supernatural strength I had remaining, I tried to push him away, but Alaric only inched closer. I began to kick, throwing my legs every possible way, hoping to find some weak spot, but no matter where my blow landed, Alaric did not flinch.

The distance between my face and his teeth lessened again. I willed my body to act like stone, tried to hide the quiver in my arms, the panic surfacing, but with the way Alaric's pupils danced, I knew I wasn't doing a good job.

"Leave her alone, Alaric," Neo screamed, jumping on his brother's back, wrapping his arms around Alaric's neck.

Alaric snarled, but Neo did not relent. He pulled Alaric's snout away from me, his grip on his brother's neck growing tighter, bringing Alaric closer to sleep. Alaric bucked, his attention temporarily leaving me.

I rolled out from under him, finding my footing just as Neo was flung at a tree stump. The sound of the impact echoed through the forest. Alaric stilled, terror in his eyes as Neo lay still. I raced to Neo, unsure how brittle we were without our wolves, knowing that if our tolerance for pain had been depleted just as much as our strength, Neo would need help right away.

"Are you ok?" I asked, pushing him into a sitting position, my fingers grazing his back, checking to see if any spots were too tender.

Neo groaned but nodded.

"Neo," Alaric whispered, now in human form, his open mouth making him look like a fish desperately trying to breathe out of water. "I didn't mean to. I was trying to..." Alaric glared at me. "This is all your fault," he announced, stalking forward, his scent already changing back to his wolf form.

I unsheathed my sword, but Neo stood and shoved me behind him, proving the lack of wolf hadn't left us with human fragility.

"Enough, Alaric. It isn't her fault. It is my choice to stand between you two, as it is your choice to move me to get to her," Neo declared through labored breathing. "Enough."

I gripped Neo's tunic, holding him in place, scared he may topple over any second, but I didn't dare let go of the hilt of my sword.

"She and I had a deal, Neo. It is within my rights to kill her," Alaric angrily snarled.

Guilt formed in the pit of my stomach. Keeping my word was the thing I prided myself most on, but in the efforts of my escape, I had thrown it away. I stepped forward, ready to apologize, to state my reasonings, but Neo spoke before I could.

"She promised that she wouldn't bring me with her, and she didn't. I followed her out. I forced her to bring me. She didn't break your deal. You don't have any claim over her life. Even if you did, she's not the villain in this story."

Alaric glared at Neo then me, debating. He began to pace in front of us.

I gripped tighter to my sword, unsure what to do.

Alaric had kept his end of the bargain in Rivelia. He had proven himself a keeper of vows, and on a technicality, Neo had just proved our bargain still held true. Alaric had to let me leave, but with his brother now in the mix, I wasn't sure if his character would hold. After all, mine had not. I had bent the rules of our deal to get what I wanted.

"Fine." Alaric stopped walking. "I will not harm her, but your escapade ends now, Neo. You're coming back home with me."

"I will not. I can't let the world keep on going as it has. I cannot continue turning a blind eye." Alaric's fists tightened. His gaze and ears fixed on Neo. I took the chance and inched forward. "The blood demons already have decimated the Artico Pack. They've ransacked their lands, and I'm sure they are killing those that pose even a minuscule threat as they travel to their castle. When they are done resting, conquering the lands around them, what's to say they won't head for Rivelia next? Yes, we'll be safe behind our walls for a while. We may even win the first battle or two, but we'll eventually waver and hope that someone will come and help, but no one will because everyone who might've come will have already been destroyed while we stayed safe behind our walls."

Alaric's chest puffed. "I wasn't asking for your opinion, Neo. We are going, even if I have to carry you home." Alaric marched forward, wholly focused on his brother.

I sprang forward and wrapped my arm around Alaric's neck, pressing my sword to his throat. If he moved even an inch, I would draw blood.

"I'd like to see you try. There is nothing more I hate than a oppressive wolf, and you, along with your father, have surpassed a level of controlling that I cannot stand. You will not take another choice from Neo," I exclaimed, more for Neo than Alaric. I would defend him just as he did me. We were partners in this now, and after hearing his story, the reasons he did the things that outraged me, I understood him. He had every right to leave Rivelia as I did. "We'll be leaving now, and don't bother to come after us again. We will be prepared this time to fight you, and even if you gather help, by the time you bring them, we'll be long gone."

Alaric scoffed, the gesture causing my blade to nick his neck.

"Neo, is there any rope in your bag? We'll tie him to a tree to give us a head start." Neo looked at me with wide pupils, understandable concern written on his face. Alaric and him, despite being on opposing sides, were still brothers and that bond couldn't be erased. They couldn't wish true harm on one another. "Your brother has been alive for more than a hundred years and has trained as a warrior for much of that time. I'm sure he'll find a way to free himself," I explained, hoping to put any of Neo's unease to rest.

Neo examined his brother then nodded and hurried to his bag, trusting my words and his brother's training.

"Neo, think this through," Alaric began as his brother approached him with some rope. "As it stands now, you will not be punished. I convinced father, thanks to your ripped dress"—Alaric bared his canines at me before turning back to Neo—"that you were both abducted. That's why he only sent me. A small party would have been easier to detect, but a singular scout could easily sneak up on these *abductors*. Please, Neo. We can solidify the story to tell father on our return trip before relaying it to him. He won't know that you left on your own accord. He won't deal out punishment. But if I return and tell him the truth, he'll—"

"Let's hurry up and restrain him," Neo barked, taking his brother from me and shoving him against a tree.

I kept the blade pointed at Alaric, keeping him in place as Neo wrapped the rope around Alaric and the tree trunk, furious that he would use Neo's trauma against him.

Alaric tracked him with his eyes. "Does it not bother you anymore?"

Neo ignored him and tied off the rope.

Alaric scoffed at his brother's quietness. "I'm surprised it doesn't bother you, Ina."

I lifted Alaric's chin with my blade, unable to follow Neo's lead and stay quiet. "Neo will be far out of Damon's reach when he hears the news," I snarled loudly. "He won't be able to punish Neo."

Alaric let out a singular chuckle. It wasn't one of amusement but of shock and disgust.

"You haven't told her," he whispered.

"Shut it, Alaric," Neo demanded, kneeling in front of his brother, taking the weapons on his belt.

"I'm sure this will make her send you home now." Alaric turned to me. "The punishment—"

"Shut up," Neo yelled again, panic growing in his voice.

Alaric swept his leg out, effectively taking Neo to the ground, allowing him to continue. "The punishment doesn't just affect him. It's dealt to others."

Neo regained his composure, tried to talk once again, but I held out a hand, silencing him. "What do you mean?"

"The last time Neo was caught—when he was child—father burned down the human village Neo had visited. He wanted the humans' screams to live in Neo's head forever so he would know never to go back. Father even found the boy whose scent was all over Neo's necklace."

"Shut up," Neo screamed, but Alaric continued.

"He made that boy watch the town burn with Neo, made the human curse us, say he hated our kind, and once he wished he had never met Neo, the king killed him too."

I paled as Alaric finished, turning to Neo in disbelief.

Neo shook, clutching the pendant through his tunic. His uneven breathing and silence proof enough that Alaric had told the truth.

Damon was a monster. He was just as bad as the blood demons. Maybe even worse.

"Why?" I uttered, a thousand questions running through my head.

How had Damon ever commanded the respect of thousands of wolves? Were the stories of his greatness before the war even real? How could anyone fall from being a protector to this?

"Because of what happened in the past," Alaric replied, not showing any sign that he would elaborate.

I stormed to Neo, forcing him to look at me, to see if he would explain, but he kept clutching his chest, staring at the ground, as if he could see the void that was his terrible memories. I glared at Alaric, willing him to tell me, but he clamped his lips tighter.

My body heated. My canines pierced into my flesh. I was done with the mystery of all of this. I needed answers now.

I bolted forward, sword in hand. "You'll tell me, *now,* what exactly happened in the past." Alaric didn't so much as blink, thinking my words were empty, but as I pushed my blade into his chest and drew blood, he flinched.

"Because the humans killed our mothers," Alaric quietly seethed.

CHAPTER 22

"**D**on't lie to me," I snapped through bared fangs.

"I'm not," Alaric retorted with an unwavering stare. "Why would I lie when there's a sword at my throat?"

I sat back on my heels, rubbing my forehead.

Humans couldn't kill wolves. They were too weak, too frail. But if they could, if they had, it would explain things. It would explain some of Damon's actions.

"They didn't," Neo interjected, finally coming out of his shock. "They just ran."

"When we needed them most," Alaric added on. "They turned a blind eye and ran, sacrificing our mothers to those beasts."

"It's what—"

"Who ran?" I yelled, tired of their bickering.

"The humans," Alaric replied as Neo once again went quiet, scared of the truth, of what my reaction would be. I cocked my head, indicating for Alaric to go on. "I can't believe your father never told you this." Alaric laughed. I applied even more pressure with my sword, wiping the look of amusement off his face. "I presume you know about the Siege of Rivelia?"

I ground my teeth at the condescending question.

Of course, I knew of the great battle, the one that ended the Blood War.

The blood demons, tired of losing, rallied all their forces and launched an attack on Rivelia. No one knew it was going to happen. No one had even predicted it. Wolf-shifter kind had been too confident in the stronghold, as the walls had never been breached. However, the blood demons made that statement false in one night.

They snuck up on Rivelia, climbed her walls, and somehow had the strength to tear open a sewage gate and enter from underneath. They had gotten half their army in by the time Rivelia had enough troops dressed to meet them. It was the greatest failure in wolf history. The demons even made it to the castle, killing more wolves than in any battle recorded, and they might have even taken the castle if it were not for my father and his warriors resting there that night. Together, he and Damon's forces fought the demons. They battled all night, held them off, and when daybreak came, they had eradicated the demon army, leaving only a few left on the continent, effectively ending the war. However, despite the win, it was the turning point for wolves.

The war had caused so much death that small packs were extinguished, and the numbers of larger ones were diminished. Everyone returned to their homelands and grieved for years, allowed themselves to feel the emotions they had suppressed during the war. For this reason, quarterly meetings were pushed back, and the sighting of a representative from a different pack became less and less until interacting with other packs seemed absurd.

Taking my glare as a yes, Alaric continued, "That's when our mothers died."

"That's impossible. The records would have mentioned that, not to mention, Neo said your mother died giving birth to him. "

"The siege was the day Neo was born. It is what put her and your mother in such a vulnerable position and made them rely on the humans. As for the records, written history can be skewed."

"You're lying. Neo wouldn't have left that out. Right, Neo?" Silence echoed through my ears. "Neo?" I called, over my shoulder, throat tightening.

Neo stayed silent, looking at his fisted hands, avoiding eye contact.

I nearly dropped my blade.

Everything Alaric was saying was true.

My head dropped. I remembered the days following the siege. My father had returned without my mother, but he had said she would come later, that she was helping heal the wolves in Rivelia. However, weeks later, he told me that she wouldn't be coming back, that she had passed on the road home a week after the siege. Surely, father wouldn't have kept that from me. I may have been five at the time, but I was old enough to understand death. There had been so much of it in my life. I was born during the war. And...

Perhaps, that was the reason why.

There had been so much death during the war, but our people always carried on through it. But when father returned from the siege, our people had grieved for days. Father too.

Could my father have kept my mother's death a secret for the good of the pack? Could they not have been able to handle losing three fourths of our warriors and my mother—the light of our village?

"During the siege, those who could not fight hid in the great hall along with my mother who was heavily pregnant at the time, even your mother was there. However, Selena stayed with them as a protector, as a friend to mine, in case she went into labor. We didn't think that the castle would be breached. However, it was, and the first place they attacked was the great hall. We didn't know at first, since most of us, including myself, were outside the castle at the time, trying to keep the bulk of the blood demons at bay. But when we saw a surge of humans sprinting from a hidden door that connected to a secret passageway in the great hall, we knew the demons had infiltrated the castle.

"Our troops changed focus. My father, Batair, and I sprinted to the great hall. We fought hard and didn't stop until every demon was dead. We kept fighting until there was only one hovering over our mothers' blood-covered bodies. He had his sword raised, ready to deliver one final blow. I jumped, murdering him, thinking I could save our mothers. But it turned out that both of them were already dead. The final swing hadn't been to finish them off but was for the babe in my mother's arms. It was to kill Neo before he even cried.

"We sat by their side for hours, mourning them as our guards threw the lifeless demons into the fire burning in the courtyard. We sat by them for hours as our guards cleaned and lined up the humans who perished in the great hall so that they could be collected by their loved ones and have a proper burial, but once our men announced they had done what we asked of them, we found that the only lifeless bodies that remained were our mothers."

Alaric's eyes met mine, waiting for me to figure out the rest, figure out why there were no other bodies.

My heart dropped.

Everyone else had gotten out.

They had run through the escape route, but our mothers hadn't because...

Births could take hours, hours in which the mother was immovable. Those who ran had to know that. They had to know that their queen would have to stay behind, unable to move, unable to defend herself. Yet, they still ran except for my mother.

I barreled over, unable to even stay on my knees.

So, this was the past everyone was hiding.

Why?

Why had no one told me? Why hadn't anyone stayed? Wolves had risked their lives for humans since the start of our existence. Why couldn't they have returned the favor just once?

"Ina, if they didn't run, they would have died," Neo said, halfway sobbing and yelling. "I'm sure that our mothers told them to. I'm certain of it. The way mine talked about the humans in her journal—"

I broke out in tears, drowning out Neo's words. The pain from this betrayal was too much.

"Do you see why we do not associate with the humans?" Alaric asked.

I didn't bother to raise my head or respond. Alaric knew the hurt and confusion I was feeling. It was why he was so confident sounding. He knew he was winning.

"If I knew this news would've broken your spirit, I would've told you this back in the palace," Alaric said. "Though it came with its own risks. You Artico wolves are always stubborn, and for some odd reason, you still associate with humans. If you had still liked humans after that tale, that would've just flamed your need to get out. You might have even made rasher decisions that I wouldn't have been able to recover from."

I dug my hands into the forest floor, dirt wedging under my fingernails, trying to ground myself.

My entire reality was coming down. My ideals were shattered.

Humans were awful. They were terrible. All of th—

Ellary.

She had been one of my friends and a loyal servant back in Artico. She had made me smile and laugh. She was kind and always thanked us. She had even risked her life once when some cubs ventured into the woods. She had searched for them with us, despite the creatures in the forest that threatened her life at night.

Not all humans were awful. Some were like Ellary. Most were like her.

People like her deserved to be protected.

My father believed that. The Artico Pack believed that. I would believe that too.

"Do not generalize the humans." I wiped away my tears and stood. "And while what happened to our mothers was horrible, they would still want us to do what's right. They would want us to protect the weak."

I grabbed the sack discarded on the ground and began to walk away. However, the speedy crunch of leaves stopped me.

"No," I growled to Neo who scampered after me. "It's too big of a risk to bring you."

"You were ok with me coming before."

"You left out some very important details," I replied without a hint of emotion.

"Ina, please. I want to help," Neo pleaded. I peeked over my shoulder, too softhearted to ignore Neo's begging completely. "If I told you, you would have never let me come, and I can't live like this anymore. It's just like you said. Our mothers wouldn't want this. I will be useful. I've already proven how dedicated I am to this." Neo gestured to his tied-up brother.

I took a deep breath. Neo was right as he always had been, but the threats and drama that followed him were starting to outweigh the benefits of having his help, especially when it would put humans in harm's way.

"Go home, Neo," I commanded softly. "You bring too many risks."

"I don't," Neo screamed.

I peered up at the sky, cursing Neo for being so persistent. I didn't have time to fight with him, but I had to if I wanted to keep going. However, before I could get out my first word, Neo interrupted me.

"Alaric has already made my father believe that we've been abducted. He will go on thinking that. He may send more men after us, but if they don't have a reason to engage with humans, they won't. Not until after they learn the truth, which by then, we'll have either died and the demons have won, or we'll have succeeded, and things will have to change." Neo placed his hand on my shoulder. "Please, think it through. You know I'm right. I would never put the humans at risk like I did to their village all those years ago. I'm smarter now."

I closed my eyes, thinking through his logic. Neo's reasoning made sense. Still, I didn't want him to come. He had betrayed my trust. He had kept things from me. He could very well have more secrets that would alter my mission or hurt me again in a world where I had so few people to trust. Yet another part of me screamed to let him come and that he had his reasons.

Neo had seen how his father and brother reacted to the news, and though he saw my need to protect the humans, he hadn't known me long enough to predict how I would react. It was just as how I had not trusted him to do the hard things in this trip, like fight his own brother.

I bit my lip and said a quick prayer, hoping that I was making the right choice.

"Promise me that you mean that. Promise me that you aren't just saying things."

"I swear it," Neo spoke, his voice so strong and so unwavering I could hear the truth in it.

I released a breath. "Alright, you can come. But if you ever"—I grabbed Neo by the tunic—"lie or keep a crucial truth from me again, I will not think twice about leaving you behind. I won't even discuss it with you. You'll just look around and be alone."

Neo stoically nodded.

I released him and threw the bag at him, gesturing to the direction I had been walking in.

"There's one flaw in your reasoning," Alaric interrupted, making me jump. I had nearly forgotten about him in all the emotions I was feeling. "Once I get free, I can always go to Damon and tell him what you two are doing. I can tell him to release hell on the humans to lure you both back."

I clutched the hilt of my sword, debating whether to cut Alaric's throat or not. He was proving to be just as terrible as his father.

"No, you wouldn't," Neo claimed, stepping closer to his brother.

"And why wouldn't I?"

"You care about me and what happens to the family." Alaric straightened and leaned away from Neo. "I may be young, but I'm not blind. I see our people becoming restless. I see their grief fading. I see them tiring of father and his ways. And I see you trying to appease them to keep a coup from happening."

I perked hearing the information.

Though Rivelia was a monarchy, and the title of alpha was traditionally passed down to the first born of the ruler, the old rule of alpha was still honored. If the King of Rivelia seemed weak or did not meet their people's needs, they could be challenged, and a new family could rule. However, if the family was replaced, it wouldn't just result in the forced marriage of someone in the original bloodline to someone in the new one like Artico did. The new family would kill off the original line, as either male or female could rule Rivelia.

If what Neo was was saying was the truth, Damon and his sons' lives were at risk.

"They're on the edge, and both of us know that they just need one more push to go over. Father going on a rampage, forcing them to fight for hatred would do that."

"I," Alaric muttered, trying to come up with an excuse. "I'd still be risking the family if I let you run off after the demons."

Neo cocked his head to the side as he crouched before Alaric. "You are, but which is the bigger risk? Father is stubborn. He thinks the people love him unconditionally. If you told him to defend against a rebellion, he'd do nothing. He wouldn't believe you until it was too late, and you certainly can't control his armies. They won't listen to you. We'd be sitting ducks in the castle, but at least with the demons, we can prepare."

A chill fell over me. From the little time I had known Neo, I had thought him a young, bright-eyed pup, overzealous and naïve to the world. I didn't think he was able to see the hidden truth of things, be able to call his brother's bluff as he just did. I didn't think he'd declare them without a sign of remorse. Yet here he was, and it was frightening. Perhaps he too had inherited a bit of Damon's monstrous ways. He just used them to do good.

Neo held Alaric's stare a bit longer, daring him to say something else, like he wanted him to say something else so Neo could say more. When Alaric didn't, Neo walked away, nodding to me, asking me if that was enough proof. I returned the gesture, promising myself that I would not underestimate Neo again.

"Wait," Alaric pleaded, sounding utterly defeated.

Neo and I kept walking, both of us convinced the rest of his threats were empty.

"I want to offer a deal," Alaric yelled. "I will aid you in your fight."

I froze.

Neo snapped to me, shaking his head, his hand on my forearm, keeping me from looking back.

I breathed deep, knowing Neo didn't want me to hear Alaric out, but I needed to. As much as I wanted to be rid of Alaric, I knew he was a trained warrior. I knew that he had seen battle and had experience against the demons. If he was earnest in his offer to help, it was worth considering. I could always say no after all.

"I'm listening," I gritted out, gently shrugging off Neo's hand while giving him an apologetic glance.

"Though you two are content to go on this death mission, I don't want to see my brother die. I will come with you. I will fight with you. I will not deceive you nor try to bring you both back to Rivelia. I won't even murder you in your sleep, Ina. I will even help you find an army so you stand a chance."

"An army?" I asked too intrigued.

One side of Alaric's lips turned up in a feral way.

"There used to be a nomadic pack that traveled near the demon's castle before the war," Alaric explained. "They were never accounted for after it though, but many of us think they went into hiding to mourn. They were always survivors."

I inched closer, enticed by the idea.

I had read about the nomadic packs. They were fearsome warriors, hardened by their continuous travel. If they fought beside us, then we might stand a chance at killing the blood demons.

"What do you want in return?" I asked stiffly, knowing the deal was too good to be without a catch.

"If we do not find them or they refuse to help, I want your word that we retreat." Alaric lifted his chin.

"There's no mention of their route in any books. It's not even shown on maps." Neo stepped between me and Alaric. "The chances of finding them are low, Ina. This is a trick," Neo warned, making his opinion of the deal apparent.

"You may have outsmarted me once, little brother, but that doesn't mean you know everything. The nomadic packs didn't like their routes documented, that's true, and even if they did, their paths changed with every season, sometimes yearly. Only those who they trusted or wolves that had to make diplomatic missions knew their many paths, knew how to find them. I was the latter before I led Rivelia's armies." Alaric turned back to me. "You can search for them all you want, but you'll only waste time. They hide their scents and trail fairly well. It may take weeks, months to find them, even with a great tracker."

Neo's shoulders curved in, knowing that Alaric had used my greatest weakness against me, the thing I always seemed to be running out of—time.

I knelt in front of Alaric, blade in hand. "You can take Neo back if we don't find them. I'll even help you knock him out so you can force him to go back, but I will remain. I will see my mission through no matter what."

"Ina," Neo interrupted.

I cocked my head sideways, eyes scowling, canines already out, effectively quieting Neo.

While I felt bad for Neo's predicament and understood his need to help in this battle, this was not up for discussion. This was originally my duty, my quest, and I would see it succeed or die trying.

"Alright," Alaric said with perfect diplomatic composure, "but we train for an hour every day."

I laughed. I was a trained warrior. I didn't need any lessons. Perhaps Neo did, but not me. "I don't—"

"I'll assess you tomorrow morning. If you truly don't need them, you don't have to hold up that part of the bargain. But if you don't meet my standards, then we train. I won't travel with any weak links, not when my brother is involved."

I held Alaric's gaze, chin high, contemplating if I should slap him for even assuming I wouldn't be up to *his* standards, but I had better morals than to hit a tied-up wolf.

I unsheathed my dagger, wedging it between the trunk and rope. "Anymore requests?" I asked, silently promising myself to make sure my fist met his face during tomorrow's assessment.

"Just a warning." I met Alaric's eyes once again. "I will keep my promise, and I will treat this like it is my own mission, but Neo's safety is my main priority. If a fight occurs and he is at risk, I will do everything to protect him, even if it endangers you. And if he's injured or falls sick, I will stay behind."

"Deal," I replied before Neo could interject, as I was certain he would. The warning—as Alaric had called it—may hurt Neo's pride, but it was far from unreasonable. I was willing to walk into a death trap for my pack. Alaric should be able to break his vows to protect his brother.

In one fell swoop, I broke Alaric's restraints and backed away, eyeing my new traveling companion, allowing him time to rub his already red wrists. Part of me wondered if Neo had taken the chance to tie the binds that tightly as payback for all the things he had endured. However, I didn't have much time to think on it, as Alaric stood, tension already filling the air.

CHAPTER 23

I had barely finished eating my morning ration of salted pork when Alaric thrusted my sword at me. Well, his, as he had given it to me when he first discovered that I was planning on leaving Rivelia. Though seeing the new shining sword that he swung around with far more gold embellishments than the one I now held in my hand, I could safely assume this one was now permanently mine.

"We're not fighting in wolf form?" I asked, surprised that he didn't want to assess me in the shape I would use most during combat.

"You still can't shift," Alaric said matter-of-factly.

My brows scrunched at the assumption, confused at how he even knew that was a problem, let alone an ongoing one.

As if I had said my thoughts out loud, Alaric explained, "It takes about three days for your wolf to come back after you've tired it out, which I'm assuming you did, based on how far away from the castle you and Neo were when I caught up."

"I didn't know I could tire my wolf," I defended, mad that Alaric was talking about it as if it was common knowledge.

"Of course not." Alaric headed a few paces away from our bed rolls, kicking a few pebbles to clear the area. "You've never had to run as hard as you did nor have been forced to shift for that long either. Only those alive during the war have."

My shoulders dropped.

So many things in the war had not been recorded due to exhaustion then were purposely forgotten in an effort to forget the war. It was something that I had wanted to blame my predecessors for but fully understood.

Many of the wolves who fought in the war would flinch occasionally at loud sounds or a snarl that seemed off. There were even a couple who could not stand the sight of younglings eating strawberry jam.

The pack always looked out for these individuals and tried to accommodate them as best as possible. Though we couldn't help those who suffered from night terrors, relived the war in their dreams.

When our warriors first returned home, the village was filled with screams at night. The most fearless warriors would wake and run around confused in a cold sweat, crying that the demons were attacking. Hardly anything calmed them, helped make the terrors go away. But after much experimentation with calming herbs, time, and meditation, the screaming lessened and lessened until it was no more. When I was little, I thought they had gotten over it. Though after I became of age, every once in a while, on night patrols, I would occasionally see one of the older wolves up, walking restless, drenched in sweat despite the freezing temperature. It was then I learned that those types of fears don't just go away. It was also why I accepted that a tired wolf was just another item that was meant to be forgotten.

"Be more responsible in the future," Alaric whispered, pulling me away from my thoughts, his tone so softly cold that it reminded me of his age.

Though he looked twenty-five, he was over a century old.

He had fought in the war, fought in those battles.

Did he suffer like those in the Artico Pack?

"If you couldn't shift when we encounter danger, particularly the demons, you'd be useless, a liability. I don't want that, not when Neo is traveling with us," he growled, back in that ever-condescending tone, causing any worry I had for him to dissipate.

"Obviously I don't want that either, but I did what had to be done. And what about you? Isn't your wolf tired? Or close to it? You ran the same distance we did," I bit back.

Alaric stopped examining the area he was clearing. "Unlike you and Neo, I used a horse for the first part of my journey then shifted when I predicted you would be stuck in human form." Alaric rolled back his shoulder and cracked his neck. "You both have much to learn," Alaric mumbled, more for himself than me. "I don't know why I'm bothering with this assessment."

I ground my teeth, my pride getting the better of me. "I was the best in my pack, completely unchallenged."

Alaric tsked. "*In your pack*, key words," he mocked, reminding me of the promise I made about my fist finally meeting his face today.

"Don't underestimate my people," I snarled, jumping to my feet.

Alaric licked his lips, eyes seemingly dancing in delight over my anger. "If you give me a reason to, I won't." He jerked his chin at the ground, indicating my starting place as he raised his sword.

"Gladly." I tied my hair into a tight bun, taking my spot.

I was ready to knock Alaric down, keep his mouth shut for this trip. But first, I wanted Neo around.

I had a night to forgive him for his secrets, and I had happily done so, as he was my friend. However, on the other hand, he hadn't so much as looked at me since I made the deal with his brother, and I was sure seeing me beat Alaric would lessen the tension between us.

I glanced in the direction Neo had left in to relieve himself. There was no sign of him or a speedy return. I waited a few more seconds.

"Is this how you won in your pack? Stalling?" Alaric pointedly asked.

"I'm waiting for Neo. He should see what's about to happen." I glared at Alaric through my brows, noting that he had set his sword down again.

"We don't need to. I already know the extent of his training, his weaknesses. He doesn't need to be here for an assessment."

I stayed silent, refusing to divulge my reason for waiting on Neo.

Alaric cocked his head, amused.

"Unless you want him here, so he can learn what not to do? If that's the case, I'm more than happy to wait. There's much he can discover from you in that field."

Alaric sheathed his sword, gloating over what he thought was a clever insult. The look had me burning. He was worse than Rainer. At least that male knew to hold his tongue, to not overestimate the power in front of him. He may have challenged me, may have announced his dreams to demolish me in battle, but he never declared his victory before he had won it. Alaric needed to be taught a lesson.

"Take out your sword," I growled, unable to wait any longer. Neo would just have to catch the end. That's what mattered anyway.

Alaric sighed. "Not only do you stall, but you're also indecisive." I gripped my sword tighter, vision turning red. "But fine. The sooner this is over, the sooner I can plan your training regimen."

Alaric held his sword high and spread his legs, strengthening his core, ready for my first blow.

I smirked.

The position was perfect for defending and delivering heavy hits, however, with his feet planted so well, moving quickly would be hard for him. A swift hit to his front as a distraction then a sprint to get behind him for a strike would end this quickly.

I shook my hips, loosening my body, and rose on the tips of my toes. Though part of my mind told me to wait and examine more, I ignored it. I didn't need to do any of that. I just needed Alaric's incessant talking to stop.

Alaric held out his hand and curled his fingers in a couple times.

I lunged.

My first strike went as planned, hitting so hard that Alaric had no choice but to keep his feet planted firmly on the ground. I spun, making sure to land behind him as my sword rebounded off his, shifting my weight so I was positioned for a slice. I threw all my strength into the move, smiling as my sword came inches from his neck. For a warrior of his age, I had thought he'd at least survive more than two hits. But then again, Rivelia had been gone from the world for twenty years. It wouldn't be a surprise if their prince had stopped seriously training during that time. Regardless, I began to tighten my muscles, slowing the sword down, making sure that it would only braise the tips of his hairs. However, before I could fight the momentum of my swing, metal collided with metal.

I staggered back.

Alaric stood in the same position we had begun our spar in. However, he had somehow moved his arms fast enough so that his blade ran parallel to his back, protecting his neck.

My jaw dropped, and the tip of my sword hit the ground. To move that fast, to be able to have the strength to block one of my attacks in such a position was unbelievable.

"Your speed is as I expected," Alaric noted, coming out of his squat, checking his sword for any nicks. "Your strength, I admit, was a bit of a surprise, but I suppose it's to make up for your ill planned attacks. Either way, I can make you into a decent warrior."

I cocked my head.

There was nothing wrong with my moves. They were calculated, proven successful over years of training.

Alaric had just...he had...

It was luck. That's all it was.

"I'm just warming up," I declared, raising my sword and my heels again, body warming from more than just the movements.

Though my first combo hadn't worked for whatever reason, Alaric was still bigger than me, therefore it required more energy for him to move his body. He would ultimately tire quicker. If I hit with an onslaught of never-ending attacks, I was sure to win.

Alaric examined me before exhaling, acting as if this was some boring, meticulous task. "I've already made my assessment," he drawled, sword lowering.

"I was promised a fair battle. You can't judge me on two moves."

"You can when you've trained enough, but if you insist on embarrassing yourself further"—he pulled out his sword but did not raise it—"so be it."

I inhaled deeply, resisting the urge to charge, somehow honoring the fact that he wasn't in the ready position.

"Well, come on." He held an arm out to the side, fully opening one side of his body. "You were so eager before." I glanced down at his lowered blade, eyebrows raised. Alaric followed my gaze. "It's out. That's all that matters."

The sheer audacity of this male.

This wouldn't be a fair fight. Still, led by anger, I charged. Step after step, I gained speed, closing the distance between us, refusing to slow.

Alaric didn't raise his sword.

I clenched my jaw, making sure to fully extend my legs and push off with my toes. The quicker I got to him, the sooner I'd end his male arrogance. I thrusted my sword forward, aiming for his gut. Alaric did not so much as flinch until the tip of my sword was a forearm's distance away from his flesh, then he parried in a rapid, effortless movement.

"Are you done?" he asked in that monotonous voice.

Angrier, I ignored the question and kept slashing as fast as my arms allowed.

Alaric blocked my attacks one after the other.

I gritted my teeth but kept going, tried various patterns, but no matter what, he met all my moves.

I wanted to scream in frustration, but I knew better than that. I needed to put all my energy into my swings.

I swung relentlessly, ignored my labored breathing, the dizziness that scratched at the surface of my head, refusing to acknowledge that I was getting tired, but even with all the denial, I knew I was. Surely Alaric was too. I dared a glance at him, only to see that he was anything but.

His lips were a straight, loose line, and his eyes were dull, like he was bored. His breathing was normal and not a single bead of sweat ran down his face.

Impossible.

I swung again, watching closer.

Alaric moved his sword with only one hand. He didn't clutch nearly as hard to his own hilt, and his muscles barely contracted as our blades made contact. He even had the gall to look around the tree line, as if I was a child who he had been forced to play pretend with.

"Fight back!" I screamed, taking his aloofness as an insult, speeding my attacks, swinging harder until my arms began to scream.

Finally, Alaric showed something other than boredom on his face. "Slow down," he commanded, nervousness in his voice.

Good. I was winning.

"Our spar is only to assess you. You'll hurt yourself at this rate," he warned. "Remember, we still need to travel today."

I ignored his words and kept swinging.

He kept up.

I growled, letting frustration get the better of me.

In all my life, no one could have a desultory battle with me. No one. Not since I was a cub. They always had to try.

Alaric couldn't be this much stronger than me. I had trained my whole life to be the best. I had even beat the warriors who trained me. I couldn't lose to him. This had to be because of my wolf. That was the only thing that made sense. But even so, I wouldn't let him beat me. I wouldn't let him have a reason to force me to train. I was my own master. I wouldn't be ordered by anyone.

Eyes darting every which way, I looked for stumps or boulders within a reasonable distance, hoping to herd Alaric toward one to offset his footing. There were none around, save the stumps by the fire, but those were too obvious.

I went back to my heavy swings, hoping that would at least make him try, but I was too tired. They were only a fraction of the power as my first move. I looked down, utterly defeated. However, as my gaze dropped, a glimmer from Alaric's belt blinded me.

A dagger.

If I had a weapon in each of my hands, then Alaric would have to put in effort to block multiple slashes at once. I removed my second hand from my sword, stilling for a moment to make sure my right arm wasn't too weak to hold the heavy blade. Thank the gods, it wasn't. With my left hand, I reached for my own dagger on my belt, but to my dismay, I felt nothing.

I curled my nails into my palm, cursing.

I hadn't bothered to put on my belt when I woke this morning, nor had I retrieved it when Alaric handed only my sword to me.

I had willingly gone into this battle with a single weapon.

A brief laugh sounded through my ears.

I looked to the source, seeing Alaric peering down at me, a mocking smirk plastered on his face.

He had deliberately given me only one weapon.

Rage pulsed through me, invigorating me.

Fine.

If I didn't have an extra weapon, I'd take his.

I flung forward, one hand aimed for his dagger, while the other held the sword above to block any potential moves Alaric could make while I exposed my neck and back to him.

"Ina," a fearful voice yelled, one belonging to Neo, "don't touch the dagger."

The warning came too late.

My hand wrapped around the hilt and unbearable pain coursed through my palm.

I fell to my knees, cradling my hand to my chest, looking up at the dagger.

It sparkled more than the steel ones wolves used. It even had a yellowish undertone to it.

I cursed, realizing what it was.

"Your dagger is made of silver," I hissed, examining my now enflamed hand.

Leaves rustled, and soon, Neo was at my side, carefully unfolding my hand, the silent anger he had for me since yesterday replaced with concern.

"That was cruel to *let* her touch it," Neo scolded Alaric.

Alaric sheathed his sword. "It was cruel to let her continue fighting with no chance. At least this way, she stopped," Alaric retorted, dropping down to pick up the blade.

My eyes widened.

Alaric held the silver in his hand unflinching, unhurried to return it to his side. He even paused to brush off the mud stuck to it.

"How?" I breathed out, fighting the pain in my hand.

"Practice," Alaric stated, sheathing the blade. "I told you, no matter what, I wouldn't find you trained enough to my liking. While Artico may have remembered the war by making sure you all stayed close to the humans, Rivelia built up a tolerance to the demons' choice weapon, our weakness."

"That's not possible."

"It's more than possible. It's part of our training if we decide to serve in my father's army. We hold it every day, each day trying to hold it longer until it doesn't hurt."

"You're immune to silver sickness?" I asked with a disgusting amount of awe.

"I said tolerance, not immunity," Alaric snarked. "We are still affected if it gets into our blood. It just doesn't work as fast, and our skin doesn't burn if we touch it."

Done with explaining, Alaric walked to the satchels by the fire, rummaging for a bit before coming back and handing some cloth and a metal canister to Neo. "Her hand needs to be healed for training tomorrow morning," Alaric announced, turning to me on the word training, eyes narrowed, daring me to challenge him. And for once in my life, I didn't, especially as I looked to Neo, to his belt, wondering if he had the same tolerance as well.

Sure enough, a dagger similar to Alaric's was at his hip.

CHAPTER 24

My back legs shook, and my claws dug into the earth as Neo attempted to throw me to the ground, but I held firm, knowing most of my shaking was due to the soreness of trekking though the woods in human form.

Though Neo had proven himself competent enough to hold his own in a fair battle with lesser opponents, our spars went quick. They seemed more like a warmup than actual training. It was far from the intensity of my fights with Alaric. He obliterated me every day, toyed with me until I was out of breath then, and only then, would he use both hands and decide to end the fight. I could have sworn some days he enjoyed it, as some battles ended with a minuscule smirk on his face.

I worried about when I would spar with Alaric in wolf form. I knew it wouldn't be like when he had finally caught up to us. He had been tired that day. It was the only reason I had been able to push him away, why I wasn't some headless corpse rotting in the forest right now. If he was anything like Neo—where his wolf was exponentially stronger—than I would be faced with even more shame.

"You're losing focus," Alaric barked, arms crossed.

I shook my head, clearing it.

Now was not the time to think about the battles ahead.

I pushed my shoulder blades together, and in one fell swoop, I pushed hard, throwing Neo onto his back.

Neo yelped in surprise, but sure enough, he got back on his feet, preparing for his next attack.

I smiled proudly.

No matter how many hits Neo took, he always got back up with light in his eyes, like he had something to prove.

"That should be enough training for the day," Alaric announced.

Neo snarled, telling Alaric he wasn't finished, and to be honest, I wasn't either. Despite my earlier rejection to the idea of training, I really did enjoy it now, as training always cleared my mind and made me feel at ease.

"Today is the first day you've been able to shift since your wolves tired. You shouldn't push them, not when we still have so far to travel, when we are so far from Rivelia. Now is the time we will start running into enemies. We need to conserve as much energy as we can. So, shift now," Alaric commanded.

I scratched at the dirt, showing my discontent but reluctantly willed my body to transform.

Though I despised the fact that I had started to listen to Alaric these past few days, I had begrudgingly realized he had far more knowledge and was better at a lot of things than me. He came back quicker from hunts. He set up his bedroll, the fire, everything faster than me. And to top it off, he had been right about when our wolves would come back.

"Take a bit of time to cool off," Alaric said in his monotonous tone as I picked twigs that poked out of my hair. "When I get back, we will start walking." Alaric turned, heading into the thicket toward a boulder, probably to relieve himself as he did every day before we took off.

Ignoring his need, knowing that it was signifying the end of our training, I asked, "Aren't we doing any additional training?"

Alaric turned to me; his brows slightly lifted as if in surprise. "You're ready for another round of sparring?" He rolled up his sleeves.

My cheeks flushed, knowing what his last action signified.

While I was ready to continue to spar with Neo, I didn't have enough energy to fight Alaric, not in a way that would leave me with any dignity afterward.

I shook my head, hurriedly following up with, "But I am ready to work on my resistance to silver sickness."

Neo froze behind me. I wasn't sure why.

Alaric had demanded that I train under his supervision if he came with us, and while I did admit that he could teach me things in combat, I could hold my own. He had to have seen that by now. The thing I needed the most work on was my weakness to silver. It had nearly killed me after all. I had been waiting for Alaric to start that training these past few days, but he never did. I assumed it was a cautionary move due to my inability to shift, but now, that problem was gone.

"You'll be fine without it," Alaric dismissively said, turning to the boulder again.

"Fine?" I yelled, my fear of being struck by silver again taking over. "I thought that you wanted to help me get stronger. Being immune to silver would do wonders for that."

Alaric threw his head back, allowing the sun rays to caress his cheeks.

I remained quiet, not daring to move my gaze off him.

Alaric sighed out, "It would, and in an ideal world, I'd have you training night and day, but you're too *sensitive* when it comes to the metal."

My skin bristled.

"It typically takes months, sometimes a year to build up a resistance, and that's with the person holding the material multiple times a day. We will be at the castle before you build an effective resistance. It's not worth injuring yourself over."

I stepped forward, my blood hot from being called weak. "How many times is multiple?"

Alaric's chest puffed. "Two or three times for a few seconds, and then when they can handle that, minutes."

"Then, in theory, if someone, per se, tripled the number and increased the time, they would gain resistance faster?" I crossed my arms.

"It would be unbearably painful," Alaric remarked, his face void of any emotion.

"I can handle it," I bit out, irritation growing.

Alaric faced away from the sun, eyes once again raking over me. His jaw was clenched, like he was in deep thought.

"Let me see your hand," he ordered.

I ran my thumb over the fabric that wrapped my hand, protected it from objects that may graze over the sensitive skin.

My palm still hurt when I touched it, but in the way a bruise would, rather than the raging fire I felt when I first touched Alaric's dagger. Still, I didn't want anyone or anything to touch it.

"It's fine," I retorted, moving it behind my back.

Alaric jolted forward, grabbed my wrist, and began stripping the fabric off, revealing red streaks. He looked up at me with narrow eyes, waiting for me to rescind my previous statement. I stared back, mouth shut.

"Stubborn as always," he mumbled before pressing into my palm.

I jerked my hand away, body folding over itself at the reappearing pain.

Quick footsteps sounded from behind. I could only assume they belonged to Neo as Alaric tossed the fabric in the direction of them.

"I can't condone pain like that, even if it would make you a better warrior. Your training will only consist of combat," Alaric announced in a voice that made me straighten. It was so demanding, so like an alpha that I didn't dare fight it as he walked away. I hated it.

"I was wondering when you two were going to have another squabble," Neo uttered, gently pulling my hand to him.

"Your brother is insufferable," I said in way of explanation, gritting my teeth to make sure I didn't say anything too terrible, unsure if Alaric was using his heightened hearing to eavesdrop. "I don't understand why you don't have more fights with him." Neo laughed to himself as he began to wrap my hand. "In fact, you've been ungodly quiet since he's started to travel with us. Why?" I asked.

Neo sighed, lowering his head more than necessary, ensuring that my hands were properly dressed. "You spend enough time with him and you realize that he has a quip for everything, that he will always be right. It makes you less susceptible to sharing your opinion. It can be very demoralizing, especially when he's your overprotective brother and"—Neo's eyes crept up to mine—"decides everything for you."

"I'm sorry," I whispered for more than just his explanation, remembering I still hadn't apologized for making the deal with his brother.

"It's fine." Neo tied the cloth off, releasing my hand. "You needed to make sure you got to your pack no matter what, and not to mention, he mainly came after us because you brought me."

I nodded, agreeing wholeheartedly with his words. However, guilt still coursed through me.

Neo's family had been overprotective of him since his mother had died, meanwhile, my father had made sure I trained hard and encouraged independence. If our roles had been switched, I wasn't sure if I could have survived his upbringing.

"Don't do that," Neo seethed. I hummed in question. "Don't look at me with pity and sadness. Don't look at me like I'm fragile. I've had enough of that. It's selfish, but it's part of the reason I wanted to come with you. I wanted to prove to them that I wasn't, that I could fight, and maybe inspire my father and brother to protect humans again, to open the gates. So, please, don't look at me like that."

My heart broke at Neo's words, at his wish. It made my urge to be Alpha of the Artico Pack seem like such a silly thing to fight over. I wanted to hug him, to apologize for everything that he had gone through, but I only nodded, silently swearing that I would do my best not to jeopardize Neo's dreams.

"Good," Neo responded in his chipper voice. It was almost a relief to hear it. "Plus, it's not that bad. I just wanted to make you feel guilty for a time. A bit of revenge never hurt anyone."

My jaw dropped. "Neo," I scolded, slapping his arm. He laughed, making me believe he was telling the truth, but I had to be sure. "You really mean that? I know I needed Alaric, but I do feel bad for you."

"I do. Alaric"—Neo sucked in his lips, thinking—"hasn't been as bad as I thought he would be. It's odd to say, but I'm seeing a different side of him. He's taking everything so seriously, and though his reasoning for it may not be right, I can at least look at him in a more forgiving light because of it."

"I'm glad to hear that." Neo moved to his pack. "But if he ever gets too much, tell me. I'll be sure to think of a way to make his life hell as well. He can't break his vow if I'm just annoying him."

Neo smiled. "Oh really? And how would you do that?"

I shrugged my shoulders, helping him pack the bedroll into his bag. "Maybe talk about humans?"

Neo paused, pushing his lips together. "I like that. We could talk about how much we love them. Oh, we could also sing shanties. He hates that," Neo offered a little too excitedly.

"I know plenty of those. My friend, Sil, she is," I stilled, shoulders dropping then softly corrected, "*was* a singer."

Neo paused and gently gripped my shoulder. "We'll avenge them soon," he cooed. "For now, we just need to train our hardest."

I nodded in agreement, but lowered my head, wishing that strength would come faster, that I could stab the demons with their own weapons.

It would be all too beautiful to see the shock on the demons' faces if I lodged their weapon into their guts, but that would be impossible while

I was still affected by silver. And while I was certain that I could handle the pain, without Alaric's dagger, I wouldn't be able to practice.

"Chin up," Neo chimed, resting his hand on the hilt of his own glimmering dagger.

"You're right. I—" My eyes widened, realization hitting me. "You have a silver dagger as well," I stated, returning to that hushed tone in case Alaric was listening.

Neo's eyes darted between the blade and me, concern already written on his face. "He's not wrong, Ina. Escalating the process will be painful beyond belief."

"But it won't affect my power to shift or my strength? It's just like this?" I pointed to my palm. "A pain similar to a bruise?"

Neo's throat bobbed. "As long as you apply the ointment the day you've been touched, and you don't do more than what you can handle."

I grinned. "Then I don't see the big deal. It's like getting a bruise from training. We still push our limits the next day, and no one bats an eye."

Neo ran his fingers through his hair. "There's no way you're going to back down, aren't you?"

I shook my head, smiling sheepishly. "It will be fine. Maybe even fun. I get to train, and you get to rebel against your exasperating brother."

Neo picked at his fingernails. "Fine," he quickly whispered, unstrapping his dagger before clipping it onto my belt. "Just make sure you keep it hidden this time. Don't leave it laying around for him to find."

I playfully pushed Neo for the lighthearted jab, but whispered back, "Promise," before unhooking my dagger and strapping it onto his belt.

"You better. If he finds it, I'm saying you stole it." Neo quickly swept up my cloak and threw it at me. "Alaric has already sworn that he'll help us, but he's also in charge of our training, and he is not one to trifle with. He'll find some way to make training hell."

"I highly doubt that. I love training, even if it is grueling. But even so, this is most certainly worth the risk," I replied just as Alaric returned.

CHAPTER 25

I rested my hand on the pommel of Neo's dagger, careful not to touch the skin that I had already exposed to the silver. Slowly, I counted, making sure to breathe in deeply as the count increased. I focused on my steps, on making sure not to trip over the jutting vines on the forest floor. I listened to the birds, the sound of Neo's ragged breathing behind me. I listened to anything to take my mind off the slow burning pain, wholly determined to keep my flesh against the silver for at least a minute today, refusing to accept Neo's claim that it would be impossible.

Fifty-five, fifty-six.

The pain was starting to burn, but I was nearly there.

I'd make Neo eat his words during our quiet talks after Alaric went to bed.

Fifty-seven, fifty-eight, fifty—

"Let her go!" someone screamed far in the distance, breaking my concentration.

I hissed, feeling the full sting. Thankfully, Alaric and Neo were looking in the direction of the sound and didn't see me jerk my hand out from under my cloak.

"They sound close," Neo stated, his shoulders tense.

Alaric peered in the direction of the cry, nose scrunched as he tried to scent what was beyond the woods. Gravely, he turned. "We should hurry along our path."

The voice sounded again. "Please, take our money instead. Just don't harm her."

"They're in trouble," I shuddered, the pain finally subsiding enough for me to talk.

Alaric stopped but didn't bother to look back. "They're human. Attacker and defender," he coldly uttered.

"They still need help," I growled, clearly furious.

Alaric cocked his head ever so slightly so he could see me from the corner of his eye. "You seem to forget that I promised to fight blood demons. Since I don't scent any there, I don't see a reason to stop."

My stomach twisted as utter repulsion coursed through me. "And it seems you've forgotten that I swore an oath to protect humans from all danger. I'm going," I announced, turning, willing my wolf to shift.

"We're getting closer to the castle," Alaric lulled, stopping me from shifting. "You'll need your wolf well rested. Shifting for *them* will put you and us at risk for when we run into the demons. Are you really going to trade in their safety for ours? For *your* main mission?"

I ground my teeth, knowing that he was right. Still, I needed to help the humans in front of me. I unsheathed my sword. "I'll fight in human form, then."

Alaric said nothing and continued to stare, hoping I would give in under the weight of his piercing gaze, but I only stared back.

Him training me didn't make me one of his soldiers.

"Fine. Do what you must," he growled, breaking our eye contact, giving up. "Meet us past the tree line by the main road when you're done."

I scoffed at his stubbornness but turned, not bothering to waste one more second on a pointless argument. I ran fast, listening to the grunts, sniffing the air for blood, trying to get a feel for the situation I was about to run into.

So far, no blood ran, but salt deluded by water filled my nostrils. Heavy breathing and cackling filled my ears, the soft whimpering of a child accompanied them. If I had to guess, bandits were attacking a family who had taken up a homestead far from the towns that speckled the continent this far west.

I ran faster, knowing that they wouldn't last long.

The tree line began to break, and through the lessening branches, I could see a field. A rickety, small cottage sat on it, a barn to its left, and a small garden to its right. It was hardly anything grand, but I had seen enough of these cottages, during my patrols, to know that the differing shades of thatch and the shiny nails that were embedded into dusty shingles meant that this was someone's loved home.

"This is all I have, please," a male begged.

I looked to the source that was a few feet from the barn. Two men stood around a female in her twenties, another held her by her beautiful blonde locks. In front of them, an old man groveled on his knees, a small leather pouch in one hand and a couple of copper coins in his other, which he extended out. Behind him, a small boy clutched to the older man's tunic, red streaks staining his pale skin.

The male holding the young woman leaned forward, peering at the old man's extended hand. He cackled. "That's hardly the amount we'd get for selling"—he pulled the woman's hair back, forcing her blue eyes to meet his—"this beauty."

My nostrils flared. They weren't just normal bandits. They were slavers.

They had been our main villain after the Blood War ended, and I had personally seen to their end, hating the stories that were brought before my father of a lost daughter or son. At least I thought I had.

Several other pack members and I had chased them from the Artico region, swearing that if we ever heard about their crimes again, we would not even allow them to grovel for their life. We had thought it was enough to stop them from ever committing their heinous crimes again, but it seemed that with the scattering of the wolves and Rivelia hiding behind their walls, the slavers had simply moved their business to the other parts of the continent, knowing that they wouldn't be stopped.

"Take me instead." The old man crawled to the three men. "I'm sure a workhouse will pay the same."

One of the three males brought up his leg and kicked the old man in the chest, leaving him wheezing in the dirt. "You're not worth anything, old man."

All three of the slavers laughed, their cruelty setting me into action.

I ran faster than I had ever run in human form, despite the blisters on the soles of my feet, and screamed, calling the slavers' attention. They looked at me with high brows and laughed, seeing me as a lone, useless female. However, their laughter quickly died as my blade sliced cleanly through flesh and bone, causing blood to sputter from the slaver's neck who had held the woman.

"You'll pay for that," sneered the man who had kicked the old man, his knees shaking.

Like an executioner, I silently stepped forward and swung my sword once more. However, this time, it was met with metal. I tilted my head, surprised—even if I was weakened from traveling—that the man was able to hold me off so well, but sure enough, his arm started shaking, and his sword lowered. His eyes widened, and I knew he felt fear. I pushed down harder, ignoring the guilt that I felt when I was about to make a kill, especially a human one. But I knew that it needed to happen. I knew that I needed to serve justice for all the lives he had ruined and the lives he had tried to ruin today.

His blade began to graze his face, and his breathing hastened. I said a silent pray to the gods, asking for forgiveness for taking a life that I was raised to protect, but as I was on the last word, the second male swung his blade, aiming for my side. Out of instinct, I grabbed the dagger strapped to my belt and blocked his weapon. Both men's breathing stopped, and their mouths dropped open in awe as I held each one off with a single arm.

"Impossible," one of them whispered.

I scoffed at the shock, but narrowed my eyes, starting to truly focus. I needed to get one of them on the ground so I could hurry and end the other.

I picked up my foot, pushing forward so both blades remained unmoving. However, as I swung my leg out to the side, my hand began to burn, some parts of the flesh screaming in more pain than others. I gulped, realizing why.

In the heat of the battle, in my anger, I had forgotten that it was Neo's silver dagger that was strapped to my side, and I was reaching my limit of tolerance for the material.

I needed to let it go before the pain became unbearable, but the minute I did, my side would be exposed to the slaver's blade. I could always jump out of the way as soon as I dropped it, but that would mean I'd have to be fast, rely on the legs that were already tired from the hundreds of miles they walked so far. It was too risky. I needed to think of something else.

I calmed my breathing, trying to think, but moments passed, and the only thing my head produced was a bead of sweat. The silver would take me soon. I had to jump.

I bent my knees and flew backward, barely dodging both men's blades.

I smiled as they grumbled in annoyance, but my joy was short lived as gravity brought me down into a slippery puddle of mud. Unused to not having two extra feet and claws to dig into the earth, I lost my footing and fell to the ground, my hand stupidly bracing on the silver dagger I had dropped. I yelped at the surge of pain, instinctively dropping my sword to cradle the burning flesh, foolishly leaving myself open. The slavers didn't take a second to hesitate.

I reached for my sword, grabbing it in time so it would block a direct hit; however, everything was happening too fast. I didn't have a firm enough grip. My sword would be flung, and I was going to get nicked. I braced myself, but no hit came. Instead, I felt a rush of wind. I peeked between my arms to see Neo between me and the men.

Angrily, Neo kicked one of the slavers in the gut, flinging him backward, allowing him to parry the other with his sword. Their blades clanged over and over again, Neo's overtaking the slaver's.

My lips parted, eyes widening, surprised that Neo was here.

I had guessed he wanted to come, to aid the humans when we heard them screaming, but when Alaric refused to help, I had assumed he would force Neo to wait by the main road with him. I had never expected anyone to show up.

"Get her while she's down," Neo's opponent screamed to the slaver that was still on the ground.

I scrambled to my feet, ready for the blow this time, but hot breath caressed my ear from behind.

"We're working on footing tomorrow," a voice growled, catching me off guard.

The owner of the voice ran past, his dagger meeting the slaver's gut. The man toppled over, blood dripping from his lips.

My heart pounded as the owner of the voice looked at me, and I realized who it was.

Alaric.

"Are there anymore?" Alaric asked, eyes surveying the land.

"Only the one Neo is facing," I informed, turning just in time to see Neo skewer the remaining slaver. "I take that back," I whispered.

"Good," Alaric snarked, stepping faster than I had time to face him. "You won't be needing this anymore, then." With little effort, Alaric ripped my sword from my hand and tucked it into his belt without the scabbard.

"That's mine," I growled, canines bared.

"You said you could handle this problem on your own, and clearly, you couldn't. We had to come rescue you. You made me and *Neo* do unnecessary fighting. You made us use the strength we needed to reserve for the demons." Alaric rested his hand on the hilt of my sword as I stalked over to him. "You are a fool, and fools don't get swords."

"Fools cannot call other people fools," I snarled inches away from Alaric's face.

Alaric slammed his thumb to his chest. "You think I'm a fool? Then explain to me—"

"Are you alright?" Neo's calm, charming voice sounded, beckoning me and Alaric to look.

Neo knelt before the young woman who had been attacked. She shied away from him, her body shaking.

I grimaced, worrying that Neo would take her fear as an insult.

I didn't want his first time rescuing a human to be like this. But I also couldn't blame the woman before him for cowering, not after what she had been through, after what she had seen us do.

Humans were always hesitant to come near us, to thank us after a battle, scared of our innate ability to kill. It had confused me the first couple of missions I had aided in, but I eventually came to understand that it was natural for them to fear strength and power, since they never knew if it would be redirected at them.

Neo retracted back a bit but paused, thinking. Finally, he offered a docile smile. "You don't look hurt; that's good. You do have a bit of dirt on your nose, though." Neo rummaged through his pocket then pulled out an olive-green handkerchief. He outstretched his arm so the girl could reach it but not close enough that he himself could touch her.

She did not move.

Neo offered one last pained smile before his lips lowered. "I'll leave it here for you." Carefully, he placed the folded cloth on plush grass, making sure it wouldn't get any mud or blood on it, then quietly stood.

I reached for Neo in comfort as he retreated to us, the only thing I could offer him right now, as I was certain that Alaric would fight my explanation as to why the human reacted that way. Even now, I was sure he was gloating.

My stomach dropped.

If Alaric was gloating, that would only cause Neo to hurt more.

I spun, ready to wipe the smug look off Alaric's face. However, as I did, I found nothing that I needed to hide from Neo.

Alaric's lips were in a tight line, and his breathing was staggered as he carefully watched his brother.

He was worried. Sad maybe.

His name escaped my lips. I wasn't sure why.

Neo was the one who I should be concerned about, not Alaric.

"Wait, please," a feminine voice squeaked. The blonde female stood up, handkerchief in hand. The two males behind her quickly followed. "Thank you," she whispered, glancing to Neo, me, and then Alaric, causing the latter to stiffen. "All of you. Without your help, I—I—would've—"

She hugged herself, unable to finish her words.

"You kept our family together, and for that, we are truly grateful," the old man said, hugging the woman, looking at her in question then the coins in his hand. "Let me give you this as payment for your good deed."

Neo peeked at me, unsure what to say, and surprisingly, Alaric stayed quiet, a veil over his eyes.

I carefully stepped forward and closed his hand, smiling softly, repeating my father's often said words, "A good deed is no longer itself if it is paid for. If it is, it then turns into a good job."

The man looked at me puzzled, unused to the kindness. "I would feel better if you did," the old man pleaded.

I silently declined him again. The man frantically looked around, trying to think of something we would accept instead.

"Let's get going," Alaric growled, heading for the road nearby. "If we're to find a place to camp before nightfall, we need to keep walking."

I sighed, hating Alaric's dismissive attitude, but I knew he was right.

If we didn't walk away now, we would spend more time rejecting the man's payment than we did fighting. I jerked my head to Neo, signaling him to follow.

"You're travelers?" We paused at the old man's startled voice. "If you won't take my money, please accept our offer to host you tonight. It's the least we can do. We don't have much, but we have blankets and fresh hay in the barn, and Rose makes a wonderful soup."

Warmth spread through me.

We hadn't had a proper meal in days, and the thought of lying on something other than a thin blanket and leaves seemed wonderful.

I looked up at the sun. It was nearly down. It wouldn't make much of a difference if we stopped traveling now.

"Soup sounds good," Neo blurted out before I could.

"Wonderful," the old man chirped, clapping his hands together. "I'll have Peter,"—the old man gripped the young boy's shoulder—"start gathering the ingredients from the garden. In the meantime, let me show you where you'll be staying."

The old man started toward the barn. Neo happily followed. I started to as well, but Alaric grabbed me, sending those shivers down my spine once again.

"We don't have time for this," Alaric whisper-growled.

I pulled away. "We do," I snarled, calling out his lie. "Look at the sun."

Alaric didn't bother looking up. Instead, he rubbed his temple. "Ina, I can't be around them, please," Alaric pleaded.

My shoulders dropped, hearing the fear and worry in his voice. "Alaric," I questioned, a gentleness in my voice that shocked me, "what is it?"

Alaric's lips moved a fraction of an inch, his scent changing to something vulnerable.

"Are you alright?" I asked, that ever-annoying side of me wanting to comfort him despite everything.

Alaric stepped back, his demeanor morphing into hostility again. "They're humans. The ones in this area have the same outlook on wolves as the ones in Rivelia. It's a risk."

I huffed, realizing that his worry wasn't anything more than trepidation for the problems he and his father had caused.

I crossed my arms. "They don't know what we are, and I doubt they'll find out unless you keep staring them down like that," I responded, not seeing Alaric's excuse as a real reason to leave.

"They won't have the chance to find out if we leave."

"Oh, they will. We've already happily accepted." I jerked my head to the barn where Neo excitedly smiled and talked to the human family. "If we take it back so suddenly, they will know something is amiss."

Wrinkles formed on Alaric's forehead as he peered down his nose at me, but he didn't say anything else. I gloated, knowing that I had pushed him into a corner, then happily headed for Neo.

Alaric would learn to tolerate the thing he hated tonight.

CHAPTER 26

I sipped from the bowl of soup in my hands, a smile forming as I savored the mixture of fresh herbs, boiled potatoes, leeks, and rich milk. It took all my restraint not to gulp down the hearty broth. Still, despite all my efforts, the soup was too tempting, and I found myself burning my tongue.

Reluctantly, I placed the bowl beside me to cool and watched the embers fly from the roaring fire we had gathered around, as the small cottage could not comfortably house its owners and our party. The old man—who I now knew as Amos—had felt terrible about the predicament, had thought himself a horrible host to his daughter's saviors. However, I was more than thankful for what he had provided us and still planned to give us, and from what I could tell, Neo was as well.

Neo sat to the left of me, watching Peter play a song on his wooden flute. It was off pitch, but neither he nor I had the heart to tell him stop, not when Peter had enthusiastically told us it was his way of thanking us. Surprisingly, Alaric hadn't either. He stood a considerable distance from our circle, falsely claiming the fire was too hot for him and barely said anything, which was more than fine by me. I'd rather deal with his silent brooding than the offhanded comments I worried he may make. However, if he tried to show his disdain for humans tonight, I was ready for them.

"Would you like some more?" a soft voice sounded behind me, close to where Alaric had taken his perch.

I speedily spun, seeing Rose inch closer to Alaric.

Though Neo had assured me that Alaric wouldn't physically harm the humans, my throat tightened, and I leaned forward, placing my weight on the tips of my toes, ready to intervene in case Rose's proximity may push Alaric over.

Alaric shook his head, refusing to look at her.

"I can take your bowl, then," she whispered, her voice like morning dew, a blush already on her cheek.

Alaric glanced at his empty bowl then at Rose. Despite the cold stare, Rose simply smiled and extended her arm. Alaric stretched his neck and rolled back his shoulders while he minutely shifted from foot to foot, his uncomfortably looking more like a scared pup then an irritated mutt. However, just as quickly as his face had changed, it returned to that hard expression as he dismissively handed her the bowl.

I relaxed my feet and rested them flatly on the ground, thinking that the interaction was over, but Rose stayed, rocking back and forth on the balls of her shoes. Alaric crossed his arms, paying her no heed. Then Rose opened her mouth and closed it a couple times, gathering her courage.

I hoped that she wouldn't find it.

Sadly, she squeaked out, "Would you like to dance?"

"Why are you asking me?" he gruffly asked, his tolerance for her proximity clearly ending.

I braced my arms on the log, ready to jump up.

Rose grabbed the fabric of her dress, her gaze askew to the ground. "I want to make sure you are enjoying tonight. You can't partake in the talking by the fire—like your other companions—so I thought you may want to dance."

Veins popped on Alaric's neck as he lifted his chin, his breathing turning shallow. "Moving would make me just as warm as the fire."

"Oh," Rose mumbled, twiddling with her fingers. "I'm sorry. I didn't think of that. I—"

A muscle feathered in my cheek.

If Alaric was under my command, if I could even land a punch, I would throttle him here and now. Though from what I knew of him, this had been the best outcome. Still, Rose's lowered eyes pulled on my heart.

I needed to do something.

"Can I dance in his stead?" Neo asked before I could think of anything.

Rose looked between the two males, giving Alaric one more chance, but when he didn't say anything more, she nodded.

Neo offered up his hand, ever the wolf prince, and Peter began to play a song that had them prancing around the fire in a matter of seconds, ending the tension. There was only pure joy now, and it energized me, warmed my chest.

I placed my hand on my heart, relishing the feeling that I had missed these past few weeks, what Neo had missed his entire life. It was what wolves needed. All wolves needed. And perhaps it was wishful thinking or plain stupidly, but I turned to Alaric, wondering if he let himself feel this, if he basked in it too. Because, maybe if he did, there would be hope for him. But when I turned back to the tree, I found his spot empty.

His hatred had gotten the better of him.

CHAPTER 27
Alaric

I stumbled through the forest, recalling the siege, recalling my mother's cold, lifeless face, refusing to acknowledge the feeling budding inside me. I had been doing so well ignoring it over the years, keeping the humans out of my heart and mind, but when Rose danced and her entire family lit up, the feeling had erupted inside me. I didn't want to feel it, not when it tempted me to go back to the old ways, not when I didn't deserve to.

I had spent the past twenty years keeping the balance in Rivelia, keeping my father from acting further on his hate for humans, convincing myself that I hated them too so I could sleep at night after another day of ignoring *their* pleas. Still, I couldn't fully turn my back on them, saying my mother's death was their fault only blinded me so far. And this night was ending that fog.

Seeing Ina and Neo's happiness tonight was ending it.

I had to get away. I needed to get away before I forgave the humans for my mother's death—the only thing keeping me from helping them. If I did, I wouldn't be satisfied just by keeping father from mistreating humans. I would need to open the gates, let them in, and protect them. I would need for things to go back the way they were before, and I couldn't do that, not when it meant a civil war and possibly loosing the few family members I had left.

I needed to remember my mother's death, needed to make sure I used it to reinforce my walls before I returned to Neo and Ina, even if it meant they hated me, even if it meant I hated myself.

I had to keep protecting everyone.

CHAPTER 28

"Let me add another pack of potatoes," Amos muttered, clipping a small bag to one of the three horses that he had gifted us.

"That's too much," I retorted, already feeling guilty, knowing farmers like Amos didn't make much.

It was almost criminal to accept as much as we already had. Food, another bag, rope, and horses, it was all too much. Though I had to admit, I didn't reject the latter nearly as strongly as I should have, not when a couple blisters had popped this morning and I knew we still had a long way to go.

The horses were badly needed, but another bag of potatoes we could do without.

"Nonsense," Amos said as he waddled to the barrels of food. "Just give me a moment to find it. Peter. Rose. You two look as well."

I fidgeted with my fingers, hearing the determination in the old man's voice, seeing the sun rise.

We needed to start trekking if we were going to make the most of the daylight, but I didn't know how to make Amos stop.

"By the gods' blood," Alaric growled under his breath, mounting a chestnut horse. "You keep saying you want to help us, but these gifts are keeping us from leaving." The family of humans froze. "Not to mention, the more weight we carry, the slower we will be."

Amos cheeks flashed red. "You're right. I'm keeping you far too long" he stuttered. "My apologies."

I flashed my canines at Alaric in discontent, wanting to stay longer just to spite him. I hated his intolerance. But I also knew that the brutal truth was needed for us to leave. So, I kept quiet.

"Mount up," Alaric snarled in response to my violent appearance.

With no amount of pleasure, I did as he bid, mounting the white horse with black swirls—Irie. However, this departure didn't feel right. Hoping to erase some of Amos and his family's embarrassment, I sweetly chirped, "Thank you, though. The thought was very sweet."

They bobbed their heads, staying quiet with the fear they may keep us longer. Neo ran forward to hug them.

"You too, Neo," Alaric commanded, making a clicking sound at his horse.

Neo glared at his brother but did as Alaric commanded, pulling himself slowly onto the saddle, glimpsing at the cottage one last time, pain and happiness clashing on his face.

I could only imagine how he felt.

For once in his life, he had finally gotten to protect humans, feel the happiness that he had helped them achieve. He had felt the feeling he had been missing his entire life.

I tugged on my reins to move closer to Neo, hoping to offer a comforting touch, but Irie pulled back as Neo's sword fell to the ground.

Alaric grunted his disapproval.

"I'm still waking up," Neo answered in response, starting to dismount.

Amos rushed forward. "I'll get it."

"Thank you," Neo breathed as Amos handed him the sword.

"I'm happy to see you have such a fine blade," Amos voiced, unable to keep quiet any longer.

Alaric clicked his tongue at his horse louder, content to walk away and force us to follow, even with Amos still speaking.

"With the frequented blood demon sightings, it's needed more than ever. They seem to have doubled their numbers in the past year."

A cold sweat formed on my brow, even Alaric halted his departure.

That couldn't be right. The blood demons just showed up on the continent again. They had just attacked Artico a few weeks ago. They couldn't have been here for a year without us knowing, even if Rivelia didn't go outside their walls. Word would have gotten around.

"I'm sorry. Did you misspeak? I thought I heard you say a year," I quavered.

Amos blinked a couple times, his head titling.

"I did," Amos replied slowly. "I thought you knew. You all seemed well versed in battling. I figured you were from the mercenaries' guild or that you were from this area. The silver daggers on your belts,"—Amos nodded to mine, earning me a scolding glare from Alaric. I was in for a lecture, but that was a problem for later—"are they not trophies?"

"No," I uttered. "None of those are our situation."

The scent of salty water began to exude from Amos.

"You should leave." Amos snatched Irie's reins and pointed me in the direction of the forest, in the direction of Rivelia.

"We can't. Our end destination is further east," I declared, trying to be vague.

Though I trusted Amos and his family, it was better if less people knew where we were headed, as it would better our chances of ambushing the demons.

"You mustn't. That's where the demons are the thickest. They'll note you, and you'll never be able to leave here."

"Never be able to leave?"

"Oh gods, you really do not know," Amos mewled frantically. "They really have made our region a bubble of secrecy. You must get out before it's too late."

Amos pulled on the reins, forcing Irie to take a step forward.

I snatched the lead back.

"Amos," I called fiercely, hoping to break through his terror. He looked up, shaking. I rested a hand on his shoulder, thighs gripping tight to Irie so I wouldn't fall. "Speak plainly, please. We do not understand you."

Amos was quiet, and his throat bobbed several times, as if he was swallowing the fear that had spewed out of him, then with a clutched hand to his chest, he calmly began, "A year ago, the blood demons returned out of the blue. At first, it was just a couple of them. We thought we could handle it on our own, but then more and more came. They claimed our land as theirs and took up residence in the old castle. We couldn't fight them, let alone kill them all. So, a few of us in different villages tried to escape, but the demons had scouts all over and found out. They hunted down the volunteers, outran them before they could get past the Woodland region's boarders, and when they found them..." Amos shuddered, and his children clutched each other tightly. "Let's just say, what they did to them, what they displayed on the posts they erected at each town, scared any of us from trying to leave and telling others what was happening here, because the fate of being owned, occasionally harvested by the demons, was better than being caught."

"So, you've been imprisoned in your lands?" Neo asked.

Amos nodded. "It is why you must go. The demons made their visit to our home the other day. They won't be back for a while."

"Then, you should leave as well," Neo added. "You'll be past the boarders before they can catch you."

"I can't." Amos stepped back to hug his children. "My sister and her children live in a different village, and the demons know that. They will be the ones to suffer if we leave. Our only hope is that someone comes. That, if you leave now and are willing to risk it, you tell people what is happening here and bring back an army."

"If the demons control the reaches of the Woodland region, a human army will not be able to free you," Alaric said coldly.

"They are not the army we hope for, nor the one we tried to run to," Amos whispered. "We need the Wolves of Rivelia."

Alaric scoffed. "You're better off trying to find the wolves that were assigned to your region. Or have they all perished?"

My gut twisted at Alaric's question, the one I hadn't thought to ask, as I was mortified by Amos's horrific news.

"No, they still exist." I released a breath. "We still hear sightings of them picking off a few demons, but nothing beyond that. They keep to themselves. They're elusive. It's like they want to help but are waiting for something. If I had to guess, they also don't have the numbers and are stuck like us too."

"Then it seems your plight will not be answered," Alaric responded. "Rivelia will never aid you."

"They might," Neo defended. "We're here after all."

"Don't give false hope when they already know the truth," Alaric growled.

Amos's head dropped.

"But we are here," Neo said again, too softly.

"We aren't," Alaric snarled. "We're not here for the humans. We're only here because of Ina's deal. Nothing more, and even now, it sounds that our agreement will come to end." Alaric eyes connected with mine. "It seems that the Woodland Pack has more common sense than you. They won't participate in a battle they know they cannot win."

My soul crumpled, suspecting that Alaric was right. He and Neo may very well leave now.

Amos met Alaric's hard stare with wide eyes. "Humans? What do you mean?" Amos trailed off as realization hit him. "You're wolves, but you don't dress like you belong to the Woodland Pack." Amos forehead wrinkled. "Are you Wolves of Rivelia?" Amos asked, stuttering. Alaric raised his chin in answer. It was enough for Amos to drop to his knees and beg, "Please, you must help us."

I raised my bottom off the saddle, freeing my feet from the stirrups in case I needed to quickly jump between Amos and Alaric.

"As I said before, we didn't come for you," Alaric coldly stated. "The gods know we would never come for the species that abandoned our mothers in the castle, the queen of the pack you beg for protection from now."

Amos froze. "You're the prince. You're royal wolves."

Alaric tugged on his reins, ending the conversation.

"No, wait," Amos called, standing.

I grimaced, wondering if I should snarl and keep Amos from talking before Alaric lost whatever was holding him back.

"I was there that night." Alaric froze, hate gleaming in his stature. "Please, I need to apologize."

I kicked Irie's sides, urging her to get between Amos and Alaric, true fear coursing through me now, urgently finding the answer to my internal debate. However, Irie refused to run into the path of fury that Alaric was omitting.

"Groveling won't bring them back," Alaric snapped loudly, causing all our horses to rear, for my foot to tangle in the stirrups, delaying the dismount I desperately needed to take.

Kind as Amos was, he was a fool to keep talking. If Alaric truly blamed humans for our mothers' death, that rage would be unchallenged, engraved into his core. Even if he promised Neo he wouldn't physically hurt humans, his wolf may take over and things would not turn out well.

"Nothing will," Alaric yelled, his scent starting to turn feral.

I ripped at my stirrup.

"The only thing that would atone for it, is if you experienced the same pain, if—"

"Alaric," Neo growled, his canines bared, "enough."

The two males looked at one another, resentment and challenge in their eyes, ready to fight if the other did not give in.

My hair stood on end.

Alaric was ready to fight Neo—the brother he came to protect.

His wolf had taken over.

Anger and rage had control of him, and if he were to fight, he would not hold back. And if I had to guess, by the way Neo did not show an ounce of fear at the thought of facing his brother, Neo's wolf had taken over as well.

The wolf trance was happening to both of them.

It was common amongst wolves—turning feral with our anger—and it was our fatal flaw. It's why wolves always traveled with at least three, so one could break up the fight before it got out of hand. However, I didn't have the strength to stop Alaric from harming Neo.

"You're going to hurt each other," I whispered, hoping a gentle voice could reach them, calm them in some way.

Neither of them budged. The musk in Neo's scent even grew.

"Please," I pleaded to them, daring to touch Alaric's hand, since he was the one within arm's reach, "stop."

Neo didn't move, but Alaric blinked. The haze from his eyes cleared, and like a sailor drawn to a siren, he turned to me. He blinked a couple more times, inhaled deeply, then stiffened at the mixture of fear and fury in the air. He looked to the humans then Neo, who had put himself between them and still remained in that anger caused trance.

Alaric's throat bobbed whilst he turned to me, asking a silent question.

I slowly nodded in confirmation.

He breathed deeply, feeling his heartbeat, forcing it to slow before gritting out, "Fine. I'll leave them alone"—Neo's eyes began to clear—"but after I say this, if the demons leave this land and you hear it was us that defeated them, know that it wasn't for you. It was for our mothers." With one last disdainful look, Alaric kicked his heels into his horse's side and rushed into the forest.

"Wait, please. I want to explain," Amos yelled, taking a hurried step forward.

I urged Irie forward, thankful she listened this time, and stopped Amos in his tracks, hoping that I blocked the wind from carrying his voice.

"Not right now," I cautioned. "He's still *calming.*"

Amos peered around me, full of regret and contemplation.

I stood my ground, ready to knock him out if need be. Thankfully, his shoulders dropped. I thanked the gods, then without moving Irie, I turned my attention to Neo who watched his brother race past the tree line.

"The threat is gone, Neo." I urged my horse to creep closer to him so that I could rest a hand on his. "Calm," I ordered in a hush toned that I had used on pack members during their trances.

Neo minutely shifted his focus to me, holding my gaze for a minute, then in the same way Alaric came out of his trance, Neo did the same. However, instead of soothing himself, Neo's breathing became rapid, almost panicked.

"What happened?" he sputtered between breaths.

I gripped his hand tighter, noticing the confusion and worry on his young face.

Could this have been the first time he had gone into a trance?

That would be impossible. The average age for a shifter to experience their first wolf trance was about sixteen. Neo was twenty. But then again, knowing how protected Neo was, he had probably never experienced such an innate urge to protect or fiery anger other than the one he was used to, other than when his father had punished him, but I'm sure the king had taken precautions for that day. Perhaps he had compelled him not to enter the trance. I needed to handle this with care.

"Your wolf took over," I explained.

Neo's pupils darted around fitfully, looking at his body. He nodded, throat bobbing, semi-satisfied that he was still in one piece, but then his heartbeat sped as he twisted every which way, examining anything that was the size of Alaric.

"Where—where—"

"He's fine," I assured, grabbing his horse's reins, stopping his sporadic turns. "He ran into the woods after he came to. It takes time and distance to fully calm."

"We need to go after him. Wolves shouldn't be alone after the trance. That's what I've been taught," he gasped, answering my earlier question.

All wolf cubs had similar educations, and the one thing we learned, was that we should never leave another wolf alone during their calming, especially when they didn't get to fight, as the energy would stay inside us and drive us to do illogical things until we used it.

Some wolves would turn to destruction or run blindly. In one case, I once witnessed a wolf run so blindly that they broke their arm ramming into a tree. However, that wasn't the case for all wolves. Some, who were experienced with the aftereffects of their wolf taking over, would walk it off or seethe to themselves. Others had an exercise routine they followed.

"I'm sure he'll be fine," I whispered, certain Alaric was one of the few who could handle himself. However, my reassurance only made Neo resume his search. "Neo, calm. Be calm."

He didn't listen.

I grabbed both his hands, realizing what I needed to do so he could return to normal.

"I'll go check on him, but right now, you can't be near each other, not until your wolves acknowledge that the threat is gone," I warned, knowing Alaric's wolf had seen Neo as a threat when they were both in a trance, making Alaric highly susceptible to entering another trance if he saw his brother again before fully calming.

"What about you? I can't let you risk yourself."

I shook my head. "Despite Alaric's normal loathing for me, his wolf didn't focus on me during his trance. I should be fine. Not to mention,

I've helped many wolves work through this." Neo continued to stare at me, unaccepting of my words. "You have to trust me," I earnestly stated.

"Ok," Neo mumbled to himself. "Should I," he began but tripped on his words.

I slumped in my saddle, meeting Neo's eyes despite his lowered head. "Stay here. Find your calm with them." I jerked my chin to Amos and his family. Neo snapped up, fear evident in his eyes. I leaned closer, making sure my voice was too quiet for human ears as I whispered, "Your wolf took over because of your desire to protect them. It won't let you hurt them during your calming. Just talk to them and hear what they wanted to say to Alaric. We can carefully relay it to him later. Can you do that?"

Neo's leg shook as he thought.

Patiently, I waited.

"Ok," he whispered.

"Good," I replied. "Come to us when you're ready." Neo held up a finger, his lips parting. "Your heart rate will slow, and the haze will completely clear," I clarified.

He nodded, allowing me to turn to Amos.

"I'm sorry," he whispered.

I raised my hand. "I'm sorry that we are leaving like this, but I promise that not all wolves have forgone their oath to protect humans." Amos raised his head, a glint of hope in his eyes. "This continent will be safe again."

Amos's children looked to one another then to their father, a smile threatening to break through their terror. They wanted hope so badly, hope that they did not have for years, and though it was Rivelia who should be blamed for that, I felt shame, because the hope I had just given to them was by false certainty.

CHAPTER 29

I pulled back on Irie's reins as Alaric came into view, taking note of his heavy steps and balled fists while he deepened the trench he had sowed in the forest floor.

I sighed before tying Irie to the nearest tree, not ready to interact with Alaric.

I understood that he still hurt from his mother's death, but mine had also died that night. Yet when it was revealed that Amos was there, I didn't lash out. I didn't tell him that he wasn't worth saving. I didn't leave him shaking in the dirt. It was clear that Amos was apologetic, regretted running with all his being, but Alaric still kicked him down. It wasn't something I could turn a blind eye to, but with his current condition, I knew I couldn't bring it up. My wrath had to wait.

I was able to take three steps before Alaric violently turned to me.

I held up my hands, palms open. "It's just me. Neo wanted me to check on you."

Alaric's chest puffed. "I can handle a calming on my own."

I cautiously took another step toward a fallen stump, realizing that Alaric's outlet was pacing.

"I figured as much, but it was what was needed for his calming to happen." I slowly sat on the stump, making sure to lean back on my hands, chest exposed to seem less challenging. "He needs to be busy and to make sure everyone is ok for his energy to be used up."

Alaric's chest dipped as he ran his hand through his hair, guilt consuming his face. "And what is he doing to keep busy? He's out of harm's way, correct?"

"Yes," I replied to his second question, refusing to address the first in case the mention of Amos and his family would set him off again.

Alaric inched toward me, folding his arms. "And what is he doing?" he asked a second time, ever the annoying, protective brother despite almost biting Neo's head off minutes ago.

I leaned forward, clasping my hands in front of my chest, making sure to discreetly protect it. "He's talking to Amos, hearing what he wanted to say."

Alaric's jaw tightened, the grinding of his teeth echoing in my ears. "Why? His words are worthless."

I pressed my tongue against the point of my canines, swallowing back the words that threatened to come out.

Alaric's head sunk back as it cocked to the side. "No argument? No defending your precious humans today?"

"Not today," I bit out, looking to the side.

Alaric smiled victoriously. "Finally see what I do?"

The flame in me flared, but I remained quiet.

I would never see the way he did.

Never.

Alaric cackled, taking my silence as a yes. "About time. Maybe now we can head back, let the humans get what they—"

I shot up, fist aimed for Alaric's gut. Surprisingly, it made contact.

He toppled over, gasping for air.

"You're pathetic," I breathed out, unable to hold back any longer. "You think that just because your mother died in a war that you can turn your back on your oath, that you can just hate humans despite not knowing them, not talking to them for twenty years. You think that they're all the same. But I have a question for you. Is it like that with wolves? Do we all behave in a similar manner? From my experience, we don't. There are some good ones, and there are some shit wolves out there. But—"

"You're right," Alaric growled, rolling his shoulders back as he stood straight.

I blinked a couple times, making sure I was awake.

"There are shit wolves, as you put it, and you're one of them."

I threw another punch. To my dismay, Alaric caught my fist. I tried to free myself from his control, but he only held tighter and pulled me closer.

"You talk about how I'm betraying humankind and how awful it is, but what about you betraying your own? Our mothers died. The humans didn't even bother to stay and fight for them, to protect them despite the years both our mothers served them. They didn't apologize. They didn't even grieve after the war for either of them. They didn't grieve for the wolves that were lost throughout the war. Instead, they asked us to help rebuild what we couldn't protect. By not being angry, you are disgracing our mothers' memories. Can you not see that?" He pulled me closer, the promise of violence written all over his body. "Or were you too little when your mother died? That's what I would guess. You weren't even old enough to know her. She's just some great wolf you've heard stories of. You wouldn't even care about her if you didn't have her blood. I honor her memory more than you."

"No," I uttered.

"Then, tell me everything you know about her. Tell me something that the general population doesn't know."

My chest tightened as I thought, as I realized the only information I knew about my mother was that which I had gained from others and books. She had barely been around once I was old enough to go to school, old enough to be alone while she and my father focused on the war. I had thought I had known enough to call her my mother, to be called her true daughter. I knew what tea she liked, her favorite season. I knew that she liked to read and what her favorite books were. Surely, I knew how to honor her memory.

I knew her.

I knew her.

I—

All those things were facts that I had learned from the pack. I didn't know the big things. I hadn't known about her past. I hadn't known that she had loved Damon, that she had lived in the Castle of Rivelia. I hadn't even known how she died.

Tears edged at the corners of my eyes.

I balled up my free hand, throwing it with all my force, hoping to land an uppercut, but Alaric blocked that too. "Take it back," I growled through gritted teeth. "Take it back."

"Can't take the truth, can you?" Alaric ridiculed, a small smile on his face.

"You don't know anything about me," I screamed, practically clawing at his arms, trying to create any distance between us.

Alaric snickered. "The same goes for me. Yet you keep—"

"Alaric," a powerful but steady voice boomed.

Neo stood with the horses, stiff-backed with somber eyes like guilt, anger, and relief were fighting inside him.

"Don't talk to her like that, not when you know so little," Neo blustered with an edge, similar to the one he had during his wolf trance.

My throat tightened.

Had he not calmed before finding us?

I had barely been able to calm Alaric when both males' wolves had taken over, and it wasn't until Alaric retreated that I could reach Neo. Now, with my heightened emotions and the tension between Alaric and I, I wasn't sure if I could do it again. However, as I examined Neo, I saw only clear hazel eyes.

He was in complete control.

"You think I know little?" Alaric shoved me away. "I was there when the attack happened. I fought in the battles, the raids, the war. I was there for the wins and losses," Alaric barked, a thin veil of mist coating his eyes.

Now was not the time to challenge him.

"Neo, he's still—"

Neo coolly shook his head, seeming more in control of his emotions than both Alaric and I combined.

What had changed in the short time we were apart?

"Alaric, I need to tell you something." Pity was evident in his voice. "I need you to listen and know that it's true, because when Amos told me what I'm about to tell you, I did not smell fear nor nervousness. I only sensed honesty."

"Amos?" Alaric cracked his knuckles. "The human? The one who abandoned our mother? The one who almost let you die?" he growled, the mist growing thicker.

Neo nodded.

"Why should I?"

"Because what they had to say will change everything. It will change you."

Alaric's wolf scent grew.

His wolf wanted to protect him. But from what?

"I doubt that. I'd be wasting time and sullying Mother's memory if I listened."

Neo's throat bobbed at the mention of their mother. "Alaric, please, listen with an open heart for once. I beg you."

"Give me one good reason," Alaric demanded, storming toward Neo.

Neo's cheeks hollowed, making him seem so much older. "If you listen, actually listen, and it doesn't change anything for you, I will go back home. I will never try to leave again. I won't even talk about the humans."

My heart dropped at the offer.

Alaric would never listen. This was a bet Neo wouldn't win. He had to know that.

"Neo, it's not worth it," I cautioned.

Alaric's hot stare turned to me, shutting me up.

"It is," Neo whispered, a pained smile on his face. "He needs to know. He deserves to. We all do."

I cocked my head at his words.

What information was Neo about to share that would affect me?

I looked between the two males, contemplating.

I didn't want Neo to do this, not when Alaric's strong resolve had been replaced with happiness for Neo's terrible deal, but as I looked upon Neo's face, I knew I couldn't stop him. This had to be done.

"Alright," I whispered, "let's hear it."

Neo shook his head. "Just Alaric right now. I need to tell him first and alone."

"Neo," I cautioned. The mist in Alaric's eyes had cleared due to his wolf's joy over the deal, but a speckle still remained.

"I'll be alright," Neo whispered, touching my shoulder, causing me to jump. He was far faster than I had given him credit for. "I just...seeing you two fight...you will both handle this news in different ways. It will be safer if you're separate for it." I swallowed hard, becoming more and more nervous about this newfound information. "There's a river nearby. Wait there for a bit?"

I bit my lip. I knew I didn't have much a of a choice, but I was scared. Scared for Neo. Scared that Alaric may enact the deal once Neo finished his story and force him to leave before I could say goodbye.

"He won't be that cruel," Neo offered, reading my thoughts, answering in a tone so calm and mature that I really did wonder if time had somehow passed for him and not the rest of us during his talk with Amos.

I nodded. "Just—" I choked on the words, unknowing of what to say. "Good luck," I whispered, hugging Neo before walking into a thicket of ferns, toward the rushing water.

CHAPTER 30

ALARIC

"What is it?" I bit out through gritted teeth, trying to keep my wolf in check. It did little to hide my anger, the feral need to fight.

Neo turned to me, sweat heavily mixing in with his scent. He was nervous, as he should be. He had made a gamble that he would not win. It was about time too.

He had dragged us too far from home, dragged us somewhere I couldn't properly protect him. And if he died out here, I wouldn't be able to forgive myself. I wouldn't be able to keep father at bay any longer. He would destroy everything in his path out of grief and rage, and Rivelia would cease to exist.

"You should sit down," Neo said, gesturing to the forest floor.

I crossed my arms and dug my feet further into the ground. I was a trained warrior that had lived for hundreds of years, lived through the war. Words no longer affected me in the way that had me swooning, no matter how horrible or shocking.

Neo looked to the ground again, grimacing. I tapped my foot. He needed to hurry this up. Our journey home would be long.

Neo sighed, "Alright, then. Just remember your promise; truly listen with an open heart."

I rolled my eyes. Neo knew more than anyone that I followed through with oaths. And even if he didn't, my traveling with him and that incessant Artico wolf was proof enough.

I knew Ina was trouble the moment I saw her and smelt her blood infused with that cursed metal. I had seen her hair and knew she hailed from Artico, guessed she might've been part Rivelian from her tan skin, maybe even predicted that she was Batair's daughter, but I had denied the latter because I didn't want it to be true.

I had fought alongside Batair, watched him and my father fight. I knew how stubborn, how strong, how loyal he was to the gods. They were qualities that had been so embedded in him that any spawn of his was sure to inherit the traits. And back when I admired them, thrived to be like Batair, I wanted those traits. I wanted to be allies with his future children. But now, I knew they were only annoyances. At least that's what Ina had proved after she revealed who she was.

She had been nothing but a thorn in my paw since that day in the throne room. She had single handily destroyed my years of work to calm Father, get him to think with a stable mind, not be driven by anger or vengeance. I had almost convinced him to open the gates for the wolves who needed to roam, prolonging the rebellion that he had refused to acknowledge before she came to us. However, all that progress halted when Ina delivered the news of the blood demons return, acted so much like her late mother that father fully reentered his craze.

I knew he wouldn't think clearly, not when Ina was around. So, when I found out she wanted to leave, I let her. I made that idiotic deal with her, thinking that her departure would return us to normalcy.

Gods, I was so wrong.

With both her and Neo's departure, Father had wrecked the throne room. I had barely gotten him to calm down with my lie about them being taken by opposing wolves. I could hardly imagine the atrocities that would have occurred if he hadn't believed me, but it didn't matter if I could imagine them or not. What mattered was that I couldn't have stopped Father's actions or lessened them as I had the last time he exploded and that Neo would have broke if father decided to punish the humans again. After all, Neo had barely survived the last time. I had barely survived the last time.

Father didn't just want to burn more than the village Neo had visited that day. He wanted to burn all the ones within a day's ride. He had wanted to for a while, and Neo's stunt had been the perfect excuse to do so. I fought him on it, knowing it wasn't right, even if the humans were responsible for my mother's death. I used any excuse I could to prevent the destruction from becoming reality. It cost me Father's trust. It made him think that I wasn't on his side, that I was a human sympathizer. I had to prove to him that I was loyal to him. Only him.

He personally beat me that day. He whipped my back until my vision blurred, and I could barely stand. He made me clean myself, dress in my nicest finery, and watch the human village burn, because if I could do that, if I stood unflinching the whole time and watched, then father would believe I was on his side, that seeing humans suffer invigorated me. So, I did. I watched until the end. I watched for Neo. I watched to earn Father's trust again.

It was the hardest thing I had to do, to ignore my pains and stay standing, to hear the cries and not help, to watch Neo beg for his friend's life. But I did it, because at the end, it proved to Father that I was on his side. It made him stop at just one village, and I would do it again. While I hated the humans for what they had done, I never wanted to harm them or burn their villages. I only sought to ignore them or deliver oral blows if they ever tried to reconnect with us. I owed that to Mother's memory, even Selena's—Batiar's mate—as no one else protected it.

Selena had shown me much kindness in the past, was so courageous during the Blood War, offering to fight on the front lines despite not having trained as a warrior all her life. It was part of the reason I had held back my strength when I attacked Ina on the day I had caught up to them. It was why I allowed us to make a new deal. I didn't want to kill her, not because I had pity in my heart for Ina, but because I knew Selena would forgive her for her stupid mistakes, but now, there was a way out of it. There was a way in which I didn't have to sink my claws into Batair and Selena's daughter and still get my brother away from danger and back home before father lost it. All I had to do was listen, and this nightmare would be over.

"Just get on with it," I seethed, making sure to take a deep breath again to calm my wolf, thinking of all the ways I would fix things once we returned.

CHAPTER 31

I sat on the riverbank, one leg stretched out, the other bent for my arm to rest on as I aimlessly fiddled with one of the countless smooth rocks surrounding the river. I knew I should have been thinking about my future plans, questions to ask if Alaric allowed Neo to say goodbye, like where to find the nomadic pack. But all I could bring myself to do was sit and wait, wallow in self-pity over the fact that I would be alone from here on out and that Alaric may have been right.

I had been so upset over what he said about me and my mother that I had wanted to rip his throat out, but now that I sat here on the bank with nothing but my thoughts to keep me company, I kept wondering if he was right.

He had known her far longer than me, had actually been old enough to guess what she would have wanted after her death, comprehend the complex emotions that came with the greyness of the world. But on the other hand, there was my father. He had known her better than anyone, had loved her with everything in his being. He would never do anything to defile her memory, and he kept protecting the humans. That had to be what was right. But then again, he could've been skewed by her death, just like Damon. His thoughts twisted with her death. He also had the pack to answer to.

Though he was the alpha, their happiness was what kept him on his throne. And if the majority of wolves wanted to keep protecting the humans, that was the side he had to fall on.

I pulled my knees to my chest, resting my head upon them, hoping that my headache and bleeding heart would stop if I gained just a bit more warmth. However, whatever relief I found there quickly disappeared, as the sound of tumbling pebbles came from behind.

I jumped up, feeling shivers down my spine, and faced Alaric.

His eyes were lowered, his shoulders curled inward, and faint red streaks began at his eyes and ended at the middle of his cheek. His hand was even blistered from punching something or—

Worriedly, I looked for Neo.

He was nowhere to be found.

My heart threatened to burst from my chest.

"Where is he?" I asked, my voice rising, scared that the conversation had taken too sour of a turn and Alaric's wolf had taken over. "Where's Neo?" I screamed when Alaric only looked on with pursed brows.

Alaric swallowed. "He's fine. He's tending to the horses," he replied, his voice hoarse.

I let out a sigh of relief, my sword dropping to my side. "Thank the gods," I whispered.

"You really thought I hurt him, didn't you?" Alaric asked, his eyes sadder than before. I didn't think it was possible.

"It's the only thing that would make you appear"—I looked Alaric up and down once more, trying to place the word to describe him—"like that." I gestured at him with my chin, sheathing my sword.

Alaric grimaced. "I thought so too. Turns out the truth of me being a monster makes me like this as well."

My pupils doubled.

What in the gods' name did Amos tell Neo to pass on?

Scared and confused, I cautiously tiptoed forward, making sure to give Alaric a wide berth. "I need to talk to Neo," I announced, barely over a whisper.

Alaric sidestepped. I stumbled back, unsure what to make of all this. At least when Alaric was angry, when he was threatening my life, I knew what to expect, what to do, but these emotions—the sadness, the guilt—that exuded off him, I had no idea what to expect. I had no idea how to handle him.

Alaric stepped back with arms raised and palms open. "Sorry." Alaric sucked in his bottom lip. "I know you probably want to talk to Neo about what Amos told him, and you can if you can't be around me, but I would like to tell you."

A silver lining in Alaric's eyes made me clutch my chest. I didn't like seeing him in so much pain, even after all the animosity between us, but I couldn't trust that urge to comfort him.

"Why?" I asked with a bit of bitterness, wondering if he wanted to tell me so he could revel in my reaction when he told me that he was taking Neo back.

"So I can apologize for everything," he whispered, his voice breaking.

I stilled.

Alaric wasn't someone who apologized. He was someone who rarely changed their mind, and even if he did, he never admitted he was wrong. This had to be a trick, but his emotions were too raw to fake.

I inhaled through my nose, running my tongue over my canines, hoping I wouldn't regret this. "What do you mean?"

Alaric slowly lowered to his knees and bowed his head.

My eyes went wide.

Wolves didn't bow to those lesser than them.

"I want to apologize for challenging you when it came to protecting the humans, for what I said about you defiling your mother's memory, and above all, for saying that you didn't know her."

I stepped back, unable to believe the words that came from his mouth. I had to be dreaming.

I pinched myself, focused on the pain, but I didn't feel the false reality shake at all.

I tried again and again, but still the result was the same.

I was awake.

Alaric was apologizing in real life. In the present. Here and now.

This was too much of a change. Just minutes ago, he had been screaming at me. He had lashed out on Amos and his family. He had told them that they and all humans weren't worth protecting, that it was about time they fended for themselves. This had to be a trick.

A mixture of a sigh and a laugh erupted from me, feeling foolish. "I'm going to find Neo," I announced, walking by Alaric.

"You don't believe me, do you?" Alaric asked, his tone a bit stronger.

I looked back at him, fingers curled in case I needed to defend myself. "You've never shown any sign that your *ideals* were changing. Why would they now?"

"Because—I—I—"

I scoffed seeing Alaric at a loss for words. "I knew you hated humans. I despised that about you, but you never once lied or played tricks. You were upfront. It was the one thing I respected about you. But now, you're apologizing for everything. Why? To get one last jab at me before you take Neo? Before you leave me alone in these woods and you return to your wondrous castle behind its safe walls? What is wrong with—"

"The humans didn't abandon them. Our mothers told them to leave," Alaric screamed, stopping my verbal assault. "I am the one who didn't know my mother well enough," he whispered too quietly. "I am the one who sullied both their memories these past twenty years. They would be ashamed of me and the hatred that blackened my heart and turned me into a disgraceful wolf. Everything that I have lived by was wrong. Every reasoning I had to defend my actions is void."

The world grew silent, and I could hear nothing but Alaric's ragged breathing, his trembling body, and my beating heart.

"How do you know?" I asked hesitantly.

"Amos," Alaric answered, still refusing to look at me despite the step I took toward him.

"But why hold on to this information until now?" I wondered, unquestioning if Amos was telling the truth. He had to be, otherwise Neo would have scented that he was lying. Humans were terrible at hiding their emotions' scents.

"He had tried to when the war ended, but I didn't know. I had been out hunting for any demons that survived the siege. Amos had told my father the truth. However, too blinded with grief, my father didn't believe him. Father threatened to snap his neck for coming up with such a lie instead of admitting to the humans' cowardice." Alaric looked away in shame, a hand in his pocket. "Amos and the others who were in the throne room that night decided to wait it out, try to tell my father again when the grief cleared a bit, or try to seek an audience with me when I came back, but by the time they decided to try again, my father had shut the gates with my full support."

I stumbled forward, dropping to my own knees, feeling agonizing, sweet relief.

I hadn't shamed my mother's memory. I knew her. I knew what she wanted. My father, thank the gods, knew what she wanted, too, despite not knowing the truth about her death.

A tear slipped out then another until I was sobbing.

CHAPTER 32

My breathing was ragged as I swung my sword overhead, and my triceps burned as I forced the blade to stop so it became parallel to the ground. Still, I lifted it again, stepping forward, ready to start the drill over, but Alaric's dull, loud voice sounded.

"That should be enough drills for the day," he announced, sheathing his sword. "We'll get back on the road once everyone is ready."

Neo silently agreed with a bob of his head, but it was of little importance, as Alaric didn't bother to look back at us, avoided my eyes specifically, just as he had done these past couple of days before walking over to his bed roll.

I waited a bit until Alaric began rolling his blanket, sure the sound of it would drown out my whispering, before turning to Neo. "I'm glad that your bet paid off and that you're still traveling with me, but I don't know how much more I can take of that." I jerked my head to Alaric. "I don't even know if he'll be of any help in a fight."

Neo turned to his brother with pursed lips. "I don't think he will. I'm really concerned about him."

My lips parted ever so slightly. This was the first time I had heard him defend his brother, and frankly, it shocked me that he was.

Alaric had been part of the reason Neo stayed locked up on the premise that humans were evil and not worth protecting, but all of that had been a false truth.

If I had been Neo, I would have been too happy with my newfound reason to do anything but what that false truth had forced him into, too happy to worry or defend the person who made my life like that.

"Everything Alaric did was because he believed it was the right thing to do. He thought that he was honoring *both* our mothers with his actions." Neo sheathed his sword. "But now, he's learned that everything he did was wrong, that he had been the injustice and evilness in this world by abandoning the humans. He's torturing himself greatly for it."

"Rightfully so," I added. "Neo, he's making up for twenty years of wrongdoings. Don't be concerned for him personally." I leaned over, making sure to meet Neo's eyes.

"Ina," Neo whispered, almost as a plea, "you have to remember the stories about him before we came to be. He was loyal, brave, strong, and kind. He battled hard for the humans, for my father. He always wanted to do what was right. That type of ideology never leaves you, not when you're a wolf like Alaric was."

"You don't know that, Neo." I squeezed his hand, wanting to ease any unnecessary guilt he had. He was too kind for this world, too kind for his horrible family.

Neo yanked his hand away. "I do," he practically screamed. We both glanced at Alaric, making sure he hadn't heard. He just kept packing his bag. Neo scooched closer to me, pivoting so Alaric couldn't see his lips. "Don't talk to Alaric about this after I tell you. If it's brought up, I really think he'll break." Neo held my stare until I nodded. "After I told him what Amos said, he broke down. He sobbed and said nonsensical things. It took me a while to understand them and a lot of thinking about the past, but I think I understand now. He chose to hate humans—using our mothers as the reason to keep his wolf from revolting—and in doing so, he was able to be an ally to Damon, became someone our father would listen to so he wouldn't kill anymore humans."

"Impossible," I mumbled. There was no way someone like Alaric would do that, and even if he had, there was no way Neo had come up with that theory with just sputtered words.

"You weren't there, Ina. You don't know what he said, and you haven't been with him for the last twenty years. You weren't there on the day my father had gone into his trance. Our father had every intent to kill, and Alaric had tried to calm him, fought against him. The proof is there for me. I know it's not there for you, but you can believe me. Alaric chose to be a villain to lessen the overall damage for both sides."

I leaned away from Neo, thinking. I wanted to trust him. I did trust him, and hearing Neo's theory after knowing the pieces he used to form, it made sense. But did it really excuse Alaric's actions?

He could have fought harder. He could've fought further on the matter to fully protect the humans, and if he still refused, he could over—

What was I thinking?

Overthrow your own father? I could never, even if I needed to, not after losing my mother. My father was the one who raised me, cared for me unconditionally. I'm sure Damon had been the same to Alaric before he went crazy, otherwise Alaric wouldn't have been so loyal throughout his life. And even if that wasn't the case, if Alaric tried to overthrow his father, there was sure to be objections to it. It would be like the forced change of power that my father had been scared to witness in Artico, what made him hold the tournament to find me a mate, except Rivelia's change in power would have been on a much larger scale. It may have even caused a civil war, and with all the death that had occurred during the Blood War, anymore loss of wolves would have sent us to the edge of extinction.

Had Alaric really thought that far ahead?

If he had used the excuse that he hated humans for our mothers' sake, all that guilt he had prevented was now rushing back to him. He had to feel terrible. He had to hate himself. His wolf had to be torturing him.

I craned my neck, watching Alaric. He knelt on the ground, putting things into his satchel. His movements had very little conviction to them, little thought. The only thing keeping them going was muscle memory. His pupils followed his hands, yet they seemed to be looking off distantly. There wasn't an ounce of light in them. There was nary a speck of the wolf I had first met in him.

My gut twisted, hating myself for reveling in his pain and suffering.

No, I shouldn't feel guilty. Even if Neo's theory was true, which it more than likely was, he still could have been nicer to those trying to help the humans.

"How long do you think it'll be until he stops blaming himself?" I asked, telling myself I was only inquiring for the sake of battles.

"I don't know," Neo whispered. "Along with denying his own needs to protect the humans, he also had to say goodbye to many of his human friends. Many of whom are close to death or have moved far away, now. I'm sure that doubles his regret."

"Oh," I murmured, the only thing I could say as a sharp pain reverberated in my chest.

It had never occurred to me that Alaric had friends he would miss. I had only viewed him as an awful wolf. I forgot the stories about him before the war, how well he was loved by both humans and shifters.

"Time will only tell how long it takes. It could be months, years, or maybe never," Neo said, sadness coating every word.

I grimaced at his words, his tone, scared at what was consuming my friend.

I reached for his shoulder, hoping to hug him, but abruptly, Neo announced, "I need to refill my wineskin."

I withdrew my hand, noticing the stale scent that exuded from him, the lack of warmth he had. I contemplated asking if he wanted company, but the way his eyes averted mine and the way his wineskin still appeared thick, I knew he wanted to be alone.

"Ok," I whispered, watching him head off to the river that had been our companion as we traveled.

I gripped the hilt of my blade needing to do something.

I still hadn't decided on if I had forgiven Alaric for everything, if I wanted his suffering to end, but I did know I cared for Neo. He had become my friend through this whole thing, someone I wanted by my side until the end. I couldn't see him saddened like this. Something had to be done. With a long inhale, I headed over to Alaric.

I stood over him, rolling pebbles with the arch of my foot, loudly and unruly, hoping that it would set him off, or at least get some form of reaction from him. I needed proof that he could be something other than an empty doll. However, Alaric didn't so much as flinch, let alone look up at me. I blinked rapidly, my chin jutting forward. I couldn't believe that this was the same man who used to scold me for turning in my bedroll when he was trying to sleep.

Neo really did have a reason to be concerned.

I kicked a few rocks and snapped some twigs, my eyes never leaving Alaric as I continued to test him. Still, nothing. I racked my brain for anything that would spark something in him.

Perhaps swordplay? He always loved to *humble* us, me in particular.

No, that wasn't it. He had talked about that this morning, and not a single thing was said with more than an instructor's voice.

Neo possibly?

No. Bringing up his brother, to the lengths where it sparked something in Alaric, would only result in tension between the two, and that was exactly what I was trying to fix.

I ran my hand through my hair. This was impossible. I needed a drink, even if it was only water.

I slid my hand over my belt, seeking my wineskin, but as I did, I felt cool metal and a slight tingly sensation.

I looked down at the glimmering hilt of Neo's dagger. The silver dagger I wasn't supposed to have. The dagger that Amos had pointed out during our dramatic farewell, which had earned me a menacing glare from Alaric—a promise of a scolding.

One side of my lips turned up.

"I'm surprised you haven't lectured me on my silver training yet," I grumbled, rolling my bedroll.

Alaric raised his head, only enough for his eyes to meet the dagger I had on display.

"It's Neo's dagger and your body. Why should I have any say in it?" Alaric stood, bringing his pack to his horse.

"What?" I almost screamed, following him. "But you were so adamant that it was a waste of my time and energy, that it would put our party in jeopardy."

Alaric tied his pack to his saddle, patting his horse's side in comfort as he neighed at the surprise shift in weight. "Stupid words," he groaned. "You seem to be handling yourself well enough."

Alaric headed for the remaining embers of last night's fire. Frustratedly, I blocked his path. He glimpsed at me before sighing heavily and averting his eyes once again.

"You're just going to rescind your words, your beliefs, just like that?" I asked, losing my patience.

"I lived by my beliefs for a long time and thought they were right. It turns out they were wrong." Alaric's throat bobbed. "I'm sure this one is the same."

He tried to step around me, but I mimicked his movements.

"Enough of this," I barked, sick of his sad eyes, his breaking voice, and his broken character. "You made your mistake. You supported the wrong side. It's sad and disappointing. And yes, you should regret those decisions. You should feel terrible about everything that you did and didn't do, but using all your energy into becoming this pathetic excuse of a male, does nothing. If you truly regret your actions, get over yourself. Stop making Neo worry. Stop making me question if you'll be a liability in a fight. Stop being this useless, sad sack of self-hatred. Start using your energy to train us, to figure out how to make amends. Swear that you'll fight fang and claw for the humans in this coming battle." I swallowed, trying to calm my hastened breathing, too worked up from my speech.

Alaric eyes met mine for the first time since the day we learned the truth. His lips parted, and for a moment, I thought he would say something, but his eyes returned to the ground. I shook my head and stormed a few feet away.

This was pointless. Alaric was lost to us. I'd have to find another way to ease Neo.

I slumped down next to my bag, packing the last of my things, but as I did, my palm—the one that didn't normally touch the silver blade and had accidentally done so a moment ago—began to sting. I needed to apply ointment to it.

I rummaged through my bag, groaning as I unpacked some things, cursing at myself for storing such an important thing at the bottom.

I pulled the tiny jar out, unscrewed the lid, and applied the salve to my hand. It was an easy task. However, as I began to dress it, the venture became more difficult than I cared to admit. Wrapping it around my dominant hand felt awkward, and when I went to tie off the fabric, I couldn't get the knot tight enough, allowing the fabric to shift with every movement.

I grumbled a string of curses, annoyed that I would have to tie it again, but still, I began to unravel the long strip of fabric.

I had rewrapped the strips around my hand twice before a larger, more calloused hand appeared under mine, supporting it. Then another hand appeared and took the bandages, tenderly wrapping them around my palm, causing shivers to once again run throughout my body.

I slowly looked up, blinking as I saw Alaric sitting across from me.

Moments of quiet passed before he whispered, "I swear it."

I straightened, knowing exactly what he meant. "To the gods?" I asked.

Alaric tied off the knot then met my eyes before shaking his head no. "I swore to them when I was little, and I broke it." I leaned away, pulling my hand back, feigning inspection of his work. Though in reality, I just couldn't bare to look at Alaric anymore. "But I'll swear to you."

My head snapped up. "Why?"

Alaric gently pulled back my hand. "Because unlike them, you'll hunt me down and yell at me if I don't keep my oath. You might even rip off my head in my sleep."

I blinked.

"Does your other hand need to be redressed?" Alaric asked, his voice light and caring, breaking me out of my stupor. I shook my head no. Alaric nodded and tucked the ointment away in my bag then stood. "I'll leave you to the rest of your matters, then." Alaric strode to our steads but then stopped abruptly. Without turning, he spoke, his voice solemn, "Ina, thank you," before continuing his walk.

My stomach fluttered, and my chest tightened at his words.

A new air was surrounding our traveling party, and it was going to change everything.

CHAPTER 33

I plopped my bedroll down on one of the few areas that roots had not taken over, groaning as I knelt, using what little energy I had left to flatten the stubborn parts that insisted on staying rolled. I tried to stand back up, but the thin padding felt too good on my knees, inviting the rest of my body to lie upon it. I knew I shouldn't, not when Alaric and Neo were still busy unpacking, but the temptation was too great. With a nod of my head, I sprawled on the bedroll and felt instant release, some parts of my body popping back into their natural positions.

"It's as comfortable as you made it look," Neo groaned out in pleasure, laying across from me in the same manner. "I'd never thought I'd find something more comfortable than my bed back in Rivelia."

"That's because you've never traveled for this long," Alaric stated, standing over his fully made bedroll—the only one in our group who had bothered to put a blanket over it. "Do you think you two can manage to light a fire before I get back?" Alaric asked, unbuckling his dagger and sword from his belt.

I lifted my head to get a better view of him, confused as to where he would even go without his weapons. He was always harping on me and Neo not to go anywhere, even to relieve ourselves, without a sword or a dagger, despite being a living weapon. He wanted us to save that tactic for the blood demons.

Seeing the question on my face, Alaric answered, "I'm going hunting, the only exception to the rule as our wolf form is much more efficient."

I quickly attempted to stand up, but I only managed to sluggishly move my legs under me and turn so I fully faced Alaric. "It's my turn to hunt," I challenged, not wanting to force my duties onto anyone, despite my body screaming at me to rest.

Alaric's eyes raked over me, but not in the judgmental way that he did before. He looked at me as if was assessing my health, my energy. He looked at me in the way that someone who cared did. It made my stomach twist and flutter. It was unsettling.

"You're tired," he said dismissively.

I pushed off my thighs, forcing myself to stand. "That doesn't matter. It's my turn. You cooked breakfast these past few days and went hunting yesterday. It's only fair I hunt on my designated day."

Alaric sucked on his lips, cocking his head so his eyes were askew to the sky. "You've been up since the sun rose, and you've been traveling all day. Your scent is becoming weaker and weaker." Neo sniffed the air. Immediately, his brows pushed together as if he was confused. "If you were to go hunt, that would surely drain the last of your energy, making you useless in a battle," Alaric stiffly said. "I'm taking your turn. That's final."

I opened my mouth to fight him, to tell him that he too had exerted the same amount of energy, probably even more than me today, but by the time any sound escaped my lips, Alaric had shifted and was leaping into the forest.

I gritted my teeth, hand on my sword, debating whether I should unhook my own weapons and follow him.

"Don't," Neo called from his bedroll.

I turned to him.

"He needs to rest," I bit out more aggressively than I had intended.

Neo's eyelashes fluttered, his head withdrawing into his neck, before sitting up.

"What?" I asked, stepping back.

"It's just odd seeing you show real concern for him." Neo crossed his legs. "I'm not used to it yet."

A deep red I didn't quite understand flashed across my face. It was fine for me to be concerned about Alaric, especially now that he was on our side and our days had become so grueling.

After Alaric vowed to protect humans, he seemed to have returned to the male I had heard numerous tales about—a driven and ambitious leader. He woke us just as the sun rose with a meal plated for each of us. He made us train until we were soaked in sweat then had us on the road just as the sun's rays warmed the earth.

It was an impressive feat that we had kept up with this routine for days but even more so for Alaric, as he was the first to wake and the last to sleep. It was admirable, almost inspiring. I didn't know how out of all of us, he seemed to be the one with the most energy. It was completely illogical and part of me worried that it was a high from his renewed passion for protecting the humans or his vow to me.

"He's part of our party," I said in way of explanation.

"He was part of our party before, and you didn't show concern," Neo rebutted.

"He was, but by a deal."

Neo rocked his head side-to-side, internally debating something. Finally, he shrugged, weirdly displeased, but didn't say anything more as he began to stack some twigs on one another.

I rolled my eyes, too tired to inquire why.

Perhaps it was good that Alaric took over the hunt, had scented that I was near exhaustion. It certainly was kind. I'd have to thank him later but also make sure he didn't do it again. He needed to be rested as well. I just needed to get used to exerting the same amount of energy he did.

"Looks like you've got a handle on the fire," I said as more of a statement than a question to change the topic.

Neo nodded as I sat on my bedroll. "Taking a nap before dinner?" he inquired, not an ounce of judgment in his voice.

"I'm going to practice my silver training."

"Have fun," Neo mused, turning back to tend to the fire as I sat down and placed the dagger in front of me, careful not to touch the silver just yet.

I breathed in deeply, opening and closing my hands. Both of them had healed from touching the silver, but still, my stomach twisted, and my heart pounded. My entire body begged me not to touch it. I pushed the feeling away, blaming it on the fact that I hadn't practiced in days due to the new tiring schedule, certain my body only remembered the initial pain when I first started and not the slight tingling that had occurred the last time I practiced. Once all the fear had left, I quickly gripped the hilt with my more experienced hand.

Pain ruptured through me, much greater than when I had first started. I began to see sporadic dark spots in the woods. My senses became dull. It was like the time I had been stabbed with a silver blade. I breathed in deeper, and against all common sense, I held the hilt tighter, telling myself that this was shock, that I needed to at least make it to the count of thirty. However, the pain didn't subside. The dots took over my vision. The world spun. A howl, a scared howl echoed through the forest.

It sounded like Alaric's.

I tried to look around, tried to let go of the dagger as the pain grew greater, but my eyes shut.

Something plush draped over my body, smelling of pine and sandalwood. The crackle of a roaring fire tickled my ears, and the scent of roasted rabbit made my mouth water, beckoning me to wake.

With great effort, my eyelids slowly opened. The world was foggy. I closed them and opened them once more, rubbing the sleep out of them, discovering that my left hand had been wrapped.

I examined the fresh linen, wondering. I didn't remember dressing my hand nor did I remember putting the dagger down.

I sat up, hissing as I foolishly pushed my hand against the ground to keep myself balanced.

Not far, away leaves crunched, and a sharp inhale echoed.

I faced the noise, finding Alaric, a bit of color returning to his pale face.

"You're awake," he whispered with relief.

I cocked my head, completely confused at the sight of him still up despite the moon directly overhead.

"So are you. Why?" I rubbed my eyes once again, starting to think this was all a strange dream.

"It was that bad," Alaric grumbled to himself.

"What?" I attempted to ask with an edge, but my growling stomach lessened the effect.

Alaric hastily stood, grabbing a stick of meat that was close enough to the fire that it keep the meat warm but far enough away that it no longer cooked. "Here. Eat this."

I accepted it and took a small bite of the tender meat, hoping that it would calm my stomach. However, the sweet juices that coated my tongue only made my stomach grow louder.

"That's a relief," mused Alaric. "Your appetite is a good sign that the silver didn't take too much of an effect on you."

Silver? Didn't take too much effect?

It was just a bit of pain. A normal day of training. I didn't know why Alaric was being so odd. I had picked up the dagger and...

I straightened, unable to recall how long I held it or when I put it down. I ran through my mind, trying to recall the memory. Finally, my heart pounded.

"I blacked out," I whispered, more for myself than Alaric.

"You did." Alaric squatted in front of me.

"Why? I've never done that before. I didn't even hold it for that long," I rambled, starting to panic, hating that I didn't know what was wrong with my body.

Alaric gingerly grabbed my wrist, pulling my hand to him, causing my stomach to flutter.

I pulled away, concerned that he had caused the feeling too many times now, but Alaric didn't let me stray too far from him.

"I believe it was a combination of fatigue and not having practiced in a while. It's been three days, correct?"

I nodded, amazed that he had been paying such close attention to my training.

Alaric began to untie my bandages, revealing my reddened palm and the tiny blisters that had burst. I gasped. Even when I first started my training, I had never gained a wound like this.

"It would have been much worse if Neo hadn't knocked it out of your hand," Alaric explained, gingerly applying some ointment to my skin.

My eyes widened, impressed with my stubbornness, but not for long as I remembered that Neo hadn't asked for his blade back, hadn't so much as touched silver in weeks. If he had knocked the dagger from my hand, he had to have touched the metal.

Frantically, I looked for Neo, worried that he had shared my pain. Thankfully, I found him on his bedroll quickly, his back turned to me. Still, it didn't ease my concern, so I called his name.

"He's fine. He's just sleeping. He's taking second watch," Alaric assured, squeezing my wrist so tenderly that one would mistake it as comfort, but I knew it was to remind me to stay still as he worked on my hand. "He's used to silver, remember? That's his dagger you practice with."

"That's exactly why I'm concerned." I turned my attention back to Alaric. "If I'm like this after a couple days, wouldn't he be hurting far worse? He hasn't held his blade in weeks."

Alaric smirked, shaking his head. "You remember how I said there would be consequences if you rushed your silver training?" I scraped my tongue on my canines, silently answering yes. "This is one of them. Normally, if you learn slowly and after you've mastered the resistance, your tolerance isn't affected if you wait a couple weeks or so. However, it seems"—Alaric resumed wrapping my hand so gently that I wouldn't have noticed if it were not for the heat radiating off him—"when you rush it, that tolerance goes away quickly."

"Oh," I sighed out, realizing that I'd have to start again. "I wish you would have told me that detail when you first said it was useless."

"It was a detail I didn't know." Alaric's hand slipped from my wrist to the back of mine, maneuvering my hand to check his work. "Would you have listened if I had, though?"

I sheepishly looked away.

"That's what I thought," Alaric said, completely taking his hand off mine. An odd sense of cold coated over me. "At least we know now." Alaric stood. "So, please, take it easy. You scared both of us."

Alaric began to walk back to his little stump by the fire.

"You're not going to tell me to stop with the training?" I asked in disbelief, sure that despite Alaric having changed his views, his arrogant personality would take over and use this as an opportunity.

Alaric met my eyes. "As I said before, you have been right about so many things. I'm sure you're right about this skill coming in handy."

My palms turned clammy. "You're not still in doubt of yourself, are you?" I asked carefully, scared that hidden sadness would claim him out of the blue.

Alaric tucked his hands into the pockets of his trousers, and his lips raised partially as he shook his head. "I just have more faith and admiration for you than I did when I first met you. Not a lot of wolves can say they were able to touch silver for as long as you did with your little time of training, nor would they have been able to keep up with my training program and still have the will to keep going. You're remarkable."

My cheeks heated instantly. "Tha—thank—thank you," I somehow managed to say, blaming the shyness on the shock of Alaric behaving out of character. He was so much nicer of a male now.

Alaric's throat bobbed, and he sucked in his lower lip, as if he was resisting something. I cocked my head, wondering what was going on, but finally, he monotonously said, "Get some sleep, Ina. Your wounds won't heal without proper rest."

CHAPTER 34

I rode next to Neo and Alaric, rubbing my fingertips together impatiently as I counted the days since the demons had attacked Artico. It felt like just yesterday with how much bloodshed haunted my mind at night, the nightmares becoming more and more vivid with each passing day.

I wanted to hurry and run to the demon's castle, finally put an end to their existence, stop them from hurting anyone else. I couldn't imagine how many lives they had ruined already. However, I knew from the way my body ached unbearably and how Alaric had eased our training, we were going as fast as we could. I just prayed we wouldn't have any more obstacles in between us and them. But as if the gods had mocked my prayer, my lower abdomen began to throb, like someone had reached inside and squeezed it until it was on the verge of bursting.

I leaned forward, clamping my hand over the pain, hoping that the warmth would sooth it. I took deep breaths, wondering what on earth was going on, until I remembered the day—a month after the mating ceremony.

My heat was coming.

A couple sniffs sounded from the other side of Neo, then Alaric asked, "Ina, are you in pain?"

I twisted, just enough to see him looking over with concerned eyes. Neo's attention followed shortly after. Though Neo's eyes flicked to Alaric before me, as if he was trying to figure out how his brother noticed my compromised position first with him in between us.

"Alaric, you don't happen to have a mate, do you?" I uttered, answering his question with another.

Neo stiffened further, whereas Alaric slumped down with relief.

"I've never found one in all my years of life," Alaric sighed, clear disappointment in his tone.

I cursed to the gods.

Of course, this had to happen now and with an unmated male around.

"We'll have to part ways for a bit, then," I said, taking a gulp of air in an attempt to calm the pain before sitting up, annoyed that my warning cramps were always so terrible. "Or," I began hesitantly, unsure if I wanted to offer the solution I had used the past years, "you and I could—"

"We're deep in enemy territory. If we separate, that would be a great risk," Neo exclaimed, leaning over, his hand hovering close to my reins.

I exhaled, wondering if Neo hadn't gotten the hint or had forgotten, after he was mated, what a female in heat did to an unmated male.

"I agree," Alaric added. "Not only are we close to the demons' castle, but this area is also known to have rogue wolves who've lost too much of their humanity to the elements."

I rolled my eyes, realizing that it was the former of the options for both males. I would have to say this bluntly.

"I'm about to start my heat," I bit out, cocking my head in frustration at both the males.

"All the more reason for you stay with us," Alaric stated flatly, taking a sip from his wineskin. "Your shifter form is weaker during your heat. You'd be helpless in a fight on your own."

"We've been traveling for weeks and haven't run into any trouble. I'm confident that luck will continue," I argued, not mentioning the other option, since Alaric hadn't either. Now that he knew we were talking about my heat, he could infer what the second option I was trying to give was. And if his silence on the topic was any indication, I was certain he didn't want it, which I didn't blame him for. Things between him and I were complicated enough as is. I doubted, even in a friendly manner, he'd want to do *that*. "Also, I wouldn't be useless. You've helped me improve on my ability to fight using swords and so forth. Me staying and my heat affecting you is the greater risk," I claimed.

"Trust me. It's not." Alaric wiped some water from his lips. "Your heat won't affect me."

I pulled back on my reins, stopping our party.

What Alaric was saying was impossible. While a male's reaction around a female in heat differed from male to male due to different variables—compatibility, attraction, how much of their wolf they let out, and of course, how similar they were to their future mate—there would always be some affect, even if it was miniscule. And even then, it still messed with a male's mind. It could make him less effective in battle, or it could make tensions rise. We couldn't afford for that to happen, not when we finally were behaving like a united, cohesive group.

"Alaric, I know you're very confident in yourself, but what you're saying isn't possible. Even if you were at the peak of your hatred for me, the heat would still affect you. There was someone in my own pack who was my rival, and my heat still made me desirable to him," I added, thinking of Rainer. Though Rainer did think I was attractive, so I suppose I had that to blame on my heat enticing him.

My eyes widened.

Could it be that Alaric didn't find me attractive at all?

My jaw slacked.

Wait, did I want him to be?

I shook my head. Of course I didn't. Well, not in the way someone who fancied another did. I was just conceited. I hadn't liked anyone before, and I wasn't going to start now.

Alaric rolled his head between his shoulders, effectively popping it. "I've just had too many disappointing"—he bit his lower lip, contemplating the word he wanted to use—"*interactions*," he drawled. "My body doesn't react anymore."

My chest puffed. So, it was the fact that he wasn't attracted to me that he felt so confident in my heat not taking hold of him.

Blinded by vainness, I quipped, "Why? Because they all rejected you?"

Neo, who had just taken a gulp of water, spat everywhere.

Surprisingly, Alaric chuckled, one side of his mouth turning up as if he found humor in my question.

I leaned away, still unused to his new character. The one that had a sense of humor, was patient and kind, and even chivalrous from time to time. It was so unlike the Alaric I knew. But then again, I only knew the one who hated me, not the one I was on decent terms with, maybe even friendly terms. Perhaps this was his true nature.

Alaric looked at me from the corner of his mischievous eyes. "On the contrary, I've had all that I've desired. Some more than once, simply because they *begged* for more afterward," he purred, his voice edged with sensuality and a sprinkle of pride. It had me grinding my teeth in something that felt like anger, and from how Alaric's smirk turned into a grin, I knew that was the reaction he wanted from me.

Annoyed but also a little pleased that he liked to play these games, I bit out, "Then, what made these interactions so disappointing? It hardly sounds like an awful time."

"It's—" Alaric froze, his nose turning up, his devilish grin vanishing in the blink of an eye.

I turned my nose in the same direction his did, inhaling deeply. I stiffened.

"That's a lot of blood," Neo faintly whispered.

My throat closed, and I grew dizzy as I smelled the too strong scent of iron in the air. However, the distinct scent wasn't what had me snapping the reins in my hand, urging Irie to sprint forward. It was what accompanied it. It was the scent of silver.

CHAPTER 35

"Slow down," Alaric bellowed a couple feet behind me.

I ran faster, refusing to listen to his words, fueled by the sickening smell of blood that grew thicker with every step.

The blood demons were here, wrecking whatever carnage their monstrous urges desired. Carnage that I had once seen before. Carnage that I swore would never happen again. However, as I cleared the thicket, I knew that promise was broken.

Smoke rose from the skeletons of several small cottages. Blood stained the earth. Lines of freshly stripped grass randomly snaked through and around the village, all of them leading to lifeless bodies that dotted the ground. Some of them had their eyes closed, whereas others were open, the dull pupils staring at one of the many gashes that decorated their owner's body, their mouths wide open as if they died screaming in agony.

The blood demons had decimated an entire village.

I quaked, my breathing hastening as I frantically searched the area below me for the monsters that had done this. There was no sign of them, except for a single trail of disfigured bodies, messily drank from, discarded like the demons were in a hurry to be gone.

I gripped Irie's reins, ready to race after them, to take vengeance for the innocent people who they fed on, but rough hands gripped mine.

I snapped around, baring my canines. "Let me go," I snarled to Alaric, who looked over me with a sense of calm and grief.

He only held tighter, even dared to pull my hands off the reins. "They're gone, Ina."

I shook my head, not wanting to fail for another time. "I'll go after them. I can catch up in wolf form." I dismounted Irie, taking a step toward the village. "I can—"

"You'll die," Alaric warned, standing only a foot away from me, his composure like that of a seasoned commander. The warrior in me had no choice but to halt. "Judging by how the blood has crusted and the nearly snuffed fires, I'd guess that the demons left a couple hours ago. You'd have to run *hard* to catch up. By the time you did, your wolf would have the energy to deal with one of them, maybe two, if you hadn't been traveling for weeks." Alaric took a step forward. "And let me tell you, Ina, as disgusting as the demons are, two cannot drink this much blood in one sitting. This is the work of twenty or so."

I examined the destruction in front of me, looked at all the signs that Alaric had pointed out, at all the truths I had ignored. My throat closed. My chest heaved in and out as I tried to get more air, tried to find the strength to keep standing, to look at the aftermath of an attack of only twenty blood demons and realized that this was what Artico probably looked like now, but I found none.

I dropped to the ground, knees roaring in pain as pebbles dug into my flesh.

"I failed," I cried, unable to contain the emotions that were bursting. "I failed again."

"You couldn't have done anything to prevent this." Alaric knelt beside me. One of his hands slipped under my chin, lifting it to meet his eyes while the other gently wiped tears—I did not know had fallen—away.

He held me like that for what seemed like an eternity, forgiving me for all the things I blamed myself for but could not control.

My wheezing and whimpering turned to shallow breaths then deep ones.

Alaric nodded, approving of my calming, not an ounce of judgment toward me. For a moment, I leaned in, resting my temple in the nook of his collarbone. It fit perfectly, bringing me so much peace.

"Don't be scared," Neo rang out, far from where we knelt, causing me and Alaric to snap to him.

Neo stood by one of the burned-down cottages in the middle of the village, the interior completely bare to the outside world, with only one wall surviving, miraculously staying up by the handful of beams. However, even those were giving way, shaking as the wind swept through, exploring what it could not before.

Neo looked up at the shaking beams then back down, holding out his hand to something in the wreckage. "Please, come here. It's not safe in there."

I followed his gaze, finding a boy of maybe five.

A survivor.

I jumped to my feet, and my adrenaline peaked as the child stepped further back into the hut, clutching the hem of his soot-covered tunic, and bumped into the worn wall. Dribbles of tiny debris fell.

The house was going to come down.

I raced forward, willing my body to shift so I could make it in time, but my wolf refused. I cursed, knowing that my heat was already prolonging my shifting time.

It would take another minute or two to rise the magic in me, and that was time I didn't have.

I ran faster, telling myself that I couldn't let another die, that I couldn't allow life to slip away when I was nearby, but the beams cracked.

I lunged, hoping that if I reached the boy, my body would be strong enough to take the weight of the beams. I even told myself I was going to make it, but when I looked up at the boy again, he was gone.

Fanatically, I spun, searching for him, not caring that I had mere seconds before the cottage came crashing down. I didn't even stop when a bigger piece of debris fell, scraping my back. I just kept looking.

I wouldn't leave without knowing if he got out. I refused to. But before I went deeper into the wreckage, a bigger body rammed into mine, pushing me out of the rubble until we both tumbled to unscorched ground.

I coughed and gasped, crawling out of the arms of Alaric and back toward the cottage, but I was too late. The wood came crashing down, splintering as it hit the earth.

"No," I screeched, my speed picking up, uncaring that wood ricocheted off the ground.

"The lumber is going to hit you," Alaric roared, jumping on top of me, using his own body as a shield.

I fought against him, but he did not budge, not until the crashing of wood stopped and all that filled my ears was the soft crackle of fire feasting on the aftermath.

"Ina," Alaric began, but I pushed him away as I sat up and stared at the rubble, at the burial site of the boy. I blinked rapidly, balling my hands, torn between crying or screaming at the male behind me. But then, wailing pierced my ears, followed by hearty coughs. I turned to the sound, my somber thoughts evaporating at the hope that mused in my ears, and through blurred eyes, I focused on the cloud of dust ahead, on a shadow that held a tinier one.

"Thank the gods," Alaric murmured, standing not too far from me as Neo and the boy emerged from the dust. "You both made it out unscathed."

My eyes widened at the relief in Alaric's tone, at the lack of rage in the fact that Neo had risked his life for the boy.

Alaric had made it abundantly clear at the start of our journey that no matter what, he would not allow Neo to risk his life. He even went as far as to claim that he would allow others to be sacrificed first before his brother was harmed. But now, as he smiled proudly at his brother, it seemed that rule no longer applied. That, despite his speed and the opportunity to try and grab Neo from the rubble, he had chosen to protect me. It made sense strategically, as Neo had been farther away from Alaric and closer to the child than I, but that would mean Alaric had confidence in his brother's ability and that he saw me and Neo as equal value, and that was a farfetched reality.

"Yeah, we did," Neo replied softly, rocking the child who now clutched to him. "Barely, though. I jumped out just as you reached Ina."

"We'll need to work on your speed," Alaric said in the way a brother trying to hide his proudness with critiques would.

Maybe I wasn't too wrong in my theory. At least in the part where Alaric had confidence in Neo. He had been excelling at his training lately.

Alaric stepped closer. The boy curled further into Neo, causing Alaric to immediately retract.

"It's alright. It's just my brother, and he's only scary when you're on his bad side," Neo whispered to the child.

"That's true." Alaric offered a soft smile that warmed my heart. "I just wanted to check and see if you were ok," he whispered with the sweetest of voices, trying to gain the child's trust. Though, no matter how sweet he sounded, the child did not show any inclination that he would talk. Both Neo and Alaric looked to the ground in utter defeat and loss as did I.

I was never skilled in comforting children nor understood their quirks and such. However, we needed the child to talk, to trust us so we could figure out how to aid him best and what our next move was.

Alaric turned up his head, taking a deep breath, as if summoning some secret skill he had buried deep inside him. He bent ever so slightly, so he was at the child's eye level, then whispered in the kindest voice, "I like your bear. He's rather charming looking." The boy perked, intrigued by words he could relate to. "He reminds me of the one I used to have. What's his name? Mine was called Pip."

The boy turned slightly, curiosity in his eyes as he clutched his bear closer.

Alaric allowed both sides of his lips to rise just a bit, ever inviting.

"Tuffy," the child mumbled against the plushie that he held tighter.

"That's a wonderful name for a bear." The boy nodded in agreement. "Can I see him?"

A sort of tension grew in the air as the child stared intently at his bear, as if he was waiting for the inanimate object to give him the answer. If he were to say no, I wasn't quite sure what we would do next.

"He's a bit dirty," the boy mumbled again, his voice a little more audible than last time.

"That's fine. It just means he's had a bit of an adventure."

The boy gave Alaric one final look before his eyes drifted back to his bear, thinking hard once again. But finally, after many quiet moments, he held out his toy, inviting Alaric to approach.

Alaric slowly did, making sure not to step on anything that may make noise. Tenderly, he took the bear, making sure not to flinch at the grime and fabric that had clotted together by blood and took a moment to *admire* it.

"He's very soft," Alaric declared, handing him back. "He must've kept you excellent company out here. I'm sure he's nowhere near as much fun as your parents, though." The boy nodded, clutching the toy to his chest. It was confirmation enough that he was out here by himself. "What happened to them?"

The child met Alaric's eyes, searching for whatever a child looked for when debating to trust someone. After a moment, with a shaky finger, he pointed at two bodies—a male and a female—cold on the ground, just a few feet away. "They went to sleep after they tried to help the people in the cages," he whispered.

"Cages?" I questioned. I had never heard of demons crating people around, as humans were everywhere.

The child nodded. "Daddy said that if we freed them, we'd have a fighting chance, but the monsters didn't let us near them at all. And the people in cages kept yelling at us to run away, that it was them that was supposed to protect us."

My shoulders scrunched up as Neo and Alaric stiffened, the air turning cold as I asked, "What did the people in the cages look like?"

CHAPTER 36

"You told me there were no survivors," I seethed at Neo, stalking the worn-down path I had made.

"That's what my father's scouts said, what my father told me," Neo sputtered, standing a respectable distance away from me as my anger was nearing a terrifying amount.

I was surprised that Alaric had even let his brother follow me into the woods, but I suppose someone had to stay with the child, keep him from the sight of me. He didn't need to be frightened any further. Though I wasn't sure why or when the child had been given to Alaric, as I had bolted once the boy had answered my question, already feeling the panic and fury rising in me. I knew I needed to burn off energy before it summoned my wolf. Still, even now, I only thought about the caged people who wore heavy furs and red dresses, described exactly as how my pack had dressed the night of the mating ritual, the night of the attack. I thought of who they were, and no matter how long I did, I always came to conclude that the caged people were Artico Wolves. I was sure of it.

"And tell me, do you think that's because they're horrible at their jobs or was it another of your father's many lies in an attempt to keep me in Rivelia?" I roared, not daring to keep my anger hidden.

A distant whimper and Alaric's consoling whispered in my ears, earning me a pointed look from Neo.

I bit my lip, calming myself. As much as my anger grew, adding to the child's abundant fear was not worth it.

"I'm sorry," I whispered. "I'm just worried. I've never heard stories of the demons keeping shifter prisoners."

Neo drifted toward me. "Neither have I, but we already know that so many things were kept from us. Maybe this was too. Perhaps Alaric knows something."

"I'm sorry to say I do," Alaric whispered, emerging into view with the child—who we now knew as Emile—curled up in his arms, fast asleep.

My skin crawled as the light shimmering through the leaves revealed Alaric's grim expression.

"It was near the end of the war, at least when we found out, which is why it's not common knowledge." Alaric bounced the child in his arm, leaning back to make sure he was still asleep.

It was odd to see him so caring over the thing he had hated so much, to see his gestures so natural, but I suppose they were, and the past twenty years were unnatural for him.

"As you both know, the war lasted a while, not because of the matched warriors from both sides but because the demons were like roaches living under rocks, always hard to find. And once we did, no matter how many of them we killed, they always came back. The number of forces was always the same as before, replenished by humans they turned by force or lulled with false promises." Alaric sat down on a boulder, a shadow crossing over his eyes, as if recalling the events that were a storm of bad memories. "It was difficult to fight it, emotionally and physically. Still, we kept going. All the packs from the north, the south, the east, and the west pushed through the hurt. We killed the humans who had turned, who begged for mercy, for the bloodlust to stop."

I stiffened, my own throat closing. I knew that blood demons could add to their ranks by turning humans, but it never seemed real to me. It never seemed like it was something the demons would actually do, that they would send those freshly turned to fight us. There had to so many faces that the wolves knew, had protected once.

"We fought until the continent was almost rid of them, until their numbers started to be fewer each battle. We were winning after so many years, but then, despite the smaller numbers, we started to lose wolves, entire packs." Alaric blinked rapidly, cocking his head so his eyes did not meet ours. "We didn't understand, especially when it was primarily the newly turned that took us down. They should've been awkward with their new bodies, their new talents, but they fought twice as hard as the older demons, moved twice as quick. It wasn't until a couple other wolves and I were sent to one of the demons' camps to lessen their numbers that we found out why.

"The newly turned demons—consumed with blood lust from all the fighting—did something that even the vilest demon deemed taboo. They allowed blood that had no business ever touching to mingle. They fed on wolves."

My breathing halted, remembering that a demon drank from Catrine. I hadn't thought much of it, as I had been too shocked during the battle and too caught up with the thought of killing the demons now. But thinking about it now, there wasn't much information recorded about demons, as we had the tendency to destroy them just as quickly as they appeared. However, what little information we had was that the demons' life source, their power was obtained by the blood they drank. It was why most survivors, if the demons' stomachs were too full that day, were children and the elderly. The stronger the human, the more energized the demons were. If they had fed on us, our strength—the strength that ran through our blood—would be theirs.

This couldn't be real. They would be unstoppable.

Seeing the denial in my face, Alaric whispered, "It can be done. I saw it that night. They feasted on wolves who were on the brink of death. They gleamed at the taste of power that danced on their tongues."

I griped my stomach and clamped a hand over my mouth, trying to keep myself from being sick.

"Why didn't they do it before?" Neo asked, his voice low, like the question itself was a terror.

"From what I overheard that night, our blood gives them strength, but it also poisons them. They must drink double the amount of blood they normally do to sustain themselves, and if they want to feel satisfied, they have to drink shifter blood again."

"Yet, they still did it?" I asked.

Alaric nodded, his soft hands turning into fists. "I believe they were desperate and wanted the war to end just as badly as us. It's why we almost lost the Siege of Rivelia. It's also why expelling them from our land matters more now than ever.

"During the war, only a handful of wolves had gone missing before the attack on Rivelia, meaning only a few demons drank. If they're collecting cages of wolves now, they will be so much stronger than all those years ago."

I backed away, chest caving in deeply.

I wanted to scream, to run, to punch something.

How was this ever kept from us? Kept from all the packs?

If Alaric had known the truth, then surely his father did, yet he still chose to live inside his walls when I brought the news of the demons return. And my pack was in cages, waiting to be eaten, for their blood to be drained.

"Why?" I raged, stalking toward Alaric. He passed Emile to Neo. "How many more secrets do you and your father have?" Alaric remained still, despite my canines inches from his face. "Tell me all of them, now," I demanded, the hate that had been fading away flooding back.

"It wasn't my place to tell you, not unless it turned out the information was needed," he replied like a soldier reporting to a leader.

"Did you not think it was needed when I walked in and told you that Artico had been attacked? That I watched my people being fed on?"

Alaric looked away, guilt apparent in his eyes. I shoved him back.

"It wouldn't have changed the outcome," Alaric said in response. "It would've just added another worry to your mind when we weren't even sure that they were collecting wolves or feeding on them again. From what you told us, the carnage was too great for them to collect a substantial number of prisoners to feast on."

I shook my head, refusing to see reason. "I don't believe that! It was to protect your father's image again, wasn't it? And don't lie to me. My people are being tortured because of you."

I went to shove Alaric again, but he caught my hands.

"I did it for your father, too," Alaric growled.

I froze. "What do you mean by that?" I lethally asked.

Alaric sucked in his cheek, regret apparent in his stature. "Your father was visiting Rivelia when I came back with my report. He knew about the demons' secret, and he chose, just like my father, to keep it from the rest of the wolves."

"My father always told the truth," I mewled, trying to come to Father's defense, but my voice lacked confidence, as nary a scent of nervousness professed off Alaric.

"He did, but he also knew that sometimes there is strength in lies. Your father, like mine, knew morale was waning," Alaric explained. "They knew revealing the truth about the demons would increase panic and would affect the armies fighting. So, they took it upon themselves to figure out how to combat the strong blood demon force. It's why your father's army was in Rivelia the night of the siege, why they took a detour."

I shrunk back, not wanting to hear anymore, but I still asked, "And what about after the war?"

Alaric released my hands. They dropped to my sides, as all my strength went to keeping myself standing.

"The war was over, and the blood demons were gone from the continent. They figured the truth was unneeded. After all, the only thing that would come of the news, would be giving wolves another item to add to their list of things that kept them awake at night, kept them from returning to normalcy." I wrapped my arms around me. "They also didn't want the information spreading through the continent or the world. We didn't know if there were other demons on other continents or other shifters. If there were, the news would invite the former to ours, and it would make the latter vulnerable. It became a secret that only a select few were allowed to know."

My heart dropped as my fury melted away. I hated to admit it, but everything Alaric said made sense and justified our fathers' actions. It was time to end this blaming game and plan our next steps.

"I'm so sorry. I'm sorry to both of you." Alaric said, nodding to Neo and me.

"We need to move faster," I commanded, pushing away the feelings of betrayal.

Alaric straightened and stayed quiet for a moment, examining me, making sure I was of steady mind. After a while he nodded. "Ok, but first, we need to figure out what to do with Emile."

"You want me to go?" Neo asked with wide eyes, wrinkles on his forehead. His expression matching how I felt.

I couldn't believe what Alaric had just suggested. I could only imagine the disbelief Neo was feeling as this was the opposite of everything Alaric had told him his entire life.

"Yes. The child needs a place to stay, and the only humans we know and semi trust are Amos and his family. However, we can't afford to go backward in distance," Alaric explained, rubbing his temple.

"I understand that," Neo faltered. "It's just, you were very adamant that we all stay together."

"Can you not handle being on your own for a couple of days?" Alaric asked with an edge of annoyance.

"No. It's fine. I mean, I can." Neo looked at me with raised brows, looking for reassurance that he wasn't the only one confused. I shrugged my shoulders. "I just don't understand the sudden change."

Alaric twisted, meeting both our eyes plainly. "We are near the nomadic pack, and I am the only one who can track them. It should take me a couple days to find their trail, time enough for you to get to Amos, drop off the child, and return," Alaric gritted through closed teeth, making it clear that he was fighting his own words. It was further proof that he was changing from the wolf I had originally met. "It's the only logical plan," Alaric claimed. I wondered if it was more for Neo or himself.

Still, Neo didn't move. Instead, he scanned the forest, his chest expanding, as if he was nervous. Alaric huffed and grabbed Neo's satchel with hurried force, not allowing anything physical or mental to stop him.

"You're leaving, now." Alaric tied the bag to his horse. Neo's stare ricocheted between his and Alaric's horse. "She's the fastest," Alaric pointedly informed.

"Wouldn't it be safer to leave in the morning?" Neo rebutted, finally having the brain to speak.

"This allows us to be separated the least number of days, since Ina and I won't travel tonight." Alaric quietly but quickly took Emile from me, so gently that the boy only mumbled incoherently then resumed his snoring. "Come on," Alaric commanded, jerking his head to his horse, signaling to Neo to get on.

Neo did so but with a shaky hand.

He was scared. But I would have thought he would have looked forward to this. To his first—

This was Neo's first mission alone.

During mine—despite preparing, knowing that it would happen all my life—my heart had hammered so hard I couldn't even hear myself think. It was natural that Neo was nervous, especially now that we knew how powerful the blood demons were.

"Keep him in front. That will make riding easiest." Alaric handed Emile to Neo then patted the horse's mane. "You keep him safe," he whispered to the steed, "and Neo, remember to travel there only by horse. You'll need your strength to get back to us in wolf form." Neo gave Alaric a look. "I want you back as soon as possible, and our wolves are thrice as fast as our human legs. Not to mention, we can't expect Amos and his family to take in another person when they've already given us so much. You must give them back the horse so they can sell it and this"—Alaric pulled out a couple gold coins—"then shift back and run straight to us. No matter what, do not stop for anything else." Neo nodded, but still looked off into the distance fearfully. A grimacing smile formed on Alaric's face. "You'll be fine. I've watched you train and grow. I know you can do this. This is what you were meant for, what you've wanted all your life. This is your last mission before you're ready to fight the demons. Now, go."

Alaric slapped the horse's behind, sending Neo and Emile into the darkness. He watched them go until they were out of sight. Then, with a heavy sigh, he turned around, his head tilted down, not allowing our eyes to meet. "Let's set up camp," he mumbled, stalking past me.

CHAPTER 37

The silence was deafening, almost unbearable, teetering on driving me insane as I sat across from Alaric for the third night in a row alone. I wanted so badly for sleep to take over, to feel my eyelids start to fall so I could escape this awkwardness. However, my body was still thrumming with worry for Neo, for his return tomorrow, and for my pack. I was sure Alaric's was as well. Not sure, certain. He glanced backward, sniffed the air, and shook his leg far too often for it to be any other answer.

His tension was as unnerving as the silence that yelled between us, and it had gotten far worse with each passing day. It was making me anxious to the point where I could barely concentrate on anything else.

I had to do something.

I stood up, taking off my cloak. Alaric looked on with interest.

"Let's spar," I declared, squatting a few feet from our fire.

He scoffed, adding another log to the fire. "We aren't doing that until Neo returns. We need all our energy to look for the Woodland Pack's trail and to defend ourselves if anything happens."

I came out of my squat. "Come on," I urged, unable to think of anything else to get Alaric's mind off his worries. "I have more than plenty of energy to burn."

"Rest," he ordered flatly, peaking at the woods once again.

I pushed my tongue against my canines, feeling the sharpness of them, knowing I would have to escalate this.

I stormed in front of him, blocking his view. "Do you not have energy to spar? If you don't, all you have to do is tell me." I shrugged my shoulders. "You are older, after all."

Alaric scoffed once. "Turning to insults, now?"

"Maybe? Is it working?"

Alaric turned back to the fire, poking it with a long, sturdy branch. "It's a waste of your energy."

I snatched the wood, redirecting his attention back to me. His brows flared.

"Well, if it's a waste, help me waste it on something useful."

Alaric rubbed his temple. "You're not going to relent on this, are you?" I stepped back into the clearing, raising my fists in answer. "Fine, but only one round."

I smirked, glad things had gone my way and raised up on the tips of my toes. Finally, Alaric's mind would be distracted, and the camp wouldn't be shrouded in concern. However, that would only last for as long as I kept the fight going. Which, to be honest, I wasn't sure how long I would last. Alaric and I hadn't fought since we learned the truth of our mothers, and back then, I hadn't lasted more than five minutes. Either way, I would give it my all.

"That's how you're going to start?" Alaric challenged, standing dismissively in front of me.

I tilted my head, jaw clenched.

"I haven't heard that condescending tone in a while," I accidentally hissed out.

Alaric rolled back his shoulders. "You wanted to spar one on one. I assumed you wanted feedback too," Alaric said with menacing sweetness.

I forced a smile. Maybe I had pushed him a bit too far, crossed a boundary that kept us cordial.

"Sure," I replied, keeping my stance.

"Good, then come at me, and I'll tell you what was wrong with it after you fall."

Alaric held up two fingers then pulled them toward himself, relaxed as ever about my impending attack. And despite my every intention for this fight to be nothing but a friendly match, the action had a fire sparking inside me. I sprinted forward.

Alaric gloated, sidestepping my attack. I huffed and threw back my arm, hoping to at least get a hit to his back, but he swirled and kicked out his leg, knocking me to the ground. I barely had time to regain my composure before his fist flew and stopped inches from my face.

"And that's match." Alaric unfolded his fist, offering to help me up.

"Again," I demanded, pushing off the ground on my own, the fire in me now roaring. I couldn't believe after all this training, I still lost so fast.

Alaric crossed his arms. "I only agreed to one."

I held up my fists, but this time, I planted my feet firmly, hoping that changing my form would help. "Let me try again. That was hardly a match." Alaric's eyes ran over me, lingering on the scrapes the twigs he had caused. His lips shifted as he thought. "Please," I added, not allowing him to think too much.

He rolled his eyes. "Do you want to hear my critiques first?"

"Not yet," I refused, wanting to prove that I could win without his help.

Alaric's shoulders dropped. "Alright. Whenever you're ready come at me."

I shook my head. "This time, I want you to attack first."

Alaric's eyes brightened, and his lips turned up. "Alright," he said, hope in his voice. He raised onto his toes, fists high, just as I had done before. I withdrew back. I thought I had lost due to my stance. If he was mimicking my first play, he should be bound to lose. "Ready?"

I nodded quickly, hating to keep him waiting and dug deeper into the earth, bracing every muscle in my body. Alaric spared no moment for me to rescind my invitation and lunged. I leaned left, dodging his fist, my grounded feet keeping me stable as I quickly ducked when he threw his second punch.

I smiled, knowing that I was doing better than before. Perhaps defense was the way to win.

"Good," Alaric whispered. "*Finally,* you're learning."

"Finally?" I growled, that fire growing. "I'm always learning." I snapped my head around to face Alaric, wanting to look him in the eyes, but just as I did, he kicked me in the center of the chest, sending me flying.

I gasped for air as my back rammed into a tree, the hit causing me to whimper.

"But still not enough," Alaric sighed, his words dripping in disappointment and contempt.

I pushed off the tree, ignoring the pain, fueled by anger. "That's not a death blow. The fight isn't over."

Alaric exhaled long and slow, just enough time for me to take one step away from the tree, but before I took another, he raced forward, grabbing my wrists with one hand and locking them above my head. I tried to wiggle out, but his chest pressed into mine, effectively pinning me between him and the tree. I thrashed against him. Rage and panic building in me as I remembered that this was the one hold I couldn't get out of, the hold Rainer had me in on the night of the attack.

"Do you yield?" Alaric rested his free hand beside my waist.

I wiggled again but did not budge. My heart raced as my breaths became more and more labored. "I can't get out," I cried, but not to answer his question. I said it for me. I said it for all the times I had felt trapped as more and more memories burst forward from that day.

Alaric straightened but didn't lessen the pressure. "You can," he assured me softly. "Just like you can always win these fights." I pushed again, using all my strength. "Not like that. You have the skill and athleticism to be the best warrior, but you lead with your emotions. Sometimes you are too rash. You need to calm down, take a step back from it all, and look at the bigger picture."

The muscles in my face slacked. *Step back?* That wasn't right. I had to prove myself, always. I had to dive right in. I had to take action and always prove that I was the strongest.

"You were doing so well on the defensive side. You were tiring me out, but then I mocked you, and you lost all control," Alaric explained as if hearing my denial.

I took a deep breath, thinking about that moment, how my chest heated. I thought about my attack before then. I thought about my anger and rage, the need to always be the best through the years leading me in fights, particularly the most recent ones. I had so many close calls because of it. For the gods' sakes, I had almost failed my mission to get out of Rivelia because I had to fight with Damon over words. Maybe Alaric was right.

My body slacked.

Alaric took a couple steps back. "One more time. This time, either one of us can attack first."

I agreed and pushed off the tree, taking several deep breaths. Alaric circled around me, his fists high. I did the same until we had created a circle in the dirt. Alaric stepped forward, I stepped back, watching his movements. He smiled then sped forward. I held my ground, just as before, and dodged each of his attacks. However, I only guarded my upper half. Alaric threw his knee forward, hitting the back of mine, staggering me. I felt that fire in me flare, demand that I take up the offensive, but I calmed it, telling it that it would get to play in a moment. Alaric nodded, waiting for me to take my stance again. I did so, but this time, I kept track of his legs.

Alaric threw punches over and over again, each one faster than the last. Several of them grazed my face, but none landed. I felt like the waiting was useless, that I was only tiring myself out, but I kept dodging, waiting for a moment when I was sure to land. Then, after what felt like eternity, Alaric stepped forward to throw a punch, but his laces ensnared a twig, distracting him. I took the chance and threw my fist, but he caught it. His lips began to rise, but not as far as mine did, as I threw out my leg, knocking him over.

"I beat you," I spoke more in awe than happiness.

Alaric groaned, rubbing his back as he sat up. "You did. I thought I had you there too, but you did well." I smiled at Alaric but froze as I met his eyes. There was something like admiration and pride behind them. It made my heart flutter. Alaric softly smiled, as if he could hear my heartbeat quicken, then rested his arms on his knees before looking up at the leaves. "Well, there goes my streak of never being beaten by a wolf younger than me. Think we can keep this a secret for a little while? My pride is going to be hurting for a bit."

I beamed. If Alaric's statement was true, that would mean we were close to equals, and for once, I didn't mind that. He was a good fighter, and I wouldn't have ever knocked him down if he hadn't helped me. Still, seeing him beg was far too entertaining. It was my turn to have the upper hand.

"Not a chance," I stated. "This is my proudest accomplishment. You'll need to offer something great to keep my mouth shut."

Alaric collapsed to the forest floor, resting one arm on top of his forehead. "Damn, another deal? Those never work out for me when I make them with you."

I crossed my arms, watching his chest heave in and out, the redness in his face fade. It was strange to see him like this, to hear him make requests out of embarrassment, and to have his guard so down. It was like we were dear friends.

"I'm sure we can figure out something that will actually benefit you this time," I replied, an undeniable playfulness in my voice as I dared to lie next to him. Alaric seemed to still, his breathing halting as he looked at me from the corner of his eyes. I ignored it, feeling an odd tension in my chest.

"Please, let's," Alaric begged, focusing back on the sky. "Ask me for something, and it's yours. Hell, ask me anything. Just don't let anyone know. At least for a while, so I can prepare for the onslaught of teasing, especially from Neo. Gods, that's not going to be fun."

I laughed again. "But do you know how entertaining that would be for me?"

"I can find more entertaining things than that for you." Alaric turned over, facing me. I couldn't help but do the same, staring at him as if we had always been friends, maybe even closer. "I'll be your personal jester and storyteller."

I rolled my eyes. "I've never been one for stories." Alaric clicked his tongue, pulling focus to his lips. My heartbeat sped.

I didn't understand why. Despite us being friends now, Alaric was far from someone I should want. He was the opposite of me. He had hidden things from me. Though, they were all things in the past. They were all things that he had a reason for doing. Still, I shouldn't be tempted, not now, not when we had so much filling our plates. Yet, I found myself inching forward.

Alaric watched with full intent, curiosity practically spilling from him. He knew what I wanted, and from what I could see, he was willing to give, maybe even wanted it himself.

"How about—"

A small change in my scent stopped my words. My heat was here. It was weak, but by the morning, I would reek of that sweet scent that lured males to me, made them lose a small part of their control.

"Ina, are you alright?" Alaric asked, a bit of panic in his voice, cupping my face, sending a shiver down my spine.

I sat up, heading to the fire, thinking it best to give us distance, no matter how comfortable I had started to feel beside him.

"My heat is here," I stated, wrapping my cloak around me.

"Oh." Alaric breathed a sigh of relief. "I'll take first shift tonight, then." He stood, grabbing his belt from the log opposite of me and strapped it tightly on, checking to make sure all his weapons were there. "I won't let any wolf come close to you."

"What about you?"

Alaric stopped checking his gear. "I already told you that it doesn't affect me."

"And that still doesn't make sense." I crossed my arms.

Though I trusted Alaric, I couldn't believe such a ridiculous claim without facts, especially after seeing him look at me in the way he did. To some extent, even if it was just fun, he wanted me, and that would let the heat affect him.

Seeing my stubbornness, Alaric sat back down, hands clasped.

"I've learned to control it."

"How?" I clipped.

He really wasn't making this easy.

Alaric studied the ground, then with a heavy sigh and somber eyes, he nodded. "Years ago, before the war, I fell in love," Alaric began, hurt coating his words. "It was with someone I had known my entire life. We had been best friends, and both of us had a natural attraction for one another. However, we refused to act on it, as finding our destined other half was something we both desperately wanted and what was expected of us."

I raised my brows at Alaric's complete opposite opinion to mine when it came to a mate, at the waiting he did. Yet, it didn't surprise me nor belittle the moment we almost had. Mates were hard to come by, and it was normal to seek casual comfort from time to time.

"But with each passing year that we did not find our mate, we began to question our desires, leading us to join during her heat." Alaric's throat bobbed, the pain and distortion on his face growing stronger, telling me exactly where his tale was going. "A false mating bond kicked in. Our feelings for each other grew stronger. Our bodies begged for one another. I was even in tune with her scents and reactions. I always felt them before anyone else. It felt like a real bond at times."

Alaric painfully smiled at the fond memory, making me want to reach out, to comfort him in any way I could.

"We kept telling ourselves not to enjoy it too much, as we knew it would fade away. We had never been declared mates after all, but time passed. Days, weeks, then months. Eight, to be precise."

I stiffened.

Never had I heard of a false bond lasting for so long. Typically, they lasted a couple of days, maybe weeks. The longest I had personally experienced had been eleven days, and that had been with Rainer. Though our false bond only made my body uncontrollably yearn for him and made his personality bearable, it was enough for me to start wondering if the females in our pack were right in their swooning over him. But thankfully, just as those ideas began, the bond ended, and I was freed. However, that little part of me who wondered, felt lost, a little sad even. I couldn't imagine what eight months would do.

"We started to think that the bond was real, and so did our priestess. We all thought, for some odd reason, that we were both immune to mating rituals. It was a phenomenon. Both her and I began to let our guards down, allowed ourselves to bask in the bond. But one day, when we were meant to go on patrol together, I injured my wrist, and my best friend—Ryder—had to go in my stead. They came back two hours later than expected, just as I was sending out search parties.

"I'll never forget the look she gave me, how her bright eyes dimmed when she saw me racing to her with a grin that could've stretched the length of the world. I was confused, but then I scented it—their scents intimately combined. They were each other's mates.

"Ryder had apparently felt the pull for years but had held off following it. He saw how deeply Evelyn and I felt for each other and wanted to give us a chance to decide what we wanted. But when they were out on patrol, they ran across a field of shineblooms when the sun began to set. The flowers began to glow, as they do when wolves who are mates are near them together. Evelyn saw, and the mating bond clicked for her. She told me it was the most primal urge. She wanted Ryder and no one else. Despite her guilt and mind telling her to wait so she could explain the situation to me, her body needed to bind herself with Ryder in that field right then and there."

I felt my jaw tighten, and my knuckles crack. This was why I hated the bond, mates, all of it. It was why, despite my devout faith in the gods and their rules, bonds were something I refused to believe in. I hated the control it had over you, how it could hurt those you cared for. Still, many wolves said it was worth it, even if they were the ones who had gotten hurt. They were glad that they went through that pain, claimed that the mating bond was a million times better than the love they had lost. But I couldn't fathom that. Nothing could feel that good.

"They went away for a couple weeks, in hopes that the bond that I felt toward her would fade away, but when they came back, it was still there. Of course, I didn't tell them. They were so happy, and I didn't want to ruin that. But the feeling lasted for a month more. I had to sit there and watch every practice, every dinner, every time we all went out. I had to watch them be happy, in love, be mated. By the time the bond faded, I was a shell. I swore to myself I'd never become that way again. I swore that I'd never join with a female in her heat unless she was mine. I think of that pain anytime my body demands I follow a scent, and it works every time."

"I—you—" I tried to speak, to apologize for making him dredge up such a hurtful past, for what happened to him, but words could not be found.

Alaric laughed. "I promise that it's been tested."

"I wasn't questioning it. I wanted to apologize. I shouldn't have made you share that story. We're a team. I should've trusted you."

Alaric smirked in a painful, beautiful way. "You needed it. If I was in your position, I would've done the same. It's your safety that's at risk. That's more important than my feelings."

My heart lurched.

"Thank you," I whispered.

He nodded. "Go to bed, Ina. I'm sure once Neo gets here, he'll be too energized after his first mission and will talk our ears off." Quietly, Alaric spun around on his perch and surveyed the darkness around us.

I slid down to my bedroll, pulling the blanket up to my chin. I closed my eyes, but as I lay there, I could only feel the sadness emitting from Alaric.

"Alaric," I called.

He hummed in response.

"If it's any consolation, I think she missed out on an amazing mate. Whichever wolf bonds with you will be lucky. You're a good male, and the gods know that. They're just waiting for the right wolf to come into existence," I whispered, the words rolling off my tongue faster than I could think. I couldn't help but cringe at how sweet they were, that I pushed aside my own beliefs to comfort him, but that didn't matter. In this moment, I just wanted to make sure Alaric felt better.

A long silence sat between us, then Alaric spoke, his voice husky, "You too, Ina. Now get some sleep."

CHAPTER 38

I stretched out, my hands extending over the bedroll, grazing over the dewy grass that beckoned me to wake. I rolled my neck, relieving it of the knots that had formed in my sleep, then lazily turned toward the warmth of the fire and the smell of frying eggs.

"That smells good," I mused out, friendlier than ever after Alaric and mine's conversation last night. However, as my eyes came into focus, I noticed that the person's hair was dark brown and had a slimmer body, a shorter stature. I stood up quickly. "Neo, you're back," I yelled joyously.

He smiled, jumping to his feet as well, ready for my embrace. The hug was warm and comforting, very sibling like. I held him at arm's length, checking his body to make sure there was not a scratch on him. To my happiness, there wasn't.

"I promise that I'm all in one piece," he cajoled, an increase of maturity in his tone. "The trip went with zero problems, and Amos was more than happy to take the boy in. I did have to force him to take the horse back, however."

I grinned, happy with the answer I had received. However, that smile was replaced with a quizzical look, as I realized the sun was directly overhead.

"When did you get here?" I couldn't believe I had slept in, couldn't believe Alaric had *let* me sleep in so late. Even though we had slowed our pace to ensure Neo could catch up and that we wouldn't miss any signs of the nomadic pack, Alaric and I had still risen as the sun was coming up. "Does Alaric know you're back?" I asked, turning to Alaric's bedroll, assuming he had also slept in, but it was empty. His blanket was even ruffled, thrown on the forest floor. My brows furrowed. Alaric never handled his things with such little care.

"I got back as the sun was rising, just as Alaric was waking," Neo said slowly, watching his words.

"You've both been awake that long." I dropped my hands to my side, stepping back with a hand on my hip. Neo nodded. "Why didn't you two wake me?"

"Alaric"—Neo pushed his tongue against the inner part of his cheek, his eyes turning up, trying to look into his mind for the right word—"thought you could use some more sleep."

"What? Why? What would ever—"

Before I could finish my sentence, rustling leaves called my attention. A large black wolf emerged, his tongue hanging out of his mouth as his chest heavily caved in and out. It began to shift to the man I knew—Alaric. Sweat beads ran down his human skin, happy that it was finally free to fall and no longer trapped under his fur. Slowly, his white tunic began to soak it up and clung to his body. Alaric chucked it off with little care, revealing a glistening, muscled chest that had me blushing, making it clear that last night's conversation rid me of the final barrier that kept me from admiring him fully.

"Oh, good. You're awake. We should get moving," Alaric announced with no familiarity, only bothering to glance my direction.

My nose scrunched. After last night, I thought we had gotten much closer.

Annoyed, I stepped forward. Alaric stepped back.

"You could've woken me. I was up just as late as you," I stated, reminding him of our conversation last night, the closeness we finally achieved.

Alaric rubbed his temple, sighing heavily. "Right. I just," he began but stopped as a breeze swept through my hair then right to his nose. Alaric held a hand to his nostrils, his chest stilling.

My pupils doubled, immediately realizing what was going on.

"You said—"

"I know," he interrupted, shifting so the wind wasn't blowing at him directly. "And I wasn't lying. I don't know what's wrong with me. I woke up, and your scent just hit me. I think it's because of the fatigue of the journey. My mind isn't remembering the pain that well."

I cursed. This wasn't going to plan at all. The gods really were throwing every obstacle at us. Obstacles we did not need. I should've forced Alaric to create a plan in case this happened despite his confidence in himself. Now I wasn't sure what to do. I couldn't ask him to lie with me as I had done with Rainer. His thoughts weren't just his own. They were controlled by his wolf instincts, and because of that, I wouldn't be able to take his word in fear that it was his wolf's. Well, unless he somehow blocked out his wolf completely. I had seen shifters do it before; however, it always was in rare and unique cases. It would take too long to figure out how to make Alaric do that, and even if he did, I was sure he'd say no. It was understandable after all. He had been through too much pain the last time he joined with a female in heat. I wouldn't ask. There was only one choice.

I backed toward my horse, grabbing my sword. "I'm going to ride ahead."

"Ina," Alaric frantically called, taking a cautious step forward but not daring to lower his hand. "We need to stay together. The blood demons are out there. Not to mention, there may be lone wolves—outcasts of the nomadic packs. There were many last time I was here, and their sentence of isolation makes them more animal than human. They won't hesitate if they scent you."

"And you will?" I snarked.

Alaric flinched at my words, as did I. I didn't want to assume he'd make unsavory advances toward me, but I could see the ravenousness in his eyes. My heat was going to be more than just a distraction.

"It's true your scent tempts me, but Neo and I tested it this morning." I glared at Neo who guilty nodded, his awkwardness now making sense. "Your scent tempted me, but if I was this far away"—Alaric gestured to the space between us—"I didn't act on it. It only taunted me, made my stomach growl like a pie does while it's baking."

"But it still clouds your mind?" Alaric looked away. The action was answer enough. "I trust you, Alaric, but you said it yourself, we are in dangerous territory. You can't have your mind clouded when we encounter danger, not when I'm the reason it comes."

"That's why I went on a run. It cleared my head, tires me out just a fraction more so I can only focus on the necessities."

I tilted back my head and laughed humorlessly. "So, you answer a problem that was caused by fatigue with more fatigue? That hardly sounds like an acceptable solution."

Alaric crossed his arms. "It's the only option we have. You'd be more vulnerable if I didn't do this."

"Exactly. I would be. Not you or Neo. This is my problem, and I won't let you two be at risk because of it." I untied Irie's reins. "I'm going. We'll meet back up in a week. This is what's best for the group."

"No, it isn't," Alaric growled, stopping me from jumping in Irie's saddle. Alaric pinched the bridge of his nose. "No matter what, my head will be clouded. If you leave, I will be worried about you and unable to think of anything else." Quietness pursued, and for a moment, all I could hear was the beating of my heart. Him caring did such odd things to me. "You'll be weaker, you won't even be able to shift, and above all, you will be alone. The risk for you to go off is much higher than it is for you to stay with us. So, please, try my plan, and if anything happens, we can come up with a different idea."

I gulped, seeing Alaric's resolve, the terror and concern on his face. It made me abandon all reason, and so, while I hated myself for it, I nodded.

257

CHAPTER 39

Alaric drowsily stood from his spot around the fire, darkness circulating his eyes. I highly doubted he could keep this routine up for another three days. But still, he persisted, proclaiming that only he would separate from the group. I had half the thought to challenge him on it, but nothing bad had happened yet, therefore our deal to make another plan couldn't be enacted. Challenging Alaric would only result in more of his precious energy being spent and wasted time.

"I'm going to scout ahead," Alaric stated monotonously. "Follow me once camp is packed up."

Neo and I both nodded, though we didn't bother to hide our worry. Still, Alaric ignored it, shifting into his massive wolf.

"I hate this," I announced, stuffing my blanket into my bag.

"Me too, but this is the best option we have," Neo said softly, giving no inclination that he was going to side with me.

I rolled my eyes.

Neo and I were the original team, and for the love of gods, that was his brother. He should be on my side for this.

I aggressively threw everything into my bag and clasped it closed. "I'll be back," I grumbled, stalking toward the woods.

"Where are you going?" he asked, worry written all over his face.

"To pee," I screamed, tired of all the fuss and sacrifices made for me.

Neo nodded but sniffed the air, searching for potential threats.

I didn't wait for the okay before I stormed off into the woods, far enough so that Neo couldn't hear me relieve myself.

I squatted down, cursing to myself about the unfairness of being female, too focused on my frustration of the situation to hear the crinkle of leaves before it was too late.

"I thought I smelt a female," a honeyed voice spoke.

I jumped, frantically pulling my trousers back up, reaching for the sword at my waist.

"It's alright," a male with overgrown blonde hair whispered as he stepped out of the shadows.

I looked him up and down, skin bristling as my eyes grazed over his tunic. It was fringed at the bottom and bore a dull green, as if it had been bleached by the sun. I breathed in deep, scared that I was about to confirm my suspicions, but sure enough, I was right. His scent was more of the earthy smell of a wild wolf than a personal scent. He was a rogue, created by a pack that had cast him out or ceased to be. They were the most dangerous of our kind, as they tended to rely too much on their wolf to survive, thus losing their humanity and their restraint.

"I just wanted to see why such a deliciously scented thing was doing all the way out here," he cooed, licking his lips, "*alone.*"

I raised my sword. Wolves were not made to be isolated. We always yearned to be with a pack, and if we couldn't, we took over one or made our own, making this wolf's desire for me triple that of a normal male.

"I'm not alone. I'm traveling with a party," I growled, appearing as hostile as I could muster, not daring to call on my wolf, since I knew his would come faster, giving him the advantage.

The wolf sniffed again, but this time not as happily, realizing his treat wasn't as easy to obtain as he had thought.

I prayed to the gods that was encouragement enough for him to turn tail and run. However, before I could mutter another word, he cocked his head to the sky, lifting his nose once more.

"The source of the scents on you," he began, an awful smile emerging, "they seem to be rather far away right now." He lowered his head, tail twitching, like any wolf once they'd spotted their sport.

I clutched the hilt in my hand tighter, making sure it wouldn't slip despite my sweating palms, spreading my stance and pointing the blade forward.

"Oh, don't be like that. I just want some more friends."

"Leave. You don't want to fight me," I warned, but it only made his eyes light up.

"I always love a good fight before a tumble," he chuckled, shifting as he lunged for me.

I barrel rolled to the side, dodging the beige wolf, knowing that the fur—despite the wolf being smaller than the ones I normally faced—was thick enough that my sword and weakened strength would not cut deep enough to force him to withdraw. It would only pierce the first layer of skin, and the force of the hit would cause me to stagger, allowing him the chance to grab me. And that was the last thing I wanted, especially when I was unsure as to if I could get free of his grasp. I'd just have to keep dodging until I found a weak spot or help came. It was something I could only do against a wolf in human form because of Alaric's training. I'd have to thank him for it later. Though as I made my third leap, I wasn't sure if I would be able to.

Sweat dripped down my back, my legs began to shake, and my throat burned as I tried to get more air and squatted low, preparing for the next jump. The wolf paused, his pupils dancing as they raked over my body, no sign of his endurance wavering. I took a moment, gathering whatever saliva I had left in my mouth and swallowed, trying to ease my burning throat. I rolled back my shoulders and squatted even lower, ready for his next move.

I was the daughter of an alpha. I would not go down this easily.

The wolf shook his head in disbelief before hunching down. In response, I took a long breath, examining his paws, just as I had for his last leaps. His back pads lifted, his weight shifted to his claws, then he jumped. So did I, but barely.

My leap was half the distance of my previous ones, landing me in a spot where giant roots had sprung, all of them intertwined. There wasn't a flat space to land at all. One foot landed on a root that curved up. The other slipped between two thick ones.

Unable to firmly plant either foot, I fell to my knees, attempting to catch myself with my hands, but the weak roots snapped, cutting into my palm. Warm liquid oozed, and I was certain that pieces of wood were embedded into my flesh, but that was something I would curse about later. Right now, I needed to focus on the wolf who was encroaching on me, too close that a leap in this state would not dodge his advances.

I made a grab for my sword, but to my dismay, I found the scabbard empty. Heart speeding, my eyes dashed all around, finding not a sign of it until I dared a glance at the spot where I was relieving myself.

All air escaped my lungs.

When I first jumped, I had left the sword, too frantic to notice that it had slipped through my hands until now, until I desperately needed it.

My chest tightened, and whereas just seconds ago I was void of oxygen, I now had too much. I couldn't find the right rhythm. I was light-headed. All I could focus on was the feral wolf's steps getting louder and the wet smack of his lips as his tongue ran over his mouth. I—I—

No.

I needed to be calm. I needed to think. I was a trained warrior. I could do this.

I felt around, not daring to take my eyes off the predator in front of me, at his slow, menacing walk. He was enjoying my panic too much. However, I only found hard roots—too thick to rip apart—and thin ones—too brittle to deal any damage. I checked my belt one last time, eyeing the silver dagger. I didn't want to use it, not when I just got my endurance back, but it was all I had, all I could do.

I pushed myself up, earning a confused look from my attacker, and grabbed the dagger. The silver stung momentarily—a warning from my body—but it passed just as it always did. I started my count, making sure that I would only hold it for a minute and no more, before sprinting to the beige wolf. His jaw dropped, but his tail wagged, amused at my desperate attempt. Little did he know the pain he was about to experience.

With a scream, I thrust the dagger forward with my remaining strength. It barely scraped his skin, but that was all that was needed for the silver to take effect. The wolf howled, thrashing to see the wound. His eyes widened as he saw the tiny scratch, smelt the microscopic bits of silver that now mixed with his blood. Whatever amusement he had before dissipated. I smirked, knowing that his body would weaken soon, but my pride dulled my common sense. I should've started running, taken advantage of his confusion. Instead, I relished my success, giving his confusion time to turn into anger.

The rogue wolf growled, raising his paw, making his intent clear. He was going to kill me.

I raised my dagger, knowing I couldn't outrun him, but I knew it was pointless. His weight would cause my arms to buckle, even if he came down on the dagger, and his claws would rip me apart before he took his last breath. Still, I had to try.

I braced myself, refusing to look away, but then another wolf came into view.

It collided with the beige wolf. Their bodies tangled with one another as jaws snapped. I looked closer, realizing the second wolf was Neo.

I tucked my silver dagger away and sprinted to my sword, making sure to wipe my palms dry before grabbing it, then charged, aiming for the weakened flesh that had been nicked by the silver blade, but I was too late.

Neo had knocked the beige wolf down and was now looming over him, snapping his jaw inches near his face, telling him to leave, refusing to take his life, as it was a mortal sin to kill another wolf if you could help it. It was why wolves were banished for their crimes instead of being killed on spot. And in this situation, when it was clear that you had lost the fight fair and square, the wolf would admit defeat and be on their way. However, that was in a civilized world. Out here, this wolf had nothing to lose.

The beige wolf whimpered, his ears lowering in defeat. He glanced at the patted down grass that he had come from then back to Neo in question. Neo nodded, withdrawing his canines, and backed away, completely leaving himself vulnerable.

I screamed his name, screamed at him not to let his guard down, cursing his naivety, but the beige wolf was already in motion. Neo barely had time to throw his arm in front of himself, preventing his throat from being ripped out.

A guttural scream erupted from me as I raced forward, sword gripped by both hands, aimed for the beige wolf's side. I did not miss.

The rogue wolf yelped as the blade dug into his already infested wound. His body jerked as he tried to get away so violently that he couldn't keep hold of Neo and flung him into a tree. The impact was enough that Neo shifted into human form. Distracted by concern, the pressure of my blade lessened, and the wolf freed himself.

I backed away, watching the blood run down his side, pool at his feet

How was he still standing?

I raised my sword as he trembled. All his attention was on me, readying for his final leap. I remained still, refusing to back down, not after he had hurt my friend. It would be me or him this time. This would be the last attack. I was ready, but just as the wolf reared up, he froze, his pupils shaking, his stare drifting from mine to whatever was behind me. I dared a glance.

Behind me, Alaric stood in wolf form, seeming more daunting than ever. Fire raged in his eyes at the sight of Neo, at me. He growled, the sound causing me to jolt, but not loud enough to make me fall to the ground as the beige wolf did.

Alaric sauntered forward, his steps slow and powerful, as if he knew he had all the time in the world to get to the rogue wolf. The wolf began to shake, thrusting his head every which way, fighting some unseeable force that held him down. Alaric growled again, stopping his efforts. Their eyes met, and for a minute, they held each other's gazes. The beige wolf closed his eyes and shifted, moving so he sat on his knees, head facing the ground in ultimate submission.

"There's an inn less than a mile from here. Head in that direction"—he lifted his finger to the left—"until you get to the main road then follow it," the wolf said, answering a question nobody had asked. Alaric looked where he pointed then jerked his head back to the blonde-haired man. "They are friendly toward our kind. I swear it. There's even a healer there, who is a lone wolf by choice. She helps others who are alone and the humans as well. That's why they aren't afraid or angry," the beige wolf speedily said, too specifically for even wolves who learned from a young age to talk through body language. This was like a vocal conversation, but that was impossible between our kind when one or more of the participants was in wolf form, unless—

My eyes widened.

Had Alaric compelled him? A wolf not of his own pack?

That was impossible. It couldn't be.

Only alphas could compel, and even if Alaric was one, he should only be able to compel those that were in his own pack. That's how it had been throughout history, apart from the original leader of Rivelia—the one who brought all the packs together, and made it so Rivelia was the center of the wolf community.

If Alaric had this power, it would be no wonder that he excelled at everything, that he bested me marginally. He could be the leader to unite the wolves once again. He would be *The Alpha.*

"You're free to go, then, but if you come back or I find out you're lying, I won't adhere to our laws," Alaric declared, his voice making me halt.

When had he shifted?

The blonde male slowly rose, his body still curled like that unseeable force still held him down. Quietly, he nodded, and without turning his back to Alaric, he limped into the darkness.

Alaric glared at the spot until the footsteps grew distant then dropped to his hands and knees, his body trembling.

"Alaric," I whisper-cried, making sure that the lone wolf wouldn't hear, rushing to him. I ran my hand down his back, planting the other on his shoulder to keep him from tumbling forward.

Alaric dug his nails into the dirt, bracing himself. "Neo first," he uttered. "Stop his bleeding."

I twisted as did my gut. In all the chaos, I had forgotten my basic post-battle training—assess the wounds of all warriors before aiding.

I sprinted to Neo and examined his arm. The gash was gushing. The bleeding needed to stop and soon. Frantically, I undid my belt. "This is going to hurt," I warned, wrapping the leather above the joint of his arm, pulling before Neo had time to think about what was about to happen.

His curdling scream echoed through the forest as I cut off his blood flow. I slapped my hand over his mouth, muting him.

The last thing we needed right now was to draw more attention to ourselves.

"Sorry," I muttered, trying to slide my fingers between the belt and his arm to make sure my fingers couldn't wedge in.

Neo gulped, his eyes watering, his jaw tense. He was struggling to breathe. Cautiously, I removed my hand, allowing him the gulps of air I had denied him.

"The worst part is over. I just need to wrap up the wound to lessen the chances of infection until we get you to a healer." I looked at the exposed flesh, the deep gashes. "It's going to sting," I informed, taking hold of Neo's gaze, knowing a brief pause would not kill him now. "Can you be quiet?"

Neo took a deep breath but nodded.

I grabbed the hem of my tunic, prepared to expose my undergarments to the world, as my outer layers were still back at camp. It was only fabric after all, and I'd rather have that uncovered than Neo's wounds. However, before the fabric could even cross my midsection, a cloak came between me and Neo.

"We'll use this," Alaric said, his voice deeper, more nasally as he held his breath.

My stomach twisted, remembering that all of this was my fault.

I should've gone my own way this week.

I made a short, low hum in agreement and slid away, allowing him to squat down. Alaric gently, but quickly, wrapped Neo's arm.

"He'll need stitches," Alaric stated in a factual voice, hauling Neo up who yelped at the movement. However, the sound didn't stop Alaric from pushing his brother into my arms. "Put him on my back after I shift. I'll take him to the healer at the inn. Meet us there after you pack up camp."

"Okay," I whispered, my breaking voice apparent.

Alaric's body seemed to slack. In a gentler voice, he ordered, "Only carry as much as you can. If some things get left behind, we'll come back for them."

I made to rebuttal, to tell Alaric that I could handle such a small task, but he shifted, reminding me of the direness of the situation.

This was no time for rebuttals. We needed to get Neo to a healer.

"Can you get on?" I asked, holding Neo's good arm, making sure he didn't fall.

Neo gripped Alaric's mane and tried to swing his leg over. He only managed to bury his head into Alaric's plush fur.

I bit my cheek. Neo needed help, but to touch another wolf's fur, while in human form, wasn't something you did unless you had an intimate relation.

Alaric made a low growl, calling my attention. Slowly, he nodded.

I took a deep breath. "I'll touch as little as I can."

Gently, I wrapped my hand around Neo's leg and pushed it over, barely grazing Alaric's fur. It was more than enough to make me stiffen, but not because I was breaking social protocol. His fur felt all too comfortable to my skin, made me want to rub my hands through it, fall asleep while I curled into him. It was alarming.

I had helped groom my father and my sisters before, and their fur never felt like this. It never enticed me to do more than stroke a brush through it and rid them of the sticks that had tangled in their mane after a run.

Could it have been that Alaric took better care of his fur?

No, it couldn't be. It glistened in the same way as theirs had and looked just as healthy.

So, why?

A small whimper from Neo snapped me back to reality.

"I'll meet you guys there. Be safe," I said, backing away so Alaric's powerful legs wouldn't accidentally hit me, eyes focused on Neo to make sure he wouldn't fall when Alaric started. Though I couldn't help but feel eyes on me, asking me to look so they could say something.

I walked into the tavern, the smell of ale and roasted mutton flooding the air. Under normal circumstances, I would've relished the aroma after weeks on the road. However, with the faint smell of Neo's blood and freshly ground poultices above me, I headed straight for the stairs behind the counter without so much of a pause.

"You'll need to buy a room to get up there," stated an older man with a bit of a gut. His large size enough to make any woman uneasy. But I wasn't a woman; I was a wolf.

"Did two males"—the innkeeper gave me a look—"men come here?" I asked not wanting to draw any more attention to us, despite knowing they were already here. The lone wolf had said they were friendly to our kind, but from what I had learned since I left Artico, there was always mixed opinions of shifters nowadays.

The innkeeper examined the three packs I held, eyes weary. "What did they look like?"

I raised my chin. "One of them with black hair, the other dark brown and injured."

The man nodded, stepping to the side. "You have the two rooms at the end of the hall on the left."

"Thank you."

I took two steps up the stairs before the innkeeper chimed, "Try not to worry about your friend too much. Alis is an outstanding healer, and"—the innkeeper looked around and lowered his voice—"she specializes in your kind."

I swallowed, my heart lightening up.

The barkeep was discreet and careful. We should be safe here while Neo healed.

I froze as I gripped the doorknob, taking one last breath before facing whatever was on the other side. I could barely smell Neo's scent with the aroma of countless herbs wafting through the air. I didn't know if it was a good sign or a bad one. I prayed that it was the former. If anything happened to him, when he protected me on my behalf, I didn't know what I would do. But praying would get me nowhere now. I needed to face the music. I pushed open the door, revealing a plain room that barely had anything in it except two beds and three bodies.

Alaric stood, looming in a corner, his arms crossed. He looked fine apart from his intense gaze fixed on Neo, who rested on one of the two beds. Neo's eyes were closed while an old, white-haired woman sat on a stool between the two beds in the room. Her hands steady as she put another application of the mushed green leaves from the bowl in her hands. And while I was happy to see Neo receiving care, the sight of his pale skin and swollen forearm broke a small sob from me.

I never should have allowed Alaric to travel ahead. It was irresponsible of me. I was a trained wolf. I should've known better.

"Get in or get out," spat an older voice.

I looked to it, meeting the healer's eyes.

"Is he alright?" I struggled to say.

The healer seethed, "He will be if you close the door. I don't want any more cool air getting in here. He's cold enough as is."

My stomach twisted.

Cold. Cold enough.

Despite the female saying Neo was ok, I knew he had come close to death. Wolves never got infections. Yet, Neo had one because of that damn wolf. Neo had been trapped in that castle for so long and the rogue wolf had been wandering, exposing himself to everything and anything. Things Neo was being exposed to now. Things his body was fighting off, like it would a common sickness, but this was so much worse and quicker because he had an open wound, and he was tired. And it was all because of me.

I sprinted out of the room and headed to the second chamber where I had dropped our bags off before checking on Neo, as I hadn't wanted to clutter the room where the healer worked, and threw open the door. I needed to go. I needed to finish this off on my own. Neo was never supposed to come with me. He was supposed to be safe in Rivelia, but I had led him here. I had taken an untrained wolf into the most dangerous region, on the most dangerous mission, and he had gotten hurt while protecting me.

"Ina, what are you doing," someone questioned sternly.

I didn't need to turn to know who it belonged to.

"I need to leave." I slung my pack over my shoulder. Keeping my head down, I stormed for the door, but a firm hand gripped my upper arm.

"Neo can't ride for another two days."

Relief flooded through me. It wasn't going to be as long of a healing process as I had thought. Still, that didn't erase the conclusion I had come to.

"Good. Rest those days, then return to Rivelia."

I leaned away, trying to break free of Alaric's iron grip, but he held me firmer.

"What?"

Alaric bent down and tried to lock eyes with me, but I twisted. I couldn't face him, not when I was the cause of the one thing he never wanted to happen.

I didn't know how he was being so calm with me now. He should be screaming.

"I'm continuing on alone," I whispered.

"Ina, I know you're worried about your pack, but two days..." Alaric licked his lips. "If you go by yourself, you won't be able to find the Woodland Pack."

"I'll go on without them."

Alaric's brows shot up. "You'll die and—"

"Neo almost died today!" I screamed, meeting Alaric's eyes. "He almost died because of me. Your brother got hurt because of me. You were right. I shouldn't have allowed him to come. I shouldn't have made that deal with you."

Alaric stiffened, and his grip lessened. I dared a glance his way. Shock was plastered on his face, but I knew anger would take over soon. In all the chaos he had forgotten to blame me, but now I had reminded him. He would start screaming soon, as was his right. But I couldn't handle that right now. I was already screaming at myself enough.

Taking advantage of his transitioning feelings, I tugged my hand away and surged forward, but I didn't get far. Within seconds, I was tugged close to Alaric's chest, his scent wrapping around me.

"Idiot," Alaric chided, his chin resting on the top of my head. I tried to look up at him, but he pushed my head back down. "My words back then, my blame for Neo coming on this journey, they were wrong. Neo would have forced you to take him, even if you told him no. This mission is something he was meant to do, what we were all meant to do because it's what's right. His leaving Rivelia isn't your fault, Ina. Don't blame yourself."

My fingers tangled into Alaric's tunic as I tried not to drop from the sincerity in his gentle words, but I couldn't accept them. I couldn't stop my self-hatred. "Even if that's not my fault, he's still injured because of me. He got hurt because he was protecting me." I pushed away. Alaric let me distance myself from his chest, but only enough so I could look up at him.

"Packs," Alaric said solemnly, holding my gaze, "protect one another."

My heart lurched forward. They did, but I wasn't—I couldn't...

Alaric continued to stare at me with that narrowed, serious gaze—the one he used when he needed us to hear him and take his words to heart.

My throat bobbed as I swallowed hard, and my elbows buckled.

"You formed this pack, Ina. It is Neo and mine's privilege to make sure you are safe. Without you, neither of us would be here."

Tears lined my eyes. After the attack on Artico, I didn't think I would ever—I didn't think I'd find somewhere to belong, a place that would accept me and I, them. I figured after the battle with the blood demons, we would all part and go our separate ways, that we would not think of one another again, as we were all forced together. Never did I think we'd bond, that we would care like this, but learning this truth only made my resolve stronger.

"Then you should understand why I want to protect you two, why I can't let you two get hurt." I backed away. "Our deal was that if anything happened, we'd make a new plan, so we are. We'll go with mine. I won't go too far away, but until my heat is done, I think it's best I stay a distance away from you and Neo."

"I said, *consider* a new plan, not actually do it," Alaric corrected sternly. "Besides, you won't be safe that way. We'll carry on in our normal way. You stay with Neo, and I will tire and keep my distance."

"I have five more days of my heat." I stepped back, canines bared. "What happens if you're on a run, and they smell me? Will Neo stand down and make sure his wounds heal or will he try to help? Whatever option he chooses, it will hurt him." I continued to back away. "At least if I'm traveling, then I'm not in a central location that has a healer for the lone wolves. It will lessen the chance—"

"It's not happening!" Alaric growled so loud that I could have sworn the pictures on the walls shook.

My eyes widened, never had I seen him lose his composure like this, not when logic was against his ideas.

"Sorry," he whispered, taking a couple of deep breaths, trying to calm himself. However, it only caused his jaw to clench and a ravenous look in his eyes to emerge.

I inhaled sharply, knowing exactly why.

I had been so consumed by my emotions, so focused on leaving that I didn't stop and think about Alaric and his urges. I didn't think about how long it had taken me to gather our things and walk to the inn. I didn't realize that it had been enough time for him to rest, for his wolf to rest.

He shouldn't have been able to last this long; he shouldn't have been able to think clearly, especially since we were in such a small room.

Alaric cocked his head so his nose wasn't pointed to me. "Don't worry. I'd rather fling myself out a window than force myself on you," he nasally said, taking shallow, pained breaths.

I pushed aside his words, trying to figure out what he had done to keep his wolf at bay. I ran through my mind, thinking, but nothing came. Then a dribble of liquid called to my ears, accompanied by the faint scent of iron. My eyes shot to the source.

Alaric's palm was bleeding, and by how tightly he fisted his hand, I knew that he was the cause of it.

His hand flew behind his back. "It will heal within a matter of minutes. It's fine."

"No, it's not," I bit out.

"You aren't allowed to venture out unprotected, and I cannot leave Neo alone, so this will have to do." Alaric held up his hand. "It allows me to be near you without—"

"Does it? Are you confident you can be around me, unaffected at all times by drawing your own blood?" I stepped forward. Alaric stepped back, the deep breaths he had taken still affecting him. "The only way that I'd allow that is if it worked fully."

Alaric avoided my gaze, the veins in his neck popping.

I nodded. "That's what I thought." I grabbed my pack and opened the door. "I'll see you in five days, Alaric."

Alaric slammed a hand into the door, effectively closing it shut. I sidestepped, but before I could get out of his range, his other hand planted firmly on the wall, caging me in.

"It doesn't, but I can't—we can't lose you. I promise that I'll find a way to deal with my urges. I'll find a way to clear my head and focus so I can stay near you and Neo. I'll do anything. I just—I can't..."

Alaric's hands pushed further into the wood, causing it to creak, pure dread and worry radiating from him. I hated seeing him this way, especially over me. If only we still hated each other, that would make this so much easier. He would let me go, or I could simply hit him over the head and be on my way. Instead, we were stuck at an impasse, because there was no way to get what we both wanted, except that one way, but I would never ask him that. Unless...

I breathed deeply. Alaric's wolf scent was light, most of his power focused on healing the wound he was constantly reopening. Alaric was as clear-minded as he could be. His answer to my question would be his and his alone. I had to ask it now, even though I knew he would say no, because pointing out that it was our only option would allow me to leave.

"So, we sleep together? Is that what you want?" Alaric's head snapped up, pupils dilated. I stayed neutral. "That's the only way I see this working.

You'll still be distracted, but at least, other wolves won't be attracted to me. Our party could stay together."

Alaric's hands slid from the door. "Ina, I wasn't trying to pressure you into that. I would never force or coerce you."

"You're not. I've lain with another shifter to end the attraction aspect of my heat before, and I'm fine with doing it now. I'm genuinely asking you—while your wolf is subdued—if you want to, if you're alright with gambling with that risk instead of the one we are facing."

Alaric shuddered. "Ina, I won't"—I felt my heart hop but also dip, knowing his rejection was coming and that I would finally win this fight—"have sex with you when that's the only reason. If it's only logic and not desire, I won't."

My brows scrunched together.

Was Alaric considering this?

No. It couldn't be possible. This was just a bluff on mine.

I stepped forward, closing a small bit of the gap between us. "And what if I told you, it's not?" Alaric raised his chin, his jaw ticking. "What if I told you, I found you attractive despite everything? What if I told you, I wouldn't mind being in your bed for fun? Would that void your concern then?" I asked, telling myself that this was only a play to win the overall argument, but as I asked the rhetorical questions out loud, I knew that they were actually statements. Somewhere along the way, while getting to know Alaric, understanding that he wasn't evil, that he was keeping the balance that threatened to sway with a single breeze, I had become attracted to him.

CHAPTER 41

ALARIC

I calmed my mind, trying to keep my composure, but the space between us was hardly enough. I couldn't believe what Ina was asking. I didn't want to believe what she was. Though it was a blessing and curse in disguise, it made sense, logically speaking. It was the best way to avoid danger from other shifters and keep the party together. However, I didn't want her to do that just because of logic. I didn't want to have sex with her merely because she thought it was the only way out of this insufferable situation. I wanted her, but only if it was out of desire, which would never happen. I had done too many terrible things. I wasn't worthy enough to be desired by her. Yet, here she was, claiming that she did. She had to be lying.

I examined Ina, watched her pupils, looked for any shaking, any sign that she was lying. There was none. But that couldn't be. She was terrible at lying. I could always scent it on her or read it in her expression.

She had to be telling the truth, or at least, she thought she was.

I had to test her declaration before I answered. I wouldn't let her regret this later.

I stalked forward, forcing her back against the door frame again, pinning her to the wood.

"I would agree, then," I whispered, admiring her lips before flashing back up to her eyes.

Ina's shoulders curled in, and her head drooped, hiding the blush that was forming on her cheeks. I pushed off the door, ready to step away again as I risked inhaling her scent, thinking I would find fear and nervousness, regret even, but instead a sweet scent—not the scent of her heat—lured me closer. She actually wanted me.

I leaned back in, ready to ask her once more if she really wanted to do this despite the proof. However, as I did, she raised her head, concern written all over it.

"But what of your promise to yourself?" Ina placed a hand on my chest, stopping me, but she did not push me away. "Alaric, even though I highly doubt I'll find my mate soon, since I tested with almost all the eligible males in my pack, I can't let you do this if you have any hesitations."

I stilled, remembering that the false bond was a risk, cursing that it was taking so much of my mental capacity to calm my wolf and think clearly about Ina that I hadn't thought to question that concern. Thank the gods, Ina was looking out for me, but also curse them. It was just another quality of hers to add to the list of things that made her so desirable, made me want to protect her. A list that I had been trying to erase for a while. If it grew anymore, I wasn't sure what I would do. Ina may very well be my next Evelyn. No, she would be worse. I knew she would be worse because I was considering forsaking my oath to myself for her, and I was okay with that.

CHAPTER 42

My heart pounded as Alaric breathed, as he thought. I didn't know what to expect anymore. When I had brought up his promise to himself, he had frozen, like he had forgotten about it. I feared that his wolf was blocking his mind, that he was no longer able to make sound decisions, but when I scented him again, I knew he was still in control.

Could it be that he was actually considering it?

That couldn't be. Surely, Alaric's heart and sanity were not on the same level as my safety. He was only considering it because he was a good male, a good leader.

"I'm sorry," I groaned out. Alaric's head snapped to me, fully alert. "It was cruel of me to ask this of you. I know there's only one answer you can give. We'll keep thinking."

Alaric stared back at me in silence, his face unreadable. I waited for him to back away, to thank me, but instead, he stepped forward with little force, watching the arm I pushed him away with. It was like he was asking a question, asking if it was alright if he got closer. I bent my elbow.

Carefully and oh so gently, Alaric cupped my cheek, the touch sending shivers throughout my body. "You've never been so wrong in a statement before," he mumbled, pressing his lips to mine.

CHAPTER 43

The kiss was gentle and cautious at first, every movement a silent question, asking permission to keep going, and of course, I kept saying yes. It felt too good. It felt better than any kiss I've had before. And Alaric, his scent was still normal. Every action he was taking was that of his own free will, uncontrolled by his wolf. Whatever was about to happen next, we were both consenting to. I was sure of that.

Without breaking the kiss, I reached for Alaric's other hand, the one that had been bleeding earlier. He still dug his nails into his palms. He was still being cautious, still waiting to see if I would back out, but I wouldn't, not when I wanted him, not when he was willing to break his promise to keep me safe. I just wanted him to stop being in pain. Slowly, I started to pry his nails from his palm. Alaric tensed, and his kisses stopped.

"Ina," he whispered in a husky, guttural tone. "Are you sure?"

I caressed the back of his hand with my thumb. "Are you sure about breaking your promise to yourself?" I answered with another question.

Alaric rested his forehead on mine, a muffled laugh coming from him. "Just promise me that if you ever want to stop, you will tell me."

I nodded, bringing his hand between our chests before unfolding it.

Alaric's scent changed completely, and he went rigid. He rolled back his shoulders with discomfort, fighting himself, waiting.

My lips turned up in a small way. I knew it was wrong, but I liked seeing him feral for me.

"Kiss me," I whispered, breaking his final restraint.

Alaric closed the little distance between us with force, pushing me into the door one last time as his lips found mind. It was so unlike our previous kiss. This one was deep and claiming. He kissed my lips like his lungs inhaled air. It made me lightheaded and weak in the knees. I even whimpered every time his tongue dashed into my mouth, exploring. I hoped that I was making him feel half as good.

Wondering, I trailed my hand down to his leathers, only for Alaric to groan as I found the answer I was looking for. He pushed it further into my hand in silent request. I obeyed and stroked it, trying to get the full feel of how exactly big his bulge was, but as I did, I felt it lengthen.

I gasped. It already filled my hand. I didn't think it could get any bigger. I kept rubbing, feeling every inch of it grow, feeling the laces of his pants loosen because of the pressure on the other side. I kept going until Alaric reached his full potential, and gods, he was huge.

I moaned, my delicate muscles already clenching at the thought of Alaric inside me. I needed him soon. Greedily, I started to unlace his leathers.

I had barely gotten them through the second eyelet before Alaric gripped just below my bottom and hauled me up, wrapping my legs around his waist. "Bed, now," he growled, pure wolf in his tone as he walked us to the back of the room, my center finding relief in the friction that occurred with every step.

My core cried for more, and I drove my hips down, oscillating them, but once I found the perfect rhythm, Alaric dropped me onto the bed.

"Alaric," I mewled, both in question and need, watching him stand at the foot of the bed, his breathing heavier than I had ever seen.

His jaw tensed. "I need a second to calm my wolf," he declared in that pained voice.

"It's fine. I promise." I sat up. "You can take me now."

Alaric stretched his neck. "Not for me. I want you to be fulfilled, ready, before I lose control. You deserve that."

I bit my lip as my entrance pulsed in selfish agreement. I held it, hoping to mute its silent demands. Though it spoke for my desires, I couldn't let it overtake me. I knew Alaric's wolf was screaming for me, causing him pain the longer he waited to obey it, and I couldn't let that continue. However, before I could tell him so, Alaric sank to the floor, and in one swift motion, he tore off my pants and pulled my knees to him so they rested over his shoulders.

"For this," he groaned, biting his lower lip as he stared between my legs, "my wolf can wait."

I bucked as his tongue grazed my thighs then licked my entrance. Alaric's hands moved to my hips, pinning them down to the bed, immobilizing me, making sure I wouldn't interfere as his tongue made its way up to that already inflamed, sensitive bit of me and sucked. It was all too much. I couldn't help but moan, to jolt at every lick he delivered. I reached for anything to ground me. I found Alaric's silky hair, fingers entangling in it. He hummed in approval of that.

"You're so sweet," Alaric mused, his praise sending me closer to euphoria. "I don't want to stop, but you look so wet, so in need."

My breathing hitched as his mouth pulled away and was replaced by one of his hands which spread apart my entrance. He looked at it with gleaming, hungry eyes before sliding a finger in and circling my bundle of nerves with his thumb.

Alaric pumped slowly, alternating between watching his work and my face, smiling in sweet, torturous bliss anytime I cried that he wouldn't let me move my hips or pleaded for him go faster. He was a wolf playing with his prey right before the kill.

"Please," I begged, actually begged, unable to take anymore teasing as a second finger joined in the torturing, "more."

Alaric's smile turned feral, evil almost. "As you wish," he mused sweetly, pulling out his fingers entirely.

I whimpered at the emptiness, but spread my legs wider, hoping for his cock to quickly replace it. Instead, three of his fingers greeted my entrance. Slowly and agonizingly, they entered, going until they reached the back.

I whimpered at the feeling, at the pure teasing.

Alaric pumped his fingers into me again, mimicking my lips that formed an O at the sensation. He pulled out, and my soft muscles contracted. He smirked, and this time, when he slid them back in, it was not slow. It was fast and wanting. Again and again, he repeated the motion until my toes were curling and my hands had moved to the sheets, scared that I would damage that beautiful, soft hair of his.

"You enjoy this," he whispered, his speed unfaltering. I nodded despite the words being a statement and not a question. "Good, because my wolf wants to take you hard today."

"Let him out, then," I said breathlessly. "I—"

"No," Alaric growled, his head ducking, his warm breath caressing that sensitive spot. "Not until you come, because once I stop holding back, once I let my wolf's urges lead me, I'm going to be selfish when it comes to pleasure."

His words left me speechless, my core aching, but not as much as when his tongue pressed against me, when his fingers and mouth worked in tandem, stroking and massaging all the parts I needed them too.

The pleasure was immense, far too great for me to think, let alone move. I moaned and pleaded. For gods' sakes, I called his name out like it was a prayer. I wanted more. I wanted him. I wanted to come.

I wanted him to make me come.

I wanted him to make me come only so he could be selfish, so I could feel the length of his cock in me, so I could finally see what it was like to be *claimed* by Alaric.

"Please, please, please," I begged, unsure if it was to my body or Alaric. Regardless, Alaric answered and drove his fingers deeper, faster. He licked harder, pulled the bundle into his mouth, and sucked, moaning like it was the sweetest thing he'd ever tasted.

My stomach clenched. My soft muscles tightened. I began to moan louder and louder, each one a higher pitch than the last.

Alaric reached up and rolled my nipple between his fingers. It was more than enough to send me over the edge. I whimpered through the pulses, the most powerful ones I had ever felt, while Alaric's fingers and tongue accompanied each one until they were completely done.

I lay there, body completely limp, overcome by the pleasure.

Alaric's nails grazed my skin as he stood, his lips glistening from my wetness. He locked eyes with me, made sure I saw him as he wiped his mouth and licked all of his fingers clean. The action brought forth another heat between my legs.

I sat up, reaching for his laces. He watched me tentatively. "It's time to be selfish," I mused.

One side of Alaric's lips turned up into a smirk. Taking that as permission, I undid the laces, biting my lip in anticipation.

I whimpered as he sprang free. The bulge had not done it justice enough. He was huge, and I had no idea how he would fit, but that didn't stop me from wanting him.

I grabbed the base, and parted my lips, but Alaric caught my chin and pivoted my gaze up.

"As much as I want these"—his thumb ran over my lips—"around me, I can't wait any longer."

I gulped, feeling too happy that his want for me was this high. I wanted him to feel good too, which is why I eyed his cock once more, at the creamy dribble that ran down it.

Gods, I wanted to taste him so bad.

"Please, Ina," Alaric pleaded. "Let me be inside you. I can't hold back anymore. If you make me wait, I'll have to run for miles to calm down."

I made some type of breathy sound that had Alaric's cock twitching.

Later.

Later, if he let me, I'd suck him until he came.

I crawled back until my head reached the back of the bed. "Take me how you need," I whispered, baring myself to him.

Alaric shuddered, and his throat bobbed, but that was all he needed.

He shucked off his pants and climbed onto the bed, his chest heaving as his cock pushed at my entrance. I gripped his forearms, ready for it, ready for the pain that came with something this huge, but I only felt pleasure.

He had warmed me up perfectly for him.

Still, Alaric was slow and gentle as he filled me then pulled out, repeating the speed until I began thrusting with him, silently telling him I was more than ready. After that, he didn't spare anymore time going slow and fully unleashed his wolf's desires.

His eyes darkened with need, the urge to dominate growing as he thrusted faster and faster, our flesh slapping together, and for once, I didn't mind that look. I didn't mind that a male fucked me to claim me, to put his scent on me because the way he felt, the way he moved, felt so fucking good.

I wrapped my arms tighter around Alaric, my legs too, as I sucked on his neck, tried not to bite it. That was reserved for mates after all. *Mates and lovers.* Still, I couldn't resist scraping my canines across his flesh. The action seemed to encourage Alaric to go faster, deeper—something I didn't think possible—and because of it, a second release began to build. I followed it, clenching my muscles around Alaric, letting him know it was coming.

"Good, come for me, Ina" he breathed, nudging my mouth away from his neck so he could access mine. "Come again so I can feel you tighten around me," he demanded, sucking on my neck. I jolted at his words, at his actions, but too much. The motion caused Alaric to slip, for his canines to brush too aggressively that they broke through my skin. He had bit me, and gods, it felt so right.

I knew it shouldn't have, knew that I shouldn't have liked it, that we had accidentally been too intimate, but the pleasure consumed me, and I found my release. Alaric did too. His cock pulsed inside me, and his warm seed filled me just as quick as I had come. It was like the bite had been his undoing as well; however, he didn't dare touch my neck again while he thrusted, working us both until we had finished. Then, with one final thrust, both our releases ended, and my chest tightened; I felt something tugging on my heart.

I looked up at Alaric, feeling joy, relief, and fear.

We had created a false mating bond between us. A bond that was stronger than any I had felt before.

CHAPTER 44

ALARIC

I balanced the two trays of food as I walked up the stairs to Neo's room, quicker than I cared to admit. I wanted to get back to Ina before she woke, before she assumed that she was easy to leave after everything we did last night. Not to mention that my wolf loathed to be away from her. It had been growling at me the moment I stepped out to get breakfast and to send a note to Alis, asking her to bring some preventative potions.

I knew that the bond would be strong, or at least, I had predicted that it would be, as they were always so random. However, I didn't think my wolf would yell at me not to leave her for such a short time nor did I think it would take so many rounds of sex to satisfy it last night. But I had to admit that the latter was hardly a problem.

Last night had been incredible, spectacular even. It was everything and more. Ina's body had moved in tandem with mine. Her moans were the sweetest sounds that I could listen to for hours. And when my canines had accidentally pierced her neck...

Gods, it had been hard not to dig them deeper into her.

Someone who wasn't my mate.

Someone I swore I'd never fall for.

Yet I had. Last night had made that clear enough. I didn't regret my decision at all. I would do it again and again, knowing that a false bond would form between us. But still, it could be worrisome.

I shook my head. I could handle this. I just needed to enjoy the situation as it was, see it as a fun fling between friends. I just needed to ride out the false mating bond, wait for it to dissolve, wait for the need to be by her side every moment to fade, then distance myself. It didn't matter if I was falling for her before this. I wouldn't let myself fall harder. I wouldn't make Ina deal with me more than she had to, despite her promising that she wasn't in the market for a mate and that I could take all the time I needed to get over the bond. At least, I would try.

"You're in much better shape than I thought you would be in," mused an older voice behind Neo's door.

I straightened, blaming the bliss I felt from joining with Ina for missing Alis's arrival. I'd have to be more cognizant of that. I couldn't let Ina and mine's bonding go to waste.

I sighed before knocking.

"Come in," Neo chimed.

I opened the door, only enough to get my body through. Though Alis had told us this was a safe place, I didn't want to take any chances. The less people who knew an injured wolf recovered in this room, the better.

Neo sat straighter in the bed upon seeing me. "Where have you been? I haven't seen you all night. Don't tell me you were patrolling."

I set the tray down on the small table beside Neo's bed, refusing to answer his question, unsure what to say. I knew he wouldn't be mad at me for leaving him all night to do other things. He was in a stable enough condition that I could, and I was close enough that if anyone tried to attack him, I would sense it before they opened his door. I just didn't know how he would react to me sleeping with his friend. I knew he admired Ina, and I was scared that he may not think me worthy enough to even kiss her. But still, even if that wasn't a factor, Neo and I hadn't exactly had the brotherly relationship where we talked about our dalliances. I hadn't had friends like that since Evelyn. I wouldn't even know how to talk about it, much less with how complicated the situation was between me and Ina.

I uncovered one of the platters and pushed it into his hands. "Eat," I commanded, hoping to distract him.

Neo scowled, but like all recovering wolves, he looked at the food as if he hadn't eaten in days and began unceremoniously scarfing it down. It was sight to behold. I had never seen Neo so enthralled with his food. Though, it was a good sign that he was healing much faster than anticipated.

"I suppose I can mark appetite as good in my notes," Alis croaked, writing in her journal.

I bristled, internally chiding myself for my manners. "My apologies," I said, turning to Alis, "if I had known you were already here, I would have brought up another meal."

"Would have been a waste. I had some rabbit this morning," she dismissed, not looking up from her journal.

Not wanting to distract her further, I silently admired her handiwork on Neo's arm. His forearm, which had been bright red yesterday, was now a soft pink. And the skin was starting to heal, slowly growing over the stitches, which—thanks to Neo's shifter powers—would naturally be pushed out of his body.

"Your skills as a healer are superb," I evenly stated, more for myself than her.

Still, the compliment pulled Alis away from her work. "They'd have to be, or every rogue wolf wouldn't agree that this inn is a safe haven for them to seek my aid."

I bobbed my head, seeing the truth in that statement, realizing that's why she had been so confident that no one would attack us here.

"In that case, I doubly thank you." I reached into my coin purse, taking out twice what I would pay a healer normally. "Without you, my brother wouldn't have survived the night, and we wouldn't have anywhere safe to stay while he recovered," I added, holding out the money to her. Alis took it with a considering hum. "Not enough?" I asked, already reaching for my coin purse again. It was better to pay her more than to argue, better for our safety anyway, if she really made the rules out here in the wilderness.

"Too much," she replied, but plopped the coins into her pocket. "Out here, we trade in services or supplies. Though seeing as how you're traveling, I don't think the latter is possible nor the former with where these coins are from. I haven't seen someone from Rivelia perform any services for a while now. I started to think I might never see a Rivelian in general again."

My stomach twisted, hating that was what was thought of us, but I could barely deny it, not when I had been one of the reasons for the thought.

"I see," I said, trying to keep as much information as I could private but still acknowledge the healer's words, "then I thank you for making an exception."

The healer mumbled something under her breath, too soft for me to hear, but proceeded to rummage in her portable box where she kept all her herbs.

"It's still gold, which to the humans is worth something. A lot of somethings," she grumbled. "Which is why your money will also cover your last-minute order." She opened her hand, revealing five vials of a greenish liquid. "She'll need to—"

I coughed, stopping Alis from saying more. "I'm familiar with them," I tried to say coolly, pocketing all but one to give to Ina. I didn't want her to think I expected anything more of her, but I also didn't want to be stuck in the middle of the woods without any preventives, just in case.

Alis side-eyed me but handed over the vials quietly, however, the damage was done. Neo had ceased his eating and was now sniffing me, each inhale growing increasingly louder and closer.

"I suppose my work here is done," Alis stated, standing up with her closed box.

I turned to the healer faster than she could blink. "He's fully recovered?"

She gave me a pointed look. "He's recovered enough not to need me anymore. Trust me, I don't leave my patients when they're still at risk." I glanced down, ashamed. Over the years, I had gotten too used to the healers in Rivelia that watched our every move, waited until the wound was healed, then watched months after. The female nodded at my sword. "He's not well enough for that, though. That will take a week, and even then, he'll have to take it slow. Let his body adjust and regain what he lost."

Neo stopped sniffing me, and I stiffened.

We were down one fighter. It was more important than ever to find the Woodland Pack.

I nodded swiftly, trying to hide the worry on my face as I bid her thanks again and walked her to the door.

"Ina isn't going to handle this well," I mumbled, already scared she would be too hard on herself. Yesterday, she had seemed to accept my words, accept the fact that Neo's injuries were not something she should blame herself for; however, this could all bring it back up.

"That's who you smell like," Neo chirped, completely past the unsettling news. "Ina. And those were—"

Neo's jaw dropped.

"I'll be back for your tray," I sputtered, turning on my heels, trying to escape before Neo inquired further. "Try to rest as much as possible. I'm going to sort out a patrol schedule."

"Wait," Neo interjected, "I have questions, and if you don't answer them now, I'll just head next door."

I rolled my eyes, fist clenching.

The joys of having a younger brother.

"Hurry up, then. Ina's food is getting cold."

Neo's grin spread from ear to ear. I snarled, unsure how to handle my emotions. Neo held up his hands, making him flinch.

Served him right for being a prying male.

"I just need to know why exactly or how? It was the last thing I ever thought you two would do."

"Things changed, Neo," I said as unfeeling as possible but couldn't suppress my smile at the irony of it all.

Neo's eyes widened. He looked me over from head to toe then sniffed. His mouth parted in shock. "Did you two finally fig—" Neo clamped his lips together, abruptly stopping his words. "How are you?"

"What do you mean?" I asked, a brow raised.

Neo chewed on the inside of his cheek, looking every which way but in my direction. "Well, I know that you were holding off joining with anyone until you found your mate, so—"

"How do you know that?" I interrupted, a little too aggressive than I intended.

Neo shouldn't have known about Evelyn, as the event had happened before he was born, and I certainly had never told him about it. Of course, others might have told him, but they considered it old news, nothing worth talking about unprovoked.

Neo ran his fingers through his hair—his nervous tick. "I did some digging a couple years ago as to why I had never seen you with anyone." I cocked my head, crossing my arms. I knew Neo was meddlesome but not that much. "I was bored," he stated defensively. "It was the summer that the guards were increased. I couldn't get out, and I needed something to do." I lifted my chin. "I won't ask you for specifics. People were very vague about it. But I do want to know if you're alright."

I stared at my brother, the one who should despise me for everything yet cared about my well-being and kept a positive light around him.

He had enough troubles caused by me. I couldn't add on to that. He needed to focus on retraining his arms.

I opened my mouth to say yes, that everything would be fine, that it wasn't anything like the past. However, no words came. I couldn't deny that I had been affected.

"Alaric," Neo whispered softly, sensing the turmoil that swirled inside me, "I need to tell you something. I don't know if I'm right, so I've been holding off on telling you, but I think I should."

I sat at the end of Neo's bed, hand over my mouth, utterly shocked by what he had said, but it all made sense.

It all started to make sense.

"Are you alright?" Neo asked.

I nodded.

I was more than alright, even if what he had told me wasn't verified just yet, because from the proof he showed me and how I felt, I knew it was. I just—I needed to—

I pushed the want aside.

I needed to wait. This news was better discovered by oneself or if proof was right in front of you. I had seen too many get overwhelmed on the matter if it came from someone else. That's why Neo had held off telling me, but I needed this. I needed to know.

But her, I wasn't sure how she'd handle this, and being so close to our goal, it was better to wait.

Safer.

If the actions of last night were doing half of what it did to me to Ina, she was already distracted enough.

CHAPTER 45

My hands bumped into the headboard I had gotten very familiar with last night as I stretched, realizing how pleasurably sore my body had become after last night. I couldn't remember when the last time I had felt like this after sex nor had so much of it with the same partner in one night. Our bodies kept begging for it, kept demanding it a few moments after we found our release. We had stayed up so late that I was surprised that the sun wasn't completely overhead, but I suppose I had the bond to thank for that, because my core absolutely ached for Alaric again. I wondered if he was the same.

Not wanting to wake him, I gently rolled over.

My stomach dropped.

The side he had slept on was empty, cold like he had been gone for a while.

I sat up, scanning the room, but there was still no sign of him. My chest stilled, and for a moment, I searched for the false mating bond to make sure someone was at the other end. But just as my mind neared the end, I stopped.

The less I searched for the bond and thought about it, the better chance I'd have of its effects lessening or simply going away. And that's what I wanted. It's what I always wanted, to be free of a bond, to be uninfluenced by it. I wanted to fall for someone of my freewill, not the gods'. But still, everything had felt so right last night. Couldn't it have lasted just a bit longer?

I mentally slapped myself, slapped away the awful, selfish thoughts in my head. Alaric wanted a mate. He wanted a bond. The sooner this one ended for him, the better. I had to limit any sensual touches as much as possible, unless our wolves were hurting, just like we agreed upon last night.

The door creaked open. I jumped out of the bed, twirling on my toes, ready to fight whoever had entered. To my relief and surprise, Alaric walked in holding a tray of food.

"Ready for a fight I see," he joked, closing the door behind him, without his amused eyes leaving me.

"Can never be too careful on the road," I retorted, lowering my guard.

Alaric nodded in agreement. "I brought you food," Alaric mused with care in his voice, nodding to the small table. Listening to his silent request, I sat in one of the two chairs. "It may be slightly cold now, though."

He placed the tray in front of me. On it were several pieces of ham, bread, some fruit, and a vial with green liquid that I recognized immediately.

"I asked Alis for it this morning. I hope you don't mind."

"Not at all," I replied, happy I didn't have to hunt her down later; however, a tinge of disappointment burned inside me at the fact that there was only one dose. "Thank you." Alaric nodded, and I turned back to my food, hoping it would get my selfish thoughts away from me. Thankfully, it did.

My mouth watered instantly. Clearly, I was at the end of my rope for the food travel allowed. I bit into some of the ham. The smoky flavor, despite it being room temperature, reawakened tastebuds I didn't know had slumbered to protect themselves from the bland food every day. A soft smile emerged.

"Still good?" Alaric asked with an absurd amount of care. I nodded. He sighed a breath of relief. "Good. Neo kept talking this morning and—"

"You saw Neo this morning?" I asked, eyes wide and focused on Alaric. "How is he? Is he in pain?"

Alaric reached across the table and cradled my chin as he used his thumb to wipe something from the corner of my mouth, clearly forgetting our avoidance rule. However, I didn't mind, especially as he was more affected by the bond than me—just as all males typically were than the female—and that the action had my entire body lighting up, proving that the bond was just as strong as it had been last night.

"He's fine," he cooed, like I was the injured party member. "He talked my ear off this morning. He has more energy than he's had since the start of this trip." My body drooped in relief. However, that feeling didn't last long as Alaric added, "I even think he might be able to fight sooner than the healer predicted."

"Fight sooner?" I gravely parroted. Alaric grimaced. "He can't fight?"

Alaric retracted his hand. "Don't blame yourself again."

I gulped, hearing the snarl in his voice. This was a topic I could not argue, one that had been discussed far too many times last night, according to Alaric. Neither one of the males would ever let me blame myself, and it was a fact I had to accept. However, guilt still drowned me.

"I won't," I retorted with my own subdued growl, "but he better let me protect him. He better play it safe once we leave the Inn." Alaric stared back at me with as much intensity, reminding me of the negative side effects of a bond. Even if it was false, it still made him possessive and protective over me. "*You* better let me protect him," I unwaveringly stated, trying to force my will onto him.

Alaric's eyes widened at the order I gave him, but then his head dropped. "Alright. But just know, I'm still going to protect you."

I gawked. This was how we had gotten into this mess in the first place. "Just because we are bonded doesn't mean—"

"It does, though. Even if it's"—Alaric chewed the inside of his cheek, eyes glancing away—"*false*, I have every right to protect you. You do too. But even if that wasn't the case, Neo, you, and I are a pack now. And packs protect each other."

I ran my tongue against the tip of my canines. We may be a pack right now, but it was temporary. They were still apart of the Rivelia Pack; they were their princes. Once this was done, they would go back, and I...

I didn't know what would happen to me. I tried not to think about the after of all this.

I knew that some of my pack was alive. However, at the rate we were traveling, I didn't know if that fact would remain. I didn't know if I would have anywhere to go, even if we won the battle the ahead. At least if Alaric and Neo made it out of here alive, they had somewhere to go, someplace to call home. It was better if they didn't take risks for me.

"Ina." Alaric knelt before me, taking my hands. "Everything will work out. We will protect each other, and we will all return."

A sense of calm rushed over me, as if someone had flung a blanket of comfort on top of me. I nodded despite the tears that threatened to let loose.

"Good girl." Alaric kissed the crown of my head.

I blinked rapidly, completely flushed. No one had done that before, not even Rainer when he was consumed by the false mating bond. Our interactions were purely sensual, not caring like this. The bond was so much stronger than I thought.

Alaric stood, beaming, proud of the blush he brought to my cheeks once again. "Gods, don't look like that. I was, now that we've resolved that matter again, going to lecture you for trying to compel me, but I—."

"Compel!" I barked, watching Alaric make his way to our bags. "I never did that."

Alaric turned his head, a brow raised. "Yes, you did. When you said *you better let me protect him,* I saw the look in your eyes and felt the energy radiating off you. It was the same as when I had ordered that rogue wolf."

"I," I began so I could deny; however, my words faded off. In all the chaos of Neo getting hurt and then Alaric and I joining, I had forgotten what Alaric had done.

"How did you do it?" I asked hesitantly.

Alaric, rummaging through his bag for something, not needing anymore words to know exactly what I was asking, responded solemnly, "I don't know. It was the first time I had done it. It was the first time I had ever compelled."

I cocked my head. With Alaric being the first-born male of an alpha, I would have expected him to have compelled multiple times by now.

Had he not known how to do it?

It would make sense. If he had known how to compel, he would've had Neo home as soon as he caught up to us. Instead, we were here.

"Do you think you can again?"

Alaric shook his head. "I've been searching for that power all my life, and I've never been able to call upon it until then. It didn't even happen because I willed it. It happened on its own accord, like it was a fight or flight response. I knew I needed to protect you and Neo, and it just happened."

"Oh," I responded, both relieved and saddened. The latter mostly for Alaric.

Compelling for a wolf was the epitome of power. It was the most blessed gift one could have. If I had the ability, it would've made my pack turn from their archaic ways without question. For me, not inheriting that power from my father was heartbreaking, but it was expected that I wouldn't get it, as the power was primarily relevant in males. For Alaric, it had to be soul crushing. He was a male and a direct descendant from one who had the power, and he couldn't control it.

"Regardless, what you did was amazing."

A smile emerged on Alaric's face, all the sorrow and disappointment from him disappearing, like my approval of him was all he needed. "Thank you, Ina."

The feeling warmed my chest and sent butterflies through my stomach. *Curse the bond for making me feel like this.*

Quickly, I nodded in welcome and turned, heading for my clothes. Needing to change the subject before I acted on my feelings, I asked, "Should we go on patrol?"

CHAPTER 46

Alaric crossed out an area of the map that sat between us, tapping his nails on the table. It echoed loudly in my ear despite all the chattering around us. Today's search had proved unfruitful, just like the days Neo had been gone, and to make matters worse, the bond had not faded even in most minuscule amount.

"We'll search here tomorrow." Alaric circled a small area to the right of where we scouted today.

I leaned forward. "That's logical," I tiredly replied.

"Good, then we can call it a night," Alaric offered, finishing off his ale.

I rubbed my fingers together.

While I was tired, it was more so in a mental capacity than physical. I needed respite from the numerous worries and thoughts that filled my head. I needed to relax and not in the way that I wanted as I watched Alaric lick his lips, especially not when we planned to share a room together. After the false bond formed, Alaric's wolf was prone to agitation and worry. It made it so Alaric couldn't be away from me for more than a few minutes without pacing about. It was not at all conducive behavior for someone like Neo who needed rest, therefore we had spent ever moment together, but it did nothing to help us lessen the bond on either of our ends. However, it was the better of the two awful results, but it was taking its toll on me, and I desperately needed to numb my mind with drink, just enough to quiet my thoughts and urges.

"After another one." I stood up with my mug and headed for the bar, feeling Alaric's eyes on me. I didn't look back, knowing his attentiveness was the cause of the bond, and leaned on the bar, pointing to my cup so the barkeep could get me what I wanted once he had time.

"Your lover isn't buying this round?" asked a red-haired man propped next to me.

"He's not my lover, and he's not obligated to buy every one of my drinks," I answered, though I felt odd saying Alaric wasn't. In a way, he was, but not in the way that mattered.

"Well, that's good."

I hummed in response, not really paying attention to his words. I was in no mood to converse unnecessarily. Thankfully, the barkeep slid an ale in front of me, along with an opened hand. I reached into my coin purse; however, before I could untie the knot that kept the coins safe, the redhead dropped his own into the barkeep's hand, causing me to fully look at him for the first time.

He sipped his drink, playfully smiling. "Whoever charms you, shouldn't make you use your own coppers."

I smirked at his attempt to woo me despite being highly uninterested in his pursuit. A free drink was a free drink, and if he wanted to gamble that it would encourage me to talk, he could. He just wouldn't win. I had to too much to worry about already, and I also had Alaric's wolf to consider. I was sure if Alaric was still watching me, it was ready to remark its territory.

"Thank you." I clinked my glass with the redhead's, pleasantly smiling. "But I'm not in the mood tonight."

The man sighed, but nodded, taking my rejection gracefully—as any male should—before I walked back to Alaric.

"You could have stayed longer," Alaric flatly claimed, though his pursed lips told me otherwise.

I slid into the chair in front of him, noting his ironclad grip on his empty mug and tapping foot. His wolf was definitely acting up, yet he held it back—which I knew from firsthand was painful—and it didn't help my resolve to avoid sleeping with Alaric.

"Alaric," I called softly, forcing him to turn away from the redhead. "I won't entertain advances while we're bonded. Your wolf would throw a tantrum," I reasoned, hiding the real fact.

"I can keep it in check for a short dalliance," he grumbled.

I chuckled under my breath at the hint of jealously in his tone. I knew I shouldn't have but seeing Alaric like this—caused by the bond or not—was too satisfying after all the grueling, torturous things he had made Neo and I do during our journey. Still, I needed to ease his wolf.

"I only care for long ones," I tauntingly hummed, sipping my drink, "like the one we had the other night."

Alaric's eyes darkened exactly how I wanted.

By now, I knew Alaric wouldn't keep me from what I wanted, and because he didn't trust his wolf to let him see clearly, he wouldn't easily believe that I didn't want the redhead. It was simpler to divert Alaric's attention to lust, just for a bit, than to try and make him see sense.

"Ina," Alaric growled.

I crossed my legs, licking my lips, knowing it was time to put out this fire, to blame my flirtations on my wolf then chug my drink and have us sleep and nothing more. However, when I opened my mouth, I found I had reached far beyond my limit and couldn't bring myself to do so.

"I thought we were avoiding *that*," Alaric stated, though there was sensual curiosity in his tone.

I opened and closed my mouth, unable to agree. We had. It had been implied after our last activity of many when we agreed that we had to try and end the bond as quickly as possible and not add fuel to the fire. And I wholeheartedly agreed. My words were supposed to be a joke, a distraction. So why couldn't I just laugh?

"I can't feel my feet," someone slurred too closely for my liking.

I looked up just in time to see a patron trip and slosh his cold ale onto Alaric, extinguishing the fire in his eyes.

"Sorry about my friend," another patron gushed out, throwing the first's arm over his shoulder. "Too much drink."

"It's fine," Alaric stated, his calloused expression unable to match his words.

The men nodded and went off on their way, swaying as they walked, happy to get away without repercussions.

"Well, I think it's safe to end the night on that note." Alaric stood, flapping his wet tunic. "To bed?"

My eyes snapped to Alaric, gulping. Though the cold ale had cleared his head, I was still occupied with my *thoughts*. However, I couldn't stay down here, not without Alaric's wolf worrying. And I couldn't let Alaric know or his wolf would come back out, so I nodded.

Alaric headed straight for the jug in our room and poured the water into the basin beside it.

I hustled for the bed, hoping to hide under the covers as he undressed. I didn't need to see him shirtless in the state I was in. However, just as I was passing, he slung off his tunic revealing—

My mouth went dry, and any urges I had disappeared.

Though Alaric and I had been naked around each other last night, the light had not been bright enough to reveal the scars that marked his body. There were too many to count.

"What?" Alaric asked, dipping his shirt in the water.

"Are all of those from the war?"

Alaric's throat bobbed, but his face remained neutral as he said, "Most."

My gaze lingered, pity already taking over. Alaric had to have experienced so much pain. I mean, I knew he fought. I knew a warrior his age had to have experienced a wound before, but not these many.

"Don't worry." Alaric patted my head. "They're just like any other scar, like this one." Alaric raised my arm, tracing a scar on my forearm. "How did you get it?"

"A bandit I had been chasing on one of my first missions cut me, and I was too stubborn to put an ointment on it, so it scarred."

Alaric pointed to a scar across his left pectoral. "A slash from a demon. It wasn't with a silver blade, but I had been too tired after the battle to put ointment on."

My cheeks puffed up, as I wanted to rebuttal that he still had more scars than me, more than anyone in my patrol unit, except for the older wolves; however, I could see that Alaric wanted to make light of the situation, as warriors often did when others looked at them, just as how I had looked at Alaric now. By the gods, I even did this act with my sisters when I came back from my own missions. It helped make us feel normal. So, I played along, knowing I couldn't just drop the conversation without creating a quiet awkwardness around us.

"And this one?" I asked, pointing at a small one on his ribs.

"Stab wound," he answered, resuming his wipe down. "It barely hurt."

I hummed in response, acting unfazed. Alaric relaxed at that and turned around to hang his shirt, exposing his back to me, which made his front seem hardly a thing to gasp over.

Whereas the scars on his front were slightly faded and small, the ones on his back were vibrant. They started from his shoulder and ended at his hips, protruding out of his back. They even made a pattern, as if someone had the time to aim, had held Alaric down.

"The scars on your back, what are those from?" I asked, though I had a good inclination.

Alaric froze. "A lashing."

"From who?" I nearly growled. My own wolf, demanding the answer, wanting to protect the male I had falsely bonded to, despite the act happening some time ago.

Alaric turned around, a darkness shrouding his eyes.

I remembered Neo's words, then. I remembered how Neo had mentioned that Alaric kept mumbling about his sacrifices and protecting everyone when he learned about our mothers.

My chest rang out in pain, not wanting to hear the answer, scared that it would contribute to that, but I asked again, "Who did that you?"

He looked at me then lowered his eyes, realizing I would not let this go. Finally, he mumbled, "My father."

I held my arms tighter to me as Alaric stared, waiting for my reaction after he told me his story—his perspective the day Damon burned the human village—but I didn't know what to say, what to do.

Alaric had sacrificed so much more than Neo and I had guessed to keep his brother and the humans safe from Damon.

"Please, don't tell Neo," Alaric pleaded, breaking the silence. I raised a brow. "I don't want him to feel responsible. He already feels too much guilt over that day."

I fought against the crumpling in my chest, the watering of my eyes. "You mean to tell me that Neo doesn't know."

Alaric shook his head. "No one does. I couldn't risk word getting out. My father wouldn't have trusted me then."

A single tear dropped. This explained so much. This explained why Alaric had been so devastated the day he found out about our mothers, why he had been so hostile toward me. He had sacrificed everything, and he had done it all alone. Without thinking, I wrapped my arms around Alaric, pulling him close. He stood there with his arms awkwardly at his side.

"No matter what, I'm here for you," I said, but inside, I was swearing that I would protect him at all costs in the future for what he had done, that I would never let him go through things alone again.

Alaric slowly lifted his arms and hugged me back. I could feel tears running off his face and onto my neck as he nuzzled it.

"Alaric?" I cooed, worried as I had never seen him shed a tear.

"Sorry. I haven't been hugged like this since the war ended," he whispered. "Can we stay like this for a little longer?"

A sharp pain reverberated through my chest, and I couldn't bring myself to say words, so I just nodded and held Alaric tighter.

CHAPTER 47

I t had been two days since the attack. Neo had been recovering much faster than we had anticipated, and Alis's word about wolves not fighting here had held true. For once, we felt safe. Well, as safe as we could on the road. Alaric and I still checked the inn for any threats before falling asleep, and we only wandered far enough away that we could still scent Neo and any potential threats that may come too close. Though, today, we had plans to push the boundaries.

While resting at the inn had done wonders for us all, we had expended too many days not traveling, especially since we still hadn't found the Woodland Pack's trail, as it had shifted over the many years since Alaric had last traveled it. It was vital that when we went back to traveling tomorrow, we had a clear path to follow.

"Any signs?" I asked Alaric, who was a few feet away in wolf form.

He shook his head, his mane distractingly dancing in the wind.

I rested my hands on my hips, sighing loudly. This wasn't going well at all. We had already pushed our boundaries to the point where Neo's scent was hardly noticeable. We couldn't go further without risking him.

Alaric nudged my side, calling my attention as he sat by me.

"I know," I whispered. "We're doing everything we can." Alaric nodded, looking at me with those intense eyes that told me to stop thinking about everything I couldn't do. I hated it, but not because he was telling me what to do.

I hated it because he did it in a caring way, and it made me want to thank him. It made me want to hug him. I especially hated it now, because he was in wolf form, and that would lead to me caressing his fur.

Though the bond was just as strong as the day we created it, and Alaric seemed not to shy away from endearments, I didn't want to push further into the boundaries that we had set, especially after seeing how I reacted when I attempted to seduce his wolf to end its jealousy the other night. I didn't want to do what lovers and mates did. And touching his fur, without plausible excuse, would definitely cross that line.

Trying to submerge my urges, I walked in a direction we hadn't tried yet. "I'm just scared that we'll waste time wandering around aimlessly." I toed a fallen branch decorated with flowers and plenty of leaves. "I just want—" I stilled as I saw the ground the branch was hiding. "Alaric, is this what I think it is?"

Alaric rushed over; his eyes widened before his paws stopped moving. He tensed and lowered his nose to the ground, to the indent shaped like a paw, far too big to belong to a normal wolf.

I held my breath, watching as his nostrils flared and took more than a few whiffs and inched forward. Slowly, he turned back to me, eyes closing as he shifted.

"Well?" I asked.

Alaric stared at me for a moment then finally a soft smile emerged. "It's them," he whispered, "and they're not far away."

"Really?" Alaric nodded, making a smile erupt on my face. There was hope. Too happy to control myself, I jumped on Alaric, holding him tightly. He hugged me back, his warmth sending shivers down my spine, the urge to kiss him coming forth again. Quickly, I retracted back, not wanting to give into my urges too much, as doing so would only encourage the bond to stay strong. "Sorry," I whispered.

"It's alright," Alaric replied softly, almost sounding disappointed. "It's good to see a smile on your face."

I blushed, unable to face his sweet words. Gods, the bond made Alaric so endearing. I hated how much I loved it. Whoever was his destined mate was going to be a lucky female.

"Should we go back to the inn?" I asked, trying to change the conversation to business matters. "I know we have a couple hours before we need to be back, but my limbs are so sore. I could use a long bath."

Alaric rubbed his chin. "We can, but yesterday, didn't you say that the bath wasn't hot enough?"

I rolled my head and rubbed my biceps, hoping to find some relief. "Yeah, but it's better than nothing." I spun on my heels, heading to the inn, but Alaric didn't follow. "You coming?" I asked, seeing his nose turn up.

"Come with me," Alaric requested. I didn't get to ask why as he hurriedly walked deeper into the forest.

"Alaric," I finally yelled after following him blindly, "where are we going exactly?"

"Don't you smell it?" I sniffed, frowning, as I smelt nothing but the woods. Alaric laughed. "There's sulfur nearby."

I inhaled again, this time looking for that particular scent. It was very faint and heavily diluted, but past the pine and grass, I could faintly smell it. My eyes widened. "How did you even scent that?" I rubbed my nose, hoping I hadn't tired out my wolf. But it seemed highly unlikely, as Alaric and I had been alternating who shifted during the days we had searched.

"Don't worry. I sensed it in wolf form earlier," Alaric explained. My brows furrowed. "I wouldn't have noticed it in human form either unless I was looking for it."

"That's a relief." I braced my hand against a tree trunk, resting for a minute. "But heading toward sulfur still doesn't tell me where we are going."

Alaric made it to the top of the hill we had been climbing, stopping in front of leaves too dense to see past. He peeked carefully through them then turned to me with a smirk, waving his hand so energetically I couldn't help but hurry to him.

"I'm surprised you don't know."

I gave Alaric a pointed look. He laughed, and it was so joyous and beautiful. I really did like this side of him. It put me at ease. But still, I continued my act of being annoyed and nudged him in the side. "Come on. Tell me already. I'm tired."

Alaric gathered the branches in his hand. "Somewhere to remedy that."

I cocked my head and licked my lips, still unable to guess before he pulled the branches back and revealed a hot spring.

With a small gasp, I rushed toward the steaming water, kneeling at its edge, feeling the warmth. It was much hotter than the bath I would have received at the inn, but not too hot that my skin would be screaming if I stayed in it for more than a few minutes. It was perfect.

"I can't believe you found this."

"Neither can I, and we can still smell Neo from here," Alaric replied, still on the other side of the wall of leaves. "You probably have enough time for an hour soak before we need to head back."

I nodded gleefully. An hour was just the right amount of time to relax my muscles.

"Well, I'll just be on the other side. Call me if you need me." Alaric began to release the branches.

"Wait," I called, already undoing my laces. "Did you not want to get in?"

"It's rather small. I didn't want to take away from your enjoyment."

I examined the pool of water. It was shallow, barely deep enough to cover my breasts if I squatted, and the size was about four tubs sat together. It would be tight, but we could both fit.

"You won't be." With skewed lips, Alaric eyed the ground, as if he still might decline. "You deserve to be relaxing in the water just as much as me. I won't take no for an answer. Come on." Alaric still didn't move. I let out a hearty sigh, storming over to him and pulling him past the branches so they closed with a snap.

"Ina," he chided, planting his feet.

"I'll just stand with you until you agree, and if you don't, neither of us will be able to bathe."

Alaric looked up to the sky, rubbing the bridge of his nose, cursing quietly. I smiled broadly, knowing I had won. "Fine, hurry up and get in."

I nodded victoriously, turning as I shimmied out of my trousers and threw off my tunic. I wasted no time running to the water, feeling the warmth hug my body, and massaging my aching muscles. I lowered in, letting it lap at the top of my breasts, humming with pleasure. I turned, hoping to catch a glimpse of Alaric's initial reaction. However, he was still firmly planted where I had dragged him, fully dressed, and his back to me.

"What are you doing?" I questioned, worried he was going to back out of his promise.

I swear if he made me climb out and abandon the heat, I would drag him in with his clothes still on.

"Giving you privacy to get undressed and into the water."

I stilled. "Why?"

Alaric's head fell into his palms. "Because it's the polite thing to do," he declared like it was a silly question.

"You've seen me naked body before."

Alaric scoffed. "Yes, and I had your permission to see it. Just because you give it once does not mean I have it all the time, especially when the time you gave it to me was because of your heat."

"Oh," I whispered softly, feeling another pang in my heart. Gods, I didn't think I would have a thing for such chivalry. I really needed to be more careful around Alaric. He kept getting more and more desirable.

"Anyway, can I?" Alaric crossed his arms.

"Can you?" My cheeks burned.

"Get in the water, now?"

"Oh, right, yes," I stammered out, completely embarrassed that I had thought Alaric had been asking about my body. Though, if he was, I would have said yes. We hadn't touched each other since the night we had first joined, and right now, everything in me screamed to touch him, for me to touch him. And I knew I shouldn't. I promised I wouldn't unless his wolf needed me.

Alaric began to take off his own clothes. I watched with fascination and longing. Hating myself for it because it was too great. It was such a stronger urge than the night we had joined, that I knew it was more than just the bond that glued my eyes to him. It was me. With the bond bringing down his walls, I was able to see him vulnerable—a warrior without his armor. And while I admired who he was before we bonded—that serious, general-like male—seeing him like this, I couldn't help but fall deeper into the hole that was my demise.

CHAPTER 48

ALARIC

"You're not looking, are you?" I asked, despite feeling Ina's eyes on me.

"No," she yelped, accompanied with the frantic splashing of water.

I smiled broadly, knowing she was red beyond belief. I didn't care if she watched. She could stare as long as she liked. I honestly wanted her to. I wanted her to want me, but I also loved seeing her flustered—the female who acted so tough until a couple days ago. It made me happy that I had that effect on her, that maybe she might feel like I did too.

I wanted to ask her if she did, but with the bond just having snapped into place, I knew she couldn't have sorted out her real emotions yet, especially with everything that was going on. And even if she did feel that way toward me, I wasn't worthy of her yet. I still had so much in this life to make amends for. Not to mention, we had our own wants to confront first.

I turned, shedding the last of my clothes and headed for the spring, trying not to ogle Ina's naked, perfect back too much. She stiffened a bit as the water splashed around, and I wondered if I had made the right choice by giving in to her. The last thing I wanted to was make her uncomfortable, but getting out now would only result in more arguing, and I wanted her to enjoy the water to its fullest. I would just have to keep my distance. I sunk down as low as I could and waded to the opposite side of the small pool.

"Alright. I'm in," I whispered. Ina swung herself around, her breasts bobbing in the water. I swallowed hard, feeling my blood rush somewhere where it had no business to and focused on a branch just past her head. "The water feels good," I stated coolly, hoping conversation would distract me enough.

Ina hummed in agreement but too sweetly, reminding me of all the sounds she had made the night we joined. "The water is hotter in the middle."

"I'll have to avoid that area, then. My heat tolerance is next to none." I brought my arms out of the water and rested them on the edge of the pool, exposing them to the cool air.

Ina nodded. "Do you mind if I use it? I like my water almost scolding."

"Go for it," I replied, gesturing to the spot, trying not to watch as she bobbed forward.

Gods, I was a mess.

Ina and I fell silent. Both of us looking at anything but each other, the tension between us undeniably loud. Then, after some time, Ina reached up to her shoulder and began to rub, the ripples in the water calling my attention.

"Is the spring not helping?" I asked, concern getting the better of me.

"My muscles have loosened, but the knots are still there." She reached further back, attempting to get her shoulder. The action raised her breasts further out of the water.

I gulped again, needing her to stop, but I couldn't very well tell her to, not when the whole goal of coming here was for her to ease her aching muscles, not when she would instantly know why when I asked her to. But still, she kept reaching back and more of that perfect bosom peeked out. Without thinking, I growled, "Turn around." Ina frantically looked around, thinking we were under attack. I slammed my hand to my forehead in disbelief.

What was wrong with me?

"Sorry. I just...there was something in my throat when I said that. That's why it came out so aggressive." Ina continued to inquisitively stare at me, her face distorted. I knew instantly that she was wondering if she had done something wrong, crossed some sort of line. She had been so careful not to these past few days, so scared that she would take advantage of the infatuation the bond had caused or even make it stronger. But I didn't care about that, at least not in regard to her affecting me. Whatever was going to happen, happened already. I twirled my finger. "Let me help you get those knots out."

"You don't have to," she mumbled, though a hint of desire vibrated in her voice.

"You can't reach the spot you're aiming for, Ina. Plus, you're making the water ripple. It's making me reposition every couple of minutes," I explained, knowing whatever guilt she had about me massaging her would be overshadowed by my excuse.

"Ok, but you don't have to rub too long." Ina turned, backing into my open hands. I nodded, despite knowing she couldn't see and began to work her tender flesh, and gods, it was more torturous than seeing her rub herself.

With every knot I rid Ina of, her body became more relaxed, falling back to where she nearly touched my chest. And the sounds she made...

I was defeated by my urges, and it was showing just below the water. Still, I couldn't stop touching her, not when it was bringing her so much joy. I just hoped she didn't fall back anymore because—

Ina inched back, far too much that she fell right into my chest, her hand reaching back to catch herself, only to grab me in the one spot I wanted to hide from her. A guttural, primal growl escaped my lips. Ina, realizing what she was holding, retracted back.

"I'm so sorry," she profusely sputtered. "I forgot to hold my body up." I breathed in deeply, attempting to calm myself, trying to stop my cock from pulsing and begging for more. "Is your wolf demanding me?" Ina asked, too concerned.

Not wanting to reveal that it was me, I bobbed my head. "But it will be fine." I stood, shielding myself with my hand, full intent to head back to shore. "You finish up. I'll wait beyond the trees."

Ina stood just as fast, revealing every inch of her wet, naked body and grabbed my hand. It took every ounce of my restraint not to take in the view, imagine all the things I wanted to do with her.

"No, it won't be. You'll get agitated and tense," she explained, acting as if I didn't know the consequences of ignoring your wolf.

"I know how to deal with it," I retorted, continuing with my lie. Ina's shoulders slacked, which would have made me happy if it were not for the sadness swirling in her scent. "Ina, it's not your fault. You know our wolves are unpredictable."

"I know. I just want to..." There was weakness in her voice, vulnerability. "I want to be of help to you, but I also don't want to see you have to do things you're not proud of."

I stopped, turning my head to see her solemn face. It was completely destroyed. She didn't think she was something to be proud of. But how could she when she was anything but. She was someone any male would be lucky to have at their side. I couldn't let her think otherwise.

"Ina," I whispered, pivoting her head up, caressing her cheek with my thumb, "it's not you. I want..." I licked my lips, not wanting to reveal too much. "You said to think of this as fun if I ever got scared about the bond, and I am. If we were back in Rivelia and this happened, I would be more than willing to join with you. It's undeniable that I find you attractive and..." I dropped my hands, hearing myself sputter. "What I'm trying to say is, I'm not saying no because I don't want you. I'm saying no because I don't want you to have sex with me for only my behalf. And I know you said you weren't the first night we joined, but that was back then, and I'm still not entirely sure that it's true or if you were desperate for another solution. I don't want you to be ok with this"—I motioned between us—"because you're worried about my wolf. I—"

Ina's lips were on mine in a heartbeat, effectively shutting me up. Tentatively, I wrapped my arms around her, my body relaxing all around her.

She pulled away, but only so she could look up at me. "Then, we're in agreement," she whispered, pushing me back to the shallows of the waters so it hit us at the knees. I let her, too focused on making sure I kept breathing.

She wanted me. I wasn't sure if it was just desire or something more. Though I doubted it was the second option. Still, if it was only desire, I would take that. I would take anything she gave me.

Ina slumped to her knees, her hands gliding down my chest then to my upper thigh.

"Ina," I growled, already guessing what she was about to do. I was supposed to please her, not the other way around.

"I promised myself that if you'd let me, I would do this," she mewled, too much wanting in her voice that I couldn't reject it.

She grabbed the base of my shaft, slowly circling it with her thumb. I groaned, fingers flexing as my hand hovered over her hair, threatening to take control. She pumped me a couple times, her doe eyes looking up at me, watching.

"You promise you want this?" she asked, but it sounded like a plea.

My throat bobbed. "I do."

She smiled, bringing me into her mouth.

"Fuck," I groaned, feeling her tongue twist down my shaft, leading the way for the rest of her mouth to follow until she was at the base, taking me whole in her mouth. She pulled away, leaving me panting, needing. I gave her a tortured look, and she laughed, relishing in my pain. I started to say her name in warning, but thankfully, she sucked me in again, making sure to lick every area as she dug her nails into my thighs.

I groaned, unable to keep my hands off her. She smiled as I entwined my fingers into her hair, but I let her work by herself. I wanted to see what she could do, what she could handle. As if taking that as a challenge, Ina went faster, her neck bobbing.

I leaned back, using every muscle in my core to keep from collapsing back with pleasure. However, that restraint couldn't be applied to the groans, the prayers of her name that I wanted to keep muffled. She was coaxing every sound out of me, and it was encouraging her to go faster, to graze her teeth against my flesh. And fuck, if that didn't bring me closer to the edge, I didn't know what would. I needed to get inside her soon, give her pleasure before I found mine.

"Ina, come here." She shook her head. "Please, I'm about to come, and I don't want to be selfish," I pleaded, but it only made her go faster, her lips tighten around me.

I cursed, holding her tighter, making her fully aware just how soon I was about to burst, that now was not the time to test me. But she only smiled, and I realized that she wanted me to come. She wanted me to spill into her mouth. She wanted me to be selfish. She really wanted me to find my pleasure and not because of my wolf.

Gods, I would be saying her name in my prayers from now on.

With one last lick, I exploded, my cock pulsing in her mouth. Ina swallowed with a smirk, causing that reoccurring shiver throughout my body to happen for the hundredth time since I met her. I pulled her up, ready to give her just as much pleasure, but she planted her palms on my chest.

"The sun is going down. We need to get back," she whispered, kissing my chest. "Next time."

I looked up, seeing the hues of orange and red. I sadly nodded, knowing she was right. I wished we had more time, but at least there would be a next time now, and that was all the hope I needed to keep my dreams alive.

CHAPTER 49

"It feels good to be outside again," Neo chimed to no one in particular, throwing out his arms, using only his core to keep him on his horse.

"Stop flailing around so much," commanded Alaric, his chest pushing into my head. "You're still healing."

Neo looked back with a minuscule scowl. "I won't fall. Calm down, but if it makes you feel better"—Neo dropped a singular arm, a devilish smile on his face—"I'll hold my reins with one hand," he announced before facing forward again.

"Gods, grant me the strength not to pummel my idiot brother," Alaric grumbled so low that if I weren't riding with him, I wouldn't have heard.

I laughed without restraint.

"Don't support his humor," Alaric whispered, bringing his mouth to my ear. "You're supposed to be on my side."

I couldn't help but tilt my gaze to Alaric in question, earning me a single kiss at the base of neck.

I shuddered a sigh, trying to calm the urges. Though I had promised myself that I would answer them from now on, now was hardly an appropriate time to act on them. Not when we were on the road. Not when Neo was just ahead. And Alaric knew that.

He had been teasing me since we left the inn, his hands always *accidentally* grazing my thigh, his body pressing against my backside. He was pushing those limits, waiting for the *next time,* and honestly, I was too.

After last night, I had nothing holding me back from wanting Alaric, from acting on those urges. At least nothing that would hurt or take advantage of others. For me, I still may get hurt. I was falling into a pit of feelings that I had been running from my entire life. Feelings, that when the bond faded, I knew wouldn't go away. He wanted a mate, and I was not it. Wolves from different packs rarely were. Not that it mattered. My thoughts on mates were still the same as when I left Artico. However, that possible hurt, I was willingly to gamble with it. As long as I remembered what Alaric wanted, I could keep myself from crossing the dangerous line I was dancing on.

I leaned away, rolling my eyes. "I was friends with Neo before you. If anything, I'm supposed to be on his side," I joked.

Alaric's grip tightened, keeping me from leaning further away, as he took back the distance I had created. "I hardly think that's the case when it's my name you've been moaning. Don't you agree?" Alaric asked, his voice sinful as his fingertips idly made circles just below my ribs.

I licked my lower lip, relishing the small touches. He was going to make me melt.

Neo gasped just ahead, pulling me out of the trance Alaric had put me in. Frantically, I grabbed a bundle of dried lavender from my pouch and sat it in my lap, hoping it would cover up the scent I wanted to hide.

Thank the gods that a peddler had arrived at the inn this morning.

Alaric laughed, briefly kissing my forehead before calmly replying, "What is it?"

"Come look," Neo replied in an excited tone. It was safe to assume he hadn't caught on to what Alaric and I were doing back here, but still, I kept the lavender close.

Alaric clicked his tongue, asking Irie to go forward, a bit annoyed. However, that dissipated as we came parallel with Neo and saw the field of blue flowers.

"Shineblooms," Alaric whispered.

"A whole field," Neo finished for him.

I sat back, both astonished and angry at the sight.

Shineblooms were hard to find, and even when you did, there were only five or so in the area. It took months to gather a bouquet of them. The sight before us was a miracle, a wonder. At least to those who wanted a mate. To me, this field was everything that I despised.

These were the plants that had magical properties inside the petals, ones that only interacted with wolf shifters. It could be infused into candles and glassware, and it would still reveal what the flower did itself. It revealed when mates were near one. It helped shifters see just exactly who they were *supposed* to fall in love with. It was the flower that made my life hell for years, forced me to be paraded around.

"Shineblooms don't grow in Artico," Neo sputtered. "Is this your first time seeing them in person, Ina? What do you think?" I bit my lip, not wanting to say anything, too busy brooding. "Ina," Neo called again, touching my arm.

Unable to lie through my anger, I seethed, "I hate them. I hate them more than anything."

CHAPTER 50

ALARIC

I sat by Ina, watching her sleep, debating for the millionth time tonight on what I wanted to do. We had come across those flowers, and my heart had leaped. I wanted to stay with her there until night fell, see if the flowers would glow as they did when mates were near, but she had revealed a truth that I could not unhear.

I knew she wasn't actively looking for her mate, but I didn't know she didn't want one, that she hated the concept, that she had the complete opposite opinion of me.

It hurt more than anything I had ever felt in my life because because I was falling in love with her. Because I was in love with her.

Gods damnit, I thought she was my mate. Neo thought so too.

He had guessed from the moment she and I had started to be cordial with one another, and I stopped despising her enough to notice a change in her scent before Neo. The strong bond between me and Ina supported his theory too, and just a few hours ago, I was so glad of it. Now, it brought me to the brink of insanity. It made me stupidly trek back two miles to pick a flower and put it in my pocket then wait until everyone had fallen asleep to debate if I wanted to bring it out and see if it glowed.

If it didn't, it would give me peace of mind. It would allow me to think on the next big decision; did I still want Ina?

Gods damn, what a stupid question.

I was willing to turn my world upside down for her, to forsake my own vow to make sure she was safe. Of course, I did. I would want her no matter what.

The real problem would be if the flower glowed.

The last thing I wanted to do was force Ina into a situation she didn't want, especially after hearing about all the mating rituals she had been forced to go through, even that absurd arrangement with the male Rainer. If we were mates, I would have to keep it a secret. I would have to knowingly walk away from a bond that would last forever. I would have to tell her I didn't want her anymore. And I didn't know if I had the strength to do that, which was why I still hadn't brought out the flower in my pocket.

I dragged a hand down my face, stopping at my mouth, silencing a sigh.

I was a coward. I had to stop being one now.

I breathed in deep and closed my eyes. With a shaky hand, I pulled out the shinebloom I had picked. I counted to ten, recalling all the memories I had made with Ina and how she had made me feel—in case it was the last time I was allowed to remember—then I opened my eyes.

A soft blue glow emitted from the flower.

I needed to end whatever was between us tomorrow.

CHAPTER 51

I forced my eyelids to lift, stretching every which way, popping all my joints back into place after sleeping on the forest floor. The sun was starting to rise, making the morning dew glisten. It was time to get up, for us to have breakfast. I sniffed, wondering what Alaric had cooked up today, but as I did, I didn't smell the fire burning nor any whiff of provisions.

Had I woken up first?

I sat up, feeling oddly proud of myself, ready to make Neo and Alaric breakfast, but as I did, I found that my theory hadn't been right at all.

Alaric and Neo glared at each other, the tension between them palpable. It was like seeing them stand off against each other the day Amos revealed the truth.

I jumped to my feet, scared of what had happened. Both their heads snapped to me with such focus that I staggered back.

"What's going on?" I asked.

Neo looked to Alaric, waiting for something, but Alaric only stared at me like his heart had been torn in two. Neo shook his head, turning his attention to me, and opened his mouth.

Zero words were able to leave it as Alaric gritted out of his teeth, "I can handle it. Just give us some privacy."

Neo opened and closed his mouth, debating on if he was going to continue to fight Alaric, but he stopped and clutched his sword for support. "Fine, but just remember what I said." Alaric ignored his brother, keeping his eyes on me. "Take care of him, Ina," Neo whispered, heading to the forest.

I waited for Neo's footsteps to become distant before asking again, "What's going on? Did we lose the trail?" Alaric remained quiet, licking his lips. "Alaric," I cooed, reaching for him. He stepped back, holding out his hand, anxious of my approach.

"I think I've made a mistake," he muttered.

"About what?" I tilted my head, heart pounding.

"About—"

A howl erupted within the forest, howls that were deeper and louder than any normal wolf or dog could make. Several others followed it, sounding closer, converging into a single area, the direction Neo had gone.

Alaric and I did not need to say anything as we went into action. Whatever conversation we were going to have could wait. We needed to get to Neo first.

I ran to Irie, mounting her just as Alaric shifted and sprinted into the forest, cursing that it would take me too long to shift because of my heat. I slapped Irie's reins, trying my best to keep up with Alaric, determined to fight in whatever battle was ahead, despite still being in human form. I wouldn't let them fight alone, not when Neo was still recovering, not when those howls were signaling an attack. We were a pack, and we needed to stick together.

I followed Alaric past the tree line into a clearing where a lake sat. Nothing was there except for Neo, standing with his sword out, conserving his wolf just in case.

Alaric leapt beside him, jerking his head to his back, telling Neo to get on. Neo did so diligently; however, it was too late. Leaves not too far away rustled on all sides.

I jumped off Irie and raced to Neo and Alaric, unsheathing my sword. We stood back-to-back, waiting, watching the woods until six massive wolves emerged.

CHAPTER 52

The six wolves began to stalk forward, canines bared and claws out. Their eyes ran over each of us again and again, sizing us up.

Alaric's hackles stood on end, his breathing heavy.

He was nervous.

My heart lurched. Still, I continued holding my stance, kept my features expressionless. I knew the odds were against us. We were as good as dead with two of us still unshifted, but our attackers wouldn't know that I was scared. It would give them power. However, that statement ceased to be true as Alaric shifted to his human form.

"What?" I breathed out, reaching for him. "What are you doing?"

Alaric glanced at me and Neo from the corner of his eyes. "Sheathe your swords," he whispered, stepping forward with raised arms and open palms.

Neo and I gaped at each other, frozen with shock and confusion.

"Do it," Alaric snarled as the wolves encroaching on us bit the air and dug their nails into the ground, as if they might lung at any moment.

Neo and I gave each other one final look but put away our blades, following Alaric's gestures.

The wolf in the middle calmed a bit but still bared their fangs. The others mimicked its motions like a pack.

Not like.

They were.

Meaning only one thing.

Alaric, taking their action as permission, began speaking, "We are wolves from Rivelia and Artico." The wolves stiffened at that, their attention leaving us to take a quick glance at the wolf in the middle. "We've traveled here to seek the aid of the Woodland Pack in our quest to hunt down the blood demons who attacked Artico." A wolf snorted, unbelieving of Alaric's words. I chewed on the inside of my cheek, trying not to growl in annoyance at the smaller wolf. Alaric looked down, rolling back his shoulders at the apparent insult before continuing. "We mean no harm. We only ask for an audience with your matriarch, and if she denies what we seek, we shall be on our way." The center wolf ceased its snarling and lowered its hackles, but it did not make a move to shift. They were thinking. "We swear it. We will peacefully leave if she says no."

The center wolf stepped forward, their fur growing thinner by the second. Another wolf snarled in warning, but the shifting wolf shot them a menacing glare that had them lowering their head and whimpering in apology, making it clear the center wolf was the leader of this pack. Or was it a patrol? I wasn't sure yet.

The leader continued to shift, fur turning to skin, claws turning to nails, and soon, where a wolf once stood was a beautiful blonde-haired female.

"You will come bound," she ordered, pulling some rope from the satchel hanging from her waist.

We walked down the path made clear by the numerous tents that graced both sides. Several wolves in human form watched as we paraded down, soft whispers amongst them, making the binds around my wrists feel tighter. Regardless, I kept my chin high, trying to seem unfazed by the prodding eyes.

We kept walking until we came upon a white tent so big that it was half the size of the main hall in Artico. One of the males at the head of the line entered the tent, not allowing more than a sliver of the flap to open.

"One wrong move and I won't hesitate to rip any of your throats out," growled the blonde female.

Soon after her threat, the flap opened again by the same male who entered. He nodded, and the blonde female shoved us forward.

My eyes went wide as they were filled with beautiful red, yellow, and green tapestries that hung from the top of the ceiling and cascaded down, covering every inch of the tent, making it feel like a grand decorated room. The floor, of course, was adorned with the same colors, however, the design was more intricate. Varying shapes and patterns were woven in the carpet, so mesmerizing that if you stared too long, it would put you in a state of hypnosis. Then, at the back of the tent, a small dais sat with two grand pillars of fire on either side, illuminating the terrifying female who sat on a throne, glaring down at us.

The Matriarch—the only female alpha in the last of the grand packs.

"Come forward," she ordered, her voice old yet still powerful, almost enchanting.

The blonde and her two of her companions shoved us again, forcing us to walk until we stood five paces from the throne.

The matriarch—Acacia—stared at us, absolutely silent. The crowd inside the tent followed her lead, waiting for her judgment.

"Why are they tied, Dahlia?" asked the matriarch, her eyes settling on Alaric.

The blonde leader stepped forward. "I thought it best that they come in as little threat as possible," she replied, bowing.

"That would be good thinking if one of them were not the firstborn of Damon." Murmurs flooded the crowd. Dahlia's eyes widened, her gaze raking over Alaric who stood stoically, unfazed by the crowd's reaction. "Untie them all."

Dahlia waved to her two companions. In unison, they unsheathed their daggers and cut the ropes from our wrists.

I relished the feeling.

"Thank you, Matriarch Acacia," Alaric began, rubbing his red wrists, sounding like the prince I had first met in Rivelia. "It's good to see that ties between Rivelia and the Woodland Pack are still strong."

Acacia laughed, leaning back in her chair. "They're not there, Prince." Alaric rolled back his shoulders. "The Woodland Pack was already distant when your father was in his prime, but we respected him because of his lineage. However, after his years of cowardice, we have decided we will not answer to him nor anyone. We are independent of the Wolf Kingdom." Alaric grimaced, the shame of his and his father's past radiating off him. "I only untie you so that if I kill you and your brother, I presume"—Acacia jerked her head to Neo, his matching scent giving his identity away—"you may have the chance to fight, and people won't call me a murderer."

"How dare you," I hissed through grinding teeth, stepping forward. The bond, or perhaps the feelings I had for Alaric, getting the best of me. "You threaten to kill him when we come in peace, to ask for aid in protecting the continent? You talk of cowardice like you don't have any negative qualities, yet you allow hate to cloud your decisions."

The matriarch tiredly rolled her eyes, resting her head in the palm of her head, as if I wasn't worth the effort.

"And who might you be, wolfling, to speak to an alpha so boldly, particularly when you've come to seek my aid?" Acacia sniffed the air. "Oh, a lover of Alaric? How quaint." She turned her attention back to Alaric. "I would have thought you'd have gotten someone demurer. That's the type of female who you're best suited for after all, ones that are too scared to leave you if they find their mate. We don't want that happening again, do we?"

Alaric flinched. It was enough to set me off.

"I am no demure, fickle female," I growled, stepping in front of Alaric, a foot on the first step of the dais.

Swords rang and were immediately pointed at my throat, but I did not waver. She had insulted me and Alaric, and I couldn't let that stand.

"Oh?" she asked in a sing-song voice, waving her hand to dismiss the wolves who pointed their steel at me.

I took a breath, unsure if my words would hold any power here. Father rarely mentioned the nomadic packs after all. They may hate me just as much as they did Alaric. Still, I stood tall and announced, "I am Ina, Daughter of Batair—the late Alpha of the Artico Pack."

Mumbles once again filled the tent, a pair of feet scampered about, and Acacia's pupils doubled.

"Impossible," she declared, leaning forward, allowing some of her many white braids to roll past her shoulder. "She was killed when Artico was attacked."

I lifted my chin. "And where did you hear that from?"

"Out of my way," a familiar voice roared, one that had me turning, exposing my back to Acacia despite all my training.

The crowd obediently parted and from it emerged Rainer.

The world slowed, and my surroundings faded to nothing.

Rainer was alive. He was here. That had to mean...

Something like a sob escaped my lips, breaking my hard exterior.

"Thank the gods." Rainer rushed forward, eyes glossing over as he wrapped his arms around me. "It's really you."

I hugged him back.

"You know this female, Rainer?" Acacia asked, her voice sharp.

Rainer gently pulled away from our embrace but kept a hand on the lower of my back, his thumb moving idly. And despite the comfort I found in our initial embrace, I wanted to be rid of the touch. It felt too much like a lover's caress, like how Alaric's hands roamed my body after a joining. However, I didn't dare to move, not when everything was so tense.

"I do," Rainer replied, a hand on the hilt of his sword. "She is Ina, the last of the original Artico bloodline and"—Rainer tugged me close to him, ignoring my resistance—"my betrothed, my future *mate*."

I flinched at the declaration, at the possessiveness he exuded. In my happiness to see someone from my pack alive, to have hope that more pack members may be here, I forgot that I detested Rainer, that he would claim me in front of this crowd, in front of—

I swallowed hard as I saw Alaric's heated glare and flaring nostrils.

The mating bond. It was acting up.

"Rainer," I whisper-growled for more than one reason, "let go."

"What? Why?" he asked, his grip unrelenting.

"We need to discuss things."

Rainer laughed. "We can discuss things later, *my* betrothed," he urged with false male confidence. "Right now, I want to show"—Rainer's thumb grazed up and down my ribs, his mouth inches from my ear lobe, acting as if he might nip. I balled up, clearly uncomfortable—"everyone that—"

"Let her go," Alaric growled, storming over to us, the promise of death in his eyes.

I muttered Alaric's name, wanting him to calm, but Rainer threw me behind him, barking, "And who are you to tell me what to do with my intended?" effectively drowning out my voice.

"It doesn't matter who I am. All that matters is that you do as she has commanded," Alaric countered.

My heart leaped at Alaric's answer. His opposition to me being touched didn't stem from the bond. It was purely because I was uncomfortable.

Rainer licked his lips, a growing smile on his face. "She commands me, but I know what she truly wants. I've known Ina all her life. We communicate in a secret way."

Alaric's temple twitched.

"Watch your words, Rainer," I warned.

Rainer cooed at me, "Don't worry, Ina. He hardly looks like a wolf." Rainer squared his shoulders. "I bet he doesn't even smell like one." Rainer bent, sniffing Alaric, trying to insult him further. However, he only tensed, and his nose twitched.

Alaric smirked, knowing exactly what Rainer had smelt.

I groaned at the show of male pride, but still, my chest warmed at Alaric's smile.

"You two"—Rainer backed away, his voice shaking—"are bonded?" Silence filled the tent. "Are you?" Rainer roared, throwing a fit.

It was a sight to behold, but it was a humiliation to my pack, as he was now alpha. I had to stop it.

"We are, but it's," I stuttered, throat tightening. I kept moving my lips, trying to get the words out, but nothing would come. Rainer kept tilting his head, and Alaric's brows drew together.

Why was this so hard?

"Enough of this," boomed Acacia. "We have enough drama over this coming battle with the demons. We don't need anymore of it, particularly when it's caused by some silly"—Acacia gestured toward all three of us, shaking her head—"love spat," she said, though the inflection in her voice made me think it was more of a question. She leaned back in her throne. "I have my proof that you are who you say, she-wolf, so you may stay." Acacia stroked her forehead. "Batair would haunt me from the afterlife if I didn't allow you to stay with your people." I nodded in thanks. "But as far as these Princes of Rivelia, your father's reputation has sullied yours in my eyes. I don't trust you to stay in my camp, even if you claim you to want to fight. You may very well spread your disease of cowardice amongst my troops." Alaric and Neo both stepped forward, their mouths already opening in hurried protests, but Acacia raised her hand. "But I also can't have you"—she jerked her chin at Alaric—"sneaking into my camp every chance you get because the bond yells at you to be with Ina, as all fresh ones do. So, you and your brother may stay. However, if I catch you doing anything to infect my pack, I will not hesitate to punish you personally."

Alaric's forehead creased at the obvious insult but graciously nodded in thanks, gesturing to Neo to do the same. Acacia watched with pleasure at their obedience.

"With that, court is dismissed." Acacia clapped her hands, and her pack dutifully left her tent. "Princes," Acacia called, stopping our party from leaving as well. "Dahlia will help you find a spare tent and instruct you where to set it up."

Alaric bobbed his head once again before stepping aside for Dahlia to lead the way. However, before she could leave the dais, Acacia whispered something in her ear that made her glare at me. Regardless of Dahlia's apparent disapproval, she nodded and continued forward, her fingers pointing to the exit. I made sure to give her a wide berth before instinctively following my party.

"Stop there, Ina." I turned back to Acacia as the rest of my party froze. "I wish to talk to you further about these claims on you."

Rainer, who I just realized had remained in the tent, grinned from ear to ear, whereas Alaric stepped closer, his chest against my back.

"What of them?" I asked hesitantly, worried by Rainer's smile.

Acacia examined her nails. "I'll tell you once we are alone," she drawled, looking past her brows, waiting.

Alaric did not move.

"Prince, do not mistake my newfound hospitality as permission to do what you like. Follow Dahlia without delay, or I will see your lingering presence in my tent as aggression."

Alaric let out a low growl that had me turning. He looked down at me with softened eyes, silently waiting for an order.

"I'll be fine. Go set up. I'll find you two later," I whispered, cupping his cheek, realizing this male would stay if I asked.

"Are you sure?"

I nodded assertively, not wanting him to get into trouble.

"Alright." Gently, Alaric kissed my brow. "Yell if you need me. I'll come running," he whispered before stalking past Dahlia whose foot tapped impatiently.

"Good riddance," Rainer uttered, stepping closer to me, his hand already reaching for my waist. "Now we can really find out what's going on."

I sent Rainer a scathing look, his words undoubtedly making my blood boil.

"*I* can find out what's going on," Acacia corrected. "Do not forget your place either. With Ina's return, your position in your pack is now in question."

Rainer cocked his head, eyelids fluttering. "I was named beta by Batair himself. The title of alpha belongs to me."

"Under the pretense that you would become Ina's mate, and as that ceremony has not happened, you are not alpha. The Artico Pack is in limbo."

"They don't see it that way. They—"

Acacia took a ferocious step down the dais. "They as in the few Artico wolves who are here. I, nor my pack, acknowledge your claim, and seeing how you are only alive because of my generosity, you will accept that, or I will have you and your wolves shown the same treatment we show wolves without a leader."

Rainer grond his teeth, nostrils flaring, but looked away.

"Smart male," Acacia mused. "Now, leave."

"As you wish." Rainer slightly bowed, but before catching my attention and mumbling, "Do what's best for the pack, Ina."

Acacia watched him leave. I waited for her to speak, but she kept focusing on the flap, ears perked up, listening for anyone who may be lingering. After a while, her shoulders dropped, and she tiredly descended her dais to a small, low-to-the-ground table with a pitcher of wine and some glasses. She poured one for herself and then another, extending it to me.

I blinked a few times, confused by the calm air around her.

She turned toward me, brow raised. "You don't drink?"

"I do. I just—"

"Then, drink." Acacia pushed the goblet into my hands before plopping down on a couple pillows arranged in a semi-circle nearby. "You look like you need it."

Heeding her advice, I took a long sip.

She let out a short laugh, her demeanor changing. "You're different than how your father described you."

I stiffened. "You and my father were in contact?"

"Not as much as before the Blood War, but yes. We exchanged letters before he passed." Acacia patted the pillow beside her, beckoning me to join her.

I silently declined, wanting to continue standing. From what I learned in Rivelia, trust was something I shouldn't give easily.

Acacia shrugged before taking another sip.

"What did you two discuss?"

Acacia leaned forward, eyeing the fruits in a small bowl that sat in the middle of the semi-circle of pillows. "How to help you."

"Help me?"

Acacia plucked a green, pebbled-sized fruit and plopped it in her mouth. "Become alpha," she said between bites.

My heart ceased to beat. "Impossible. That rule cannot be changed. That's what my father told me."

"He didn't want to get your hopes up, and rightfully so." Acacia set her goblet down before clasping her hands together on her lap. "You could have never become alpha in the position you were in."

I gripped tighter to my goblet.

What was the point of this conversation?

"Getting angry, little wolfling?" I narrowed my eyes, evoking a laugh from Acacia. "Your father talked about that too. He warned me about it when he made me promise I'd help you after he passed. Though I'm starting to regret that promise after seeing how much trouble you've brought into my camp, but a promise is a promise."

I took deep breaths, calming myself, before speaking, "You just said it was impossible for me to become alpha. How are you going to keep a promise you can't achieve?"

"The promise wasn't to make you alpha. It was more generic than that." She flicked her braids back, mumbling under her breath, "Batair, you're lucky this is payment for saving my life years ago," before speaking normally. "It was more generic in the sense that if you needed aid, I would grant it. It ranged from providing you shelter if you denied Rainer, to sending my army to defend your boarders if Rainer or you were threatened. Anything and everything. I'm basically your safety net."

Despite my anger mere minutes ago, my heart warmed, but also sadness coated it.

Father had prepared so much. It made me wonder how long he had known he was weakening.

"However, one scenario I hadn't seen coming was defending you in a lover's spat. Batair said you had no interest in relationships, let alone one with a Prince of Rivelia. How did you even meet Alaric? Get him, let alone that poor younger brother Damon keeps hidden, past their walls? That is a victory within itself."

I stared at the female who sat so openly, so ready to listen. I was hesitant to answer her questions, worried that whatever I told her would be used against me. However, if father had really written to her, had made her promise to help me, I couldn't squander this opportunity. Before, I had a clear concise plan—get to the Woodland Pack then fight the demons.

And while that plan had stayed the same for the most part, it had become far more complicated.

I needed to tell her my story.

"So, it is a *false* mating bond that has formed between you two," Acacia repeated back. Her countenance even more grim as the sun began to lower and most of the light came from the flickering flames that were stationed around the tent.

I nodded, drinking more of the wine.

Acacia sucked on her lips, popping them out before she spoke again. "And what do you intend to do about it?"

I shrugged. "Keep sticking to it." Acacia raised her chin. "It will break him if I move on."

"And what of Rainer? Will you choose to reject his claim?"

I swirled the wine around in my goblet, watching it come close to the rim. "I was hoping to explain to him that our arrangement needs to be put on hold for a bit."

Acacia muffled a cynical laugh. "I highly doubt that will tide over well. You should know that too."

I spun the wine closer to the rim. "I do, but I was hoping, since you said you're here to help, that you could *talk* to him with me." Acacia raised a brow. "When he refused to leave, you seemed to handle him well. I was hoping you could do that again."

Acacia humorlessly snickered, reaching for the pitcher of wine she had moved down to the floor and refilled her glass. "That was because it was my right to do so; he is my guest. Your promised bond to him is an affair pertaining to your pack. For me to meddle with that, would be me declaring that I am a part of it. And while challenging Rainer does sound enticing, I have no interest in causing needless conflict for my pack before we face the blood demons."

"But if I don't convince Rainer to stop pursuing me for a while then…" The wine swirled just at the rim in perfect balance. "You saw what happened. They wanted to fight. They—"

"*You* must choose." I stopped swirling my goblet, and the wine spilt. "They do not have to do anything. Alaric is fighting not to be heartbroken, and Rainer is fighting to ensure that he gets what he was promised. Both of their reasons are valid, and both males have no reason to stop unless you give them one, unless you reject a bond publicly. And even if you somehow made one of them relent, it would still result in you *actually* choosing." I raised my head to Acacia, asking her to explain, as I was too deep into my emotions to see what she was getting at. "We've already established that Alaric cannot temporarily ignore his feelings for you due to the bond, and because of that, Rainer is the only one you can ask. However, if he does, even if it is temporary, your pack may become unstable as they wait for things to become more permanent, and what your pack needs, more than anything, is stability right now. They will demand it, and they will find it on their own if not given. And it won't result in a way that you would have wanted. So, you need to choose, Ina. Whose claim will you take? What do you want to protect? A heart or to bring your pack out of uncertainty?"

I set my goblet down, wanting to wrap my arms around myself. This should have been an easy decision. Yet I kept flipping on what to do. I kept thinking about Alaric and how devastated he would be, how he may never let anyone in again. How if he stayed for the battle—which I knew he would—how his broken heart would affect him. I may as well sign his death warrant. I kept thinking about how my pack would create its own stability. Would they lean solely on Alaric? It would forsake our rules about the original alpha's bloodline staying in control, but they had already forsaken it when they named him alpha after they thought me dead. It was a highly probable solution. And at first glance, it wouldn't be so bad. I would be free from the forced mating bond, but if it did happen, I wouldn't have a say in the rulings of my pack. I wouldn't have Rainer's ear.

No matter what I chose, I would lose something.

"Gods, why couldn't I have been alpha in my own right. None of this would even be a debate right now," I grieved to myself, resting my forehead in the palms of my hands.

"Because the world is unfair," Acacia answered, taking up that ancient voice again. "Sometimes those who have every right to something, who deserve it, do not get it." I shuddered a breath. "Do not decide right now. Think on it. Visit your pack. Speak to the Rivelian Prince. But decide before they rip each other apart, before the option of choosing is ripped from you."

"How can I? How do I know what is right?"

"I cannot help you with that," Acacia whispered before hitting a gong. "But whatever it is, be strong in what you decide, and remember, I did not become alpha in happy times. But now, the stage is the same."

I scrunched my nose, wondering why Acacia was speaking in riddles. I wanted to ask her what she meant. After all, she had said I couldn't be alpha. She had told my father there was no way I could. Why was she bringing that up now? But before I could utter a word, Dahlia entered the tent.

CHAPTER 53

Dahlia left me alone in the medium-sized tent with little conversation. I knew she was furious about having to give up her tent and not just because of the glares and scoffs she directed at me. She had made sure to inform me that the matriarch *forced* her to give up her tent so I could be situated in the center of camp, equal distance from Rainer and Alaric. It made sense, as it made Acacia look like she wasn't favoring either males' claim, but Dahlia was still angry about being misplaced. However, it was an inconsequential when compared to my situation with Alaric and Rainer.

After calming my emotions, the choice I had before me was obvious. I needed to choose my pack. I needed to see my father's final order through. It was what was right, and I was sure Alaric would let me break my promise to him. But still, I couldn't let him go.

I shouldn't have let my feelings for Alaric keep me in his bed. I shouldn't have let them keep growing. This would hurt us no matter what. It would hurt me. I needed to find a way to lessen the blow or make the bond fade faster.

I slunk down on the piles of fur and pillows—the Woodland Pack's version of a bed—holding my head in my hands. The pressure helped with the ever-growing migraine.

Today had been a whirlwind of emotions and—

"Her scent gets stronger over here," a familiar female voice stated. It had my head turning and my stomach flipping.

"But that's Dahlia's tent," another familiar voice whimpered, her voice soft and delicate. "She won't like us looking, especially since we received—"

"Rainer received orders not to go looking for her, not us," the first voice snarked.

My eyes began to water.

Could it be?

"Alright, but I'll look. You and Dahlia already argue too often. If she catches you snooping, I'm not sure that Acacia's orders not to harm us will be obeyed," whispered the second voice.

There was a brief grunt of agreement before delicate hands pulled back the flap of the tent, revealing blonde hair and two beautiful blue eyes that I had known my entire life.

The owner and I stared at each other for what felt like an eternity before I sprang to my feet and rushed to Ala, sobbing, "You're alive." I sent up a prayer of thanks to the gods. "How?" I mumbled through tears.

"Aspen and Rainer," Ala mewled, wiping away tears. "Aspen got us out after—" Ala's arms slacked as she struggled to finish the sentence.

"After Catrine's death," the first voice finished for Ala.

I raised my head to it, finding Sil standing stiffly at the entrance of Dahlia's tent.

"Sil," I whispered, gently releasing Ala as I walked forward, sending up another prayer. However, I went still as I saw Sil's balled up hands, and her pinched expression.

You killed her. Those had been Sill's last words to me.

"I'm sorry," I whispered but not for the decision I had made, but because I had to.

Catrine's death had been inevitable and denying her that quick death would've resulted in hours of pain. But that didn't excuse the anger Sil had for me. She didn't know what was going on. She didn't know the two options I had. After all, she wasn't a warrior or a healer.

Sil stormed forward, fists still at her side.

I closed my eyes, bracing for whatever she needed to do, hoping that it would quench some of her anger, that maybe she could stand to be around me, but I only felt warm, gentle arms wrap around me, her head burrowing into my shoulder.

"I'm sorry," Sil sobbed. "I shouldn't have blamed you for it. I shouldn't have told you to go away. Ala and Aspen explained what you did." Sil quivered. "I had no right to say that to you, and when I realized it, I wanted to apologize, but Rainer had said you went into the building. He saw it collapse and—I never thought—we thought—"

Gently, I pushed Sil away, holding her at a distance so I could look into her eyes.

"It's alright, Sil. You didn't know," I whispered, trying to smile despite the tears that ran down my face.

"But—"

I brushed a strand of hair back from my friend's face, somber happiness overwhelming me. "It's okay. I'm just happy both"—I extended a hand to Ala who took it with the same hurting smile I felt to my core—"of you are here and safe. I'm sure Catrine is too. She wouldn't want us to focus on the mistakes of the past."

There was silence as Sil digested my words, as she licked her lips, trying to find more words to apologize with, but I didn't want anymore. I knew her words were not because she hated me but out of fear. I just wanted to be happy with my sisters once more, mourn the death of Catrine together, and make sure they weren't hurt.

"But," I began, making sure my voice was light in hopes that we could move on, bring back the joking air that always followed us. It was all I wanted after so many emotions and revelations today. "If you still feel guilty, you can always sing me a song. I've missed your voice."

Ala, understanding what I was doing, piped in, "Just not the one about the sailor and the siren. That one always creeps me out."

Sil's mouth dropped, and her brows furrowed. "That one is an artistic treasure. It's not my fault you get creeped out so easily."

"It's about a man falling for some creature and her drowning him to death," Ala exclaimed. "How is that artistic?"

A hearty laugh erupted from me, pulling both of them from their squabble. It was just like the old times before the attack, before all the complications of life.

"I've missed you two," I said, pulling them into one more quick embrace, scared that a long one would bring back the intense emotions I was trying to flee.

"Same here, but I don't miss you not choosing a side," Sil snarked.

I chuckled again, sitting down in the pile of furs, using both hands to pat it, beckoning them to take a seat.

"If I did, it wouldn't end the argument. It would only prolong it. One of you would be vexed, and the other would be sinfully prideful. I rather not deal with that, particularly since we need to spend our energies telling each other how we came to be here."

"It's a long story," Sil grumbled.

"It really is," Ala chimed, climbing onto the blanket, stealing one of the pillows to hug.

"We have time," I retorted, seeing their reluctance, knowing they didn't want to relive what had to be the scariest moments of their life, but I needed to know, needed to understand what they and the pack had been through. I had missed too much.

Sil and Ala looked at each other, hesitantly sighing, but they understood and replied, "You first, though. Rainer said you arrived here with some Rivelian dog guarding your feet?"

I rolled my eyes at Rainer's blatant insult but agreed and told my tale for the second time today.

"So, that's why Rainer was steaming when he got back to our section of the camp," Sil said, her jaw resting on her hand.

I nodded. "He always loses his cool when things don't go his way, even at training. I'm sure he'll be over it in a couple of days or hours, especially when he hears it's false. It's just his male pride acting up over the fact that another male is touching something that he is supposed to have claim over."

Sil and Ala looked at one another with discomfort.

"What? What's wrong?"

They sighed heavily before Sil began.

CHAPTER 54

ALARIC

I jumped between shadows, careful to avoid the eyes of sentries as I followed Ina's scent. I knew I wasn't supposed to venture to the center of the camp, unless I was summoned to the area. Acacia had declared it, but I needed to make sure Ina was ok.

Though Acacia was just in her rule, she was unpredictable and left no vengeance unserved. And while she had no quarrels with Ina, she did have them with me and my family. She would make sure that punishment would come to me, even if it meant using Ina and mine's bond.

I passed two more tents until I came to one where the flap bared an emblem of a wolf's head and three trees behind it—the crest of the Woodland Pack. Only a few people would be able to stay in a tent with that crest—the matriarch, her family members, and her prodigy. Judging by the size and that Acacia still had not borne children, I knew this was Dahlia's tent, and she was the person I needed to avoid most after Acacia. I needed to get out of here, however, I could scent Ina just behind the fabric, and I needed to see her more. I needed to know she was safe.

I creeped closer to the tent, further into the shadows, debating whether I should enter. Dahlia's scent was weak enough that I could conclude that she wasn't in the tent, but two other aromas tangled with Ina's. I didn't recognize them at all. I couldn't discern if they were friend or foe.

It was best to wait for Ina to be alone or find a way to signal to her that I was out here. I crouched down, accepting my fate of an unpredictable wait.

"Ina," a voice like morning dew said. "Rainer"—my skin crawled at the name of the male who had tried to lay claim to Ina in Acacia's tent—"he—what do you plan on doing?"

"What do you mean?" a second voice that I recognized as Ina's asked.

There was a sigh, followed by a third voice—this one deeper and sultrier compared to the first—chiming, "This Alaric. I've never seen you talk about anyone like this."

A sly smile crept onto my face, though, guilt quickly followed. I was supposed to end Ina and mine's relationship today, not relish in the way she talked about me. Though after seeing Rainer caress Ina in Acacia's tent, seeing her so uncomfortable around him, my resolve on that matter had wavered. Everything inside *me*—not my wolf—wanted to claim her, to rush to her side and rip Rainer's hand off. I was starting to think that Neo was right, that maybe I should tell Ina my feelings before doing anything rash. Not only that, but this conversation was casual, and the third voice was alluding to times of the past. The other two scents had to belong to wolves she knew. Wolves from her pack.

Surely, they wouldn't run to Acacia.

I should reveal myself.

I gripped the flap but stopped upon hearing Ina's response.

"Why does that matter?"

There was silence for a bit.

"Because we need to know if you're going to choose Rainer," the second voice said with a bit of tension, almost fear, "and we need to know soon. The whole pack does."

Feeling the energy change in the tent, I peeked inside. There were two other females with Ina, all of them sitting on the plush furs and colorful pillows. All of them rigid.

"I think it's fairly obvious," Ina replied in a confused manner. "I know what's expected of me."

"Are you sure? From what Rainer was saying—"

"From what Rainer was saying?" Ina's voice rose. "Sil, why would you even take in account for what he's saying. We already discussed that he was mad because someone else had a bond with me. A bond that I already told you was false."

Sil stood. "But you didn't tell Rainer that. You didn't say it in front of Acacia."

Ina pushed her tongue into her canines, as she always did when she was upset.

Now, even more unsure who these females were to Ina, I slid a hand around the curtain, ready to intervene if need be.

"What Sil is trying to say," the girl with the dewy voice softly spoke, "is that the pack is now divided." Ina's brows fell. "Many of them think that the male you came with is truly bonded with you, which means he should have claim to be alpha. However, the other half thinks that Rainer should still be alpha with or without you, which would mean—"

"I'd be outcasted," Ina whispered, her face falling.

It took every ounce of my strength not to jump through the tent flap and defend Ina. I knew how much her pack meant to her, how much she worked to get back to them. She had every right to rule, no matter the male she was bonded to.

"There's already a divide in the pack, and it's going to grow every second you wait on bonding with Rainer, or you leave us again."

"Why?" Ina muttered. "Our pack has always preferred my family's blood and strength over the strength of a new line when choosing alphas."

"Rainer proved himself these past weeks." Sil moved past her dewy-voiced friend, the panic in her voice almost gone. "After the battle, when we heard that the building crashed on your father, after we assumed the same happened to you, the pack was a mess. We didn't know where to go. We didn't know what to do. With the human village below destroyed and the screams of our people being dragged through the forest—either be fed upon or stuck in a cage—echoing around us, we were in shambles. But Rainer stood strong. He rallied us, said, that you and your father were a terrible loss, but both of you would want us to fight and get our people back. He took us here, where we found the Woodland Pack, and Rainer begged for their help, for their aid. He's a hero in so many eyes."

"I—" Ina began, about to make her choice. I listened closely, hating myself for eavesdropping, but I needed to know my fate, needed to know what to expect. Because though I was starting to doubt my initial decision, this was the push I needed to go back to it, to understand exactly what Ina wanted without making her choose. And no matter what, I was ready to support her anyway I could, no matter my want. However, before she could answer, Dahlia's snide voice sounded a couple tents down.

Quickly, I jumped into the tent.

CHAPTER 55

I snapped my head around, alarmed by the whip of the tent flap opening, a cold sweat already starting down my back as I saw Alaric, my resolve wavering. I wasn't ready to see him yet.

I had planned to wait a day or two to figure out a way to lessen the bond. However, after hearing that the theories about my pack were coming true and seeing the panic in both Ala and Sil's eyes, I knew I couldn't wait. This was the first break in the Artico Pack, and I couldn't be the reason it grew further.

"Alaric," I stuttered, "what are you doing here?"

"I wanted to see if you were alright." He glanced at Ala and Sil. "But I see that you are well and that you have company. I'm assuming they're from your pack. That's wonderful. Dahlia was telling me quite a few survived," Alaric rambled.

He never rambled.

"Alaric, are you—"

"I'll leave you be."

He began to turn, but Sil interjected, "We were actually leaving." She turned to Ala and jerked her head to the flap then turned back to me. "Decide, now, before the meeting tomorrow."

Ala waddled over to me on her knees, giving me a tight hug and whispering, "Whatever you decide, we'll support you. You seemed happy when you talked about him."

I gave Ala a confused look as she pulled away and walked out with Sil. She knew how much the pack meant to me, that I dreamt of leading them.

Alaric and I stood in silence, long enough that the loud crunch of Ala and Sil's synchronized steps were no longer audible.

I didn't know what to say. Well, I did. I just didn't know how to start.

I was sure he was looking for an explanation. He had to be terrified that his heart was going to break again. I was terrified of that.

"Ina," Alaric called, softly with a crooked smile, "let's go on a walk."

"Alright," I whispered back.

Alaric and I walked from the civilization of the camp, far enough that no one could hear us, and we couldn't hear them. He hadn't spoken once during the walk here, but neither had I. I had been too busy going over what to say, what to do. But one thing was clear, I needed to do this sooner rather than later.

Alaric stopped at a tree and turned to me.

"It's been a crazy day, hasn't it?" he gently asked.

I nodded, still unable to find the words.

"We found the Woodland Pack. We found your pack. All that's left to do is defeat the demons then after that—"

"Alaric," I whispered, arms wrapped tightly around me.

I didn't want him to finish that thought, that sentence. I didn't want to know what he expected to happen after this all came to an end. If he wanted us to stay together after the fight, it would make what I was about to do so much harder. I didn't want to hurt him. I didn't want to see his smile fade. And I didn't want to break my promise to protect him, but I also couldn't ignore the duties of my birthright. They were always supposed to come first.

"We can't," I breathed out. "I can't." The words became lost as my heart began to strain, and air became hard to come by. "I know the bond hasn't ended, but the male from before...I need to...my father was the one who arranged it. I didn't think he had survived, otherwise I wouldn't have—"

Alaric stepped back, sighing. I thought I saw his lip quiver, but he looked back at me with a soft smile and retraced his steps, pulling me into an embrace. "I understand, Ina." He tucked my head into his shoulder. "I understand."

I tried to look up to explain, but he kept his hand on my head, firmly but gently keeping me planted, unable to see anything.

"You have your own duties to attend to. Don't feel bad." His throat bobbed. "The bond was fading for me anyway," he whispered, his voice trembling. "It won't hurt that much to be apart from you, and with your amazing devotion to your pack, I'm sure your wolf's happiness in doing right by them will make ignoring the bond easier for you."

I clutched to his tunic. Alaric was so wrong. It would hurt so much. I was already hurting but not just because of the bond. "But," I began as silent tears began to fall, and my legs grew weaker, looking for any excuse to make him order me to stay with him. Because, if I was being honest, the rebuttals were no longer because I was scared of hurting him. They were for me. Now that I was doing this, I realized I wanted him and not out of lust. I truly wanted him. I didn't want my pack. Rainer had done a well enough job. He would keep doing so, and I could leave with that knowledge. I wanted the pack that I had found. The pack that accepted me for me. The pack where they saw my worth with or without a mate by my side.

"Don't worry. It's just"—he paused, and I swore I felt something wet drip onto my head—"it's just a *false* bond. It will fade, and I will be ok. We will be ok. This is for the best. Right now, we have bigger problems to worry about than my feelings."

I froze at his emphasis on false.

That was right. He wanted his true mate, not me. Even if I somehow made this work, made it so we were together until the bond faded, I would still lose him.

"You're right," I whispered, dropping my hands. "This is what's best for everyone."

CHAPTER 56

I woke the next morning, eyes stinging from last night.

I had stayed out in the woods far longer than I should have after Alaric departed, and even when I finally returned to my tent, I lay on my bed awake, my chest in too much pain for me to even think of sleep. But I had no right to complain or dwell. Last night, I had given myself time to be weak, but today, I needed to return to my pack and unite them. I needed to stand strongly by Rainer's side. I couldn't let Alaric suffer for no reason. I pushed the heavy blankets off myself and dressed before packing my few belongings and throwing them over my shoulder.

I marched through the camp, trying to ignore the eyes that followed me, that noticed the bag I carried. I closed my ears, trying to ignore the mumbles, the ones that whispered, "Looks like she made her choice."

It wasn't mine. It wasn't what I wanted.

I made it two or three steps past the first Artico tent by the time someone from my pack recognized me. She was an older female that had lived on the outskirts of our village and walked with a hobble. However, her weary body seemed to brighten up, despite the foggy breeze, as I passed her. She beckoned others to come look, a smile on her face. One by one, each wolf realized who she was pointing at. Their bodies froze, and their mouths parted in surprise. Some ran to get more of our people. Others placed a fist over their hearts, as they had when they greeted my father.

I stood unsure what to do, emotions overflowing as I counted the number of wolves who stared, who were dragged out half asleep from their tent by excited children. It was more than I had anticipated.

My people were survivors, warriors.

The old female stepped forward and bowed her head slightly. "Welcome back, Ina. You've been missed."

I returned the gesture, blinking away tears as others mimicked the motion and words.

It felt good to be back, but guilt over Alaric dulled it. I missed him. Feeling tears edge at the lining of my eyes, I realized I couldn't linger much longer.

I rolled back my shoulders, pushing down my emotions, and smiled. "I've missed all of you, and I'd love to stay and talk, but I need to find Rainer."

The female nodded, beaming with a mischievous grin. "You'll find your *betrothed*"—I grimaced, an action I'd have to learn to stop doing—"further in. He's in his tent. The white one or as we've been calling it, the Alpha's Tent."

"Thank you," I whispered, dipping my head once again, and proceeded to walk through the camp, nodding as more wolves saw and acted in the same manner the first set had.

The walk was short, yet it felt like it took an eternity—longer than the journey here—and when I reached Rainer's tent, it took all my strength and concentration to push open the flap and enter, so much so that I didn't hear the voices before entering.

"What do we do if she chooses him?" Sil asked the group—their backs to me—as they faced Rainer, who leaned against one of the poles that held up the tent, his head in his hand, looking seemingly destroyed.

I went to interrupt, to announce my arrival, but Aspen, like the well-trained warrior he was, countered, "Well, we can't let there be a civil war."

"We can't exile Ina, either," Ala argued. "She's family!" Ala stepped toward Rainer. "Remember that Rainer. Remember what drove you. Your lov—"

"Enough," Rainer growled, raising his head "there's no sense in—"

Rainer's chest stilled as his eyes met mine.

"Ina," he whispered, summoning the others to look.

It barely looked like they breathed.

"Hello," I mumbled, resting my bag on the ground, which all their eyes followed. The tension in the air lessened.

"You've decided," Rainer uttered, his forehead pinched in what seemed to be confusion.

"I did," I said, trying to feel the room.

With how tense and worried everyone had seemed a second ago, I thought they would have been jumping for joy. Instead, the tent seemed to radiate worry and confusion.

I expected this reaction from Ala and Sil. They knew how much the bond had affected me, knew how deeply I cared about Alaric. However, I didn't expect it from Rainer.

"What about Alaric?" Ala asked, finally breaking the silence. "Did the bond fade or did you—"

"Ask about that later, Ala, please?" Rainer pleaded.

Ala's cheeks reddened, consumed with what seemed to be sympathy for Rainer, but she nodded her head.

What was going on?

Rainer should be happy. With me at his side, everyone would accept him as alpha.

Before I could say anymore or think about the surprising actions of everyone, Rainer stepped forward.

"Acacia is holding a meeting to discuss the plans for the battle," Rainer said matter-of-factly, not an ounce of the arrogance he always showed when he won. He held out his arm. "We should go together so we can show an undivided front, and end any bickering." I studied his outstretched hand, wondered at his asking instead of him just taking. "That is why you're here, isn't it? To make sure the pack stays together?" Rainer asked. Though there seemed to be an underlying question with it, one that I didn't understand.

Still, I rested my arm on his, the way a mate of an alpha would. "It is. Why would there be any other? You know I treasure the pack. I would do anything for them."

Rainer chewed on his bottom lip. "I know." He closed his eyes and took a deep breath. When he reopened them, he seemed to be back to normal, not a trace of his previous feelings. The others noticed it too, their own faces turning from dismay to neutrality, as if that was their signal not to speak of something ever again.

CHAPTER 57

Rainer and I walked into the war tent, side by side. Aspen followed a few steps behind us, acting as Rainer's second. The wolves already inside shuffled to let us pass, but the fit was still tight. I could barely notice anything else in the tent besides the path that was made and the long, outstretched table in the center of the tent that took up most of the space. It was decorated with a map of the area, chipped wolf figurines of varying colors, and another set of figurines that appeared to be human. However, with the ghastly faces they made and the faded red paint that colored them, I knew they were to represent the blood demons.

"You're late," Acacia snarled, calling my attention away from the positions of the little figurines I was memorizing.

"We had Artico business to attend to this morning," Rainer replied flatly, picking up an unplaced white wolf figurine that was slightly bigger than the others on the map, with the exception of one other white figurine and an orange-brown wolf.

"I can see that," Acacia mused, bobbing her head at me. "I see the news you delivered about her choosing Rainer was true." Acacia's eyes drifted to her right. I followed, seeing Alaric and Neo for the first time today.

The air in my lungs suddenly dissipated. The bond began tugging, feeling hope and frustration all at once. I balled up my hands, focusing on the nails that pressed into my flesh, trying to calm the feelings that bubbled, reminding myself of the promises I made. But those promises seemed to be empty now, even more so as Alaric stared blankly back at me.

It was like we were strangers forced to work together. The only proof that we had been friends, a temporary pack, or even lovers—if that's what you called falsely bonded wolves—was behind him in Neo. His brows pursed together, and his attention flicked between me and Alaric, unsure what to do.

"I have no reason to lie, Acacia," Alaric replied, his gaze coldly leaving mine.

Acacia hummed in contemplation. "I could think of a reason or two, but since we are already short on time"—Acacia shot Rainer and I a grimacing glare—"we will proceed with the final meeting before the battle."

Everyone around the table grunted in agreement, edging closer to the map.

I mimicked their actions, unused to a war meeting. With the time of peace, I had only attended small briefings with patrol pack members. However, that would not stop me from representing Artico well.

Acacia pointed to the castle. "As we all know, the castle is home to the blood demons' army, and their numbers are three-fourths of our size. Under normal circumstances, we would not balk at this. However, as many reports have stated, it's taken two of us to take one of them down. We still have no idea how, but—"

"They're feeding," Alaric interjected, already grimacing, "on the Artico wolves. It makes them stronger."

A wave of mumbles filled the tent.

"And how would you know that? I thought Rivelia hadn't interacted with a demon since the war," Acacia growled, canines already showing.

I tensed, recalling my initial reaction to Alaric's life changing news. I had wanted to tackle him, and I was on good terms with him back then. Acacia, she hated him, hated the Rivelia wolves. She had threatened

Alaric's life already. The only thing holding her back was the need for more fighters, maybe the bond between us. But the bond was no longer a factor now, which meant one less thing to hold her back. If she knew that Rivelia had been keeping the truth from everyone else, even if it had been Damon's order and not Alaric's, I was sure what little reason she had for keeping Alaric around would mean nothing to her.

"Because my father told me, and I told him," I blurted out before anyone could take another breath. All eyes turned to me. Alaric's too. He shook his head and went to correct me, but I continued quicker than he could. "Back in the Blood War, the blood demons had an unexplained spike in power, just like now." Acacia ran her nails across the table as she closed the distance between us. "My father sent out a party to investigate and discovered they were feeding on captured wolves. They even heard the demons talking about how it made them stronger."

"And why didn't Batair tell the rest of us?" Acacia asked, leaning in, ready to rip out my throat, regardless of her promise to my father.

"It was the end of the war by the time he figured it out. He didn't want the news to affect his fighters, then when the war ended, he didn't think it was worth telling, as the demons were gone. It would turn into a tale that kept their memory alive. He didn't want that," I rushed out, making sure to keep my voice even and my scent level as Acacia examined me, testing me for a lie.

Alaric raised his chin, the veins in his neck popping. He even gripped the pommel of his sword. Still, I held Acacia's gaze, refusing to acknowledge Alaric's wrath. I didn't care if he was angry or not. All I wanted was for him to walk out of this tent alive.

"Batair never hid things," Acacia growled.

"He hid this," I pressed.

Acacia held my stare again, debating.

Rainer stepped between us, blocking her view, changing her focus.

"Does it matter that much?" Rainer asked with unflinching confidence.

"It does when someone I trusted has betrayed me."

"Someone you trusted? He was my alpha, and you don't see me staring down his daughter, ready to rip out her throat." Acacia sneered. Still, Rainer did not move. He really wanted his transition of power to go smoothly. "What matters is that we know and can prepare better."

"The Artico wolf is right," Alaric chimed in, his waist brushing the corner of the table. A wave of gasps swept over the tent at the agreement between the two males everyone had expected to kill each other. "There's no point in fighting over some silly mistake of the past."

Acacia looked out to her pack. Her face redder than fresh blood, making it clear that she wasn't used to being questioned.

"Fine," she snarked under her breath, gripping the table as she leaned over, "but know the Artico Pack treads on thin ice."

I nodded, knowing whatever sense of protection she had for me was over, along with her unwavering loyalty to my father.

Seeing my understanding, Acacia returned back to the map. "Because of their newfound strength, we cannot have everyone fight head on. We need to split the demons' numbers. A portion of our army will draw out the blood demons while a second group flanks them." Acacia pointed to the back of the castle. "I will lead the majority of the Woodland Pack on the attack of the castle's backside after the Artico Pack—graciously volunteered by Rainer—attacks the front along with any extra Woodland Wolves."

I snapped to Rainer, who stared unflinchingly at the map, fear coursing through my veins.

What had he done?

Though we were not a pack who backed down from a fight, half our numbers were gone, and the few who remained weren't even our best fighters. Putting Artico wolves on the front line could very well mean the extinction of our pack. We couldn't afford to take that risk. Any smart leader should have seen this, especially a warrior. Rainer should have seen this.

I willed him to look at me, to try and tell him that we needed to take back our promise, but he ignored me. I licked my lips, wondering if I should let Acacia know that we couldn't, but as we were already on thin ice with her, I had no doubt that she would come close to killing us on the spot. There was no way out of this.

"As you can see, the plans still remain the same; however, we do need to place our new fighters—Alaric, Neo, and Ina." Acacia pulled out two green wolf figurines, the same size as the one Rainer held in his hand, the same size as the one that represented Acacia on the board. "Though they are just two more units, they are the best fighters of their packs," Acacia said through gritted teeth. "But as I said earlier, the Rivelia Princes cannot be trusted, so they will be at the back and help clear up whatever my pack misses at the rear of the castle. They will also act as backup for the inexperienced wolves positioned there as well." Acacia set the two green pieces down.

Alaric looked at them with hate, mad that his skills were being used to clean up, but he didn't rebuttal, at least not for himself. "My brother is still recovering," Alaric stated calmly. "He will not be in the battle, but he can stay behind and guard those who cannot fight." Alaric picked up one of the two green pieces and firmly placed it in the camp.

I waited for Neo to fight it, to shout that this was his purpose, but he remained quiet, trusting his brother.

"I highly doubt any action will reach the camp, but an injured wolf is not needed on the battlefield. I shall accept your request." Alaric bowed in thanks and removed his hand from the figurine. "Moving on to Ina," Acacia breathed out, reaching out to where the second large white wolf figurine had been. An eyebrow raised as her hand gripped nothing but air.

"She will be here," Rainer finished for Acacia, placing the figurine he had taken at the start of the meeting on the backline.

I gawked at him and the sheer audacity that he would ridicule me with such a position.

"No, I won't," I interjected before Acacia could approve of the position.

Fuck being united if trusting Rainer led to calamitous battle plans.

I wouldn't let my people fight alone, not after Rainer had practically sacrificed them.

"I need to be with the Artico Pack. I've been away from them long enough. They need me and my skills on the frontline," I growled to both Acacia and Rainer.

Rainer considered me for a moment before taking his hand off the figurine and crossing his arms, showing that's where it would stay. "You need to stay safe for them."

"Acacia," I called, hoping for her to oppose the ludicrous idea.

She didn't.

She didn't so much as look at me.

I pressed my tongue against my canines and reached for the figurine, but Rainer caught my wrist.

I shot him the glare I always used when he challenged me in training, challenged my rank over him. It always had him bowing his head in apology; however, this time he did not do so. He held my gaze and pulled my hand away from the piece, wedging himself between me and the table.

"I am your alpha," Rainer growled, his canines out, inches from my face. "My word is final. You will be at the back of the lines."

I tried to pull back my hand, but Rainer held strong.

"Aspen," I whispered, expecting him to follow my lead, just as he normally did during missions, but he turned away, refusing to meet my eyes.

"You know he must answer to me, Ina. Your choosing of me this morning solidified that. Don't cause your friend pain," Rainer whispered in my ear, his grip growing tighter.

I remained strong despite Rainer's words, but the more I watched Aspen turn, smelt his sadness grow, the reality of the situation finally hit me. I was in the powerless state I had wanted to avoid my entire life. No one would come. No one would interfere because I belonged to Rainer. My entire pack did, and to question his word was to challenge him. It was why Acacia hadn't challenged him. It was why Aspen remained silent.

My eyes turned watery.

I blinked rapidly, trying to rid the tears that threatened to come loose.

I didn't want to cry in front of these strangers, in front of Rainer.

I needed to be strong.

I looked to the ground, trying to hide them, but felt numerous eyes on me.

Everyone would see.

"I know you do not trust me, Acacia," Alaric said smoothly and without a bit of emotion, "but I do believe that we should have another strong fighter on the frontlines with the Artico Pack."

My head snapped up.

Was Alaric standing up for me? Was he breaking the cardinal rule of not interfering in another pack's affairs?

The questions pushed back my tears.

"The Artico Pack's Alpha has decided," Acacia bitterly bit out. I wasn't sure if it was because it was Alaric speaking or because she didn't agree with the decision.

Alaric countered, "I would never dare to question a leader regarding decisions of their pack, not when my family has been absent in the rulings. Instead, I offer myself up to fight alongside the Artico Pack. The battle will be hard, since they will get the blunt force of the blood demons' army, and I believe that my claws will be of better use if I stand with them."

"I've already told you that—"

"I know, but do you really think I would flee?" Acacia tilted her head, straining her neck. "You claimed that the only reason I was here was my bond with Ina. She's already denied me. If the bond was what drove me here, then I would have left last night. I would have taken my *injured* brother—the only reason I was forced to start this journey—and gone to the safety of Rivelia. Instead, I am still here, begging to be sent to the front." Acacia crossed her arms as Alaric leaned over the table, gripping the green figurine in his hand. "I want change in Rivelia. I want to honor the old ways, and I will do so starting now and will continue to do so when I return, even if that means I have to go against my father. Do not lose more wolves than necessary because of his mistakes."

A silence fell over the room, even I unknowingly gasped.

Alaric loved his family, even if his father was psychotic, and saying those words, declaring that he would have his own civil war if need be, couldn't have been easy.

I felt myself moving forward but stopped as Acacia finally replied, "Fine."

Alaric nodded and began moving the figurine.

"But," Acacia said coldly, stopping Alaric midway, "if you betray us, if you flee, know that I will not hesitate to hunt you down and tear you limb from limb."

Alaric gave a single nod before slamming the piece down, agreeing to the deal.

I raced through the crowd that was exiting the tent, trying to catch up to Neo and Alaric.

I desperately needed to talk to them, needed to thank Alaric for volunteering to protect my pack, but I also wanted to wish him luck. Though I was sure he'd be fine, the thought of him fighting on the front lines made me worry.

"Alaric," I called out as he and Neo came into view, a considerable distance from the tent, making it seem that they had sprinted away.

Neo stopped but Alaric kept walking. I called out once more. Thankfully, Neo grabbed Alaric and made him wait.

"What is it, Ina?" Alaric asked distantly, his back still turned to me.

I stiffened, confused at his response.

I had thought he was cold in the meeting to keep his guard up around Acacia, but that clearly wasn't the case.

"I just wanted to thank you for moving to the frontline. I didn't—"

"I didn't do it for you." Alaric turned a quarter. "I won't do anything for you anymore, Ina. Just as how you shouldn't have claimed that your father hid the truth."

I confusedly laughed. "Yes, I did." I looked to Neo to see if he had a reason for Alaric's behavior. I knew that he may still be raw from our conversation last night, but I didn't think Alaric would be like this. "Acacia nearly attacked me when I told her, and she had no quarrel with me. If it had been you—"

"That's none of your concern." I shuddered at the harshness in Alaric's voice. "You broke the bond last night, Ina, for your pack. So, protect them. Do not risk your life for mine."

Alaric walked away without so much as a glimpse back.

My chest tightened, and my throat grew dry as I watched him grow further away.

His words were right, but they still hurt.

After everything we had gone through, the claims that were made, I had at least thought we'd still be cordial, that we would look out for each other.

"Give him time, Ina," Neo whispered, a hand on my shoulder, causing me to turn from Alaric. "He needs to get over the bond in his own way."

"But he said he was getting over it," I added, my chest feeling like it would cave in at any moment.

Neo looked at me with pity and licked his lips. "Ina, you can't be that—"

"Ina, where are you going?" a voice that had my sadness replaced with pure rage asked.

Rainer hurried toward me and Neo, Aspen on his heels.

I huffed as he eyed Neo territorially.

We were in for a fight, one that I looked forward to after how Rainer talked to me in the tent, but one I didn't want Neo around for.

"I'll talk to you later," I whispered.

Neo glimpsed at Rainer with a weary, annoyed look but nodded. "I wish I would have trained more so I could stay."

I laughed, pulling him into a hug that I was sure would have Rainer steaming, but I didn't care. Battles were far too unpredictable.

"Be safe."

Neo hugged me back. "You too," he mumbled, racing after Alaric, just as Rainer reached me.

"You can't run away like that, Ina. Not after such a tense meeting. The Woodland Pack already thinks we are divided because of that business with Alaric and even more so after you challenged me," Rainer growled.

"Challenge you?" I scoffed with even more ferocity, spinning around to face him, knuckles white. "Is that what you call it when I want to protect *my* pack?"

"You'll be protecting them in the back." Rainer stepped forward, his forehead almost touching mine. I didn't shrink away.

"I'm the best fighter in the pack. My skills are better in the front. You know that. Or do you need a reminder of how often I bested you in the ring these past years?" I shoved Rainer's chest.

"Do not challenge me, Ina. I am your alpha, your betrothed," he seethed, closing the distance between us once again.

Without thinking, I gripped Artico's Fang, hoping the ancientness of it could change my fate. Rainer eyed it then ripped it from my neck.

"Know your place," he ordered, retying it so it adorned him.

My nostrils flared, and the veins in my neck threatened to pop.

Rainer had taken the last thing my father had passed to me—even if it was for temporary keeping. I wanted to lunge at him right then and there, but Aspen inched closer, ready to intervene and do his duty of protecting his alpha. And while, I was more than okay hurting Rainer, I couldn't hurt him. So I did the only thing I could do and lashed out.

"Only because I wasn't allowed to fight for myself. If I was, you'd be nothing," I bit out.

Rainer flinched.

Taking the chance, I turned. However, as I did, Rainer's fingers wrapped tightly around my wrist, stopping me.

"So, it meant nothing all those times?" Rainer asked.

I stared at him blankly, unsure what he meant, but as time passed, it became clear. He was talking about all the nights that ended with him in my bed.

Of course they meant nothing. They never did. I told him that numerous times.

"Did it mean anything when you slept with him?" Rainer questioned, taking my silence as an answer to his former question.

"How is that any of your business?" I pulled my hand back.

Rainer didn't have the right to know the answer to that question. He was already taking far too much of me. He didn't get to know about the happiness I found. Not to mention, that depending on the answer I gave, he may very well challenge Alaric, despite my choice to leave him, as any lingering feelings threatened Rainer's reign.

Rainer's eyes darkened, and he stepped forward, clearly angrier than before. "Do not make me compel you for an answer."

My chest stilled. Compelling wasn't something that was supposed to be used lightly. It especially wasn't supposed to be used to coax answers out of your mate.

"We're attracting attention," Aspen whispered, stepping between me and Rainer. "If you two continue this, you need to do it at the tent.

Both Rainer and I froze, turning our heads to see every wolf within our sight staring.

This wasn't good, even Rainer knew that, despite his prideful ignorance.

"It's fine. We're already finished," I remarked, taking advantage of the situation, and stormed off.

CHAPTER 58

I stormed through the camp, not bothering to look back or sniff the air for Rainer or Aspen. I didn't care how close they were or if they had fallen behind. All I knew was that I needed space from Rainer before I chewed off his head. However, as I got to the Artico section, my legs stilled.

I had come too late in the morning to have my own tent set up, and I was certain that with my choosing of Rainer, Dahlia was reclaiming her tent. And as far as the alpha's tent, it belonged to Rainer now. I would find no peace there. I had nowhere to go.

"You're back from the meeting already?" a honey-dew voice asked from behind.

My shoulders slacked, and I allowed all the fear and sadness I had been holding back to wrap around me and ran into my sister's arms.

"Ina, what happened?" Ala asked, adjusting the basket of herbs on her arm so she could hug me back, worry evident in her voice.

"It's a long story."

Ala leaned back, cupping my face. "You know I always have time for you."

My throat bobbed as I forced back down tears. "Do you mind if we find Sil and head to one of your tents before I start?"

Ala moved her basket to the arm that was the farthest from me and held out her now free one. "I think Sil's in her tent."

Sil and Ala sat in silence, far longer than I thought they would, as I finished relaying the events of the meeting and Rainer's ludicrous decisions. I had expected them to jump up, to curse his name, as we did with all males who crossed either one of us, no matter how small their error was, but they didn't. They didn't so much as sneer at the thought of him. They only looked at each other with utter confusion.

"Do you think he was right?" I asked, scared to hear the answer.

"I don't think he was right to make those decisions," Sil began, "but I know why he made them."

I leaned away. "What do you mean?"

Sil once again looked at Ala, who shook her head, whispering, "We promised."

Sil gripped the mug in her hand, eyes averted. "It's not our place to tell you."

I gawked at the two females in front of me. They were supposed to be my closest friends, family even. Yet they were holding secrets for Rainer.

I knew he was alpha and that they needed to obey him, but I never thought they would hide something from me, especially when we were alone. I thought that they'd always be faithful to me. Things really had changed since I had been gone.

"He threatened to compel me," I refuted, trying to get them to see reason.

"Which is wrong by all means, and we will face him together on that aspect, but he did so for your protection, Ina," Ala defended.

Another pain shot through me. I stood, unable to face any more of this.

"Where are you going?" Ala asked, sounding as if she may very well cry.

I fisted my hands, trying not to yell. "Somewhere else. Somewhere I can find answers."

"But it's the night before the battle. You should rest. We should be together," Ala pleaded.

Hearing Ala's voice like that hurt almost as much as the betrayal. She wanted me to stay with them, to spend time with them before tomorrow; I did too. Battles were always erratic, and the night before, you had to make the most of it, spend it with those you cared about. And with us having been separated for so long, because of the same enemy we were attacking tomorrow, it felt even more important that we cherish this time together. However, I couldn't bring myself to stay.

Quietly, I turned and walked to the door.

"Fuck this. This isn't worth it," Sil hissed.

"Sil, we promised," Ala interrupted. "He said he was going to tell her himself. He—"

"He's had plenty of time, Ala. I know you like to keep promises and believe that people will do what they say, but that's not always the case. This isn't a secret worth losing a night that could very well be our last one together."

Ala didn't say anything else, her battle of morals and loyalty coming to an end.

"He's in love with you, Ina," Sil declared.

"What?" I spun around.

"Rainer is in love with you. That's what he told Aspen, who told me."

I shook my head, looking to both Ala and Sil to find any inclination that they were joking, but there was none.

"He doesn't. The way he treats me...he treats me as if I was some fragile thing. If he had his way, I'd be locked up," I stammered.

"That's how he loves, Ina," Ala whispered. "He wants to protect you. It may not be how he should love *you*, but that's how he does it. It's what has driven him to make every decision. It's why he put the pack on the front lines. He wanted to be the one to rip off the head of the leader of the demons. He wanted to avenge you, because that was the only way he could live with himself for letting you die. He was willing to do anything to amend the mistake he made by letting you go to your father by yourself. It nearly destroyed him. It's why he's putting you in the safest place he knows. He wants to keep you safe, to keep the promise he made to your father."

Love. Alaric loved me, and he wanted to show it by risking my pack. Anyone with common sense would know that wasn't what I needed, what I wanted. They would know that keeping me from protecting my pack would result in me hating them.

My brows pursed together as I tried to calm myself.

My sisters had answered my initial question only to lead to more.

Why did they know all of this?

Why had they hidden it? Why did Rainer hide it?

And better yet, what promise had Rainer made to my father?

I stepped toward my friends. They looked sheepishly at me, knowing that they had opened a box they weren't going to be able to close for a while. However, just as sound passed my lips, screams were heard from outside, and the flap of the tent flew open.

Aspen limped into the tent, carrying a crying pup and an older wolf who, despite her bleeding leg, still managed to support half her weight.

I rushed over, as did Ala and Sil, each of us taking hold of the wolves who had entered.

I lowered the older one onto a pillow, grabbing whatever cloth was nearest and blotted at the blood that was running, revealing the already festering wound.

I stiffened, knowing there was only one thing that could cause an infection that quick.

Silver.

"They're here," Aspen breathed out, stating what I had figured out.

I tied the cloth above the older wolf's wound before quickly standing, taking guard at the tent's entrance, and peering out to see wolves shifting, biting down on the heads of demons who darted every which way in search of prey.

"Their attacks are chaotic," I whispered, already heading for Alaric's sword and Neo's silver dagger in the corner of the tent, thankful I hadn't had time to return them yet.

"We suspect it's the recently turned," Aspen groaned. "They're clumsy, so we've been able to cut them down because of it, but a few have been able to run off with some pups."

Fear coursed through me now knowing the demons had come here for supper.

"Where are the bulk of them?" I asked, strapping my weapons to my waist, despite the fact I would soon be in wolf form, but if I had learned anything from Alaric, it was to always be prepared for when your wolf tired.

"They came in through the other side of camp. The side closest to the castle. It's also where many of them are retreating to."

"Then, that's where I'll go," I announced, determined not to let anyone else become food for the demons.

"I'll go with you," Aspen grunted, trying to get up but was swiftly pushed back down by Sil.

"You're not going anywhere. You can barely walk," she cried, panic clear in her voice.

"I'll be fine. I need to protect the pack. I need to—"

Aspen gritted his teeth, muffling a scream as Ala poked his leg with the hand that wasn't covered in blood.

"It's broken," she said flatly, ever the calm healer. "You need to stay."

Ala turned back to her other patient, pulling out ointments from her basket though her lip quivered.

She was scared, scared of losing more people. As was Sil. She just wasn't as contained.

Tears ran down her cheeks, and her hands trembled as they pushed on Aspen's chest. Though despite his weakened state, Aspen began to rise.

"Sil, you know that there is no greater disgrace for an Artico warrior than to shy from battle," Aspen sighed out, a hand over Sil's as he admired her like it was his last time to.

"Please," Sil begged, "I can't lose you." Still, Aspen rose, none of us except Sil doing anything to stop him from doing so. After all, he was right.

Never run from a battle when you're needed. That was the rule ingrained into us from the first day of training, and right now, based on the thickening blood in the air, we all were. This was a pivotal battle.

"I can't lose my mate," Sil sobbed, throwing all her weight onto his chest.

Everyone stilled at her words, at the word mate. Ala even stopped the stitching she was doing.

I bit my lip, thinking of Alaric. It had hurt almost unbearably so to cast him aside, and he was nothing but a false bond. I couldn't imagine what it would feel like for a real bond to be broken by death and not by choice.

I pushed my tongue into my canines, knowing Aspen would hate me for this, but I couldn't let that happen to Sil, not when it already happened to Ala.

"Aspen," I roared, "as future wife of the alpha, I command you to stay."

Sil nodded to me in thanks. However, that thanks was short-lived.

"Nice try but"—Aspen pushed off the ground, fighting Sil who had wrapped herself around him—"Rainer already gave me orders to go where you go. So, the only way I'm going to stay is if you do too."

I groaned, watching more and more of the battle go on.

I needed to fight. I needed to protect the pack, but I couldn't allow Aspen to leave. For him to fight with a broken leg, would mean his death, and for him to willingly disobey Rainer, would mean a demotion for him, possibly a banishment from the pack.

I was going to have to choose.

I cursed Rainer as I paced the tent and listened to the screams and cries grow louder, as the air became so thick with the scent of blood that my nose burned. I needed to go, but I couldn't allow Aspen to die. I sunk to the ground feeling utterly useless.

"Damn it," Ala bit through her teeth, the first time I heard her curse.

Ala grabbed a clean towel, and poured some liquid onto it, then planted it firmly over Aspen's nose and mouth. He gave her a look, squirmed a bit, but whatever she poured onto that towel had his eyes closing.

Sil gripped tighter to Aspen, her chest stilling, fear creeping into her eyes.

"He's fine. It's just a sleeping potion to calm terrified patients. A really strong one," Ala assured, tucking the towel into her pocket.

Sil lowered her ear to Aspen's chest, exhaling with relief as she heard his heartbeat.

"Go, Ina," Ala whispered. "Do what you were meant to."

"Right," I whispered, my heart lightening.

My sisters, despite hiding Rainer's secret, had chosen to side with me in the end. I wasn't alone, not everyone had chosen him. Some still believed in me.

I closed my eyes and called on my wolf. My feet and hands turned into deadly, clawed paws. My arms elongated into strong, powerful limbs made to leap, and my teeth sharpened.

I was going to kill them all.

CHAPTER 59

I sprinted through the camp, biting the head of any demon that came into my path, not caring that their thick black blood splattered onto my white fur or hit the back of my throat. Seeing the carnage around me, I just wanted them dead.

Wolves whimpered as they tried to stand on their injuries. Children's' screams could be heard far off in the distance. Elderly cries and pleas too. It took every ounce of me not to run after each one, but I knew where I needed to go, knew where I would stop the majority of the demons from taking anymore wolves.

I ran and ran until there was nowhere to go, until a congested camping site filled my vision.

Wolves of every color leapt, their teeth finding purchase in any blood demon that got too close. Most of the demons ran, not bothering to even fight, reaching for whatever poor wolf they could grab, but only a select few made it past the barrier that Dahlia and her two underlings made, decimating the demons easily. It was hardly like the time Artico was attacked.

Aspen was right. These were the recently turned. Still, that didn't make this fight any less dangerous or serious. If I had to guess, the demons had figured we were going to attack soon and sent out their recently turned to get the key thing that allowed them to compete with us. Our blood.

This battle was just as important as the one we would take part in at the castle.

I jumped into the mob of demons and wolves, slashing, and snapping at anything that didn't have fur. I took down two, then three, then four, then five. The coating of their blood on my fur started to weigh me down, but still, I traversed. The more we killed today, the less there would be tomorrow.

Bit by bit, the ground became covered. I couldn't take more than five steps without having to maneuver over the dead.

It was hard to tell who had more losses, as all who lay on the ground appeared to be human, red and black blood covering them, covering their scent.

Still, I kept fighting. I kept biting until I couldn't find anyone else, until I kept turning so fast in search of my next target, that I bumped into another wolf, into Rainer.

His eyes went wide at the sight of both wolf and demon blood on my body. He searched for any harm done to me, and when he found none, he looked around, no doubt, for Aspen. When he didn't find him, Rainer growled and thrusted his snout in the direction I had come from.

I dug my claws deep into the dirt. I would stay here.

I would always choose to help rather than seek safety.

Rainer encroached, looking as if he may very well drag me back himself, but he stopped when a long, proud howl echoed through the camp.

I looked over to find Acacia, the last demon in the camp dying at her feet.

The battle was over.

Several other wolves joined in the howl, relishing in the victory, mourning those who could not make the sound.

I began to raise my own head, but as I glimpsed a black wolf, my heart stopped.

Alaric whipped around frantically, his eyes going every which way. Finally, they settled on a cloak, one that I knew well, one that belonged to Neo. Alaric sniffed at it, his hackles rising at whatever scent was mixed in. He turned his nose to the sky, sniffing deeply, body turning to wherever the scent was leading. I did too, trying to figure out what was wrong. It wasn't until Alaric let out a low, mournful howl, begging for help, that I caught Neo's scent and realized where it was coming from.

The castle.

Neo had been captured.

Wolves beheld Alaric, saw him near the cloak, and wondered where the second Rivelian prince was. One by one, they understood and looked to Acacia and Rainer for orders. Both shook their heads.

Alaric's snout scrunched up, a judging snarl emitting from him. Still, Acacia and Rainer didn't change their mind, didn't so much as move when Alaric turned and began to sprint into the woods.

My gut twisted, and I let out a low growl of my own.

Though Alaric was strong, he was not strong enough to infiltrate the demon's castle by himself. He would die.

However, my growl did nothing. I highly doubted he even heard it. It was nothing but another whisper in the wind.

I couldn't let this happen. I couldn't let both males I had traveled with, had become family with die while I sat here doing nothing, waiting for tomorrow.

Sensing what I was planning to do, Rainer stepped in front of me, his large frame blocking my view of Alaric. I snarled, telling him to let me pass. He didn't move. He only held my stare with those controlling eyes from earlier. I stepped around him. It didn't matter if this affected the pack's view of him or me. If Rainer was going to lead this way, I didn't want any part of it. Wolves were supposed to help the weak, not protect the strong.

Rainer lunged for my neck, but I dodged him, throwing my paw with enough force that I threw him to the ground and pinned him, calling the attention of all the other wolves. He squirmed underneath me, snapping and snarling, spit sputtering from his mouth. However, I pushed down harder, evoking a whimper from him, making sure he understood that if I wanted to, I could end him, before sprinting after Alaric.

CHAPTER 60

I sprinted through the trees, the scent of decay and death becoming so thick that I couldn't find Alaric's scent. All I had to follow were his faded tracks. Part of me worried I was going the wrong way, scared that the tracks belonged to another, but then cackles sounded not too far away, a low growl too.

I ran faster until a castle loomed in front of me, vines climbing up the dulled stones, not a single living thing surrounding it. Light was even rare around and in the structure. Everything felt wrong. It was death personified.

"I recognize you," a voice boomed from across the bridge. "You took down so many of my men in the war."

I peered across the bridge, finding Alaric at the open gate, demons slowly pouring out, surrounding him as the same demon whom my father told me to run from sauntered to Alaric.

Every instinct in my body wanted to surge forward, to aim for Marcellus's throat, and cut him down, seek revenge for my father. But if I had learned anything from Alaric, it was that I needed to wait. I needed to control my emotions, even if that meant hiding until I could make a strategic move.

I burrowed down in the grass.

Alaric's claws extended, scraping on the stone under him as he squatted down, making sure he could handle any attack. He bared his canines, showing off the black blood that dripped from them, looking utterly terrifying, despite the sheer number that surrounded him. The demon laughed.

"I suppose you're here for your brother. At least that's who I think he is. He sure as hell smelt like you." Alaric growled, but it didn't affect the demon. "Would you like to see him?" the demon asked in a sing-song voice, curling his fingers. Two demons dragged a barely conscious Neo in human form forward. Alaric stalked toward them, murderous intent in his eyes. "Stop there, young prince"—the demon pulled Neo to him until his back was against Marcellus's chest, his fingers softly running up Neo's neck—"or I'll end him now."

Alaric shifted his weight, and his ears tucked down.

"Good little prince. I must admit, this turned out much better than I thought. When the wolves chased us from the continent, my people and my father swore they would never return, but I never did, not after your kind killed my sister. My beautiful, dear sister. She deserved so much more. She inspired our people to come here, to come out of the dark and claim lands that we deserved as immortals. I swore that day that I would return, that I would ensure that I'd make every wolf suffer, especially the leaders. I killed Batair and practically made his pack go extinct. The Woodland Pack was supposed to be tomorrow, but my armies got hungry, so they'll be a slow kill, which in a way is better. If I remember correctly, Acacia hated the slow route. But as far as Rivelia, I didn't know how to hurt Damon or you, not when your father kept his walls so high and seemed to care so little about anything. I didn't expect to see you or your brother outside, but now, I have both. I have two things to lure Damon out of his castle, making it so much easier to rid the world of you wolves. I will become master of this continent, and my vengeance will be complete."

I quaked, realizing that there were more of them in the world. Hiding. Waiting.

"But I'm suspect that will be a while, so I'll have to make do with entertaining myself with my hostages," hummed the demon before sinking his teeth into Neo's neck.

Alaric lurched forward, fear controlling him, while Neo's eyes began to close, and the scent of his blood spread.

The demon threw Neo to the ground, holding out his hands to stop Alaric. For a moment, the demon's arms began to tremble, and Alaric's canines grew closer to his face, but then Neo's blood hit him.

The demon gloated, cackled even, as he pushed Alaric back and threw him to the mob of demons that had formed a ring around them. Alaric scrambled to his feet, ready to pounce again, but with a nod from their leader, the demons jumped on him, using all their combined strength to keep Alaric down.

Marcellus proudly closed the distance between them. With his foot, he pivoted Alaric's head to him, earning several growls.

The demon smirked. "You're a lot more fun to play with than your brother, but I will confess, the years haven't dulled your strength. Without your brother's blood, you would have knocked me down." The demon frowned. "You're a bit too dangerous to keep around, and I can't be drinking wolf blood at all hours to keep you tamed. I suppose one son will have to be enough." The demon walked back to his castle, and with his back still turned, he offered to his army, "Go ahead and kill him. Taste him if you wish. His blood will be a glorious surge of energy for all of you, but it will curse you with unbelievable cravings."

Drool seeped from the demons' mouths. They circled around Alaric and pushed one another to get closer, ready to pounce.

My stomach dropped. It didn't matter if there was an opening or if the numbers were still the same, I needed to attack now, or Alaric would die.

I stood, claws already out and sprinted to the horde of demons, sending prayers to the gods, asking them to watch over my pack. Because with the sheer number of demons, I knew my chances of coming out of this battle would be meager, but I couldn't sit by ideally. Alaric had no one. At least my pack had Rainer, and as much as I hated him and thought his decisions were ludicrous, he had kept them alive. With one great snarl, I leapt, ripping demon after demon off Alaric.

Alaric's face fell at the sight of me, sheer surprise taking residence on it. I held his stare for a moment, waiting for the anger. Instead, only relief was shown.

"Who?" stuttered Marcellus as he ran back to the middle. I picked up Alaric, hurrying to get him back on his feet. He nuzzled me and, gods, the touch made me want to cry, made my heart lighten despite the monsters surrounding us. I couldn't help but keep from cuddling into him as we stood, the touch reassuring me. And based on how Alaric mimicked my movement, he was too. "You're Batair's daughter," the demon leader whispered in disbelief. "Impossible. You died. You should have." Marcellus bared his fangs in frustration, but Alaric and I held our ground, looking stronger than ever. "I—"

Several howls sounded not too far away, enough to be an army.

Marcellus's pupils doubled. "To your defensive positions!" he roared, the scent of fear secreting from him.

Several demons ran past us, ignoring us as they made their way to the castle and scrambled up its walls, while Marcellus sprinted to Neo and threw him over his back before rushing to the gates.

Alaric snarled, barely able to hold himself up. I pushed on his chest, hoping to hold him back. The army would be here soon enough. We would get Neo back then. We just needed to wait. Still, Alaric blindly stormed forward, too tired, too high on emotions to see the powerful punch Marcellus had prepared.

Alaric fell to the ground with enough force that he shifted back to human form. Marcellus gloated and brought Neo's throat to him. Slowly, he licked the delicate flesh, relishing the pain that danced in Alaric's eyes. Alaric tried to get up, tried to crawl to them, but Marcellus kicked him down once again and stepped on Alaric's throat, immobilizing him as he drank from Neo a second time and replenished his strength.

"You should have just let me take him," Marcellus cooed, wiping away blood resting at the corner of his lips. "Now you're going to die before the battle even begins."

Alaric gripped Marcellus's ankle, tried to push him off, but the demon only pressed down harder.

I raced forward, forsaking my plan to wait for the pack, for the help that would have guaranteed that we made it through this alive, because it wouldn't end like this. I wouldn't let Alaric die.

With both paws, I brought the demon down to the ground and flung Neo from his shoulder, far from the battle. He was going to wake up with so many bruises, but it was better than being dead. Marcellus fought against me, using all his force to try and push me off, but I pushed even harder. I wouldn't let him get back up, not until the rest of the wolves arrived. He would stay here on the ground until his strength waned and I was able to rip out his throat or until others did it for me.

The howls got closer, the scent of both Artico and Woodland wolves covering up the vile scent of tainted blood.

They would be here any second, and Marcellus would die.

I gloated down at the demon, giving one final push to ensure he would stay down. However, it did so much more than that. Marcellus's elbows bent.

The effect of Neo's blood was finally wearing off.

My eyes widened. Maybe I didn't have to wait for the other wolves to take my revenge.

I pushed again, and this time, I was able to shake off one of Marcellus's hands.

Revenge was about to be mine. Revenge for my father, my pack, Neo, and Alaric.

I opened wide, canines aimed, but instead of feeling his flesh tearing, I felt mine. I felt my side burning. I felt the pain spreading and my body weakening.

I looked to the source, cursing as I saw it. A dagger made of silver lay deep in my flesh.

Marcellus cackled.

He had never been tired. It had all been a ploy.

Doubt and hatred for myself began to cloud my mind. All my training and I had let it be a waste. I was going to die and—

Not all my training.

I was still standing. I was still coherent because of my silver resistance. I could still fight; I could still move, a fact that Marcellus didn't know. I could use the same tactic. I just needed to move but fast.

I purposefully swayed and drooped my eyes as I stepped away from Marcellus. His smile grew wider.

"This time, I'll watch the light leave your eyes," he mused, standing without a care for anything else.

I breathed deep, waiting until Marcellus inched closer. Then, once his hand reached out to take his blade, I lunged. My canines dug into his flesh, met his bone, and with one swift movement, I tore off his arm.

"You bitch," Marcellus cried, black blood sputtering all around us as he used his remaining arm to smack me.

I hit the earth with little resistance, the silver slowing me down. Marcellus stalked forward, vigor fueled by hatred emitting from him.

Why couldn't he just die?

"You should have let the silver kill you," he whispered in my ear, kneeling beside me as he twisted his dagger and leisurely pulled it out. I cried at the pain, wishing that it would stop, but not in the way that Marcellus was about to make it.

He raised the dagger dripping with my own blood, ready to plunge it into my heart. I screamed at my body to get up. It didn't listen. The dagger started to come down, but a snarl, accompanied by several howls, sounded just behind the trees.

The dagger stalled. Fear showed on the demon's face once again and a blob of wheat-colored fur flew over me.

Marcellus screeched as he was hurled straight into a wall. He clutched his head, trying to get over his daze. Now was the perfect time to kill him. I crawled to him, but Rainer stepped over me, making sure the numerous wolves rushing the gates would not accidentally trample over me.

The army was here.

Incoherent orders were given, indecipherable growls mutely sounded in my ear. I didn't know what was happening, but based on how the demons ran, we were winning.

Once the initial rush was done, Rainer nuzzled me and lifted my paw. No, not my paw. My hand.

I had shifted back. The silver had started to take its toll on my body. It was a wonder I was still conscious.

Rainer, seeing my half open eyes, gently glided my hand to his back, then grabbed me by my tunic and threw me over him, turning for the woods.

"You must stay and fight," I quietly ordered, trying to slide off, knowing that the trip back would cost him precious time in the battle, our allies a valuable player, and our pack their leader—their morale.

Ignoring me, Rainer thrust upward, forcing me back on.

"No," I mumbled, pulling his coarse fur as hard as I could, attempting to make him see sense.

Still, he didn't listen. He didn't stop trying to get me secured on his back until the leader demon attacked once more.

"I will not let you flee again," Marcellus grunted, kicking Rainer in the side, sending me back to the ground. "You will die. Batair's heir will die," he screamed, stalking to me. However, Rainer jumped on him, hoping to stop his assault. Instead, Rainer was thrown and kicked again and again until he barely had energy to flinch from the pain.

I watched, my vision blurring, my lids closing.

I needed to get up. I needed to finish him off. But I was so weak.

I couldn't even shift and the sword I carried was too heavy. The only thing I could lift was a dagger.

Neo's dagger.

The silver blade.

But I could only hold it for a minute. Killing the demon leader would take so much more than that. Not to mention, I had silver running through my body already. I would instantly pass out, maybe even die. I couldn't. There was no way. Perhaps this wasn't what I was meant to do. Perhaps I wasn't as strong as I had thought.

The sound of battling began to die down.

I roused enough strength to lift my head and see the reason why, praying that the battle was finally ending. Instead, I found eyes turning to us—the future leaders of the wolves succumbing to Marcellus.

Doubt was forming. The deadliest thing in war. Not even Acacia would be able to fight by herself.

I had to try. I had to wield the dagger.

I pushed my palms against the stone, my grip slipping, but I kept going. I found friction in the sharp rocks digging into my flesh until I was on my feet. My entire body yelled at me, told me to lie back down. I shook my head, taking a step forward, making sure my hand hovered just above the hilt of the dagger.

"Your time here is done," I growled.

The demon turned, took one look at me, and laughed. "You really think you can declare that? You can barely stand." I stared him down. Marcellus sighed, "I'll get to you in a second, little one. I have better prey to hunt right now."

"I am not your prey," I roared. "I am Ina, Daughter of Batair, and you will die by my hand today."

Marcellus straightened. "Will I?" He stormed forward, clear agitation on his face, and reached for my throat. I didn't move to dodge it, didn't so much as struggle as he grasped it and raised me up in the air. "You want to die that badly?" he snickered. "Then, give your parents my regards."

Marcellus squeezed tighter, a smile emerging so wide that his glistening eyes narrowed. He was completely enthralled with my gasping, with the color slowing leaving my face. It was just what I wanted.

I ripped Neo's dagger from its sheath and drove it up through Marcellus's chin. Blood sprayed from his mouth, and his grip loosened as I wedged the blade to its hilt and dragged it through his throat. Marcellus's head tilted to the side with only a few strands of flesh keeping it attached to his body. His knees started to bend, but it wasn't enough. Not for me. With one last thrust, one last scream, I cut the remaining flesh.

His head fell beautifully, then his body, the thud of it hitting the ground like a symphony to my ears. But I did not get to enjoy it as much as I liked, as I fell too, too tired to hold myself up, to keep my eyes open. And when I hit the ground, the world went black.

CHAPTER 61

I jolted up, gulping for air as my heart roared. I was in danger. I needed to find a dagger, a sword, anything.

My hands raced around, bracing for the jagged rocks I was sure to feel as they slid about, waiting for my cloudy eyes to clear. However, I felt nothing but soft, lush blankets.

I rubbed my eyes, forcing them to focus.

Everywhere I looked, colorful tapestries lined the walls of a tent. A low table filled with fruit sat in the middle, surrounded by multiple pillows that had clear dents in them. There weren't any signs of havoc or carnage in sight. There were no signs of the demons. There were only signs of the Woodland Pack, that I was in one of their tents.

Slowly, I pushed the heavy blanket off, revealing a strange, white shift that was cut in half. I may have very well thought it was a skirt and tunic if it were not for the thin material that undergarments were made of. However, I didn't have time to think about it, as my body was now fully awake and screaming at me to attend to it.

I twisted, trying to find the chamber pot.

"Ina," a soft, almost sobbing voice gasped, accompanied by the drop of something.

I turned, finding Ala, Sil, and Aspen gawking in the flap of the tent.

I was barely able to register Ala's swollen eyes, the dark circles on Sil, or Aspen's scruff—that would have taken him days to grow out—before Ala pounced on me.

"You're awake," she sobbed, holding me tight, stirring pain in my side, eliciting a whimper from me.

"Careful, Ala," Sil scolded, sitting on the blanket beside us.

Ala hurriedly pulled back and hiked up my top, revealing my torso wrapped in bandages. I flinched as memories of the battle and Marcellus stabbing me flashed back. Carefully, Ala undid the bandages and examined an almost-healed wound. I stiffened. I shouldn't have even been alive after that battle. It was completely impossible for my wounds to have healed already. It would take days, maybe even a week.

Had I been asleep for that long?

"Looks like I didn't do any damage," Ala mused, proud of herself. "My new salve has made the wound almost nonexistent, resistant to anything, even me. But I'll apply some more just in case." Ala retrieved a small metal canister from a basket that Sil had brought over—the object that I had heard drop, if I had to take a guess based on how disorganized the contents were. Thank goodness none were glass.

"Someone needs to take away that title of best healer from you," Sil mumbled.

Ala stuck out her tongue before working on my torso. Sil shook her head before placing a gentle hand on my shoulder.

"How are you?"

"Confused," I squeaked out, my throat too dry to properly speak.

Ala and Sil perked up, both of them scrambling for the pitcher of water on the table. However, just as they took their first step, Aspen held out a cup.

I nodded in thanks, gulping down the cool liquid without so much of a breath in between. The feeling was glorious, and before I had time to lower the cup to my lap, Aspen handed me a second one filled to the brim. I took it, but this time, only to sip on.

"Better?" Aspen asked.

"Much. Thank you," I replied, my voice still a tad husky, like it was out of practice, making me ask my silent question out loud. "How long have I been asleep?"

Sil's hand slid down to mine, gripping it tightly. "Only a couple of days. Thankfully, after you passed out, you were taken to an amazing healer right away."

"You mean fighters had to leave the battles because of me? That didn't affect the casualties, did it?" I asked, panicking, despite assuming we had won the battle, as we were all here.

Aspen shook his head. "The battle ended shortly after your infamous slaying of the demon leader. Without him, the rest of the demons had no plan. They all started running. According to the scouts, who were sent out to terminate any stragglers, some even jumped into the ocean and swam to only the gods know where."

I sighed in relief. We had won, and better yet, my fallen pack members and father had been avenged. Everything I had sworn to do had finally come to fruition. Though, despite the happiness that was bursting inside me, the trained warrior side of me asked, "Have the reports for the battle been finalized?"

"Enough about battles, please," Sil begged.

I exhaled, a tad disappointed about Sil's request. Though the battle was short, it didn't guarantee that the casualties were low. If they were high, it was even more important to start planning our defenses for returning to Artico. However, seeing Sil and Ala's worried faces, I knew they didn't want to rehash the horrors of the battle. And if I was being honest with myself, even if I went against their wishes, I wasn't sure I would be able to fully understand all the information. My head still felt cloudy, and my thoughts were slow.

"Alright," I whispered, taking another sip of water, pushing my bladder just over the edge. I clutched my abdomen, groaning.

"What's wrong?" Ala put down the ointment, eyes raking over me.

"Chamber pot," I sighed out.

"Oh," Ala exclaimed, already rushing to retrieve it.

"Can you stand?" Sil held out her hands, inviting me to use them if I needed.

I nodded, pushing up with little pain, and took the few steps over to the chamber pot Ala had brought over.

"Are you guys going to watch?" I asked, noticing that all eyes were still on me.

"Oh. I—I'm sorry," Aspen stuttered. "I'm too used to staying through everything in case Sil and Ala needed help lifting you." I grimaced, realizing just how severe my wounds were. "I'll go. I need to report that you're awake anyway." Aspen stumbled back, rushing out of the tent.

Sil laughed. "For such a strong warrior, he is such a bashful male."

I gave a shallow nod in agreement, waiting for Sil and Ala to follow him or at least turn around. However, they both kept staring. "What about you two?"

"I still need to bandage you," Ala remarked from her basket, preparing some fresh linen.

I cocked my head to Sil.

"I'm here to catch you in case your legs give out. Plus, we've all peed together before," Sil snarked in way of saying she wasn't letting me out of her sight. I raised a brow. "Drunk nights at the human tavern. We always had to pee halfway up the mountain, remember?"

I crossed my arms, wanting to fight that logic, but with how adamant these two were, I knew this was an argument that would take too long, according to my throbbing bladder. But who could blame them? I barely wanted them out of sight after I found them again, and I had only lost them once. They had to go through it twice.

"Fine," I grumbled. "Turn around at least."

Sil crossed her arms. "I don't trust your legs to hold you. I need to be close in case you fall."

I rubbed my temple. There was no winning this battle. I reluctantly shoved down my undergarments. "Then, tell me about this amazing healer. I can't go without a distraction."

"Well, for starters, she's in this tent." Sil gestured to Ala. "Every wolf has been demanding her attention after they saw how she was able to bring you back from the brink of death. Her new salve did wonders for you. It practically rid you of severe silver sickness in a night."

I blinked, eyes wandering over to Ala. I knew she was good but not that amazing.

"Thank you, Ala," I whispered, reassembling my clothes so I could return to the bed and let Ala finish her work.

Ala disagreed with a hum, ever the shy, humble female I knew her to be. "It was mainly thanks to your stubbornness and also Alaric and Rainer." I perked up, cursing the fog around my brain. I should have asked about everyone as soon as I woke up. "I think the gods knew that if they took you, those two would ruin the world above and below to get you back."

"Alaric and Rainer are alive? What about Neo?" I asked frantically, gripping Ala's hand, ceasing her wrapping of my torso.

She gave me a reassuring smile. "Alive and doing well. None of them were touched by the silver. Their wounds only took hours to heal, then they were here day and night."

My brows scrunched. "Rainer and Alaric waited together?"

Ala and Sil gave each other a sheepish grin.

"They did," Sil mumbled.

"Rainer let Alaric in here?" I asked, still in disbelief.

Sil nodded. "There wasn't much choice, though. Once Alaric found out which tent you were in, he stormed over here and refused to leave.

Even Acacia couldn't get him to depart with a summons. Alaric always sent Neo to deal with her."

"I actually worried that he may have to be bedridden soon. He slept so little and only ate when someone brought him food," Ala added, clicking her tongue in disapproval. However, a hint of admiration coated her tone.

I softly smiled, reveling in the fact that Alaric still cared, that he had been with me this whole time. Though I shouldn't have. It meant that I still wanted him, that the false bond was still in effect. At least for me.

"It's almost a shame that you woke up during the one time he had to step out," Sil remarked.

Ala gave her a scolding look. "Don't make the gods think we're ungrateful."

"I'd never be ungrateful for them waking Ina up." Sil plopped down next to me on the pile of blankets. "I'm just ungrateful that the Rivelian army showed up."

I snapped to Sil. "The Rivelian army is here."

Sil nodded, playing with the strands of fur in the blanket. "They arrived this morning, demanding to know where Neo and Alaric were."

I jumped up just as Ala tied off the bandages. "Where are my clothes?" I asked, feverishly looking for them.

I didn't know why the Rivelian army was here, but whatever the reason, it couldn't be good. Damon was more stubborn than his son, and he was willing to sacrifice human lives to make a point. Luckily, the latter had mostly been prevented these past years because of Alaric, but I wasn't sure what he would do against an entire army, not after they were given orders. I had to be there with him. I had to help. I had to say goodbye in case he was taken back.

"They're in that chest." Sil pointed to a medium sized trunk next to a mirror.

I threw it open, pulling out a simple tunic and trousers, not caring that the colors didn't complement each other. I dug deeper, trying to find boots, but when I found none, I stormed over to the ones Sil had taken off before plopping onto my bed.

"Hey," she protested, but I was out of the tent before her hands could reach me.

I sprinted through the camp, ignoring the throbbing pain coursing through my body. Many wolves turned to me. Some reached out, mumbling some incoherent greeting. I didn't stop, didn't slow to hear them or to nod until I saw the flags of Rivelia and the field of soldiers.

I braced my hands on my thighs and breathed deep, allowing myself a bit of respite now that I knew I still had time.

"Ina," a curious voice came from the side.

I turned to it, finding Neo, perfectly healthy and not a mark on him.

"Neo," I breathed.

"You're awake." He speedily walked to me, a broad smile on his face, as he extended his arms to me. I walked into them, holding him tight.

"I just woke up," I mumbled.

"I can tell," Neo teased, patting down my hair.

I brushed away his hand. "I came as soon as I heard your father's army was here. I had to make sure everything was alright."

Neo stepped back, his smile growing broader. "Everything is fine. More than fine actually."

I tilted my head. Judging by the size and how the army was still geared up and ready to leave at a moment's notice, I wasn't sure Neo had his facts right.

"Aren't they here to take you guys back?"

Neo laughed. "Originally, but let's just say that after they had some fresh air and the use of Alaric's newly found skill, they won't be escorting us. We'll be leading them. Change is going to come sooner rather than later for Rivelia."

My eyelids fluttered. "Wait, he compelled the general?" I whispered.

Neo nodded.

My hand flew to my chest as a small, surprised smile creeped onto my face. To my knowledge, Damon didn't have the power to compel those out of his own pack, meaning that Alaric was now the stronger of the two without question. Change would come easy, now. Alaric wouldn't have to fight his father. At least not in the brutal way he would've had to before.

"That's amazing," I declared. "How did he figure out how to call the power on command?"

Neo glanced coyly at the ground. "You should ask Alaric about it. It will be better if you hear it from him." Neo cocked his head to the back of the Woodland camp. "Come. He's in our tent, hammering out details with Thomas."

Neo pushed open the flaps, revealing a male with red hair and green eyes. His armor sparkled and showed the reflection of the male across from him—Alaric.

He looked as strong and regal as ever, focusing on the map between him and the redhead. He pointed with assertiveness at a spot that was too tiny for me to make out and mumbled something to the male across from him—Thomas, if I had to guess. Alaric's mind was entirely focused on his plans. He would take hours to notice us, but that was okay. It was one of the traits that I admired about him.

"I'll talk to him later, Neo. He's busy," I whispered, already turning.

Neo gripped my wrist, stopping me, before yelling into the tent, "I have a surprise."

Alaric turned ever so slightly, a scowl already on his face as he ran his fingers through his jet-black hair. "Neo, I told you not to interrupt. I want to get the plans ready as soon as possible so I can get back to—"

Neo swung me in front of him, effectively quieting Alaric.

Alaric's breathing shallowed. We stood in utter quietness with him just staring. For a moment, fear coursed through me, unsure what silenced him, wondering if he still needing to treat me coldly because of the bond. I hoped he didn't. Gods, I hoped not. I couldn't handle that. I searched my brain for something to say, but before I could, Alaric was before me in four large strides and pulled me to his chest.

"You're alright," he mumbled into my neck.

"I woke up just a bit ago," I replied, taking in his comforting scent, leaning into the hug while I pushed away guilt.

I was relieved we were both okay, but I was enjoying the feel of him. I was tugging on the false bond, finding relief that it was still there, that he was still mine.

"Thomas," Neo whispered, "you must be hungry. Let's get you some food before you and my brother finish your plans."

There was a grunt of some sort and feet shuffling. The sound was enough to pull me back to reality, to make me see sense that it was cruel to keep holding on. My arms slacked, allowing Alaric to let go so he could tell Thomas to stay, but he only gripped tighter, nuzzled further into my neck.

"Alaric," I whispered after the footsteps fell away.

Alaric raised his head, putting enough space between us so we could look at one another. My heart hammered as I sheepishly met his eyes, glanced at his lips, and licked mine. This had been the closest we'd been since we decided to go our separate ways, and while I knew I needed to ignore the bond, I wanted nothing more than to rise on my toes and kiss him. Alaric leaned forward a bit, seemingly having the same urge. I made to meet him halfway, but as I did, Alaric coughed.

"Sorry," he grunted, pulling away, leaving me a bit colder than when I had come in. "I just didn't—I was really worried."

Alaric's hands glided down my shoulders to my upper arms, his gaze sliding to my hands, but he only patted my arms then withdrew his touch.

I laughed, trying to hide the disappointment I felt from the lack of it. This was for the best after all.

"As I was told by Ala and Sil," I joked.

One side of Alaric's lips turned up while his eyes dashed to the floor, and he scratched his chin. "They outed me already?"

I nodded. "Those two cannot keep secrets to save their lives. Though, I will say, I think they like you."

Alaric smirked, taking a step back. "That's a relief. When I first showed up to your tent, they watched me like a hawk. I don't think they trusted me very much."

"They're very protective."

"I believe that." Alaric straightened his tunic. "I'm honestly surprised they even let you out of the tent after just waking up."

I bounced my head from shoulder to shoulder. "They didn't have much of a choice." Alaric crossed his arms quizzically. "I kind of ran to you as soon as I heard the Rivelian army was here." I sucked in my lips, popping them out as I rocked on my heels, trying to ignore Alaric's lecturing gaze, the same one he always gave me before adding on extra exercises as punishment.

He rolled his eyes. "Ina, I told you that you're—"

"You can't use that excuse," I interjected. "You were worried about me when I was recovering. I heard that you stayed by my side even though Acacia called for you."

Alaric braced his hands on his hips. "You're as annoying as ever." I smirked, feeling the same energy we had between us before we found my pack. "Without you, Neo and I would be with the gods by now. We're forever in debt to you. It was only right for me to stay by your side."

"It's what friends are for." Alaric's jaw tensed, as if he might say something, but I quickly declared, "That's what we are, Alaric. I know that you think that we shouldn't meddle in each other's affairs, since our packs are separate, but you also said you wanted Rivelia to change. So let's do that. Let's stay friends. Let's be there when the other calls." Alaric stiffened, seemed to lean back as he registered my words. It was selfish of me to ask. I knew that he was still struggling with the bond, but I wanted him close. I needed to know that I would still see him again, since what I really wanted to ask would be too selfish. "It'd be best for our packs," I followed up with, trying to convince him and ease my own conscience.

Alaric loosened, a melancholy smile emerging on his face. "Alright, then, Ina. Friends."

He held out his hand, but I slapped it away and pulled him in for another hug. "Friends. Always."

"You two are still hugging?"

I separated from Alaric, finding Neo and Thomas in the tent's opening.

"It's our second one," I snarked, rolling my eyes at Neo, annoyed and thankful for their interruption. I didn't know if I would be able to pull away again, not after feeling that warmth that only Alaric brought.

"Well, whatever it is, I need to interrupt." Neo stepped into the tent. Thomas too. "Your pack is looking for you, particularly Rainer."

I bit my cheek in annoyance. I didn't want to leave Alaric nor see Rainer. I cared about him, yes, but Ala and Sil had already told me he was fine. They probably told him I was fine. I was sure this summoning was to lecture me, punish me for disobeying orders. Still, he was my alpha, and I needed to obey. It was best for my pack.

"I'll see you all later." I straightened my clothes and pushed down my hair.

"You won't, actually," Alaric said somberly.

I whipped around.

"We need to get back to Rivelia as soon as possible. Both before my father does something more than just send armies, but also because of Acacia." Alaric bit his lip. "She may not have a quarrel with me or Neo now, but that doesn't mean she's alright with an army of Rivelian soldiers at her door." Alaric rested his hand on his pommel, rubbing it anxiously.

"I promised her that we'd leave as soon as you were awake, and seeing as how that's today, I guess she gets her wish."

My throat bobbed. I wanted Alaric to stay. I wanted to tell him not to go. I wasn't ready to be apart from him, but Acacia had every right to tell him and his army to leave.

"I see," I whispered, quiet following. Not even Alaric said a thing. He just kept staring with pleading eyes, but I wasn't sure for what.

CHAPTER 62

ALARIC

"What are you doing?" Neo asked, looming over me.

I gripped harder to the table, studied the map more intensely, scared that if I let myself feel or think of anything other than my plans to take Rivelia that I would run after Ina.

"Alaric," Neo roared.

I continued to ignore him despite his attitude being far different than his carefreeness. But then again, when it came to Ina, Neo was always different. He was braver, stronger, and outspoken. She really did have a knack for bringing out someone's suppressed qualities. Just as how she brought out the good in me. Just as how I could only compel when it was detrimental to keeping her safe.

"Gods damnit." Neo slammed his fist on the table, wrinkling the map. "Do not let her go like this. She is your mate, Alaric."

"You do not need to remind me," I snapped, unable to hear the word I was so desperately trying not to think of, tried not to think of since the day I damned myself and plucked a shinebloom. "I know what she is to me. I know how I feel about her. I don't need you to remind me or make this harder. It already hurts too much."

I slouched, resting my forehead in the palms of my hands, finally feeling the full bulk of the hurt.

"Then, why won't you go after her?" Neo asked so much softer than before.

"You know why," I uttered, recalling the plentiful discussions we had time and time again.

"I know that you kept you two being mates a secret because you were scared of what she would say. I know that you ended your relationship because it was what she needed at the time. And I know that you think you aren't worthy of her." I nodded with each of Neo's sentences, ready for him to give up. "But I still don't understand why."

I raised my head and looked at Neo with pursed brows. "You just don't understand."

"No, you don't. I have a mate Alaric. I know how the bond works. I know how much the bond affects someone. I can tell when someone does something because of a bond or of their free will. And—"

"Enough," I yelled, grabbing Neo by the collar of his tunic.

"Ina loves you," Neo proclaimed, gripping my wrists. I stilled. "Do you think she would have run after just anybody, knowing her chances of survival were slim? Do you think she would have taken the fall for the secret about the wolves' blood, knowing that Acacia may rip off her head when she just found her pack—the thing Ina so desperately fought to find again? The answer is no, Alaric. She wouldn't do those things for just anyone. She wouldn't give up the thing she cares most about for someone she didn't love. She wouldn't have cried so much the night you told her you two needed to go separate ways. She would have been sad, yes, but she would have been happy because things worked out for her pack. Instead, she cried and cried. She showed up to that meeting with swollen eyes. With or without the bond, she loves you."

I thrust Neo away. "No, she doesn't. That's impossible. She's good, and I'm..." I choked back a sob. "I was a monster for years."

Neo rested a hand on my back. "You did so to protect everyone. She knows that. We all know that. You sacrificed so much already. Don't sacrifice her because of a misunderstanding. Don't miss out on the chance to tell her how you feel, even if you don't believe me. Ina is strong. She's not the type to give in, even if you tell her you're bonded. If she doesn't love you, she'll say it. She'll reject you. You'll both hurt temporarily, but you can move on. But if you don't tell her, if you don't give her that chance to reject you, you are subjecting both of you to a lifetime of pain and regret."

A shaky breath escaped me as I wondered when my little brother had become so wise. As much as I hated it, his words were right. At least the ones about Ina being strong. She wouldn't go along with something just because the gods destined it. She never followed orders. I knew that from the moment she had entered Rivelia. I was just scared. I was coming up with excuse after excuse not to tell her in case she rejected me, because if she did, I didn't know if I could handle it. But now, I was out of them. The continent was free of demons. Ina had her pack, the respect of them, and I was certain that if she wanted to reject Rainer, she could do so safely. There was nothing holding me back except myself.

"You're right," I whispered.

Neo perked up. "Then, you'll tell her?" He raised on the tips of his toes. "I can tell Thomas to delay the march so you can find her."

I shook my head. "Not right now." Neo dropped. "I will, but after I right the wrongs of my past, after I fix Rivelia. Because if she rejects me, I can walk away knowing that she rejected *me*, not the coward I had become because of war. That's the only way I can live with that."

Neo chewed on his lip, though understanding showed in his eyes. "And what if she chooses someone else in the meantime?"

I painfully smiled. "You said Ina isn't the type of person to just go along with things. If she chooses to mate with someone, then it's her own choice. I'll be happy for her."

CHAPTER 63

I walked back to the tent I had woken up in and wiped my face, trying to ensure the streaks from the tears that I had shed moments ago blended in with my skin. I didn't want anyone else to see me so vulnerable. I didn't want Rainer to have another reason to hate Alaric or another reason to lecture me. I hated myself for giving him one, but no matter how hard I commanded myself not to cry when I said goodbye, my stubbornness did nothing, especially when Alaric gave me one final hug, one final kiss on the forehead.

I knew I would see them again. I just didn't know when. We were all about to be so busy, and I was sure none of us would be alright leaving our packs during this crucial time. It could be months, probably a year before we even saw each other again, before I would be able to hug Alaric and be reunited with the warmth that ignited in my body.

I shoved the thoughts from my head. Friends. That's what we needed to be. We couldn't be anything more. He wanted his mate.

"Thank the gods your awake, Ina," an Artico wolf mumbled, bowing as I passed, pulling me from my thoughts. I nodded in thanks.

"You saved us," a wolf covered in bandages said, bowing as well.

"Slayer of the Demon Leader!" yelled another, his fist raised high.

"May you live a long life."

The comments continued as I passed every tent, feeling more and more like a victory procession. Some wolves even handed me flowers, and I wish

I could have said I accepted them graciously and with confidence, but I had never received praise like this, even when I came back from the hardest missions. It felt odd to do so. It felt like I was a hero, like I was the most important person in the pack, the most valued, and I didn't know how to respond to it. And I didn't learn by the time I disappeared into my tent and the cheers stopped.

"They love you."

I jumped at the voice, fists already in the air as I faced it.

Rainer lounged in the semi-circle of pillows, a glass of wine sloshing around in his hand.

I rolled back my shoulders, shaking off the urge to fight and defend myself.

"What are you doing in here?" I asked, taking a place in the semi-circle, trying to pat down my hair again, mad that my original plan of fixing my appearance before receiving my scolding from Rainer didn't work out.

Rainer chugged the remainder of his wine then set it next to an almost empty wine bottle. "I figured it'd be easier to wait for you here while you were with *him*."

I held back a sigh as Rainer refilled his glass then poured a drink for me. His jealousy was going to be the death of me.

"I wanted to make sure he and Neo were okay," I tried to say calmly. "They did get injured in battle, and the Rivelian army—"

"I also got injured," Rainer exclaimed, slamming down the jug. "Your betrothed had been injured, and you still went to Alaric first."

My temple twitched. "Yes, but as I was saying, I also went to him first because the Rivelian army had arrived. I thought he may need help to calm the situation. Rainer, the Rivelia Pack is close to us. It is best to keep peace with them."

"Keep peace? Is that what you call prioritizing him?" Rainer scoffed. I remained quiet, watching him down his second glass. "Tell me, Ina, if they hadn't shown up, who would you have run to first? And don't lie. I've known you long enough to tell."

I crossed my arms. "Rainer, you're drunk," I accused, wanting to get on with the lecturing. I was too tired to deal with his jealousy, to confront the twisted love he had for me. "Let's talk about this once you've sobered up."

"Answering my question by sending me off?" Rainer laughed. "I guess I have your answer now. It makes sense, though. You did keep calling out his name when you were asleep, and his touch was the only thing that would calm you." Rainer chugged his freshly poured glass and reached for the bottle once again. "I'm going to need more of this tonight if I'm going to do what I must," he mumbled.

I snatched the bottle away from him, seeing his dilated pupils. "Do what?" I asked.

Rainer pushed off the ground, swaying as he stood. "End our engagement."

I nearly dropped the bottle. I figured Rainer would have been infuriated by me seeing Neo and Alaric, but I didn't think he would be nonsensical.

"Rainer, our people. They need this. They need us. You know that. With me, your claim to be alpha will not be questioned ever. Don't let jealousy cloud your mind. Your sons—"

"I can never be with you while you love him. I can never be with you when I've seen how you love another, when I know that will never happen to me," Rainer mewled, barely holding himself up.

"Love?" I blinked rapidly. Ala and Sil claimed that Rainer loved me, that it made him overprotective of me, but I didn't think it made him stupid. "Rainer, I don't love him. I told you before, love isn't for me. It's the bond and attraction that makes me—"

"That's a lie," Rainer growled. "I don't know if you know that it is, or maybe you've been lying to yourself, but I've seen you. I've been with you when a false bond snaps into place. You've never behaved the way you do with him. You were never like that with me. Whatever you feel for him, it goes beyond your wolf's desires."

"Don't be dramatic, Rainer. This is all in your head." I marched toward Rainer, desperate. After all the bloodshed, our pack couldn't survive a civil war.

"Am I? Tell me, Ina. Do you remember all the times we bonded, the weeks you told me to keep my distance when we were around others because you didn't want them to know? Do you remember when someone asked if we were falsely bonded because they smelt me on you? Without a thought, you denied it. You know who you couldn't do that with? Alaric. You looked like the world was going to end if you denied it, and you looked like that again when you saw him go after Neo alone. You raced after him, knowing that none of us had plans to follow, when you knew that if it was just you two, it would be suicide, but you still went. You followed him, knowing you would leave the pack that you've wanted to lead your entire life to me. You love him."

I parted my lips to correct Rainer, but I just stood there like a gaping fish. Realization hitting me.

I had been lying to myself about it this entire time. It wasn't just admiration, an addiction to the pleasure he gave, or even the obsession that came with having a worthy opponent. I loved Alaric.

"I can't be mated to you like this," Rainer whispered, hurt and pain in his voice.

Slowly, Rainer approached me, taking the hand I had unknowingly used to cover my mouth. He dropped two metal rings, one thinner than the other but both with wolf engravings—the rings of the alpha and his mate—and Artico's Fang into my palm.

I raised my eyes to his, breathless.

"The pack is yours. I rescind all claim to it." Rainer began to walk away.

"You can't. The pack, the tradition. They won't accept me. I'm a female."

Rainer peered over his shoulder, tears shimmering in his eyes, forcing tears of my own. He did love me. I saw that now. So much of what he had done in the past made sense. But he could never love me in the way I needed, and I could never love him because of that. That's why he was letting me go.

"Don't you remember how Acacia came to be the matriarch of her people?" I shook my head, causing Rainer to scowl. "She gained her packs' respect in the war by showing them her true strength, just as you did when you killed the demon leader with a weapon only they can wield."

I clutched the meaningful items to me, remembering Acacia's words. *The stage is now the same.*

Back then I was confused by her words, but now I understood them. The circumstances that allowed her to prove herself to be alpha were now mine, and if I acted well enough, I could change the rules.

But would my people really accept me as alpha? Had I done enough?

They had been cheering loudly for me.

It could be. But...

"What about your power to compel?" I asked, still in disbelief.

Rainer sadly laughed. "I never had it. If I did, do you really think you would have made it to the castle?"

My eyes widened at the realization. Rainer had never once compelled me since our reunion. He had only raised his voice. "But you were in my head the day of the tournament. You must have the power."

"After I won against your father in a spar, saw that I had made him bleed, he took me to see Azima. He told me that if I didn't say a word to anyone, he would guarantee that I won, that I would finally gain your respect by appearing stronger than I was for a day." I raised a brow. "Azima preformed a ceremony that allowed your father to share his power with me for a night in exchange for my silence and an oath that I would protect you, which back then was to claim you and be your alpha. But now, that isn't even close to what's best for you. It's not even what's best for the pack. You are what's best for it. You can be alpha, Ina, and no one will say a thing. You're free," Rainer whispered with congratulatory melancholy before walking out of the tent.

I stood for a minute in total shock, wondering just exactly what to do. Everything I knew was changing. I was going to be alpha. I was going to get everything I ever wanted, yet I didn't feel like I had won, not completely. I felt cold and alone and knew of only one person that could rid me of that. Alaric. I needed to find him. I needed to talk to him before he left. I needed to—

I couldn't.

I couldn't do any of those things.

He wanted his mate. That was his dream, and I refused to get in the way of it.

I needed to stay quiet, hope that he would find her soon, that maybe I could move on. Until then, I would focus on rebuilding Artico, healing and proving to the pack day after day that they were right to put their faith in me.

A new age was about to begin.

CHAPTER 64

One year later

Light blazed through the bustling great hall through the copious number of windows that lined its walls. Banners from Rivelia, Artico, and the Woodland Pack—the latter just in case they decided to come, however, it was highly doubtful, as they kept true to their statement of being independent—hung from the ceiling above, stopping ten or so feet away from the long tables covered in plates, goblets, and cutlery. The middle of the tables were open and ready for the plentiful food that was being prepared and scented the entire village, no doubt, making everyone's mouth water and their stomachs grumble, just as it was doing to me. The preparations were nearly done for the feast tonight and everything was going to plan. Yet, my heart pounded, and my throat felt tight. I was finally going to see Neo and Alaric again.

Though we had exchanged letters, mainly Neo and I, as Alaric was far too busy with his new role as King of Rivelia, I was nervous to see the two. In particular, I was nervous to see Alaric.

It had been a year since the war, which we named The Fall of Blood and Snow—named for the end of the Blood Demons and the old Artico ways—and I still had the same feelings for him as I did the day we parted. I still thought fondly of him, thought about the kisses that were exchanged, missed the warmth that left with him on our final hug. By the gods, I even jumped for joy like a silly, stupid maiden whenever I received a letter from him. It made my day. Though each time I did receive one, a small part of my gut twisted, wondering if the letter would contain the information I knew would kill me to hear—that he found his mate.

Of course, I'd be happy for him. It was his dream after all, but it didn't make it any less heart wrenching of an idea, not when my feelings for him hadn't lessened despite my attempts to do so. At this point, I ironically wished to find my own mate so I could feel a fraction of what I did for Alaric.

"Scouts have reported the Rivelia party approaching, Alpha Ina," informed a male from behind.

I finished rearranging some misplaced decorations before turning and smiling at Rainer—my second in command.

Though we both had left the Woodland Pack hurting from broken hearts, Rainer's loyalty to me did not waver. He kept true to the oath he swore to my father and made sure no harm came to me. He pushed down any—though it was only three wolves who were ghastly old—that fought against my claim to be the alpha. It was only right to give him such a high position.

"Let's gather in the Alpha's Hall, then. Could you assemble everyone?" I asked, already heading for the grand double doors.

"I already have," Rainer informed, following close to my heels. "Well, I at least told everyone to gather."

"Oh?" I raised a brow, stepping into the square where a giant bonfire was being prepared, admiring the newly built village and my happy pack members racing about.

Construction had finished a couple of months ago, and while we kept the layout fairly similar to how it was in the past, we had erected more buildings and a larger main hall to host guests from any pack that needed help or wished to visit. My people should have been tired beyond belief.

However, they were anything but. As soon as we were reestablished, my pack quickly volunteered to go on missions to nearby human villages and help them rebuild. Some even offered to travel to the Rivelia region and help regrow the trust that had been ruined. It was truly a time of peace. My father would've been so happy to see all this change. My mother too.

"Ala and Aspen are already inside."

I nodded, expecting that from both of them. Ala was our head healer now, so renowned that wolves and humans visited us just for her care. And Aspen, though he was no longer second in command, he was my third. He was also the head trainer of our armies and the leader of our scouting units.

"However, Sil is too busy preparing the entertainment tonight. She insists that her choir needs to practice once more," Rainer grumbled.

I laughed, causing my entire body to shake. Sil, while she didn't have a place on my governing board, had become quite the connector of humans and shifters by running a choir that consisted of both species. They sang beautifully and occasionally traveled around the continent, particularly the areas that were still weary of wolves, all to help in bridging the gap.

"Poor souls," I joked. "Her choir is going to be practicing until it's time for them to perform."

Rainer grunted in agreement, evoking another chuckle from me as I opened one of the doors to the Alpha's Hall and passed the many statues lining the narrow halls, each one honoring the past alphas. I stopped at my father's and placed a fresh flower I had found on my morning walk before heading to the dais.

"Alpha Ina," chimed Ala and Aspen as I passed them, bowing their heads ever so slightly with fists over their hearts.

I blushed. Even in a year, I wasn't used to that greeting.

"You two haven't been waiting long, have you?" I asked, taking a couple steps back, forgoing my place on the dais as nerves started to kick back in.

Ala shook her head as did Aspen.

"You know how quickly Rainer works," Ala chimed. "As soon as he told me, he sprinted off to find you and Aspen."

"It's good to be diligent," Rainer grumbled, a slight rouge forming on his cheeks.

I raised a brow and glanced at Aspen, slightly jerking my head at Rainer. Aspen looked over then turned back to me with pursed lips as he nodded. I smiled broadly, knowing that he was starting to agree with me that Ala and Rainer were becoming a little more than friends—a union I would happily bless.

Though Rainer's way of loving someone was torture to me, his overprotectiveness was good for someone like Ala. She was too sweet for this world, and enjoyed the help he offered, enjoyed his visits and overbearingness. But with both of them still healing from broken hearts—Rainer from me and Ala from the mate she never got to bond with—I hadn't thought either of them had given much thought to how well they molded together. However, recently, I had noticed one too many easily won blushes and lingering eyes. It's also why I wasn't too worried about how Rainer would be once Alaric arrived.

"There they are!" someone shouted just outside.

My gut twisted as nerves and excitement hit me at full force. I spun around, trying to figure out where to stand when they entered, thankful that only my inner circle was in the hall.

"Just stand by us, Ina," Ala whispered, positioning me so I was at the bottom of the dais with them. "It'll be alright."

I agreed, but I could feel my face paling.

"I'll go get them," Rainer added, already heading to the doors.

I counted, trying to calm myself. However, I didn't even reach five before the doors slammed opened.

"There she is," Neo happily yelled, his arms already open as he walked past Rainer, who looked a tad annoyed that he took a couple steps for nothing.

"Neo," I replied, rushing into his embrace, nerves calming a bit upon seeing the smile that hadn't changed in a year.

He hugged me just as he would have a year ago, shaking me side to side in his overly friendly ways. However, this time, the hug was a lot tighter and stronger. He had gained muscle, quite a bit, judging by how deep his biceps dug into my upper arms.

"It's good to see you again," came a soft, almost too quiet voice.

I looked over Neo's shoulder to see sweet Lillian looking as beautiful as ever, holding a small babe in her hands.

I pushed Neo away, quickly closing the gap between me and Lillian.

"Is this yours?" I asked, bending down so I came face to face with the adorable bundle.

"Can't you tell?" Neo rounded his arm over Lillian's waist. "I know he's only a couple months, but I thought his features were prevalent enough."

"A couple of months," I gasped, rising. "He's so small. How was the journey? It must have been tiring for you all."

"It was fine. He slept more than he did in the castle. I think it was the rocking," Lillian assured.

"Still," I replied, "I wish you would have told me. I could have delayed the event a bit. I'm sure traveling with him a bit older would have been less strenuous."

Neo scoffed, "I don't think you could have postponed it if you tried. We were all so excited. Alaric had even packed weeks in advance."

My heart skipped, knowing Alaric was excited was a relief.

I peered over Neo's shoulder, half expecting him to be rolling his eyes for being outed, but as I looked, he was nowhere to be found.

"Where's Alaric?" I asked, my smile already fading, thinking the worst.

Neo's lips parted as one hand rested on the lower lip, tugging at it. "He's running a bit late," he drawled.

"Oh," I mused in confusion.

"He shouldn't be long," Neo assured. "He's just getting a present for his *mate*."

I whipped to Neo, a pain searing through my chest, too strong for me to hide my shock.

"His mate?" I asked, trying to fight the breaking in my voice.

Neo smiled, unaware of my emotions. "Yes. She'll be here all week as well."

My breath caught in my throat.

"She's quite—"

Lillian smacked Neo on the arm, earning a confused scowl, but she narrowed her eyes, forcing him to be quiet. "We'll let him tell you about her," she whispered.

I nodded, the only thing I could manage.

I knew that this was bound to happen, but I didn't think it would be today. I didn't think I would learn about it in person with so many people around. I had to keep it together. But I couldn't move. I couldn't speak. It hurt too much, and everything was spiraling.

"I'm sorry to interrupt," Rainer started, helping to get me out of my stupor, "but would you like to be shown to your rooms? I know you've had a long journey, and the feast will be long. A bit of a rest may do you good."

I inhaled deeply, refilling my lungs with the air I had forgotten I needed. "That's a good idea, Rainer," I replied for Lillian and Neo. "Feasts here can go until dawn." I waved over my healer and my third, knowing they would be friendlier than Rainer. "Ala and Aspen will give you a tour of the grounds and show you where you will be staying. I would do so myself, but there's one more thing I need to see to before tonight," I lied through a shaking voice. Though I doubted it worked, as Neo reached out for me and everyone else looked at me with pity filled eyes. I jumped back, forcing a smile. "Well, I best be off. The sooner I get this done, the sooner I'll get to see you two and Alaric and his mate. It will be fun," I chimed, racing for the doors before the tears started to fall.

I stood alone in the cave with only a torch to illuminate the unlit candles, staring at mine in particular. Once Ala and Sil's used to sit next it, but now theirs were gone, taken away when they found their mates, leaving mine all alone. I shouldn't have felt sad about it. I wanted it to be that way after all. I had prayed for it to be that way. By the love of gods, I had everything I had dreamed about before the night the demons came and changed everything.

I was the alpha. My pack loved me. I loved them. We now lived in a time of peace, and I never had to be bonded to achieve it all.

I should be happy, but I wasn't.

Yes, I was glad that I had achieved my dreams without having to be bonded to a male, but some part of me felt empty. The part of me that had loved Alaric, had found comfort around him, was empty. It was so empty that it hurt.

I almost wished that I had found my mate years ago before I even met him. Then I wouldn't be feeling like this. I wouldn't be wishing that he hadn't found his mate, that for some odd reason he changed his mind and felt for me as I did for him, but that was a selfish wish that would never come true.

I needed to move on. I needed to stop hiding and face him and his mate. But before that, I needed to make a wish, a prayer, just as I had done every day before the mating ceremony, because it was all I could do for the pain I felt.

I picked up my candle, gripping it to my chest, and closed my eyes, silently wishing for the thing I never wanted. Because, maybe, if I found them, the pain would stop.

Help me find my mate.

A rush of wind swept through the cave, its coldness causing me to shiver, yet it carried a scent that had my heart warming.

Pine and sandalwood.

I gripped the candle tighter, not daring to open my eyes. I wasn't ready yet. I needed a couple more minutes.

"Ina," he whispered, his voice like music to my ears.

I bit my quivering lip, scolding the emotions that were bubbling up.

I needed to be happy for him.

I exhaled. "Alaric," I breathed out, forcing a smile as my eyes opened slowly, "it's good to see you. I—"

Everything in me froze as I spied the glowing flower in Alaric's hand.

A shinebloom.

But those only glowed when mates were near each other.

I gulped, peering around Alaric.

"Is your mate near?" I asked, gesturing at the flower. "I heard from Neo that you finally found her. I'm so gla—glad." My cheeks heated, embarrassed that I couldn't act as well as I wanted.

I was such an awful person.

I *needed* to be happy for my friend.

I strode forward, forgetting to put my candle down, and looked past Alaric into the darkness, forcing myself to look for her with a smile. "Where is she? Shineblooms only work when a mate is a few feet away. Is she outside of the cave? You need to introduce me to her. I want to meet the female who finally swept you off your feet," I overzealously declared.

"Ina," Alaric whispered with great concern.

I cursed. He knew. He knew I wasn't happy.

Gods.

I needed to try harder.

"Let's go find her." I broadly smiled and stepped past him.

"Ina, we need to talk."

I ignored him and continued on, but Alaric grabbed my upper arm and swung me around.

I looked away, not daring to stare once again into those hazel eyes. I couldn't. There were too many memories. I needed to interact with him slowly.

"Ina, please, look at me."

I shook my head, eyes lowering to my hands. "We really shouldn't keep her—"

My chest stilled.

My candle. The wick. It was on fire.

But it could only light if mates were touching.

Slowly, I looked to Alaric.

"I'm sorry," he whispered, releasing my upper arm. "I couldn't keep it a secret anymore. I know that you don't want a mate, and that will probably never change, but Ina, what I feel for you is more than any bond could force me to. You're amazing and incredible. You're kind and caring, yet one of the fiercest wolves I have ever known. I've tried to ignore the feelings I have for you, but even after a year, they haven't left me." Tears lined my eyes. "I want you, Ina, not as someone I can claim but as someone who I can walk through life with, who makes me want to do better, be better. I don't expect you to reciprocate. I remember what you said when we traveled, but I had to tell you. My feelings have mocked me too much since the day we stumbled upon that field of shineblooms, and I foolishly plucked one. They have hurt me ever since the day I let you go without telling you. For that, I'm sorry. I just—"

I threw my arms around Alaric, pushing my lips to his, savoring the taste, the feel of him.

I couldn't believe this.

He wanted to be mine. He was mine.

Tears spilled and a happy sob broke loose forcing me to stop.

Alaric wiped away my tears, his eyes raking over me, utterly confused.

"I love you," I sobbed. "I have thought of you every day, every moment since we parted. I have been so confused about whether I should feel happy or nervous each time I get a letter from you, as I never knew if it would contain information about your mate, about you finding that mate. But now I see that wasn't information I should've dreaded."

Alaric blinked a couple of times, processing words he never thought he'd hear. "Does that mean you'll accept the bond?" he asked.

I laughed, unclasping the chain I wore around my neck that held Artico's Fang and two rings—the ring of the alpha and *her* mate. I put the thinner one on then slid the bigger one onto Alaric's finger. "I accepted it long ago before I even realized I had," I whispered, pressing my forehead to his.

Acknowledgements

After writing one book, I thought the second would be easy. Oh, how wrong I was. This book was so challenging to write, and honestly, I don't think it would have seen the light of day if it were not for the amazing people around me.

David, my best friend and amazing husband, thank you so much for not letting me trash this book. When I wrote it, I was going through major imposter syndrome, and I didn't think I could write another book, let alone one that people would enjoy. I wrote a third of this and stopped. I told myself it wasn't good, and you still read it in all its incomplete glory. You told me it had potential and encouraged me to keep going. I didn't believe you, but I did. I cried a lot but you held me through it. Without you, this book or the cover wouldn't exist, so thank you. Thank you for always believing in me, even when I can't believe in myself.

Katherine, tiny human, you are literally the best hype woman any writer could ask for. Thank you so much for listening to my numerous audio messages that ended up being your personal podcasts, and thank you for replying, for showing interests in the characters that are so dear to me. I loved every text and voice memo you sent back and every time you called me to tell me you were thinking about my book. You really know how to make an author smile.

Sake and Inari, my fur babies, I know you guys can't read, but I will give you credit where credit is due. Thank you for keeping me company during long writing sessions, for the cuddles when the imposter syndrome got bad, and for reminding me I needed to take breaks. Love you little fluff balls!

To my long-distance writing besties—Mel, Cait, and Maz—you guys are the best. Thank you so much for letting me slide into your DMs and rant, for letting me bounce ideas off you, and of course, sharing endless, encouraging reels. So thankful to have you guys in my life.

Finally, to the readers, thank you. Whether you were a beta, alpha, or someone buying this book, thank you for taking time to read my story.

Always follow your heart,
Renee M. Palstring

ABOUT THE AUTHOR

Renee M. Palstring has not always known she wanted to be an author. In fact, she originally started out on a completely different path. She earned a Bachelor of Science in Mathematics and Computer Science and set off on an adventure to become an engineer/programmer. However, after marrying and moving during the pandemic, she realized that her passions were somewhere else, she just didn't know where. She finally realized this when she started reading again. This small act sparked the creative writer in her. She started writing as a fun hobby, which ultimately turned into her debut book, A Misplaced Love, thus starting her writing career.

When Renee is not busy chasing her newfound dream of being an author, she can be found doing a variety of activities, ranging from lounging near the garden to trying to survive a three-hour hike. She'll jump at the chance to travel and experience another's culture, but she also loves the comforts and familiarity of home.

ALSO BY RENEE M. PALSTRING
A MISPLACED LOVE

An arranged marriage, a secret love, and one mistake

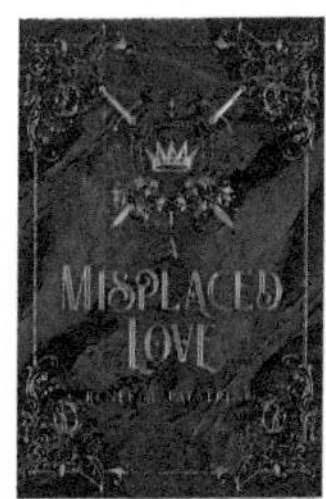

Estelle, Princess of Isara, has always known one day she would wed, that it is her duty as a princess. However, as long as she can remember she's dreamed of marrying her best friend, Griffith. She's always lived in this fantasy, kept her feelings a secret till the day she had the courage to speak them. That all changes when the neighboring kingdom—Modare—takes Astra and Ula. A feat that no one thought possible.

Scared that Isara will be the next kingdom to be taken, Estelle's hand in marriage is offered to the King of Modare. A man rumored to be so evil, so power hungry, that he has been deemed a tyrant king.

Ripped away from her secret love, Estelle panics, making choices that will ultimately change the future of her arranged marriage. Will she still be able to protect her kingdom and her heart under these new conditions?